AMAZO

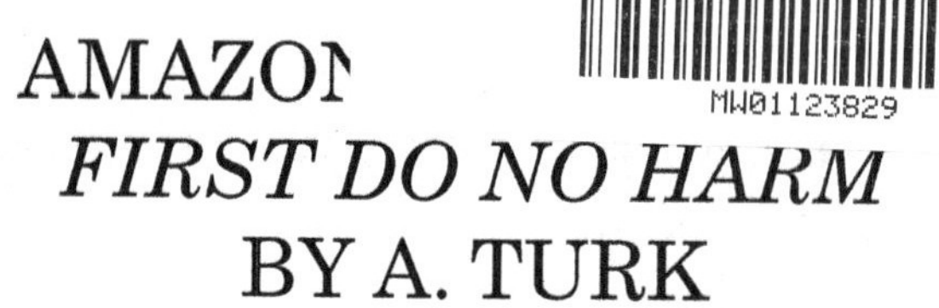

FIRST DO NO HARM
BY A. TURK

This was one of my top picks. I was spellbound and couldn't put it down. *First Do No Harm* was Grishamesque. Loved it.

A. Turk's first novel is a legal thriller that is both a fun read and an interesting one as well. The characters in the story are well developed and rich in personality.

As a practicing attorney in Nashville for nearly 36 years, I have recommended this book to clients to read so that they can get a clear understanding of the legal process.... Whether you are a Plaintiff or Defendant in any piece of litigation, this book is a MUST READ!!!. A. Turk's three decade career as a litigator is shown in his attention to detail, and the reader becomes a part of the litigation. And if you love the city of Nashville as I do, this thriller is a guided tour of Music City USA. It is an enjoyable journey to Nashville, Middle Tennessee, and its judicial system.

"First Do No Harm" accurately captures and conveys the excitement of a real blood and guts lawsuit. The stakes are high for all concerned, and the suspense is compelling. We get to see inside the mind of a dedicated litigator, and we are privy not only to what he does, but why he does it. The portrayal of the legal system is the most accurate I have read in any book of fiction.

A thoroughly enjoyable read. I hope we see more of A. Turk and his protagonist, Ben Davis.

Attorney Ben Davis takes on the case of the estate of Rosie Malone (amongst others), who died as the result of the incompetence of two doctors who together are complicit in performing unnecessary expensive tests and surgeries. The author A. Turk is a born storyteller and brings to life a difficult court case all the while explaining the intricacies of the legal procedures to the reader.

AMAZON REVIEWS OF *SECOND DEGREE* BY A. TURK

This second installation of the Benjamin Davis series was better than the first. I found this work more thrilling than the first and appreciated the nods to the first book. Kudos to Turk for stepping up his game and making me want more from good old Davis.

A great legal thriller with sex, politics, medical "practice" and a lot of greed. Davis and associates fight to the finish for justice to be served.

Alan does a really good job with legal stories. I can't believe anyone could make depositions interesting, but he did. Looking forward to his next book.

Great storytelling. The plot is very good and the protagonists are in great form. The outcome is somber but sets the stage for more action.

So happy to find this author. He explains so much about the law and procedure wrapped up in a great story. He gives insights into why juries often surprise us with their verdicts.

AMAZON REVIEWS OF *THIRD COAST* BY A. TURK

Who is Morty Steine and why is he so beloved as a lawyer, mentor, confidante, and friend? In Third Coast, A. Turk tells Morty's story while remaining true to the series theme of legal thriller involving Attorney Benjamin Davis. This is the third book that reveals more about Morty and Benjamin. Each novel can stand alone as a read, but together, the entire Benjamin Davis series is a testament that our legal system is a crucible where justice prevails. Third Coast is the best A. Turk book to date, mainly because Morty is so endearing as a character and person. This is a definite must read.

So I've now read Turk's third book. Hard to put down. At first, I thought that perhaps he'd gone just a little overboard with all the legal terminology. And after the first third of the book, though, it seemed to smooth out and was a nice read. Learned a LOT about the complexities of a civil trial . . . very enjoyable.

Fourth of July

A Benjamin Davis Novel

A. Turk

Fourth of July is the fourth novel in the Benjamin Davis Series by author A. Turk. This is a work of fiction. Any names or character, event, or incidents are fictitious.

The image on the book's cover is the state flag of Tennessee.

Printed in the United States of America

ISBN: 978-0-9892663-7-6 (Paperback)
978-0-9892663-8-3 (Ebook)

Cover design by Dan Swanson • van-garde.com

Book design by Darlene Swanson • van-garde.com

CAST OF MAIN CHARACTERS

Davis Team and Family

Benjamin Abraham Davis—protagonist
Morty Steine—mentor and partner of Davis
Sammie Davis—partner and niece of Davis
Bella Rosario—office manager of Steine, Davis, & Davis
George Hopper—investigator
Liza Davis—wife of Davis
Caroline Davis—daughter of Davis
Jacob "Jake" Albert Davis—son of Davis
Larry Davis—father of Davis
Shelly "Nana" Davis—mother of Davis
George Davis—older brother of Davis
Victor "Vic" Browne—nurse and Sammie's fiancé
Dr. John Caldwell—Davis's father-in-law
Patsy Caldwell—Davis's mother-in-law
Anthony "Tony" Rosario—husband of Bella
Abbott and Costello—Davis pugs

January Family

Rachel January—missing wife/daughter
Daniel "Dan" January—husband of Rachel
Franklin "Frankie" January—son of Rachel/Dan
Gabriela "Gaby" January—daughter of Rachel/Dan
Phillip January—younger brother of Dan

Sinclair & Sims

Tyree "Ty" Sinclair IV—father of Rachel/lawyer
Rita Sinclair—mother of Rachel
Harold "Harry" Sims—partner of Tyree Sinclair
Beverly Sims—Wife of Harry Sims
John Timmons—partner of Sinclair & Sims
Mary Forsythe—associate of Sinclair & Sims
Peter Mitchell—associate of Sinclair & Sims

Keller Family

Martha Keller—deceased matriarch
Stanley Keller—second husband, newspaper mogul
Harold Hamilton—first husband, Tommy's father
Thomas "Tommy" Hamilton—gambler
Maureen Wagner—stepdaughter/trustee
Robert Wagner—husband of Maureen
Betty Andrews—stepdaughter/substitute trustee
Sam Andrews—husband of Betty

Steine, Davis, & Davis Clients

Laura Chapman (sex for legal services/divorce)
Rebecca "Becky" Taylor (wife/elevator)
William Taylor (deceased/elevator)
Richard Sasser Sr. (NSA)
Richard "Dickie" Sasser Jr. (drunk driving/NSA)
Chris Addams (banker/age discrimination)
Karl Moore (former DEA agent/ contempt)
Johnny Cash and June Carter Cash
Howard Longfellow (commercial pilot)
Maria Lopez (bookkeeper/sexual harassment)
Brandon Tell (negligent construction of pool)
Gloria O'Hara (real estate agent/missing husband)
Larry Davenport (deadbeat client)

Adversaries of Davis

Agent-in-charge Brian Greene (Sasser)
Keith Rogers—president FANB (Addams)
Stan Hamm—umpire (Longfellow)
Richard Feeder—contractor (Tell)
Caleb Dean—construction worker (Sasser)
Bobby Dean—construction worker (Sasser)
Ralph Kramer—guard (Taylor)
Lawrence Kennedy—inspector (Taylor)
Thomas Brooks—inspector (Taylor)
Oscar Brand—supervisor (Taylor)
Terry Thompson—EVP of Safeway Ins. (Taylor)
Warren Kroner—EVP of Olympus (Taylor)
Jon Leek—Crystal Tower Management Company (Taylor)
William O' Riley—EVP of Aetna Insurance Company (Taylor)
Dr. Bobby O'Hara—vagrant (O'Hara)
Robin Gaines—sex partner/alibi (January)
Robert Gaines—sex partner/ alibi (January)
Helen Cooper—sex partner/ alibi (January)
Albert King—sex partner/alibi (January)
Elliot Richardson (R&R Construction)

Extradition Team

Carlos Ramos—ex-DEA agent
Roberto Mendez—lawyer who met Davis in St. Barts
Hermando Diaz—lawyer/fixer

Cubans

Raul Castro, Defense Minister
Major Pepe—assistant to Defense Minister

Attorneys

John "Jack" Henry (Rachel Sinclair)
Amy Pierce (Daniel January/ Phillip January)
Robert "Bob" Sullivan (Barry Chapman R&R Construction)
Charles Brody (Taylor)
Lowell Thomas (Crystal Tower Management Company)
Kurt Lanier (First American National Bank)
Bradley Littleton (Tommy Hamilton)
Brian Ellis (co-counsel in Taylor case)
Thomas Joseph (Moore)
Pamela Ziegler (Chief Disciplinary Counsel)
Jim Neal (Brand)
Jerry Shames (Tell)

Psychiatrists, Therapists, Experts

Dr. Virginia Ames—psychiatrist (Rachel Sinclair)
Dr. Paula Milam—therapist (Laura Chapman)
Dr. Karen Richards—therapist (Laura Chapman)
Dr. Edward George—medical examiner (Taylor)
Jackie Samuels PhD—handwriting expert (January)
Solomon "Sol" Rosen—accounting (January/Taylor)
Dr. Carl Weaver (Taylor)
Dr. Thomas Peeler (Addams)

Law Enforcement/Prosecution

General Johnson Tory—district attorney general
Assistant General Belinda Little (January cases)
Assistant General Sue Beck (Sasser)
General Larry Carpenter (Sasser)
Chief Gerald Neenan—police chief
Officer David Tanner (January)
Detective Sharon Duncan (January/ Keller)

Judges/ Court Officers

Judge Paul Billingsly (Moore/ January contempt)
Winnie Bray—Billingsly court officer
Judge Robert Rutherford (January probate)
Judge Mark Carlson (Oscar Brand)
Judge Katherine Russo (January murder trial)
Honorable Sandra Palmer (Addams)

Jurors

Judy Monroe—Foreman
David Jackson
Katie Poe
Roy Baker

A Legal Glossary has been included in the back of the book to assist the reader with legal terms.

Dedication

While I was writing this book, on June 6, 2016, without warning, the world lost Gerald David Neenan, age sixty-two. Gerry was a great husband and father, and his wife and two sons will love and miss him for the rest of their lives. Gerry was an exceptional lawyer; he cared about his clients; they trusted and loved him. I am confident that each and every one of them were touched by him. Gerry had a way of making a lasting impression on you; he was a man of substance. I know that other lawyers trusted and respected Gerry. He set the bar for our profession and was an example for his peers to strive for.

Gerry was my best friend. I miss him terribly. Some days, when I think of him, I just start crying, I can't help it; I really loved him. We shared almost forty years together, I don't remember a harsh word; he was a true mensch.

God bless you, Gerry.

CHAPTER ONE

A REAL TRAGEDY, NO JOKE

Monday, April 1, 1996

Davis never knew his client William Taylor. He wasn't really Davis's client. His wife was. In preparing her case for trial, Davis got to know William and his activities of April Fools' Day, 1996. He was sure he would have liked the young man.

William Taylor stared blurry eyed at his client's tax return as he considered whether to risk the deduction of a medical expense for a Siberian tiger named *Thriller*.

Why the hell would a big cat need his tonsils out anyway? A zoo with thirty-four exotic animals, owned by a pop musician, that in five years hadn't been profitable and wasn't open to the general public posed a great risk of being declared a hobby by the IRS.

William, a very smart accountant, knew that the IRS, on good basis, could declare more than $23,600,000 of deducted operating expenses invalid. That would create a taxable event of more than $8 million, trouble no matter how rich his eccentric client.

William pulled his micro recorder from his breast shirt pocket and began slowly speaking into the device, "Tomorrow review holding in Burrus vs. IRS, local counsel for the plaintiff, Steine, Davis, & Davis." Then he put the recorder back in his pocket, forgetting to turn it off.

A few minutes later at midnight he called his wife, Becky, for moral support. They'd met in college and married the month after graduation. That was ten years ago.

At thirty-two, William had been an accountant seven years. He was about to sit for the last and fifth part of the CPA exam. He looked the part: bookish, with thick glasses, short-cropped brown hair, short stature, and bad teeth. His parents neglected his dental care. His wife was the polar opposite: tall with curly auburn hair and a great smile. Her killer smile was what first attracted William to the shy girl from the upper Michigan peninsula. William, a native Nashvillian, couldn't resist her the moment he laid eyes on her that Monday morning the first day of freshman English class at the University of Florida.

"I won't be home for dinner, and I may not even be home for breakfast," he joked to Becky. "What'd I miss?"

The young professional stated the obvious to his neglected wife. It was the fourth night this week he'd missed dinner with the family. Becky reported she'd served their three kids hot dogs and fries six hours earlier. "Hebrew National." William joked that they were "blessed by a rabbi."

I didn't miss much. He rethought, *I bet those were pretty good dogs. At least I know the company would have been outstanding.* William and Becky cherished family time.

"Rosen ordered in Chinese food from a new place, The Dynasty. It just opened around the corner. We should take the kids there. They'd love it."

The Taylors had three children: Gary, age seven; William Jr., age five; and Cora, age two. The youngest was spoiled by her two older brothers and had them twisted around her little fingers. The three kids kept their mother busy, and with her bearing all of the parenting responsibility, she wished she saw her husband more.

Although William was ambitious, he felt real guilt that work preoccupied his time from Halloween through April 15th. His boss and mentor, Sol Rosen, took a liking to William, guided him through his profession and through office politics, which could be insurmountable. The goals were an equity partnership and large bonuses. To achieve those goals, one needed to secure clients and keep them happy and paying large fees.

"When do you plan on coming home? It's already tomorrow," Becky asked.

"Rosen's still here. I'll be damned if I'm leaving before he does. I want to watch him walk out the door. It's important for him to see me still here when he leaves. It's not just a matter of principle. It's a matter of dollars toward my year-end bonus."

Becky groaned, "Money isn't everything!"

Solomon "Sol" Rosen was the cigar-chomping senior partner of Lamar, Gleason & Rosen, an accounting and management firm that specialized in representing country music recording artists. The firm represented more than twenty Grammy winners and several artists who'd crossed over into movies and television. Although the firm's principal place of business remained in Nashville, it had opened satellite offices in both Los Angeles and New York to meet the special needs of its clientele. The firm also managed trusts for wealthy Nashville families. That was Rosen's specialty. He was connected to the wealthiest families of Nashville. Rosen let the younger partners deal with the music divas and prima donnas. They were generally far more demanding, difficult, and time consuming, but there were always exceptions.

A few minutes later Rosen got up, walked past William's desk, nodded at him, and was out the door. The younger man told his wife he loved her, "and I'll be home soon."

Becky felt less neglected and responded, "I love you too, William."

Five minutes later, William locked Michael Jackson's thick file in his desk drawer, grabbed his suit coat, and headed for the elevator. The building was empty except for the security guard, whose nameplate identified him as Ralph Kramer.

The offices of Lamar, Gleason & Rosen were on the tenth floor of the twenty-two-story Crystal Tower office building in downtown Nashville, part of the city's new skyline. The building featured three glass elevators suspended on the outside of the building offering a breathtaking view of the city, the Cumberland River, and the under construction Titans' Stadium. Taylor pushed the down button and waited for one of the three elevators to take him to the ground floor where he'd switch elevators to then go to his car in the underground parking lot.

The doors opened, he got into car #3, pushed L, for Lobby, and daydreamed about passing the last part of the CPA exam, audit. He'd failed it twice before. He'd passed the other four parts the first time around. He just couldn't get that audit shit, and the funny thing was he'd never use it in connection with his work. His mind jolted back to reality. "What the hell?"

The elevator jerked hard, plummeted three floors, and abruptly stopped. It was the type of noise that makes you cringe, like gears of an engine seizing up.

William looked up at the smoked glass ceiling and saw his reflection. Fear was in his eyes. *Relax, these elevators have backup systems, and then there are backup systems to the backup systems, and then finally backup systems to those backup systems. There's nothing to be concerned about. You'll be driving home in fifteen minutes. Relax, man.*

Confined in the car, William couldn't know that the emergency brake started sparking. That wasn't true of Ralph Kramer. The retired sixty-year-old police officer loved his job with Bradley Guard Service. Basically, he was paid eighteen dollars an hour to read, listen to books on tape, or snack from 10:00 p.m. until 6:00 a.m. at the Crystal Tower. He'd been employed there the last three years since retirement from the force. It was easy, quiet work. He had almost nothing to do and almost no contact with people. He'd gained fifteen pounds because the work was so sedentary; he'd lost his hair before he'd started the job.

Kramer's sensors picked up the sparking emergency brake, but he didn't know what to do. He had almost no training for such an event. His instinct told him to determine whether the car was occupied. "Anybody there? Push the black button to reply."

William couldn't answer. The violent force of the abrupt stop threw him to the floor. On the way down, he hit his head so hard that he cracked the paneling of the elevator. Blood poured from the deep gash on the back of his head and started to pool on the elevator floor.

William looked down. *That's a hell of a lot of blood. Damn!* Concerned, he put his right hand on the back of his head and brought it back in front of his face. The tips of his fingers to the palm of his hand were covered with blood. *Shit, I'm losing a lot of blood.*

He reached into his pocket and pulled out his cell phone. It was immediately covered in blood and so slick that he had trouble punching the numbers 911. Another problem was that his eyes couldn't focus. He had to redial twice.

He could hear someone answer, "911, state the nature of your emergency."

All of a sudden William's mouth got so dry no words came out, no matter how hard he tried. Finally he squeaked out, "William Taylor, injured in an elevator in the Crystal Tower."

"Mr. Taylor, is that at Fifth and Church?"

Establishing location of a caller was the most important priority; the details were secondary. "Are you injured, sir?"

"Yes, bleeding pretty badly from the back of my head."

"Sit tight. Help is on the way. Is there anyone you want me to have the police call to let them know about your situation?"

William didn't reply. He disconnected the 911 operator. He'd given her the information he needed to. Now he had to make the tough call to Becky. He didn't want her to hear about this from some police officer over the phone or, worse, to see a police car arrive in their driveway at two in the morning to report his predicament.

Dazed, William lay on the elevator floor, trying to gain his composure. His mind racing, he figured the elevator fell a few floors and then the emergency brakes caught it. He was right, but he didn't know that those emergency brakes were defective.

"Is anyone in car #3? This is Ralph Kramer." Kramer used his cell phone to first call 911 and then the emergency number for Olympus Elevator Company. He reported, "The emergency brakes of car #3 engaged and are sparking. I've got an elevator stuck between floors at the Crystal Tower, Fifth and Church. Unknown if anyone's in the car. I'm trying to make contact."

The dispatcher at the company responded, "We're already on

our way. We heard from 911. They got a call from an occupant, a Mr. William Taylor. He reports bleeding from the back of his head." The police department's computer system maintained elevator service records for such emergencies.

During Kramer's exchange with 911, Taylor momentarily became more alert. He managed to struggle to his knees and push the black call button.

"Help! Help! Help!" William called. His head was pounding, and the blood continued to gush. From the speaker he heard, "Keep pushing the black button to communicate."

William was back on the elevator floor, exhausted from his efforts. He thought and almost yelled out loud, *What fucking idiot designed this communication system? Couldn't they anticipate that someone might be knocked to the floor, unable to get up?*

He worked his way to his knees but fell back onto the bloody floor. Frustrated, the button four feet away, he yelled to no one, "William Taylor, Taylor . . ."

Barely conscious, William mustered all of his strength, got to his knees, crawled the short distance, and pushed the damn black button. "Taylor, William Taylor," he gasped "Cell, 400-7163."

Five seconds later Kramer called William on his cell phone. Contact with the outside world, and William didn't have to push that damn button. He was proud of his ingenuity, but his head was pounding harder, and he was feeling nauseous.

"Mr. Taylor, help is on the way. Hang in there. How badly are you hurt?"

The answer was obvious by the weakness in his voice, "Hurt bad, hit my head . . ." He faded.

Kramer tried to keep him talking and asked, "Are you married?"

"Yes, ten years. Becky. Tell her I love her," he choked out.

"Don't worry. You'll get to do that. Children?"

William closed his eyes and started to sob. Kramer repeated the question. No answer. Kramer yelled into the phone, "Wake the hell up, Taylor."

He did, and William, agitated, insisted, "I'm calling my wife" and hung up.

Kramer began to protest, but it was too late. He knew that the injured man was right.

William slowly dialed his home number. He misdialed twice.

Finally Becky answered, "If you're calling to impress me with your dedication to work, I'm not. I was in bed trying to fall asleep. I've got a day tomorrow too."

She waited for some snappy response. There was none, so she continued, "By the time you get home, get to bed, and do your morning routine, you'll be operating on three hours of sleep. I wouldn't want you doing my taxes."

Still no response, so she decided to provoke him, "Are you thirteen years old, have nothing better to do than harass some poor housewife trying to get a good night's sleep so she can care for her children and family? What's wrong with you?"

During her rant, William had been mustering all his strength to get out a coherent sentence. He managed to say in a very weak voice, "No, I'm hurt, sweetheart. I'm bleeding in the elevator, which is stuck between floors. Help is on the way."

His words were choppy. Her attitude immediately changed from smug to concerned. "Where are you hurt, darling?"

"My head, bleeding badly, feel weak, fading . . ." His voice trailed off.

"William, William, William, William!" Becky yelled into the phone, louder and louder each time. The last time was almost a shriek.

It worked. His eyes shot open, and for the first time he noticed the name of the elevator company, Olympus, and the names of the last two inspectors, Lawrence Kennedy and Thomas Brooks. As William read the name of the last inspector, he felt a jolt accompanied by a horrific grinding noise.

Becky heard him say, "Fuck you, Olympus, Kennedy and Brooks." Then the elevator fell the remaining seven floors. The crash shook the Crystal Tower. The sound was unmistakable, even from the other side of the phone.

Becky screamed in horror, her entire body shaking. She knew what happened. She screamed, "William!" and said a little prayer for her poor husband. She was sure he was dead. Then she heard a slight whisper, "Becky . . ." She knew she heard something, but it was extremely faint, ghostlike.

"Becky . . ." There it was again. He was forcing out her name between measured breaths. She cried as she pictured him alone and dying. Then she heard another voice. She didn't know who it was.

Feeling helpless, Ralph Kramer kept saying, "Mr. Taylor, help is on the way."

Dying, William wondered, *Who is this idiot?* The still working phone was only five inches from William's mouth. Becky could hear his shallow breathing, and between breaths, he mumbled words that she couldn't understand. After a few minutes, his incoherent words turned to sobs and then complete silence. She kept yelling his name again and again. No response.

The impact caused severe trauma to many of his organs and internal bleeding. However, according to the autopsy report, the smoked glass ceiling cut him so badly that the cause of death was from cuts made by the falling smoked glass. According to the autopsy report prepared by Dr. Edward George, William was "cut to ribbons and bled to death." The report also found that William survived the second elevator malfunction and crash by fifteen minutes, in pain, conscious, knowing he was going to die.

The police investigation lasted two full days. Olympus Elevator Company was allowed access to the site on the second day.

Two days later, William Taylor was buried at Woodlawn Crematory and mourned by his widow, Becky, and three children.

WILLIAM TAYLOR SR.
BELOVED HUSBAND AND FATHER
August 22, 1964—April 2, 1996

CHAPTER TWO

A FULL HOUSE

Monday, April 1—Tuesday, April 2, 1996
(SAME NIGHT AND NEXT DAY)

I'd been a fuckup my entire life, and that reputation was well deserved. I walked into Jack Darby's basement, an infamous poker den, and was greeted by the three hundred-pound host, "Tommy Hamilton, you've got a lot of nerve showing your ugly face around here. If I were you, and I'm glad I ain't, I'd turn around and let that door hit me in the back before I'd let the wrong persons see my sorry ass. I suspect every player in this room holds paper on you. No one 's going to sit down with you."

I was a bit offended by what old Darby had to say, even though what he said was true. Sometimes the truth hurts so bad you can hardly stand to bear it. But when necessary bluff, and bluff big.

"Darby, don't count other people's money or other people's debt. I've got more than enough money and/or credit to spare. I'm sure I can round up a game based on my good name and reputation alone. I've got green, and I'm ready to play."

Darby looked straight at me and spat out, "I know it's April Fool's Day, but these players ain't fools today or any other day. Tommy, they ain't going to give you credit on your name. It ain't worth shit."

Darby knew his customers. I had a big problem; I was drowning in my gambling debts. To make matters even worse, I had only $6,000 in my pocket. I couldn't afford to sit down at the games hosted in Darby's basement. It was no limits Texas hold 'em poker, with a one hundred and two hundred blind. Six grand wouldn't get me very far. A player with limited funds would have to bluff right out of the box in order to survive, maybe the fifth or sixth hand or be lucky and be dealt a monster hand right away

As I was pondering my strategy, I heard, "What about the three grand you owe me?" It was an old acquaintance, Red Douglas. We'd played softball and cards together.

"With the vig, it's closer to fifty-five hundred. I'd have to put pencil to paper, it's been so long that you've been ducking me, you son of a bitch."

"I've been around, Red. It's just that our paths haven't crossed, that's all."

The truth was I was ducking Red and six other guys. Two others were sitting in the corner of the room.

After quick calculating in his head, Red came back with, "It's fifty-six hundred and forty dollars on the button to be exact. Cough it up, Tommy. I want my money now!"

My God, that's my entire bankroll. I've got to do something quick to reestablish myself with the room. "Tell you what, I'll cut you for the full debt right now, double or nothing."

I quickly peeled off the amount of the bet and slammed my cash on the table. Nobody but me knew that was all the money I had on me except a few hundred. If I lost, I didn't have the duplicate amount to cover the bet.

Red gave me a hard stare and then a smile. "Tommy, you're half crazy, but that's one of the things that I like about you. Darby, a fresh deck, please."

Darby brought an unopened deck of blue Bicycle cards. Red and I each in turn inspected the deck and nodded our approval to Darby, who opened it with some ceremony. As I had hoped, both games had stopped and the thirty people in the room focused on our little contest. Darby, our self-proclaimed official, announced, "High card wins. If the card is the same, spade beats heart, heart beats diamond, diamond beats club. Hamilton has put up his fifty-five hundred against his existing debt owed Red, winner take all. Any questions?"

Dead silence. Darby turned to Red Douglas and said, "Since he put up cash, I think it's only fair that you draw first."

Red looked at the deck hard, like a man might look at a beautiful woman. He didn't pull right away, but when he did, it was a ten of spades. He smiled and threw the card on the table.

I wasn't happy. Red had pulled a pretty good card. I did the calculation in my head. *There are fifty-two cards and only sixteen cards can beat Red's card, so he has a seventy percent chance of winning. Shit, there goes the money on the table, and I'd still owe Red the debt. What the hell have I done? Stop with the negative thinking. Nothing was ever accomplished by thinking negatively. You're going to pull a Jack or better.* I grabbed the cards and cut them. I came face-to-face with the most beautiful queen of hearts I'd ever seen.

The room erupted in laughter, even Red Douglas. "Tommy, that took brass balls. Pick up your money. Not only did you win back the three thousand you owed me but the twenty-five hundred of accumulated interest as well. How about I buy you a drink and then we play us some poker?"

With a straight face I suggested, "How about another go?"

Darby jumped in, "Tommy, don't press your luck. Accept the drink and move on. Be happy you cleaned up one of your messes and have gotten an invite to sit down in a game rather than been thrown out on your ass, like you should have been."

Before I could answer old Darby, Kurt Swimmer, who'd been watching my exchange with Red, spoke up, "Tommy, you owe me thirteen hundred. I'll cut you for what you owe me right now!"

I grabbed the deck from Darby and handed it to Swimmer, who shuffled the cards for good measure and then placed them on the table. "Same rules as before. My debt of thirteen hundred for cash." I peeled off thirteen hundred, put it on the table, and waited for Swimmer to make his move. He pulled an eight of hearts.

There were twenty-five cards that could beat him. My odds were just under 50/50, not bad. With a little luck I'd erase another debt. I closed my eyes and drew the queen of diamonds. I sighed with relief. "Anyone else? I'm ready."

The room went silent. After a minute I announced, "How about we stop this foolish bullshit and play some poker?"

About the fifth hand in, I was dealt two aces in the hole. The flop or the three common cards laid face up were a three of hearts, a three of spades, and a jack of hearts. I casually bid the pot up with my two pair aces over threes. Two other players followed, and one kept raising five hundred dollars. The fourth exposed was a ten of clubs, which seemed like it was no help to anyone. My last hole card was a third ace. I had a boat aces over threes. I looked at the board, and my opponent who'd been betting, Palmer Lee, his only winning hand would be four threes.

"I'm all in, fifteen hundred," Lee said.

My choice was to call or let him have the pot of about four thousand dollars. Odds were that he didn't have four of a kind. "I'll call.

I've got to keep you honest." I turned over my boat with some fanfare.

Lee smiled and with an almost sinister bravado said, "Read them and weep."

Over the next six hours I played no limit Texas hold 'em and lost fifty-five hundred dollars.

I got beat on a couple of big hands. I lost with another boat to four of a kind, and three aces lost to a flush I didn't see coming. The cards just weren't falling my way. That happens some nights. A smart man walks away from the table before much damage is done. An addict like me loses his bankroll and then some.

Blurry eyed, I walked out of Darby's with five hundred dollars in my pocket and the rest of the month of expenses to pay for. I saved enough for a good meal, gas money, and maybe some female companionship to make me feel a little better about my situation and myself.

I'm in big trouble. I have a lifestyle to maintain. I have to call my accountant Sol Rosen later today for an advance on next month's allowance or I'll be in a real financial pinch.

Tommy was under strict instructions to direct all financial questions to Rosen. His mother refused to discuss money with him at all. Their relationship over the last few years had become tumultuous because of his gambling, more specifically because of his losses.

At ten I dialed Rosen's office. "Lamar, Gleason & Rosen, may I help you?"

"Sol Rosen, please."

"He's unavailable. May I take a message?"

"Yes, this is Tommy Hamilton. When will he be available? I need to talk to him. It's an emergency."

"Mr. Rosen is occupied with another matter and won't be available today and may not be available tomorrow. Could someone else help you?"

"No, I need Rosen. Give me his cell number!" I demanded.

"I'm not permitted to do that, sir. Only Mr. Rosen can give anyone that number. I can take a message and hopefully he'll be able to call you tomorrow."

Look, missy, I pay a substantial fee to your firm every year. I'm an important client. Now give me the goddamn number."

"Mr. Hamilton, I can't do that. Would you like to talk with the office manager, Mr. Wilcox? He's my supervisor. If not, please give me your telephone number, and I'll have Mr. Rosen call you when he can."

I gave her my number and didn't pursue it any further until nine o'clock that evening when I called Rosen at home. Mrs. Rosen answered the phone. She had a very pleasant voice. As soon as Sol got on the phone, I started in, no hello, how are you, nothing. "Sol, I need an advance on next month's allowance." I could tell right away he was pissed.

"Goddamnit, Tommy, it's the second of the month and you're out of money already? Is this a joke? This firm directly pays your mortgage, your health insurance, and your car insurance. Your only expenses are food, clothing, and discretionary costs. Your allowance is six grand a month. You're a degenerate gambler. Let's face it. That's the problem. You need help."

Thank you, Dr. Rosen. You're an accountant, not a psychiatrist, so deposit another three grand in my account."

"Drop dead, Tommy. I don't know whom the hell you think you're talking to. Don't ever call me at home again. I had a rough day. An associate of my firm died yesterday, and I've been consoling his widow. I'll deposit fifteen hundred in your account, and you better stay away from the poker tables the rest of the month or starve. I don't want to hear from you again this month. I'm tired of your bullshit." Rosen slammed the phone into its cradle.

CHAPTER THREE

PARENTING, A DIFFICULT TASK

Thursday, April 4, 1996

I wish Mary Catherine would keep her opinions to herself. Like most folks, I think she just likes to hear herself speak, bless her heart.

"Well, I'll sure take that under advisement, Mary Catherine. Any other old business?"

The conference room at the Cheekwood Botanical Garden and Museum went silent, a good sign to proceed with the meeting of the planning committee for the Swan Ball. The ball was the main annual fundraising event that sustained the grounds and gardens of the property once owned by the Cheeks, the Maxwell House Coffee family dynasty, now operated and maintained by a charitable foundation. Rita Sinclair, and her co-chair Doris Paine had been imposed upon to perpetuate the continued survival of the site since relinquished by the family in 1959 and falling into the public domain.

Rita Sinclair understood her responsibilities of chairing a successful event, but she felt comfortable that she had some breathing room. The ball was two months away, and most of the legwork was done. Rita knew how to pull it all together.

"I think the silent auction is the biggest issue. Beverly . . . " Just as Rita called on Beverly Sims, the wife of her husband's partner, John Martin, the estate manager, walked into the room. Rita was slightly annoyed by the interruption. He'd been told to interrupt only in the case of an emergency.

"Will lunch be served at noon as requested, Mr. Martin?"

"Yes ma'am." Martin whispered in Rita's ear. The other women in the room strained to hear but couldn't.

"Ladies, I have a phone call I must take. I suspend the meeting until my return. Talk among yourselves in my absence."

I followed Mr. Martin to his office. He led me to his desk and the phone on his credenza. I sat down, and he left the room.

"Mom." It was my only child, Rachel. "Hi, honey, what's wrong? Is there an emergency? What are you doing calling me here? You know I'm in a meeting."

"I'm leaving him. I'm taking the kids, and I'm leaving him. Can I come to your house? Can you come over and help me pack? I've got to figure out what to take. I know I need to take clothing. . ."

Overwhelmed but still thinking.

Slow down. What's he done?"

"Don't you dare take his side. He's unfaithful, and he's sexually demanding. I've got to live with the worst of both worlds. I don't know which offends me more: his demands or the fact that he still isn't satisfied and he needs other women. He didn't come home last night. He was probably with one of the women he swings with. You have no idea what disgusting things he wants me to do. He's perverted."

I'd had this conversation with my daughter. At least I'd started it. I stopped at a point. It was none of my business the sick sex acts my son-in-law wanted to perform. I couldn't ask my husband, Tyree, to speak to Rachel. That just wasn't going to happen. I thought about having

Tyree talk to Dan, my son-in-law, but talk about awkward. No, Rachel needs to talk to a pro.

"Look, dear, can this wait until I've finished my meeting, say about five? We've got real problems with the silent auction."

"He's coming home early tonight, about five, and he expects me to satisfy him. If you get here at five, you'll be here just in time to see that happen against my will. That should be a pretty sight. You can tell your grandchildren all about it. What's more important, your silent auction or me?"

"I'll be there in fifteen minutes. You don't need any winter clothing, only spring and summer."

Returning to the conference room, I needed to quickly dismiss my fellow members. "Ladies, we'll have to address the auction issues tomorrow. I've got to get home."

"But Rita, American Airlines has changed its pledge from four first-class tickets to four coach tickets that will greatly impact the price the New York trip will bring at auction. My notes from our meeting clearly acknowledge that Anna Braun, American's customer service representative, committed to first-class tickets. There are three other pressing auction issues we need to address."

"Tomorrow, they'll all hold till tomorrow."

I stood and left the room. *I was in charge. It was my meeting to start and end. Who the hell was that Kate Wilson to take over my meeting and tell me when an issue needed to be addressed? If she's not careful, she'll be demoted to the cleanup committee.*

Rita got in her dark blue Cadillac parked in its reserved parking space in the Cheekwood parking lot and drove through Belle Meade to her home.

Met at the door by her crying daughter, Rachel, she immediately knew she'd left one confrontation for another.

Between tears, Rachel blurted out, "I spoke to him an hour ago. He didn't come home last night. When I asked him where he was, he told me he worked till three preparing for the Swanson trial next week and was too tired to drive home, so he checked into the Radisson next to the office. He's done that before. He keeps a fresh suit in the office, just in case."

I didn't want to minimize my daughter's concerns, but so far Dan's explanation seemed plausible. Her father had done the exact same thing before many such trials. The Radisson was a convenient watering hole and resting place for most of the firm's partners who had to work late and be back at the office before the crack of dawn. We wives had come to understand. We also knew that the Radisson could also be a place of infidelity if a husband so desired. Rachel wouldn't be the first victim to the long hours and the long legs of another woman. I was confident that my Tyree was faithful, but I knew that many of the other partners had something on the side. It was almost an occupational hazard, I was sorry to admit. It wouldn't surprise me if my daughter had fallen victim to these bad circumstances. I decided to listen rather than voice any opinion just yet.

"He claims after a few hours of sleep, he went straight back to the grindstone this morning. I don't believe him. I just know he was with another woman."

"What makes you so sure he wasn't working late and wasn't just tired?"

"Because when he didn't come home or call last night, on a hunch I called the Radisson at 9:30, and he'd already checked in. He obviously had dinner out or room service in, and by 9:30 he was enjoying dessert in the room. At the very least he lied to me. He didn't work till three and then decide he was too tired to drive home. That was pure bullshit."

Dan and Rachel January had been married ten years. Rachel

was Tyree and Rita's only child, and Dan was a law partner in the second largest law firm in Nashville, Sinclair & Sims. Dan's infidelity was a serious problem on many levels.

"Mother, I can't give him what he wants sexually."

This is a conversation I'm not capable of having. I was awkward having the sex talk with my daughter when she was thirteen more than twenty years ago. I'm certainly not having it now.

"Rachel, stop. I love you and I'm here for you, but I can't have this conversation with you. What about seeing a therapist? Someone you can talk to openly about Dan's sexual demands. I'm afraid if we get into this conversation I'll never be able to look at Dan the same way again. Besides, I know so little about the subject. I'd be of little or no help. A professional, who can guide you through this difficult time and help you deal with Dan, would be a better alternative than a heart-to-heart with me. Maybe there's some sort of compromise that a therapist can provide you with that can save your marriage. Maybe joint counseling is the answer."

"Mother, if you only knew what he wanted, you'd sing a different tune."

Rita paused and weighed the moment. She was faced with opening the door and learning the intimacies of her daughter's relationship with her son-in-law. She hesitated and then choked out, "Your father and I would be happy to help you find a therapist and would be happy to pay for him or her, but it would be inappropriate for me to get in the middle of your sex life and marriage and its problems. We love you, and we love Dan."

Rachel didn't like her mother's answer. She needed to talk to someone, and no therapist was readily available. Rachel continued to reach out to her mother. "Can we at least talk in general terms, without details of Dan's sexual demands?"

She sounds desperate. How can I refuse her? She's my daughter.

I've got to lend a sympathetic ear. Listen, let her get whatever she wants off her chest. The less you say, the better.

"I know he's sleeping with other women. Six weeks ago he took me to a swingers' party."

I should have stopped her right there. This was more information than I wanted to know. These were the details that I didn't want to know because I didn't want to form vivid images in my head. As she finished her story, I tried to think of what to say.

"No one should tell you what to do with your body and who you should have sex with. Dan should be satisfied being a monogamist. It sounds like he needs to see a therapist. In my opinion he's a sick man. Without going into detail, a wife should try her best to satisfy her husband's reasonable sexual needs. I don't know and don't want to know what efforts you've made. You might seek help and guidance in that regard. If you've made reasonable effort, and Dan still insists that he can't give up other women, then you'll need to accept his infidelity or divorce him. If you accept the other women, you risk disease, public humiliation and/or severe depression. It will definitely affect your family and your children. If you opt for divorce, short term, your life, your family, and your children's lives will be disrupted, but long term, you have an opportunity to find happiness. Divorce will change the lives of your children and have an impact on your family forever. Neither alternative is a win for your children. Divorce holds the possibility of a happy ending for you after years of hurting. The best alternative is for Dan to change his behavior."

I had said far more than I intended. I hadn't listened, and I avoided the details of my daughter's marital problems. Both my daughter and my son-in-law need couples therapy and individual therapy. I hoped that Dan still wanted to save his marriage and didn't see divorce and his sexual freedom as the only solution.

CHAPTER FOUR

A BROKEN MARRIAGE

Thursday, April 4, 1996

Barry Chapman came home after a twelve-hour shift tired and in no mood for a fight with his estranged wife, Laura. They both worked at Saint Thomas Hospital, she a registered nurse, he a physical therapist. They had two children, Hannah age five and Lily thirteen months. They'd married because of an unexpected pregnancy. They'd argued over abortion, but Laura was adamant that she was having the child, and Barry finally after a bitter life-changing decision agreed to marry her. Now six years later the couple struggling from the strain of parenthood and the demands of their work schedules were losing their sanity and turning on each other.

What am I going to do? He's going to explode. I don't have to tell him today. I'll have to find the right time. He'll eventually be in a good mood. I've got at least three months. If I'm careful maybe four.

Barry used his key and walked in the door of their two-bedroom apartment located less than two miles from the hospital. He called out, "I'm home."

"We're in the kids' bedroom."

I was on the bean bag, and the two girls were sitting on the carpeted floor in front of the television. Big Bird of *Sesame Street* fame was on the screen. A plate of cookies was on the coffee table.

"May I join you?" he asked Hannah politely.

She smiled and said, "Of course. Would you like a cookie?"

"Please."

I joined Barry on the couch. He remained silent. *It was a nice family moment. Why couldn't my life feel more like this? Maybe this was the moment to tell him. Nah, why ruin this moment?*

I let silence prevail. Despite the fact he'd been a reluctant father, Barry wasn't a bad father. He wasn't a bad man. He wasn't a very good husband. He no longer loved me if he ever did.

I asked him, "Are you on tonight?"

"Don't you know my schedule?"

I didn't appreciate his smart response. "Sorry, I forgot. If I knew, I wouldn't ask."

"I'm not. Next time remember. I'm not your secretary," he said angrily.

Asshole, what did I say? What did I do? Nothing. One minute we're sitting around having a nice moment with the kids, and the next minute he's abusing me. What's wrong with him? It's not me, it's him. I can't keep living like this. It's not fair to me, it's not fair to the kids, and it's not fair to him. We need professional help if we're going to save our marriage. I've got to have the strength to raise the issue with him, or I've got to have the strength to leave.

Laura picked up Lily and asked, "Who wants grilled cheese sandwiches for dinner?"

Hannah jumped up and followed her mother from the bedroom into the kitchen. Barry remained where he was.

Laura called back, "Aren't you coming? How about soup with those grilled cheeses?"

"Sure, tomato okay with you?"

Barry joined them in the kitchen, and they ate with almost no conversation. Hannah finished quickly and returned to her television. Lily ate most of her dissected grilled cheese sandwich, and then Laura carried her into the bedroom and sat her next to her sister.

The room began to spin. I felt my supper come up, and I rushed to the bathroom. I just made it to the commode. I straddled the porcelain throne like a queen holding court. I was concerned about the reddish puke that came up but then remembered the tomato soup and was relieved. I vomited again and produced a much clearer fluid. The third time I only gagged.

After completing my disgusting task, I sat down on the cold tile floor, leaning my back against the tub and using a damp washcloth to cool myself off. *I know what's wrong with me. I don't have the flu. This isn't a stomach virus. I've had this problem twice before. I'm pregnant. I need to buy a pregnancy testing kit to confirm what I already know.*

I put the kids to bed and told Barry that I was heading to the store. "I feel like a beer, and there's none in the fridge. I'll be back in five. Do you want anything?"

"Bring me some peanut M&M's."

With that I was out the door and drove to the West End Super X. I picked up two pregnancy testing kits, just to be safe, and a king-sized bag of M&M's.

As I walked in the door, I tossed the candy to Barry, who made a good catch. Then I went straight into the bathroom. It took me only a moment to pull down my pants and pee onto the stick.

Holly shit! A happy face wasn't what I wanted to see.

I grabbed the other kit from the bag and ripped open the box. After three minutes, red letters appeared on the stick and read "yes."

I'm pregnant again. No sense in getting third and fourth tests. I'll just have to wait for the right moment. Well, there's no time like the present. I have to face reality.

"Have you given any thought to how we might celebrate Hannah's birthday next Tuesday?" I asked as I emerged from the bathroom. "I checked our schedules. We're both off three to eleven on Tuesday, her birthday."

"That works for me," he replied.

"Birthdays are important milestones in a child's life, right?"

"Absolutely, I wouldn't miss it. You know I love birthday parties. What's up? You sound strange."

"Well, I've got some big news." I paused, and Barry figured it out before I could say anything else. I guess I didn't have a very good poker face, or maybe I just didn't give a goddamn anymore.

Whatever it was, he became irate. "You're goddamn pregnant, aren't you? Holy shit. Well, I don't want another one. This time you're having an abortion. No argument. This time I'm making the decision."

"Like hell you are. This is my body, and I'll decide what's going to happen to it. You've got no say in the matter. I'm having this baby. It's living inside me, and neither you nor anyone else is going to tell me what to do. Fuck you. I'm taking him or her to term. It's your child, Barry. Grow up and accept your responsibility."

That was the wrong thing to say. It was an unfair thing to say. Barry for the last six years had accepted full responsibility for his situation. He'd married a woman he didn't love and supported two children he did love to the best of his ability.

I tried to reason with him. "We need to talk about this. We shouldn't refuse to listen to each other."

"Look who's talking. You argue it's your body and claim I've got no rights? I've got rights too. It was my sperm that made that child. He or she is half mine. I'll have to raise him or her alongside you, and I don't want to do that. I don't want to go through those sleepless nights and diaper changes. I don't want to have another mouth to feed and another child to educate. We're talking about splitting our attention and love away from Hannah and Lily by a third. We already work ourselves to death to make ends meet. It will be one-third more difficult."

"Stop thinking in dollars and cents. This isn't about money. It's about a tiny little piece of you and me that's fighting for its life right now. This family can make it work."

"You're being selfish to me and your children. I can't make it work."

"Then leave," I said angrily.

I'd said the wrong thing again. I really didn't want him to leave, at least not right at that moment, without any notice and advance warning. If Barry were to leave, I needed time to plan his exit and make sure the girls and my unborn child were protected legally and financially. I needed to get him to back down and cool off.

"Look, let's get counseling. Maybe we can save our marriage, but if not, at least end it on friendly terms. We've got Hannah and Lily to think about. No one is to blame here. This pregnancy was certainly unexpected. I was on the pill, and you were using condoms. Besides, we weren't having sex that often, maybe once a month. What are the odds?"

Barry had calmed down several levels although the problem still existed.

"I'm getting a vasectomy as soon as possible. That will prevent a repeat occurrence. Let's try to figure this out together. Counseling will be a good start, but you need to be open minded."

Counseling will buy me time. I'm not getting an abortion. I'll be getting a divorce and raising these three children on my own. I'm going to need one hell of a lawyer.

CHAPTER FIVE

VACATION UNDER PRESSURE

Monday, August 31, 1998

(TWENTY-NINE MONTHS LATER)

Davis was in big trouble with his wife, Liza. He'd be the first to admit that wasn't unusual. For a good guy, he just seemed to stay in trouble.

He had all the right qualities. He was a loving and caring husband, an exceptional father, a good provider, and a great lawyer, but he always seemed to fall victim to circumstance. He was also humble and realistic, with a good sense of humor. At least that was his defense, and as he pondered his predicament, he was sticking to it. His current problem was the standing promised anniversary vacation and his grueling work schedule.

He had good reason to be distracted from the anniversary trip. He'd committed to complete the discovery in the Taylor case, and he had the pressure of that looming deadline. There were eleven depositions to be taken in ten business days. The length of each deposition varied with the importance of the witness. It would be very difficult to get them done in the limited time allowed.

The Taylor case had been pending two years, but Davis had been involved in the case only two months. It all happened at his July 3rd party. His niece, Sammie Davis, who recently passed the Bar, introduced him to her date, Brian Ellis, another young lawyer.

Sammie joined the firm of Steine & Davis in 1992 as a paralegal. After a few years as a support staffer, she went to Vanderbilt Law School, and now as a recent graduate, she practiced with her uncle and Morty Steine, the senior partner. Sol Rosen, the employer of the deceased, had also exerted pressure on Davis to accept the case and rescue the widow from the incompetence of her current lawyer. Rosen, an experienced forensic accounting expert witness, had assessed Ellis's mishandling and prosecuting of the lawsuit and implored Davis's association.

Sammie was tall and beautiful with long blonde hair, usually worn in a ponytail. Like her uncle, she had piercing blue eyes. Men desired her, and she encouraged them, much to the disapproval of her uncle. She was young and argued, "I have my needs, and so do they. Everybody's over twenty-one. We're consenting adults." She reminded him, "Grandpa told me you weren't any angel." Davis came of age in the late sixties and early seventies and was forced to remember that he lived in a glass house. Now happily married, he had conveniently forgotten his youthful exploits. He cringed every time his father brought them up in front of Sammie and embarrassed him.

Sammie was currently being pursued and frequently caught by Ellis. He asked to accompany her to the July 3rd party because he wanted to meet and ambush her famous uncle.

He got right to the point: "Mr. Davis, I represent Rebecca Taylor. Can I bend your ear for fifteen minutes?"

"I'm hosting a party of more than two hundred people, I feel obliged to . . ."

Sammie cut him off. "Please give him a moment for me, his client, and her children." She knew just how to manipulate her uncle. He had a real soft spot in his heart for her and found it difficult to say "no" to her. He scolded, half angry and half joking, "You don't play fair. I bet you learned that from your Nana Shelly. She really knows how to apply the guilt, like all good Jewish mothers."

"Maybe so," said the younger Davis as she smiled impishly.

Davis respected his niece's opinion, and despite all his complaining and his obligation to his party, he gave the young lawyer a half hour to tell the tragic story of William Taylor. Hooked, he met with Becky Taylor on July 5th and three days later accepted employment, despite his existing heavy case-load. He'd act as first chair and co-counsel to Brian Ellis, who'd been struggling with the case for two years.

Ellis hoped that the elevator negligence case would settle quickly and he'd earn a big fee and a good settlement for the wife of his college roommate. Unfortunately, he'd seriously misjudged the defendants, who took advantage of his inexperience.

Since the case was filed, the defendants used delay tactics and his dreams of settlement against him. Now with a November 15th trial date and a September 15th discovery cutoff, the case was in trouble. Finally realizing he'd been played the fool, Ellis begged Davis to take over the case and, if necessary, try it with him. Davis accepted employment with the proviso that the last two weeks in September had to be set aside for his pre-scheduled anniversary vacation.

"I'll throw myself into the case. It will anger several of my clients whose work won't get done on time, but I'm going on vacation September 15th, no matter what. I'll stay at the office right until the plane is about to take off, but I've got to be on that plane."

Sammie agreed to pick up the slack and work with his other clients while he tended to the Taylor case during the summer, and she agreed to whatever was necessary during his extended vacation. His clients were used to his unavailability because of the small size of the office and the personal attention he gave them when it was their turn for their case. That was the nature of his practice. There was only one of him. Sammie could help and Bella was amazing, but he could be in only one place at a time. For years he had Morty Steine in the office, but recently he was less and less reliable. At seventy-eight, he'd taken the word *retirement* seriously and ventured out of his apartment only when he felt like it, which was rare.

In regard to the Taylor case, the first thing Davis did when he accepted employment in early July was to file a notice of appearance that specifically provided that he was unavailable from September 15th through the end of the month to conduct any business. It was a smart precautionary move when dealing with defendants who had unlimited resources.

Ellis roomed with William at the University of Florida, and both moved to and worked in Nashville. Sammie also attended UF, but was several years behind them.

After his friend William entered an elevator on the tenth floor of a downtown Nashville office building and plummeted to his death on April 2, 1996, Taylor's widow, Becky, called Ellis.

Taylor's employer, Lamar, Gleason & Rosen, paid Becky $175,000 under the Workers' Compensation Act because William was leaving work at the time of his death. Becky deposited $75,000 in Ellis's escrow account for expenses, which he spent poorly. Ellis wasn't dishonest, just an inexperienced attorney. Rosen expedited this payment, so that experts could be obtained. He didn't agree on who Ellis hired; another reason to seek Davis's advice and counsel.

Ellis confided to Davis, "The defense wore me out with mountains of paper, deposition after deposition, expert after expert. They took me down unnecessary forks in the road that I never should have taken. I wasted time and money. I realize it now. I didn't know how to stop it. I was too afraid to go to the judge, and they knew it."

When Davis entered the case and reviewed the expense ledger, he couldn't believe how the funds had been spent. Sammie defended Ellis, "He's never handled a complex litigation before . . ."

"That's no excuse. He accepted employment, and Ellis held himself out as competent. You wouldn't have done that."

"You're not being fair. I worked as a paralegal for years under Bella and learned the office side of the practice of law, and I had you and Morty to guide me in the law. He had no one. He was thrown in the deep end of the pool and had to learn how to swim on his own."

"The boy nearly drowned. He didn't even know how to dog paddle. I've got to give mouth to mouth to this case and revive it. There's still life in it, but barely. The only thing he did right was to sue the right parties."

Ellis had sued the elevator manufacturer, which also had a continuing inspection contract, the LLC owner of the building, the management company, which operated the building, and the guard company. In other words, he'd sued everybody using the shotgun approach to litigation. It wasn't sophisticated, but it was cautious.

Sammie and Ellis had been dating five months. Davis thought she could do better. He might have felt that way no matter which young man she was dating. He had very high expectations for his niece. Ellis was good looking enough with jet-black hair, blue eyes, pale skin, about six feet and well built. He jogged almost every morning at 5:00 a.m. and worked out at a gym on weekends. Davis hated exercise. He'd run only if chased, and then only if he didn't think he could fight his way out of the confrontation.

Sammie claimed Ellis had a good sense of humor. Davis didn't see it. He wasn't jealous, just particular. Sammie had lived with his parents since she was a little girl and had been under his wing the last six years. He just wanted what was best for her. Sammie didn't share with her uncle what Ellis did best. He satisfied her sexually, and that was no easy task. She'd been disappointed by many men.

At forty-four, Davis was rapidly losing his boyish looks, but not his charm. His sandy hair was thinning, and his weight was a constant struggle, roller-coastering from two twenty up to two sixty. Looks fade, but personality and charisma do not. In a courtroom at six foot two, with a radio announcer's voice, he remained an imposing figure. His most powerful weapon continued to be his steel blue eyes and the stare he could deliver a jury during argument or when questioning a witness. He had a real presence in a courtroom.

Davis was on his third cup of coffee when Bella Rosario, his secretary, buzzed in and identified Ellis, who said, "Go check your fax machine. We've gotten a letter from Charles Brody, and you're not going to like it. Call me back."

In the hall Davis was met by his partner and mentor, Morty.

"You look glum."

"I'm about to read a letter from Charles Brody, and I've been warned by Brian Ellis that I'm not going to like it."

"You sound surprised. You're in a lawsuit with Brody's client. You might as well expect you're not going to like whatever he sends you unless it's a settlement offer, and even then you should expect that the offer will be so low, you're still not going to like it."

Davis quipped back, "You're a real optimist, aren't you?"

Morty said with a grin, "I'm a realist."

The two men walked the ten feet, and Davis retrieved the fax from the machine.

Sent Via Fax and US Mail
(Names and Addresses omitted)
Re: Taylor vs. Olympus Elevator Company, et al

Dear Mr. Ellis and Mr. Davis,

In reviewing the current deposition schedule and the identity of those witnesses, please be advised that the defendant has decided to retain the following additional expert, Dr. Carl Weaver. Enclosed please find Dr. Weaver's resumé and his Rule 26 statement setting forth his professional opinions in the Taylor case. If you'd like to depose Dr. Weaver, he can be available for a deposition on September 18th, 19th, or 22nd. If you have questions or if you wish to discuss the scheduling of Dr. Weaver's deposition, please contact me.

Yours very truly,
Charles Brody

Cc: Anthony Korn
William Patton
Lowell Thomas

Davis didn't overreact. There was nothing to be gained. He showed the letter to Morty, and without a word, he knew what to do. Morty followed him into his office and sat in one of the rich teal blue chairs across from Davis's desk. Davis pushed the speakerphone button and connected with the offices of Hecht, Brody & Lewis, a twenty-five-man (there was one woman associate) firm located in the Life & Casualty Tower in downtown Nashville. He got the receptionist and asked for Charlie Brody.

"Hello, Charlie, I've got you on speakerphone. Morty's sitting in on the call."

"Hello, Morty. Ben, when do you want to set Dr. Weaver's deposition?"

"I don't."

"Well, my Rule 26 statement describing his opinions must have been pretty clear if you don't need to take his deposition. I must be getting better at this than I thought."

"You've misunderstood. I won't be taking Weaver's deposition because he won't be testifying at trial."

Brody's voice changed. It went up an octave or two and was definitely louder. "What's that supposed to mean?"

"I mean you've missed the deadline to disclose experts. All defense experts had to be disclosed two days ago. You calendared your deadline wrong. Go look at the scheduling order. I sighed with relief when your deadline passed on Sunday, so under the rules it extended until Monday, yesterday, the first business day. You're one day late, Charlie."

"Then I'll file a motion for an extension, and it will be heard the week of the 15th."

"Wrong again. Go look at my notice of appearance filed July 8th. It puts you on notice of my unavailability for that week and the week after."

"I don't care about your unavailability. Let your co-counsel Ellis argue my motion."

"You're through pushing that young man around. Steine, Davis, & Davis represent Becky Taylor, and you'll find Morty Steine will argue that motion. I'll be sending you a response to your letter by the end of the day. It will inform you if you seek your extension after the deadline has expired that the plaintiff will seek sanctions if you file such a frivolous motion, including attorney fees. In fact I'll argue and plant the idea in the minds of the judge and your client that by missing the deadline, your firm committed malpractice. How'd you like to take that chance, Charlie? After we get a judgment in the Taylor case, your client, the big bad insurance company, sues your firm for malpractice and you lose the client forever. I'd let sleeping dogs lie, don't you think."

Morty interjected, "By the way, Charlie, my hourly rate is $500, and I plan on walking very slowly to the courthouse. If I have to argue your motion, I'll be enunciating each word and plan on being long-winded."

Brody hung up without another word. Both men knew he wouldn't be filing a motion or offering Weaver as an expert witness. He was clearly surprised. Some poor secretary, paralegal, or associate would be getting canned over this.

Morty chuckled and asked, "How did he think he'd get away with that? He must know I've taught you better than that."

"He's been dealing with Ellis for almost three years, and he's gotten complaisant. He and other defense lawyers have been walking all over him, and I guess they forgot that there's a new lawyer on the case."

Davis shook his head and added, "What bothers me is that Ellis didn't have a clue the deadline had expired, and he's my co-counsel. I don't think I can trust his work. I don't mind doing all the heavy lifting, but I'm going to have to carry him the entire trial. How about helping out?"

Morty shook his head and said, "You know you can count on me, but you can't have three attorneys at counsel table representing one widow. It just wouldn't look right."

Davis agreed. He called Ellis and told him to forget about Weaver. He wouldn't be testifying at trial. He didn't provide details. Ellis was impressed that Davis had gotten Brody to withdraw his expert. It was a good thing for Becky Taylor that Ellis brought Davis into the case. He had also caught the eye of the beautiful Sammie. *Lucky guy, in more than* one *way,* thought Davis.

CHAPTER SIX

PROMISES MADE

Monday, August 31, 1998

Davis had a busy afternoon. He signed six letters he'd dictated the night before, dictated six others, and made eleven calls, leaving five messages to clients. The name of the game was phone tag. People were usually unavailable, and you had to get back to them. One letter, as promised, was to Charles Brody concerning the expired expert witness deadline. He smiled as he signed it and told Bella to fax it and also send it via U.S. mail. *I hope you choke on it, Charlie. You're not dealing with that kid any longer.*

He spent more than an hour working on an appellate brief in a royalty dispute case involving Johnny Cash and June Carter Cash in which Davis had been awarded a verdict of $480,000. Both performers were originally Morty's clients. He'd represented them for years regarding their music careers and Johnny's brushes with the law. In this contract dispute, which Davis handled, all three issues raised by the appellant, the losing party, came in during Johnny's testimony. At the time Davis debated the importance of the documents and testimony, and in the end he pushed for their admission. He was now paying for those calculated decisions on appeal. Johnny did a great job on the stand and the case was won, but now the victory had to be defended on appeal.

He buzzed Sammie as he quickly switched gears. "I don't want to see the Longfellow brief again. I'm sick of polishing this document. Proof it one more time and then file the damn thing."

Howard Longfellow, forty-two, father of three, a commercial freight airline pilot, and former Air Force captain, lost his cool at a Little League baseball game and got in an argument that resulted in a pushing match and ended with a right cross that broke the jaw of Stan Hamm, home plate umpire, and put Hamm in the hospital overnight.

Criminal charges for aggravated assault and battery were brought against Longfellow, a felony. Hamm filed a civil suit against the Brentwood Community Baseball League and Longfellow, individually, alleging intentional wrongful conduct, recklessness, and outrageous conduct. The league cross-claimed against Longfellow, asserting that he was the proximate cause of Hamm's injuries, not the league. The firm was filing a brief to dismiss the claim of outrageous conduct because it was unclear as to whether Tennessee law recognized the existence of the tort. The Tennessee Supreme Court had not yet ruled on that issue, and the Tennessee appellate courts were split on the question. The Middle Section of the Court of Appeals, where Nashville was located, previously allowed the tort of outrageous conduct, while the Eastern and the Western Sections refused to recognize the cause of action. Punitive damages, damages for the purpose of punishing Longfellow, could be awarded if outrageous conduct was recognized as an actionable tort by the court. Davis hoped the trial court would follow the majority of the sections and dismiss Hamm's claim for outrageous conduct despite the fact they were located in Nashville, which was located in the Middle Section. It was a long shot because geography was geography, but it was important to preserve the issue for appeal. This disputed matter would probably go to the Tennessee Supreme Court if Davis couldn't get the matter settled because the three sections were not in agreement.

As he proofed the brief, he was forced to eat at his desk, something he generally didn't like to do. He enjoyed eating lunch and having a sit-down meal. However, the back door of Davis's office building, the old Steine Department Store, was on Printer's Alley, so he had access to various take-out alternatives. The firm maintained an account at the famous Captain's Table, an upscale restaurant, and Davis had a New York strip steak and fries delivered by a waiter to the office. He ate alone, reading between bites.

The afternoon was devoted to three client meetings. The first involved an age discrimination lawsuit filed six months earlier in the U.S. District Court for the Middle District of Tennessee, which alleged that Chris Addams's employer, First American National Bank, violated the federal Age Discrimination Act. That statute protected employees over forty from discrimination based on age.

Addams had been a senior vice president of international banking and a member of the bank's executive committee. In February he was demoted to manager of the main branch. Furthermore, he was directed to report to the senior vice president of operations who, prior to his transfer, the lawsuit argued, was his equal. His $100,000 salary as a senior vice president was red lined or frozen because it exceeded the salary cap of $90,000 for bank managers.

Addams had come to the office today to review his proposed answers to interrogatories (questions) and the request for production of documents that were due in three days to verify the accuracy of the answers. The document had been bantered back and forth between Davis and Addams, with Bella making changes each time. They hoped to finalize the document today so that it could be sent to the bank's attorney before the expiration of the deadline and be taken off Davis's to-do list.

Davis wasn't looking to pick a fight with his client, but he suspected his next suggestion would invoke one.

"I've decided to let my niece, Sammie, take Rogers's deposition."

"What! You've got to be kidding. She's green. He'll eat her alive. I hired you. You should take the deposition. It's the key to the case."

"It will throw them off balance. They're overconfident and arrogant. They won't know what to think. Trust me."

Client and lawyer argued for more than twenty minutes, but Davis prevailed. Addams left in disgust, and Davis returned to his work.

Davis maintained his to-do list on a yellow pad in his own handwriting, which only Morty, Sammie, and Bella could read because of Davis's illegible handwriting. He also used shorthand to describe the tasks to be completed. They included correspondence, phone calls, pleadings, deadlines, and so on. Addams's discovery responses were third on the list.

As Davis completed an item, he crossed it off the list. At least every other day, he rewrote the list, always moving uncompleted tasks to the top. The list changed every day, with Davis moving items according to his random system that only he understood. It kept him organized and helped him be a better lawyer. He learned such techniques from the best, Morty, who was more than twenty-five years his senior and his mentor.

Morty had taken in Davis more than twenty-two years earlier as a young, inexperienced Vanderbilt law student and taught him how to practice law. After all these years, he elevated Davis to a junior partner. Davis was Morty's first and only partner, and that in and of itself said something about the young New Yorker's ability and charisma. Morty and his wife, Goldie, had adopted Davis as the son they never had, even though Davis's parents were very much alive in Woodbury, Long Island. In return the Davis family had extended an open invitation to the Steines to be a part of their family.

Over the more than two decades an indescribable bond developed between these two men involving love, respect of each other, and mutual admiration of the law, but there was something more: a desire to serve their clients and do the right thing. The older man in an effort to teach the younger one the law and how to conduct himself when dealing with others led by example. More amazing was how both men had approached the education of the newest member of the firm, Davis's niece, Sammie. Each man was committed to making her a better lawyer and person than either of them, a lofty goal.

The second meeting of the afternoon was with Brandon Tell, the owner of Aquamarine Swimming Pools Inc. Richard Feeder and his wife, Glenda, sued Tell for negligent construction of a swimming pool. Feeder owned a used car lot in Columbia, Tennessee, and their home was in Spring Hill, near the General Motors plant. This was a first consult. Davis had never represented Tell or his company before.

The meeting started out friendly, each exploring the other's background.

"How did you come to call me for a consult?"

"It's funny. You were recommended by my competitor, Bob Simmons of Clear Water Pools. I'd asked Bob to look at the Feeder pool as a favor to see if he could figure out the problem. He couldn't, but during the conversation poolside, he admitted to me that Clear Water had been sued last year and that the judge found against them. I asked him who represented him in the lawsuit, anticipating that the Feeders might file one if I couldn't solve the problem. His response surprised me."

"What did he say?"

"He told me not to hire his guy, but to hire you because you kicked his lawyer's ass, even though he thought they should have won. Bob claimed that you made the difference, and he confided that if he got sued again, he'd be hiring you."

That was the best advertising Davis could hope for.

"Simmons told me that you were relentless in your questioning. Despite his preparation, you rattled him on the stand. He called you a junkyard dog."

Davis thought about it. *That was a backhanded compliment. I've been called worse.*

Davis spent ten minutes reviewing the contract between the parties. Ninety percent of the document was standard language, boilerplate. It had been prepared by Tell himself from a document he'd seen and copied. *That's usually a big mistake. A pool contractor playing lawyer. Tell would have been better off having his contract prepared by his plumber or electrician. Both had about the same amount of legal training as Tell.*

Davis offered to improve the document for Tell. "There's no reason to have a clause that provides that the successful party is entitled to legal fees and costs. In general, under Tennessee law, each party must bear its own legal fees and costs unless you include this clause in your contract. If your contract was written, as I suggest, then you could collect attorney fees and costs if the customers failed to make full payment, but if you screwed up, the customers would still be liable to pay their own attorney. The fact that customers will be responsible for their own legal fees makes it much more likely those problems will be resolved without the need for litigation. I'm sure their attorney, Mr. Shames, has told the Feeders that they will reimburse the fees he's paid. They'd have been less likely to pursue the claim if they knew they'd be five or six thousand in the hole."

Davis asked if the pool could be repaired by Aquamarine or another company. Tell was uncertain. Davis indicated that identifying the problem was the first step. He knew the Feeders' attorney, and he'd secure access to the pool for another competitor to examine it and "get another pair of eyes to look at the problem." He assured his new client that the rules didn't require any action for thirty days. "But there is not any reason why we shouldn't be proactive."

Davis informed his new client that his hourly rate was $350 and that he needed a $3,500 retainer to bill against. Davis's hourly rate varied. It ranged from $300 to $450 depending upon the nature of the case and the nature of the client. Tell was a business client, of modest means, so his fee was mid-range. Morty had taught him that whenever possible, he should demand a retainer from any new client for a new case. He said, "They need to have some skin in the game, and if they are an unknown commodity, there is no need to extend them credit." They signed a one-page contract, and Mr. Tell felt better when he left Davis's office. Davis also felt better. He had a new client who was referred by an adversary, possibly the highest compliment of all.

Davis was a businessman and Steine, Davis & Davis was a profit-making enterprise. Fortunately, Morty Steine was a wealthy man and could subsidize the business if it had a bad month or two, so the firm had the ability to take on contingency cases that didn't have the luxury to quickly pay off and also could accept many pro bono cases that helped people in need, with no promise of economic reward. The firm had plenty of big paydays that could offset its non-profitable actions.

Davis returned several phone calls. He reached two clients and answered their questions about the status of their lawsuits. He left messages for three others whom he tried to reach earlier in the day. Telephone tag continued.

The last meeting of the day was a sad one. Mrs. Vinson, age forty-six, had a son who suffered from both drug abuse and mental illness. Because her son was over eighteen, her options were limited to get him help.

"If he's willing to voluntarily commit himself to treatment, that's the way to go. If not, you'll have to get two doctors to be willing to swear under oath that he's a danger to himself or an imminent danger to others. That's a hard opinion to get from a psychiatrist or any doctor. Start with his treating physician and then call me."

Davis didn't have much hope she'd get the cooperation from the doctor that she needed, but if she did, he'd represent her free of charge.

It was almost seven, so Davis called it a day. Home to wife and family.

CHAPTER SEVEN

THE OLD COLLEGE TRY

Tuesday, September 1, 1998

What can he possibly be thinking? He doesn't love me. He feels trapped and wants out. Why do I even want to try to save this marriage and for whose benefit? The children hear the arguments and see the anger on our faces.

Laura sat with Barry in the waiting room of Dr. Karen Richards, a family therapist. It was their third session. The first two had yielded no progress, other than to reveal the seriousness of their marital rift.

Barry leafed through a *Golf Digest,* intentionally not making eye contact with Laura.

"Would you look at me, please? What are we doing? You thought you could bully me into an abortion. Well guess what? You were wrong. I'm five months pregnant. There's not going to be any abortion now."

Barry tightly grabbed the arms of his chair, and his face turned red.

I'm not sure why I was pushing his buttons. I think I want this to be our last session with Dr. Richards. Why waste the time or the money? In retrospect, maybe I shouldn't have provoked Barry so much.

"You need to explain to me why you need to not only be right but also have to be cruel about it in the process. I'm not only going to file for divorce on the grounds of cruel and inhumane treatment, but I'm going to challenge the paternity of that child. Who knows? Maybe I'll get lucky and I'll only have to pay child support on two rather than three, and I'll have grounds for divorce on the basis of infidelity to boot."

I remained silent for a moment before responding, "What a hurtful thing to say." Barry and I had our problems, but I never looked at another man. "You're bluffing. You know that I've been faithful to you. Our marriage may stink, but that's not because either of us has anyone else."

Barry looked at me hard, and said, "I need someone else. I need someone to share my thoughts with, to share my dreams, to share my life, and that person isn't you. Somehow we got off track and went in different directions."

"So accept that, and let's just move on in our different directions without trying to harm each other."

Barry jumped out of his chair, and it fell to the floor. "How can I? We've brought three children into the world. I'm going to be paying for that financially at least till they're eighteen and emotionally for the rest of my life."

As he completed his sentence, the doctor came out. "Are we ready for our session?"

Barry turned to the door and over his shoulder said, "I'm out of here. You ladies try to figure this marriage out without me. Laura, you'll be hearing from my lawyer."

As I walked into her inner office my therapist asked, "What got him started?"

"I did. I'd had enough of him and this marriage. I saw no point in continuing a charade and trying to a save a dying marriage. The man didn't love me, and he didn't want to have our third child. I don't think he wanted our first two either. We weren't a real family, and it would have gotten worse. I saved my family."

Dr. Richards waited for me to finish my little speech and then said, "I couldn't agree more, but I wouldn't be surprised that by the end of the week you're sued for divorce. You just stopped working? Who pays the bills and is familiar with the finances? Where are the last three years of tax returns? Do you know a good divorce lawyer? Do you know any divorce lawyer, good or bad? Do you have the money for a divorce lawyer? Do you know how much money a divorce lawyer should cost? You shouldn't have provoked him without a plan."

She was right. "Do you know an attorney?"

"Not personally, but a client of mine is represented by Dan January with the firm of Sinclair & Sims. I am familiar with the firm. It is one of the oldest in the city. According to my client, January specializes in divorce, and she seems very happy with him."

I asked, "May I please speak with your client so I may personally hear her recommendation?"

"Sorry, that would violate doctor-patient confidentiality. The important thing is that I heard he's tough; he's a fighter. My patient says he's on your side. He gets that bone in his mouth, and he doesn't let go."

"That's who I want, but how am I going to pay him? Lawyers don't come cheap."

Dr. Richards took my hand and simply said, "You better figure it out for the family and that unborn child. They need representation in this divorce just like you do. January should be a reasonable man. Lay the facts out for him, and he'll help you Nothing is free. You'll have to work for it; it won't kill you. What doesn't kill you makes you stronger."

What bullshit. I'm in for a fight. I better hire a gunslinger, and I better find the cash to hire him or her. I may have to beg, borrow, or steal because whoever I get isn't going to fight for me for free.

"Dr. Richards, I want to thank you for your honesty and guidance. I brought you a dying marriage, but you helped me recognize its death. I'm going to contact Mr. January or someone like him today. My plan to defend my family and children begins right now."

I stood, and despite our professional relationship, I gave the doctor a hug. Surprisingly, Richards hugged me right back. I turned and walked out and drove straight to the day care center and picked up Lily. As we drove home, I pondered my exchange with Barry at Richards's office.

Would Barry really declare war against me? Would he pull the grenade pin and risk killing everyone he loves around him, his children, including himself? Maybe he doesn't love anyone, including himself?

At home, I put Lily down for her nap. I made a cup of tea and then used my cell phone to call the law office of Sinclair & Sims. When the receptionist answered, I said, "Dan January, please."

After a short wait, Mr. January got on the phone. "Good afternoon. I understand you need a lawyer?"

"Yes, sir. My husband, Barry, is about to sue me for divorce. I have two girls and another child on the way. I'm five months pregnant. I feel very alone right now."

There was a brief silence. Then he said, "You're not alone. First you've got your children; then you've got the joy of your unborn child. There's life inside you. You've got me and the resources of my firm, and let me assure you that is considerable. You are definitely not alone."

I need to warn you that I don't have much money. I'm a registered nurse. Barry's a physical therapist. He keeps the family's checkbook, and I don't know the details of our finances. How will I pay you?"

There was a longer pause. "You'll come in for a free meeting so we can get to know each other. Look each other in the eyes and make sure we're compatible. If we're comfortable with each other, then we will agree on a retainer and an hourly rate to charge. My rate varies based on circumstances, and your ability to pay is an important consideration. I think you'll like me and feel comfortable with me. I don't want to mislead you, though. This isn't going to be easy or happen quickly. Let's not try to go any further over the phone. Can you come in tomorrow at 3:00, and we can begin to get to know each other?"

"I'll be there. Thank you, Mr. January, for agreeing to meet with me and considering to represent me."

"Call me Dan. I'll see you then."

He hung up, and I felt a whole lot better.

CHAPTER EIGHT

HOME SWEET HOME

Tuesday, September 1, 1998

Davis exited the back door and emerged onto Printer's Alley. At night, the Alley awakened, only beginning to come to life. The neon signs screamed come in and have a drink and listen to some good music. He was tempted. *It's been a long day, and I'm a little thirsty.*

Printer's Alley, originally a publishing center, hence the name, now offered all types of music: country, western, bluegrass, blues, and rock 'n' roll. A basement poker game could be found. Other establishments offered a look-see at half-naked women. Locals knew and tourists could find out, for the right price, where to get a little something extra on the second floor. The Alley could be a seedy place.

Davis thought about getting a drink at the club of Boots Randolph, the sax player/bar owner. The music was good, and he knew the bartender, who poured three fingers of Jack. He decided against it and headed for the Commerce Street garage. There she was waiting for him, his twenty-fifth anniversary Vette, silver with dark cherry interior, a gift from his client Albert Wilson after winning his case. He rarely drove it, trying to keep the mileage down. He slipped in, lowered the top, and exited the garage faster than he should have. *Good old Albert Wilson, a man of substance! A blessed memory.*

The drive down West End Avenue brought back memories. On his left was Vanderbilt University, where he'd gone to law school and graduate business school, and most important where he met his wife, Liza, who'd attended nursing school. Farther down the road he drove through Belle Meade, the ritzy part of town, where, as a Jew, he'd be a little out of place, forcing his way in. He then turned right into the Hillwood area, where he and Liza had chosen to raise their family, right off Hillwood Country Club.

Jake, age eleven, met him at the door, with his book in hand. They'd been reading *The Hobbit* together, and Davis alternated voices with each character. He could control his deep, booming voice pretty well but had difficulty with Bilbo's high, squeaky voice. Jake was a fantasy junkie. It was something that father and son shared together. Davis knew it was important for a father and a son to share common hobbies. He'd shared the 1960s New York Yankees with his father. They'd gone to games in the Bronx at the House that Ruth built and watched on television as Mickey Mantle, Yogi Berra, Roger Maris, Whitey Ford, and other legends brought home pennant after pennant and several World Series back to New York. It was something that Davis and Morty shared also. Interesting, although Morty was born in Nashville in 1920, he'd been a Yankees fan during the era of Babe Ruth and Lou Gehrig in the late 1920s and early 1930s.

"Hello, my little monkey boy."

Jake acted perturbed by his pet name but really wasn't. He tried to imitate the high voice of Bilbo Baggins and had it down pretty well: "Dinner is being prepared for our mutual enjoyment."

They walked into the kitchen, and Davis's wife of more than sixteen years was bent down looking in the oven. Davis admired her backside. With his son present, that's all he could do. He restrained himself. *Maybe later?*

The room smelled delicious. Davis's nostrils flared as the aroma of her mother's recipe for pot roast with roasted potatoes and carrots overcame him. *Beauty, brains, and she can cook, a deadly combination. I'm a lucky man. I'd better remember to tell her that.*

She scolded him when he dunked several pieces of bread in the gravy. "Can't you wait? What kind of manners are you setting for your son? You need to wait and sit down with us as a family and not eat like an animal."

That's a little harsh. "I'm teaching him that's the best part," he insisted. Davis was already dreaming about leftovers, which he'd consume later tonight away from the eyes of his loving and complaining wife.

Like his father, he worked long hours, but he still felt it was important for the family to eat together. That meant the kids weren't fed by six and weren't in bed by eight. The Davises were a late night family, a very non-traditional family, and proud of it. Often the four of them piled into the California king-sized bed and watched TV together. It made them uniquely close, but that was happening less and less as Caroline became a teenager. She preferred alone time to family time. "A teenager's prerogative," Liza would insist. Davis was less understanding.

Caroline entered the room while listening to her Walkman. Davis gestured for her to take the earphones out of her ears so she could participate in the family conversation. He hated how she got lost in a trance with those things on her head.

Davis opened the floor for discussion, and Jake brought up the anniversary trip. Davis insisted that he was in charge of planning the trip and "didn't need any help from the peanut gallery."

Liza groaned and rolled her eyes.

"This is your mother's and my anniversary. We'll be making the arrangements to take care of you. Both sets of grandparents will be pitching in. Sammie and even Morty will be contributing his fair share. So it's none of your concern."

Usually family discussions were far more democratic, but Jake had abused his position by offering outrageous destinations that infuriated his mother. Davis's tone was his attempt to protect the boy. Despite their father's remarks, both Jake and Caroline continued to make suggestions.

"How about Africa?" Jake proposed. "You can see lions and tigers and bears, oh my." He was repeating the line from the *Wizard of Oz*, his favorite movie. Caroline brought up Disney World, but she was joking. Her father had dragged her there six times over the last fourteen years.

Davis perked up and said, "That's not a bad idea." (He was joking.) Liza gave him a dirty look that ended the conversation. She didn't like any of the suggestions, and although she loved her children, everyone in the room knew the children were staying behind. They had to attend school, and two sets of grandparents would alternate taking care of them. This was an anniversary trip for the parents; an opportunity for them to be alone and rekindle their relationship. Davis had made promises, and he needed to keep them.

After dinner, Davis roughhoused with Jake. They pretended that they were professional wrestlers, and Davis pinned his son several times after tossing him around like a rag doll. Davis had a hundred and twenty pounds on his son. His final act of domination was to hold both hands down and blow hard on Jake's belly, tickling him and making a loud farting sound at the same time. Jake loved the attention and the horseplay. Davis's older brother, George, had done the same to him almost forty years earlier.

Davis finally turned his attention to what he really wanted, other than the leftovers. He entered his bedroom with a devilish look in his piercing blue eyes.

"What do you want?" Liza asked, pretending a protesting tone.

"Only a few minutes of your valuable time, my lady."

"It's ten fifteen. I've given you the time. What more do you need?"

"You know what I want, and I don't have time to dillydally."

Now it was time for Liza to be coy. "What's more important: your work or satisfying me? If we start something, I demand snuggle time."

She was making Davis negotiate for what he wanted, and she knew she had the upper hand. She could tell when he was horny, and he was.

"Have I told you lately how beautiful you are? How wonderful and brilliant you are, and what a wonderful wife and mother you are to our children?"

"No, not lately. It's interesting that you bring those points up here and now when you want something."

Davis contemplated his next words carefully. *How little snuggle time can I get away with and still achieve my goal?* He fixed on his strategy, asked for more than he expected, and settled for what he really wanted. "What would it take for you to . . ." and he whispered his most secret desires in her ear. It only took a moment.

There was a pause as his wife contemplated her response, "That will happen only when aliens invade Nashville, Tennessee."

Without flinching, Davis made another sexual suggestion equally abhorrent to his wife. "Well, how about a quickie and five minutes of snuggle time, since I can't get what I really want?"

She nodded, and the fun began. Fifteen minutes later, Davis was at his desk, satisfied, working on the Taylor case. Liza rolled over, not satisfied, but ready for bed and another day. Davis, deluded, thought to himself, *I'm a good negotiator,* while Liza acknowledged, *I'm a good and supportive wife.*

One of the depositions scheduled later in the week was Becky Taylor's. William's cell phone records revealed that he called 911 and his home number twice that fateful evening. The second call lasted an hour and forty-one minutes before the battery went dead. It took the Nashville Fire Department three hours and fifteen minutes from the time of William's 911 call to extract his body from the wreckage. Becky would testify that she estimated she spoke with William for about fifteen minutes before the second crash. Surprisingly, her testimony was not without support. There was a partial record of what was said. William failed to turn off his micro recorder that was left on in his shirt pocket. That recorder was returned by the fire department with William's personal effects, and a sworn transcript was turned over to the defendants during discovery.

Dr. George, the medical examiner, would testify that in his professional opinion, William survived the final crash about fifteen minutes. Becky would confirm hearing her name whispered several times. That was confirmed by the micro recorder.

As he sat at his desk Davis thought, *Thirty minutes of hell, and I've got to get a jury to understand what William was going through and get them to feel his fear, pain, and anguish.*

Davis returned to the task at hand. The depositions scheduled for tomorrow were those of two engineers. They were very technical in nature. Davis found a consulting expert to explain the dozens of documents and help him draft questions. Under Rule 26 of the Tennessee Rules of Civil Procedure, Davis was not obligated to disclose the identity of his consulting expert because he didn't intend to have him testify at trial. Davis wanted to keep this expert's identity and testimony secret, so he'd already decided to use someone else for trial, who Ellis had already disclosed as his expert.

Davis was studying the defendant elevator company's incident report of the 1996 event and at the same time looking at various photographs of parts of the death chamber that were taken soon after the elevator imploded. Many parts were severely damaged during the crash. One of the theories of the complaint prepared by Brian Ellis was that the safety brake was defective and failed to work and prevent the tragedy.

Davis was staring hard at the picture of the safety brake and then moving his eyes to the report. He compared the information. Something was not right. He'd get it clarified at the deposition. He was pleased and felt confident about tomorrow.

The last thing Davis did before he went to bed was to look over his yellow pad list of things to do. It was extensive. He had thirteen unanswered phone calls, six returned calls where he left a message, three letters to write, five correspondences that needed responses, four pleadings to prepare, two briefs, two end of the day client meetings, and the ten Taylor depositions over the next two weeks. He tried to figure out which tasks he could delegate to Sammie and Bella. It was two when he finally went to bed. Liza, sound asleep, looked satisfied. He was exhausted.

CHAPTER NINE

UP AND DOWN

Wednesday, September 2, 1998

Davis arrived at the office earlier than usual because he'd be in depositions all day and wanted to address some items on his long to-do list. He glanced over the document and contemplated how best to address the complex issues presented. He spent most of the early morning dictating correspondence to clients and adversary counsel in varied cases. Several of these correspondences tried to solve problems, while others were mere delaying tactics to buy time or draw matters out. Unfortunately, sometimes there wasn't a good solution to a problem, and the best option was to force a settlement down the road. He also worked on a motion to compel discovery. It was his stab at a first draft. He figured, *That will keep Bella busy all day, not that she needs things to do.* The more than thirty-five-year veteran secretary was critical to the operation of the office. In recent years Morty had delegated all administrative responsibilities of running the office to her, and she'd shined in that capacity.

He attempted three phone calls, no luck. The parties hadn't gotten to their offices yet. He left a message but knew he wouldn't be available for the call back. The vicious cycle continued.

He quickly wrote out instructions to Sammie about how to

begin drafting the three other pleadings and the necessary research for the two briefs that had to be written. She could get the documents started. Then he'd polish them. *Under the circumstance that's the best we can do. Sammie makes a good point. Compliment her.*

Almost seventy-eight, Morty could no longer do everything. Davis was stretching himself and doing all he could, and Sammie would have to shoulder more and more responsibility. *She's ready. We've trained her well.*

With his blood-stained, initialed BAD briefcase in hand, he walked the short distance to Charlie Brody's office. Brian Ellis was waiting along with their client, Becky Taylor, who greeted him with a good luck hug. As instructed, Becky was dressed in her Sunday best, no jewelry except her wedding ring. She was an attractive and extremely sympathetic witness.

Becky wore her curly auburn hair extremely short, much shorter than when William was alive. She was usually soft spoken, but her testimony concerning William's death was powerful, and her dramatic description of the last thirty minutes of William's life was chilling and would bring any juror to tears. Only William and Becky shared those last few minutes together. No one on the face of the earth would dare refute whatever she said.

That testimony would be corroborated, in part, by Ralph Kramer, the guard on duty that morning, whose employer was a defendant, and then there was the recorder in William's shirt pocket. Davis wanted the insurance executives who controlled the purse strings to hear Becky's testimony so they'd come to fear it.

Defense counsel, all business, quickly took their seats. Lowell Thomas represented the management company that operated the Crystal Tower and hired Bradley, the guard service. Thomas nodded hello to Morty but didn't waste a breath in his acknowledgment of

Davis and for good reason. He hated Davis. It all stemmed from bad blood between the lawyers. Most of the time after a heated battle the combatants could set their feelings aside and behind them, get paid, have a beer together, and wait for the next fight. A pharmacy malpractice judgment ten years ago, and then five years later an almost $5 million medical malpractice judgment in the Malone case, one of the Plainview cases, for a total settlement of $10 million had made Thomas a bitter man and a very sore loser. *Hello to you too,* thought Davis. *Nice to see you again too.* He didn't like Davis, and the feeling was mutual.

After the court reporter and the videographer set up, the parties were ready to proceed. Davis had filed a motion with the court to videotape all eight of the depositions he was taking. Defense counsel filed a similar motion for the three they were taking, including the deposition of Becky Taylor. Davis loved the idea of Becky on camera, but at the same time he realized that it placed additional pressure on his already nervous client.

The videotaping of depositions was done for two reasons: one for safety and one as a pressure tactic. The video preserved the demeanor of the witnesses' testimony, body language, and so forth. In the event they died or became unavailable due to illness or travel outside the country before trial, the video would be available. The pressure aspect was that most people were uncomfortable on camera. It was harder to lie and be evasive with the eyes of a camera on you. The lie was preserved forever and not just on a piece of paper in a deposition.

First up was Thomas Brooks, the Olympus inspector who last inspected car #3 of the Crystal Tower on January 4, 1996. Davis slowly went into Brooks's background and training. He challenged the extent of Brooks's training and his qualifications as an expert to inspect elevators. Davis established that Brooks followed the company checklist when he inspected car #3 and that the elevator did pass the inspection.

"It passed with flying colors, right?"

"Yes, sir."

"No parts had to be replaced?"

"That is right."

"In fact, please look at Exhibit 3, the maintenance log that was filled out prior to your January 4th inspection. Was a major part replaced?"

"No, sir, only minor general maintenance was performed. No major part was replaced."

Davis asked another half hour of questions and then turned the witness over to the defendants, who had no questions. The parties took a five-minute comfort break.

The next witness up was Lawrence Kennedy, an employee of the defendant elevator company who'd prepared the incident report.

Davis started by inquiring about Kennedy's education and prior employment. He was forty-six years old and had been with the company six years. He'd worked two years as an inspector, who would approve the condition and operation of elevators sold by the company and maintained under a continuing contract.

"During that two-year period, how many elevators did you inspect?"

"At least one a day, sometimes two, rarely three."

"Worked five days a week and got two weeks of vacation?"

"Objection, compound question," Brody announced.

Through a series of questions Davis established that during the two years, Kennedy inspected approximately a thousand elevators.

"How many of those failed inspection?"

Before Kennedy could answer, Brody objected, first on the grounds of confidentiality and then on relevancy. Davis argued that the state required all inspections to be posted on the wall of each elevator, so the information was readily available to anyone who wanted to visit each of the elevators and keep a running total.

"It's relevant because it's clear this elevator failed, and you know how broad Rule 26 and Rule 401 are. So let's stop wasting time or I'll call the judge, and he can tell you to reserve your objections to what is really objectionable."

Brody backed down because he knew Davis was right, and he knew that Davis wouldn't hesitate to call the judge and embarrass Brody.

Davis finally got his answer, three or 1/300th of a percent.

"So a failed inspection doesn't happen often?"

"I guess not. I think that's a pretty low percentage."

"How many of those three that failed your inspection caused an injury or death?"

"None."

"In the six years you've been with the company, how many injuries and deaths have occurred?"

Davis already knew the answer to the question through written questions and requests for documents to the company.

"There was one other fatal incident when I first started with the company in 1992. Four people died in Bowling Green, Kentucky, when the elevator they were in fell six floors. I had nothing to do with that matter. I just heard about it through the company grapevine and in training."

Kennedy admitted that after his two-year stint as an inspector, he was transferred to the investigation department.

"That would have been January 13th, 1996?"

"Yes."

"Describe your training."

Kennedy testified that the training lasted a year and consisted of schooling and field training. He admitted that at the time he prepared the Taylor incident report, he was still in training and that the Taylor report was counter-signed by his supervisor, Oscar Brand.

"This was your first field incident? You'd never investigated a falling elevator incident before?"

"No, sir. Mr. Brand was with me every step of the way."

"But you prepared the incident report, and he counter-signed it?"

"Yes, sir."

"All the information is accurate?

"Yes, sir."

Davis made the report an exhibit to the deposition.

It was agreed they'd take a fifteen-minute comfort break. When they resumed, Davis pushed a picture of the safety brake in front of Kennedy.

"You took this picture, right?"

"Those are my initials on the left-hand lower corner."

"The date is three days after Mr. Taylor fell to his death, right?"

"Yes, sir."

"You and Mr. Brand began the report as soon as possible even before the police completed their investigation?"

Just then there was a knock on the door. It was Morty carrying an overhead projector. Davis quickly rose and took the machine from his friend. The machine was heavy, and the old man was struggling with it. Davis realized he should have had Sammie bring it over instead of Morty, and he started feeling a little guilty.

"Perfect timing, Mr. Steine."

After plugging in the overhead and asking Brody if he could turn out the lights, Davis placed the picture on the machine and magnified it. He worked the image to a specific spot of the brake.

Davis apologized for the interruption and had the court reporter read back the question.

"We were allowed into the shaft the day after the incident. Mr. Taylor had been removed, but the elevator and its parts were undisturbed. We were actually on the scene within six hours of the incident, but the police and fire department were down there. It was a very confined space. There was not enough room for our entire team. We had to go down in shifts, one at a time. We were never down there together."

Davis pulled out a picture and showed it to Kennedy. "This item was pretty badly damaged in the crash, wasn't it?"

Kennedy hesitated and then said, "I think the picture speaks for itself. I'd say it was badly damaged. I guess it could have been worse. I'm not sure how to answer that question. It's a matter of degree compared to what?"

"Can you read the number that we're looking at?"

Kennedy read, "03089412567."

Davis spent the next thirty minutes reviewing with Kennedy the maintenance records of Olympus, from the time the elevator was installed in 1989 through the date of its last inspection in January 1996. Kennedy confirmed that the maintenance records indicated that the safety brake in the photo was the original brake and that according to company protocol, the brake was not scheduled to be replaced until June 11th, 1999, ten years from installation.

Davis suggested that they take a half hour break and start with Rosen and then go to lunch. He'd be a short witness.

CHAPTER TEN

HOLY SHIT

Wednesday, September 2, 1998

Davis and Morty met their old friend Sol Rosen in reception and walked out into the hallway by the elevators away from prying eyes and ears for a little privacy. Rosen had a worried look on his face, and he didn't sound very happy.

"My partners don't like this one bit. This is private information. I had to stick my neck out to convince them to share this with you, and now you have me giving it to some other lawyers. They think I'm out of my mind. I've told them I trust you."

Davis took the documents and studied them for five minutes; they were very straightforward. He handed them to Morty, who did the same. They had a brief conversation, Davis asked Rosen three questions, and then said, "Wait here."

"In the hallway?"

"Just for a few minutes."

Davis and Morty marched back into the conference room. They'd been gone only a total of twenty minutes. The defense team never left the table.

"We're ready, but we need to get something settled first. We do need to agree that this document shall remain confidential and be placed under seal." Davis handed Brody a compilation of the earnings of the partners of Lamar, Gleason & Rosen over the last five years. Brody looked at the piece of paper, crinkled his nose, and spit out, "Why are we taking Sol Rosen's deposition anyway? He's available to you at trial."

"Charlie, you know I have a right to preserve Rosen's testimony. He could become unavailable or even die; so can we agree that the document is under seal?"

"Why should I cooperate?"

"Because Rosen's testimony is relevant as to lost wages, future lost wages, and character, and his deposition date and time were agreed to. If I call the judge, that will at the very least get you yelled at by the judge for being unreasonable, possibly far worse."

Brody knew Davis was right. He agreed to put the document under seal. No problem going forward. Brody was under control.

"We'll do Oscar Brand after Rosen."

Davis went back out to the elevators to get Rosen, who by now had lost his patience.

"What the hell am I doing here? Why did I get a subpoena? I would have showed up if you just told me to and why. I've been standing here for ten minutes. I expect my friends to treat me better than this."

"Sorry for the dramatics, but I wanted you to make an entrance. I issued the subpoena because I wanted it to look official. You're here to establish that William Taylor would have definitely made partner and what his future earning would have been."

"My partners are not comfortable with this information being shared with other people. Are you sure you've got it tied up?"

"Absolutely. It's under seal. It will be used in your deposition, and then those pages of testimony and the document itself will be sealed in an envelope under the court's control."

"Okay, let's get this over with."

Rosen and Davis entered the room, and introductions were made. He took the oath and provided his background and his knowledge of the events of April 1, 1996. He had no personal knowledge. Davis asked about William Taylor's character and then about his likelihood of becoming a partner.

"At the next partners meeting in December 1996, William would have become a partner."

"You sound so certain."

"I am. You see, I own 33 percent, and the management committee, consisting of three, owns 55 percent. We'd already discussed William's inclusion, so he was a shoo-in."

"How much was William Taylor earning at the time of his death?"

"Eighty-nine thousand dollars per year plus bonus."

Davis reviewed with Rosen the earnings exhibit. They established that partners last year earned between one hundred eighty-one thousand dollars and one million two hundred eleven dollars per year. Using average earning, life expectancy, and a retirement age of sixty-one, Rosen projected William's present-day lost future earnings at five million one hundred and seventy-two thousand dollars and forty-two cents ($5,172,000.42).

Davis invited Morty to lunch, but he passed. Davis, Ellis, and Becky ate lunch at Satsuma, a well-known meat and three in downtown Nashville. Davis had roast beef, a double helping of mashed potatoes and gravy, squash casserole, fruit tea, and banana pudding to top it off. Everybody else ate light. Becky and Ellis kept asking Davis how he thought the Kennedy deposition had gone, and he kept assuring them, "Just fine."

Back in Brody's office, Davis was face-to-face with Oscar Brand, vice president of investigation for Olympus. Morty resumed his position at the conference table. He didn't want to miss this.

Brand had been with the company twenty-six years and in his current position, fifteen. He had six inspectors reporting to him. Their territory was divided geographically. He confirmed that Kennedy's territory was only two states, Tennessee and Georgia. He admitted that the prior investigator who serviced those states also serviced Kentucky. He admitted that Kennedy's territory was smaller because he was less experienced. He admitted that the Taylor tragedy happened during Kennedy's field training and that Brand, because of Kennedy's lack of experience, supervised every aspect of the investigation. Brand admitted that the shaft was too narrow for more than one person to occupy at a time. He got Brand to authenticate the incident report and the photo of the safety brake.

Davis reviewed the maintenance records for the elevator in question and established that the original safety brake was still on the unit. Davis put the photo on the overhead and focused on the number he'd questioned Kennedy about.

"That safety brake has been pretty badly damaged, hasn't it?"

"Well, it fell three floors, held for some period of time, and then fell seven more floors. It's been through a lot."

"It's also been through almost seven years of use, right?"

"Yes."

"Can you read that number, sir?"

Davis directed the videographer to focus tightly on the number on the photo and then asked him to return to the witness.

During that exercise, Brand didn't answer. The color drained from his face. He just sat there, obviously upset. He knew what was coming but couldn't do anything about it. He was caught, and he had nowhere to run. It was all on video. Most people in the room didn't understand what was happening.

"Did you hear my question?"

Again, Brand didn't answer.

Davis turned to the court reporter, "Please note for the record that Mr. Brand is refusing to answer my question."

"Why don't we take a break?" Brody suggested. Brody and Thomas understood. Their clients from the insurance companies didn't have a clue. Ellis and Becky Taylor were also in the dark.

In a commanding and angry voice, Davis stated, "Absolutely not. Not until I finish this line of questioning. Madame Court Reporter, please read my pending question back to Mr. Brand."

The court reporter did. There was no testimony in response.

Davis waited three full minutes before he asked, "Are you refusing to answer my question?"

A hundred and eighty seconds is a very long time when a camera is fixed on a witness. Brand sat there unable to say or do anything. The silence was deafening.

No response, so Davis took another tack. "Isn't it true that the part number for the safety brake is 12567?"

Again, no response from Brand. He started looking at the defense lawyers for support.

Brody tried to jump to his aid by insisting, "We need to take a comfort break right now."

Davis's retort was louder than he intended, but he said it with such authority that even Brody, a seasoned litigator, wouldn't challenge him.

"Sit down and put your backside in that chair. This deposition will proceed until I adjourn it. You're an officer of the court, and that imposes on you certain duties and obligations, which you may or may not have already violated.

"Now, back to you, Mr. Brand. Do you know what the numbers 030894 reference?"

Brand was consistent, no response. Davis let the camera keep rolling for two full minutes. One hundred and twenty seconds is a long time when you know you've been caught in a big lie and the camera is just staring you in the face.

"All right, since the cat's got your tongue, I'll ask the same question another way. Isn't it true that the 030894 indicates that the safety brake, which was reflected in this photograph, was manufactured March 8, 1994?"

Still no response from Brand.

"How do you explain a safety brake that's been on an elevator since 1989, that's never been replaced, has a manufacturing date in 1994?"

Dead silence. Charles Brody began to speak, but Davis interrupted, "Mr. Brody, I'd be real careful what you're about to say. You don't want to be an accessory after the fact to a crime. I remind you, you're an officer of the court bound by the Code of Professional Responsibility, and just about anything you might say at this point that interferes with this witness answering this question other than advising him of his constitutional right to remain silent will violate your oath as an attorney."

Brody remained quiet.

"Isn't it true that you substituted the original safety brake with the one in this photo at the time of your investigation?"

No response.

Davis suggested, "Mr. Brody, why don't you tell your client to take the Fifth Amendment before he further perjures himself, and then you can take that comfort break you desperately need. I wouldn't want you to soil yourself. The plaintiff's side of this lawsuit will excuse ourselves and go back to my office. I will expect a phone call before four o'clock today to discuss how best to proceed."

Davis, Morty, Ellis, and Becky got up and walked out the door.

CHAPTER ELEVEN

A CONSPIRACY UNRAVELS

Wednesday, September 2, 1998

When Davis got back to the office, he deposited Becky and Ellis in his conference room. Becky was completely lost. Ellis may have had a basic understanding of what had transpired but did not grasp all its implications. Davis hadn't shared his late-night discovery of the substituted brake with either Ellis or Becky.

In an overly excited voice, Ellis began, "Does this mean what I think it means? That bastard removed the original brake and replaced it with a brake manufactured in1994 to cover up that the original brake was defective?"

What a dolt! He still doesn't understand the full implications of the extent of the conspiracy. He needs to find another line of work.

Davis looked hard at Becky, who finally, after Ellis stated the obvious, grasped the full implications of what Brand had done. For the first time she became angry. Her whole body changed. She stiffened, and the once grieving widow became a vengeful crusader. From a litigation standpoint, her intensity was welcomed. From a humanity standpoint, Davis feared for her sanity and judgment. She was beyond furious. He decided he'd better intercede.

Davis commented, "He didn't kill William, but he did try to

cover up the reason why he died, and he did try to prevent you and your children from receiving your rightful recovery for the loss of William's life. He's a very bad man, and I will make him pay and Olympus pay for what he's done. I need you to trust me and let me guide you through this difficult time. I can't bring William back. If I could, that's what you'd want and what I'd do, but that's impossible. I can promise you this: I can make those responsible pay money damages that will benefit both you and your children, and we may be able to impact the company's policies and how it and its employees conduct themselves in the future."

Becky started to cry. All of the anger drained from her body. She ran over to Davis and gave him a big hug. She squeezed him so tight he could hardly breathe. He crumbled in her arms. He wasn't nearly as tough as he thought he was. In fact, in many respects he learned from a wise old man compassion and a sense of caring for his fellow man that stemmed from an even older Jew named Abe Steine.

"Thank you for your help. I trust you, Sammie, and Morty with all of my heart. Do what you think best."

Davis thought, *She didn't mention Ellis. She realizes the case is far beyond his capabilities.*

"William didn't like liars. If he were here, he'd tell you that. I know they didn't kill him, but their cover-up was a horrible thing, and they got caught red-handed thanks to you. Now they should be punished."

Davis couldn't have agreed more. "The two of you make yourselves comfortable in here. We'll be hearing from the defendants shortly. I dropped a bomb at the Brand deposition and insisted that they contact me before four o'clock. They'll be contacting me before that deadline expires. I need to confer with Morty before that conversation." Davis intentionally excluded Ellis and left him with the client.

Davis went back to his office to think. *Too often people don't take a moment to just stop, contemplate the facts, and digest them.* He actually put his feet up, opened his desk drawer, pulled out an orange Tootsie Pop, and started sucking hard. With each suck he formulated his strategy. He smiled as he came to his next moves. They'd be painful for the defendants and their counsel.

From the faces of his adversaries at the deposition, Davis could tell that Lowell Thomas figured out the substitution first. *It was clear from his reaction and his whispered conversation with Brody that defense counsel was unaware of what had happened prior to the deposition. Therefore, none of the defense counsel could be accessories before the fact to any crime. I wasn't watching any of the company representatives. I wonder whether they knew of the cover-up, or were they also surprised at the deposition? I need to ask Morty if he could tell from their faces whether they knew about the substitution. I'm sure he was watching. Morty doesn't miss anything. I should have been watching them. Rookie mistake. Stop being so hard on yourself. You had a good day, and I suspect it's going to get even better.*

Davis replaced the Tootsie Pop with another. He tried to put himself in the place of defense counsel with a lying witness on their hands. *What to do?*

He started to mentally run through various scenarios that the defense lawyers and the company representatives might contemplate, and he envisioned what his response should be. Brody, Thomas, and the others were in trouble. Their conduct would later be scrutinized by a criminal court under a microscope. *Any action taken by them could be considered an overt act as part of the conspiracy, including giving legal advice in an ongoing conspiracy to defraud Becky Taylor. I pity them, on the one hand, but I'm enjoying their predicament, on the other. At least I'm being honest with myself,* thought Davis. He wouldn't share that thought with Morty. His teacher would tell him to be the bigger man and feel sympathy for his fellow lawyers if he believed they were unaware of the switcheroo. Whether the old man really believed that or not, Davis wasn't certain, but he knew that's what he'd say. Sometimes the old man said the right thing, but Davis wasn't sure that he actually believed it. Nobody could be that pure at heart.

Once the defense's three lawyers knew about the fraud, they were obligated as officers of the court not to further perpetrate the fraud. *The action of directing Oscar Brand, who on his own refused to respond to direct questions, to take the Fifth was appropriate. Anything further, other than withdrawal as counsel of record, was suspect and subject to attack.*

It was now three o'clock, and Davis's deadline was in an hour. Neither doubted that Brody and his gang wouldn't let that deadline pass.

Davis and Morty entered the conference room together, and Davis spoke first, "I want to start by apologizing for not including you both in conveying my suspicions. The conspiracy came to me about ten o'clock last night, and I was up most of the night filling in the details. There are still a few unknown pieces to the puzzle."

Ellis spoke first, "Brand sat there like a statue, right on camera. They can't let this go to trial. Do you have a plan how to turn this into a settlement and money?"

Becky understood less than Ellis and was still digesting what she knew.

Davis explained, "During the first few days of the investigation, Brand swapped out the actual safety brake for a newer undamaged one, and then he damaged the new brake to make it look like it was the one in the crash. That will not sit well with a jury. He fabricated evidence. I will destroy him on the stand, and defense counsel knows that."

Becky naively asked, "Why would he do that?"

Morty answered the question. He'd been listening intently at the depositions, watching the two witnesses, and focusing on Brody and the company representatives. "He made the switch to cause confusion. The real brake failed and was the proximate cause of your husband's death. Replacing the defective brake with a good one creates a dispute between the experts about what proximately caused the elevator to fall. Hell, take away the real reason, and the experts on any given side might render different opinions. At trial it's the plaintiff's obligation to prove proximate cause. The substitution creates doubt, which hurts the plaintiff and helps the defendant."

Ellis asked, "Who do you think is part of the conspiracy?"

Davis handled this one. "That's a very good question, Brian. My speech to Brody about being an officer of the court was intended to bring home that he'd better step softly; any affirmative act on his part at this point could be construed by a court as joining the conspiracy. I don't think he was part of the switcheroo. He was just as surprised as you were. To be a part of a conspiracy, you've got to commit an overt act."

Davis paused. The young lawyer must have missed those two or three days of law school when conspiracy was discussed and when he studied for the Bar. Davis figured that the kid barely passed it. As Morty always remarked when dealing with stupid lawyers, "The Bar is a minimum qualification. A monkey on a good day may be able to pass the multiple guess portion."

Trying to educate Ellis, Davis continued, "If defense counsel knew about any part of this before today, then he's a co-conspirator, and how we proceed will be far more complex. We would then amend our complaint and allege bad faith and sue the lawyers, their firms, and the insurance companies as independent defendants. That's what Brody and the other lawyers will want to avoid at all costs. They will need to throw Brand under the bus if they are to be exonerated."

Morty continued the answer. The two men were completely in tune with one another, teacher and pupil. "Brody owes certain fiduciary duties to his client Oscar Brand, but he owes an even higher obligation to the Circuit Court of Davidson County. He cannot perpetrate a fraud on the court. He cannot suborn or permit perjury. Besides, from a practical point of view, either Brand or Brand's employer, Olympus, the elevator company, does not pay him. Their insurance company pays him. That's where in Brody's heart, mind, and soul his real loyalty lies because the insurance company sends him dozens of cases a year. He's going to protect that relationship. I watched him carefully. Until Lowell Thomas figured it out and whispered in Brody's ear, he didn't have a clue."

Davis speculated, "My guess is that Brand acted alone, but I'd argue differently. As a twenty-six-year veteran of the company, he reported to the most senior people. Hell, he was the company. I'd argue he was a managing agent with apparent authority, and there's plenty of case law to support that proposition. Olympus is screwed, whether they knew about Brand's actions or not. The company's management would be smart to settle."

Davis predicted they'd get a call prior to the expiration of the deadline. He was right. At 3:53 the phone in the conference room rang. Davis let it ring five times before he picked it up. He was just playing a little game with Brody.

"Ben Davis, can I help you?"

"Cut the crap, Davis. We need to meet."

"Why's that, Charlie?"

"I want to talk settlement and try to contain damages to my client."

"Which client is that? Brand, Olympus, or its insurance company?"

"All three if I can. If necessary I'll prioritize them during the negotiations."

"Unacceptable. At the very least you get Brand his own attorney. Charlie, I suggest that it should be a good criminal attorney. You might also consider getting separate counsel for Olympus. Brand was high enough in the organization to be considered an agent who bound Olympus by his conduct. Olympus is in big trouble too."

"Thanks for the ethical advice. I don't think the company needs separate counsel. It was in the dark. I'll keep the defendant company and its insurance carrier."

If I were in your shoes, Charlie, even if only for the sake of appearance, I'd bring in a friendly co-counsel to represent the defendant, but that's your call.

"I also need you to make some disclosures that you're not required to do under Tennessee law. First, the name of your insurance company, and whenever we meet, a fully authorized representative must attend. Second, I want you to disclose your policy limits for individual events and then aggregate for the year."

Under Tennessee law, the identity of an insurance company and the dollar amount of its liability limits are not discoverable. You simply can't find out that information. It was a decision of the Tennessee legislature. In contrast, if a case is filed in the federal court system, that information is automatically provided as a matter of course.

Brody interrupted, "That's not discoverable . . ."

Davis returned the favor and interrupted him, "The rules just changed. Besides, if Ellis had correctly filed this case, it would have been in federal court, and the rules of civil procedure there compel discovery of policy limits. Stop interrupting me and listen."

Brody shut up and took his medicine. He had no bargaining chips. Brand had put him in that position.

"Last, I want the two highest-ranking officers of the corporate defendant to attend this meeting. I'll accept nothing less than these conditions. Let's cancel depositions tomorrow, but we resume on Friday unless a meeting is scheduled for this week. Invite all the rest of your defense team and whomever they need for authority. If we meet, it will be in your best interest to make a deal. If not, I'll see you in court. I suggest you settle quickly. If settlement is not achieved before Becky Taylor's deposition, then the cost of settlement automatically increases a million dollars from whatever my last settlement offer was when we break from our talks."

"What the hell does that mean?"

"If you put that poor woman through a deposition and force her to retell the last thirty minutes of her husband's life, that story will cost your clients a cool additional million dollars. Is that clear enough for you?"

"You know you're crazy?"

"Let's face it. I am crazy, but it's a good crazy. We understand each other, and that's what's really important, isn't it?"

Davis was just trying to add to Brody's anxiety, and he succeeded. Davis hung up the phone, turned to the others in the room, and said, "I think I sounded half-crazy, didn't I?"

He looked at Sammie and smiled. It was a teaching experience. "You don't want to screw around with crazy people. Remember that. They're unpredictable and dangerous."

She smiled back at him and nodded in agreement. "I'll remember that."

Davis continued, "Before this meeting, we need to decide what we want from the defendants and ask for a lot more. Brody and his client will probably call tomorrow and set up a meeting for Thursday or Friday, so we don't have much time to get our ducks in a row."

As usual, Davis was right. Brody called the next day and set up the meeting for Friday at his office. Davis insisted that the lost days of depositions be taken before the 15th so his vacation would not be disturbed. The agreement was confirmed in writing.

Davis looked over the draft pleading prepared by Sammie. He made minor adjustments and approved them for filing. He read and highlighted the cases Sammie copied for the two briefs that needed to be prepared. He dictated one of the briefs, which Bella would type, and called Sammie into his office to discuss the other. He returned five calls and connected with three of the parties. He kept going by replacing one Tootsie Pop after another. He tossed the sticks in his ashtray, creating a small pile of eight partially chewed sticks.

Davis went home that evening earlier than usual and surprised his family. Liza hadn't started dinner yet so Davis suggested they go out. Jake and Caroline wanted Chinese, Davis's favorite. Liza frowned at the suggestion. The family compromised and went to Houston's on West End Avenue. Davis had ribs and loaded baked potatoes. Jake misbehaved the entire dinner and would suffer the wrath of his mother when he got home.

After the kids went to bed, Davis approached his wife and was pleasantly surprised that no begging was required. He went to bed satisfied, looking forward to the next day and sticking it to Brody, Thomas, and particularly Oscar Brand.

CHAPTER TWELVE

UNCONDITIONAL SURRENDER

Friday, September 4, 1998

The Davis team filed into Charles Brody's conference room precisely at nine. As designated spokesperson, Davis greeted defense counsel and was introduced to Terry Thompson, executive vice president of Safeway Insurance Company (insurer of Olympus Elevator), Warren Kroner, president of Olympus Elevator Company, Jon Leek of Crystal Tower Management, and William O'Riley of Aetna Insurance Company (insurer of Crystal Tower and Bradley Guard Service).

Brody had laid out quite a spread of food and drink. Davis was confident it wasn't for his benefit, but he dug in anyway, unashamed, and never to be deprived of a good meal. After a cup of coffee and two apple fritters, he was ready to go and took his seat at the head of the table, assured that by assuming the head of the table he would annoy Brody. Starting the meeting was only the primary goal; annoying Brody had a certain secondary sweetness.

"Gentlemen and ladies, I called this meeting to avoid protracted litigation" *and to remind everyone that Oscar Brand is a no good fucking liar.*

Brody really was miffed by the seating arrangement. He added, "We all want that . . ."

Shut up, Charlie, this is my meeting. Davis interrupted, determined to maintain control of the meeting and the conversation. "Some of us want to avoid litigation more than others. For Becky Taylor it will be a horrible experience, but for us, the plaintiff, there will be only one trial and one appeal. It will take years, and she will have to relive the death of her husband, William, and she will tell her horrific story to a jury at a trial."

Davis pulled the micro recorder from his jacket pocket. He said, "I don't know if you gentlemen have listened to this tape." The insurance men shook their heads; the lawyers had heard it multiple times. "Well, there's no better evidence of what the last thirty minutes of William Taylor's life were like than this tape, so here goes."

The tape started with William's conversation about what his kids had for dinner, through his need to stay after his boss so he could earn a larger bonus, to his exchange of "I love you" with Becky, to telling Olympus to "go fuck itself," to his last dying breath. When the tape ended, Davis looked at the executives. They were defeated men. They'd heard what a jury would eventually hear and base their award upon. That didn't make them happy; it made them concerned. In the end, they knew that a jury would be awarding a bunch of cash to vindicate William Taylor's death and to punish Oscar Brand's cover-up. Davis said, "The defendants will appeal, payment will be delayed, and the money will earn ten percent interest by law."

Davis paused and then said, "Someday years from now, after Becky Taylor and her children have suffered both economically and emotionally, they will receive millions of dollars for the death of William. That inevitable day of reckoning of payment for the defendants will arrive."

No one said anything so Davis continued, "The plaintiff's lawyers will be forced to work hard. I might miss a few nights or Saturdays with my family, but I can assure you I won't miss a meal." *Although, that might do me some good.* "In the end I'll earn a one-third fee plus ten percent interest."

"Let me tell you what will happen if we don't settle this case. The current lawyers representing all of the defendants in the case will resign. I know Mr. Brody will. He will for two reasons. First, there is a criminal conspiracy in connection with the substitution of the safety brake, and at least two, probably more, of his clients are co-conspirators. He doesn't want to join that conspiracy. Second, he has the most serious conflict of interest any lawyer could possibly have: one of his clients is about to sue another client. I'm referring to the lawsuit between Olympus and Safeway and the counter-claim filed by the other. I suspect that Crystal Tower Management and Bradley Guard Service will be thrown in for good measure by one or both of them. That means Aetna will have to hire two sets of lawyers and will have to worry about two possible judgments based on the actions of two separate defendants. All of these parties will hire their own lawyers. Each party will be blaming Oscar Brand and arguing it wasn't part of the conspiracy. All of these claims and counter-claims will cost hundreds of thousands of dollars in legal fees, expert fees, and expenses, and even if you are successful, and Oscar Brand is left holding the bag in the end, the costs will still be incurred."

The attorneys, except Ellis, understood what Davis was saying was true, but Kroner looked perplexed. Brody never explained Olympus's biggest problem because he represented both Olympus and Safeway. Brody had a clear conflict of interest, which he failed to disclose to either of his clients. Because of his greed, Brody did a disservice to his clients and thereby jeopardized that fiduciary relationship with both.

Davis counted on that. "If we don't settle the Taylor case, we will go to trial, and I'm confident we will be awarded both compensatory damages and punitive damages. How much, no one knows, but it will be millions. Quite frankly that dollar amount will vary from jury to jury. How much, not whether, is the plaintiff's risk. Collection isn't a problem. Safeway, Aetna, and Olympus are all solvent."

Davis paused, knowing Brody would jump into the conversation.

Brody said, "You're simplifying the issues. An award of punitive damages is a long shot, no matter what the facts are. This isn't New York or LA. This is Nashville, Tennessee. Our juries have common sense and are conservative."

Brody could be counted on to say just the right thing. Morty predicted he'd make that point.

Davis countered, "Under normal circumstances, Charlie is absolutely right, but the people of this city have a good sense of right and wrong. They'll strive for justice. You've got on one side Becky Taylor, widow, and her three young children, and on the other side Oscar Brand, who will be the face of Olympus."

Kroner didn't like that last statement and argued, "He wasn't acting with the knowledge of management of my company. We're a company with integrity, providing an excellent service to our customers. It's unfair to lump us in with Brand. He acted inappropriately, without authority."

Davis couldn't let that last remark stand. He asked, "Where did you go to law school, sir?"

"I didn't."

"Well, that's not the law in the state of Tennessee or anywhere else for that matter. Mr. Brand supervised all six company's investigators. He's been in the position for fifteen years and has worked for your company for twenty-six years. He's part of the company's management; he has apparent authority and binds your company. That's the law. That's not subject to dispute. I tell you what, you can go to Mr. Brody's law library and pull a book on Tennessee law of torts or agency and look up apparent authority, and I'll wait. Or you can ask Mr. Brody if that isn't the law?"

Davis looked at Brody, who shrugged and said, "That's your opinion. I'm not making any admission. Move on, he doesn't need to go to the library. We want to settle the case."

"Fine, Mr. Kroner, what are the liability limits of Olympus?"

There was a brief discussion about discoverability and admissibility. Davis cut the conversation short. "Forget all that. If you want to settle this case, then you must disclose the company's liability limits, or we're walking out right now."

Silence.

"I wouldn't test me, gentlemen, or you'll find yourselves in a trial."

Brody believed him. The limits were $5 million and $10 million.

That meant Olympus had coverage of $5 million per person, up to $10 million per event.

"Okay, that's $5 million for the life of Mr. Taylor and $5 million for Mrs. Taylor's claim for loss of consortium."

Everyone understood that Becky Taylor had a separate claim.

"The plaintiff will settle the estate's claim and Mrs. Taylor's claim for $10 million."

In bold letters using a black felt tip, Davis wrote the offer on a yellow pad.

$5,000,000 William Taylor

$5,000,000 Becky Taylor

Brody almost yelled, "Get real. Why would we settle for policy limits? That's absurd."

"So you reject our offer?"

"Absolutely."

"Would you write 'rejected' and make a counter-offer on the legal pad? We'll adjourn to the reception area."

Davis stood. Morty, Ellis, Sammie, and Becky followed him out the door.

A long twenty minutes later, Brody came and got them. When everyone was seated, Brody handed Davis the legal pad. As promised the offer was rejected, and the defendants counter-offered.

"Rejected—$1,000,000."

Davis looked at the piece of paper and cleared his throat, "Let me explain what just happened. We offered to settle within policy limits, and Safeway rejected that offer. For your information, Mr. Kroner, Olympus now has a claim for bad faith against Safeway Insurance because Safeway has exposed Olympus for liability over its protected coverage. If a jury awards more than five million dollars to the estate of William Taylor, Olympus is liable and has an action against Safeway. Mr. Brody now has a real conflict."

Brody became very angry and lashed out at Davis, "That's bullshit."

"No, it's reality, and you would have seen that if you weren't trying to represent two clients who have conflicting interests. I warned you. You have no one to blame but yourself."

Brody was now furious. He was about to tell Davis to get the hell out of his office, but the president of Olympus interceded, "Make a counter-offer, Mr. Davis. You're here to settle this matter. You've made your point about Mr. Brody's conflict and the fact that is a potential claim for bad faith. Get serious, and let's try to settle the matter."

Davis recognized that Kroner understood the situation and wanted to end the Taylor case. "Before I make that counter-offer, I'd like to remind you that William himself, in his dying breath as the elevator plummeted, blamed Olympus and its inspectors for his death. That's what a jury is going to hear."

Although Thompson, Kroner, and O'Riley may have read the transcript of April 1st, hearing the audio of William's voice was much more powerful than reading the same words on a piece of paper. A jury would turn his dying words into dollars for the Taylor family.

Davis pulled three pieces of paper from his inside pocket and handed a copy to Brody, Kroner, and Thompson. He intentionally didn't bring a copy for Thomas. He could look over somebody's shoulder.

SETTLEMENT OFFER

1. OSCAR BRAND IS FIRED BY OLYMPUS.
2. KENNEDY IS GIVEN A VERBAL REPRIMAND.
3. THE DA MAKES AN INDEPENDENT JUDGMENT WHETHER TO PURSUE CRIMINAL CHARGES AGAINST OSCAR BRAND.
4. PAYMENT BY SAFEWAY TO BECKY TAYLOR AND THE ESTATE OF WILLIAM TAYLOR OF $ 5,000,000.
5. PAYMENT BY OLYMPUS OF $200,000 IN TRUST FOR EACH OF THE TAYLOR CHILDREN (EXEMPT FROM ATTORNEY FEES).

6. PAYMENT BY AETNA OF $100,000 IN TRUST FOR EACH OF THE TAYLOR CHILDREN (EXEMPT FROM ATTORNEY FEES).

THIS OFFER SHALL REMAIN OPEN UNTIL 4:00 P.M. ON SEPTEMBER 7TH, 1998.

BENJAMIN ABRAHAM DAVIS

"We'll leave you gentlemen to discuss our offer."

Then they dramatically walked out.

CHAPTER THIRTEEN

PRETTY PLEASE

Monday, September 7, 1998

The day began with three strong cups of coffee. I was a little nervous. In seven short years, I'd gone from party girl at the University of Florida to taking the deposition of a bank president. Not bad, but my uncle thought I was ready, and so did I. My first call was to Chris Addams, the age discrimination plaintiff, related to the deposition of Keith Rogers, the president of First American National Bank, scheduled on the 10th.

I assured the client, "I'll be ready. I still have to review the bank's document production and decide how to use that at the deposition. Remember, you'll be right next to me, ready with a legal pad to write me any note or question I need to ask him. You're my most valuable asset. You worked at the bank more than twenty years. You know the ins and outs of the systems and its operations. If Rogers misrepresents a fact, it won't get by us because it won't get by you."

I got the sense my client didn't have complete confidence in me as he should. I didn't know if it was my age, my sex, my lack of experience in this type of case or what, but there was something in his voice that just didn't invoke the type of confidence I'd hope to get behind me. Maybe he just expected the great Ben Davis to be his lawyer since he'd hired Ben Davis. Well, he had me, and I'd get the job done just fine. In fact, I was better than fine. I'd win the case big and make the bank pay for discriminating against him. I'd show him and them who they were dealing with. I wasn't some party girl from the University of Florida any longer.

I knew that Addams was depressed. Because he filed the lawsuit, the bank had blackballed him in the local banking community. Friends in the banking and business community wouldn't return his phone calls. Addams specialized in international banking, and Nashville wasn't New York or London. It was a small international banking community. The market was tiny, with only a few positions to begin with. He was seriously considering moving out of town and giving up his profession. Davis urged him to hang in there, but that was easier said than done.

"My brother in Huntsville offered to let me purchase a third of his Thrifty Car Rental franchise. He makes a pretty good living."

"I love Huntsville. Years ago when I was a young girl visiting my aunt and uncle, they took me to the Space Center there. It's a nice small town, but it's no Nashville."

I told him, "I don't want to be negative, but going into business with a sibling can get dicey. Second, a third of a business from a control standpoint is the same as owning one percent of something. Last, do you want to be in the car rental business? Hold off doing anything until after the Rogers deposition. We'll assess after that."

I needed to connect with the client. I told him a little bit about myself; about my parents' divorce and being raised by my grandparents. He told me that he was a Boy Scout and that he was still active as a Scout leader of Troop 34. I explained that I was in Indian Guides with my grandfather rather than Girl Scouts because he wanted to be directly involved in the activity. It gave us some common ground from which to build. We had a good hour-long conversation and got to know and like one another. He left feeling a lot more comfortable with his lawyer.

Addams paused and then conceded, "Fair enough, I'll call you on the ninth."

"If I have any questions before that, I'll give you a call.

I looked at my yellow pad; preparation for the Rogers deposition was at the top of the list. Like my uncle, I maintained a to-do list. I circled it with a red pen to emphasize my need to get ready. I made three quick phone calls, leaving messages for two of the persons. I dictated responses to adversary counsels to four correspondences in my in-box. I started looking at the documents pulled from the bank's production to prepare questioning for Keith Rogers when Bella walked in holding a fax in her hand. "You've got your response in Taylor from Brody."

My uncle and I didn't want to wait for Morty, who was still asleep in his apartment. Instead, we adjourned to the library that had a portion of a wall that was a white board equipped with colored markers and a dry sponge.

I reviewed the lengthy letter and mumbled, "I don't think you're going to like this, but we're obligated to present it to the client. It is Becky Taylor's decision whether to accept, counter, or go to trial. It does have a forty-eight-hour deadline."

Davis was already angry. That wasn't the best frame of mind to consider a settlement offer, but that was the reality of the situation. "Just jot the crux of the offer on the big board."

I selected the green marker, representing money, and reread the letter to myself before writing on the board:

1. Complete confidentiality of terms and dollar amounts of the settlement.
2. Oscar Brand retires from Olympus without any civil or criminal actions taken against him.
3. Oscar Brand receives his full pension and severance from Olympus.

"Bullshit," Davis interrupted, "that's not going to happen. I'm not letting that bastard off without any consequences, and I'll be damned if Becky's going to agree to that."

4. Payment by Safeway of $2,100,000.
5. Payment by Aetna of $100,000 in trust for each child (exempt from attorney fees)

Davis stared at the board, trying to appreciate Brody's logic of his last offer. First, he was protecting Brand, almost rewarding him despite his conduct. That told Davis that Brand had damaging information against Olympus that Brody wanted to bury. Davis suspected that if he exerted even the slightest amount of pressure on Brand, he'd crack and other heads at the company would roll. The big question was how much would Olympus pay to prevent that from happening? Second, it was commonplace to impose a confidentiality clause on a settling plaintiff, but maybe this time there was more at stake requiring that the deal be sealed to avoid criminal prosecution. Third, Brody's dollar amount was proposed because it was divisible by one-third, the standard attorney fee contingency contract. He liked the fact that they bought into the concept of an education trust for the children exempt from attorney fees.

Ever the optimist, I pointed out, "At least they doubled the dollar amount of their first offer."

Bella buzzed in, "I've got Brian Ellis on line two."

Davis directed me, "He got the letter too. You deal with him. I don't have time for him now. I don't understand what you see in that guy. He's useless."

"He's a good guy. You've misjudged him."

"No, you've confused a good lawyer with good sex. Let me remind you that they're two different things. Just because he's good at one doesn't make him good at another. And just because he's good at one doesn't make him a good guy. You need to be looking out for your client Becky Taylor and no one else. I'll call Becky."

That last comment bothered me. It was uncalled for. *My uncle usually didn't get involved in my personal life. He was disrespectful. Why didn't he like Ellis?*

Fifteen minutes later, we reconvened in the library. I went first. "I spoke with Brian. He wants to settle: he believes it's a lot of money now, a bird in the hand argument."

Davis smiled and countered, "Well, I spoke with Becky. She told me that she has complete confidence in my judgment, and I have her complete authority in these negotiations. We're not taking the settlement offer, and it's your job to keep that putz Ellis away from me while I figure out how to maximize our recovery."

We sat there just staring at the board with no conversation. Morty taught us that deep thought at times was the best course of action, and we were zoned out, thinking. Finally Davis spoke, "Oscar Brand is the key."

Morty walked in the library then, and we brought him up to speed. His response came in less than a minute, "Turn over Brand's deposition transcripts to either the state district attorney or the federal DA's office. Better yet, send the deposition and video to both of them."

I offered, "What if we threaten to . . .

Davis and Morty simultaneously yelled, "Extortion!" Davis added, it's not only unethical; it's an actual crime. Let's go back to the drawing board."

Morty asked the $64 million question. "What do we want? Is it money or something else, something intangible?"

Davis answered, "We want money to help Becky Taylor and her kids through life, and we want Brand put out of business, unable to falsify an inspection or investigation again. We also want his conduct evaluated by a DA and let that professional determine whether he should be prosecuted. It wouldn't bother me one bit if Oscar Brand went through a criminal trial. If a jury of his peers decided he needed to spend a few years in prison, then so be it. It's not my call."

Morty kept the analysis going, "How much is enough money?"

"The kids will need to be educated, so we need the trusts. Maybe a hundred thousand in each trust is sufficient. The kids are young. The corpus of the trusts would grow."

"Okay, that's three hundred thousand for the kids. That's half of what you previously asked for. The attorney fees are one-third. So how much do you need to put in Becky Taylor's pocket for the settlement to be fair?"

I objected to this cold-hearted analysis.

Morty responded, "William Taylor's dead. We can't negotiate him back to life. All we can do is secure money for the widow. You'd better learn that reality, or you're going to get better practicing law."

All of us talked for another half hour, and via speakerphone Davis called Brody. Becky Taylor had delegated authority to Davis. *So here goes.*

"Charlie, I got your offer, and I have a take-it or leave-it response. This offer expires tomorrow at four. If this isn't acceptable, I want to resume Oscar Brand's deposition, as we agreed, before my scheduled vacation on September 15th. You can characterize Brand's termination any way you want, firing or retiring, that's Olympus's business, but we are providing the DA's office with Brand's deposition and video. We'll cooperate with law enforcement and the grand jury. I suspect he's going to be charged with several crimes, and unless he agrees to jail time, he'll be tried. Becky Taylor and I will be testifying at his criminal trial. The confidentiality clause should reflect those limitations. I propose we limit confidentiality to dollar amount paid and let the chips fall where they may."

Davis paused to let Brody absorb that information. That probably meant others at Olympus were at risk. Then he said, "Here are the amounts: "$100,000 in trust for each of the three kids paid by Aetna exempt from attorney fees; $100,000 in trust for each of the three kids paid by Olympus, and $4,500,000 paid by Safeway for Becky Taylor; sweet and simple. Take it or leave it. I'll wait to hear from you." He hung up.

Two hours later Davis had a written acceptance of all terms. Davis picked up the phone, called the Davidson County DA, and told him he was sending via messenger two depositions for his consideration and would answer any questions he might have.

Becky was relieved. She knew that she'd have financial security the rest of her life and that there would be funds for her children's education.

Ellis was ecstatic. He bungled through and made $500,000, one-third of the $1,500,000 fee.

Steine, Davis & Davis's fee was $1,000,000. Not bad for less than three months of work. The firm divided the fees as follows:

Bella—$33,333.33

Sammie—$66,666.66

Davis—$200,000

Morty-$700,000

Morty received the lion's share because he paid all of the overhead, everybody's salary, all expenses, and he owned the building.

Ellis called me, his voice low and sweet, "We just earned almost six hundred thousand between us, enough to start a life together. Would you consider . . ."

I stopped him mid-sentence. "Brian, I love you, but not in that way. You are a wonderful, caring man, who will make some woman an incredible husband, but I'm looking for someone else. I haven't found him yet, but I'll know it when I do. I'll always be your friend, but it can't be anything more. Good luck."

Dejected, Ellis suggested in a parting jab, "I know what you're looking for. Your uncle is married to your aunt. I'm pretty sure relationships like that are against the laws of this state. Good luck too."

I love my uncle and respect his opinion. He obviously saw no long-term future between me and Ellis, and truthfully neither did I. He was fun and the sex was wonderful, but I knew he wasn't the one. What was the point to continue in the relationship? My uncle was right. He always is.

CHAPTER FOURTEEN

GRAY AROUND THE TEMPLES

Thursday, September 10, 1998

Chris Addams arrived at eight. I had already been at the office reviewing documents and my questions for the deposition. My uncle figured that the defense team would be shocked by my substitution for him as the questioner of Keith Rogers, president of First American National Bank.

Bone, Lanier & Bass, the largest law firm in Nashville, had recently merged into the legal giant Covington & Burling, out of Washington DC, which boasted offices in New York, Boston, Denver, Chicago, Miami, Birmingham, Atlanta, Los Angeles, London, Paris, Madrid, and now Nashville.

Kurt Lanier and three associates met me and Addams at the conference room door. He said, "Hello, sir, and Miss...?"

"I'm Sammie Davis. I'm the second Davis on the letterhead of my firm's stationery. I'll be taking Mr. Rogers's deposition this morning. Where's Mr. Rogers?"

"Where's Mr. Davis? I thought he'd be..."

"No, I'll be taking it. Where's our witness?"

"Mr. Rogers called to let us know he's been detained in a meeting at the bank. He apologizes for his unavailability. Can I offer you a cup of coffee? He promised to get here as soon as possible."

In a calm and collected voice, I asked the court reporter to preserve the exchange that was about to occur. "For the record, I am Sammie Davis, counsel of record for Mr. Christopher Addams in Addams vs. First American National Bank. I'm here with my client to take the deposition of Mr. Keith Rogers, president of the bank. It's 8:30, and Mr. Rogers is not here at the designated time and place of the deposition."

Kurt Lanier knew exactly what I was doing, and he didn't like it. "Let's go off the record."

"No, sir, I'm going to make my record. When I'm done, you can make whatever statement you want, but I'll make my record right now! After that's done and you say your peace, then we're going to call the Honorable Sandra Palmer, the presiding judge in this matter. I don't think she will appreciate your client ignoring a lawful subpoena."

"Let's be reasonable, Miss Davis..."

I wouldn't be swayed. "No, sir, Mr. Lanier."

I turned to the court reporter, "On the record please." I directed my next words toward Lanier, "Please confirm that Mr. Rogers's meeting is at the bank's main office at Third and Commerce."

"Yes, he's sorry . . ."

I didn't want to hear the rest of the sentence. I said, "This deposition was scheduled by agreement for this day at 8:30. I let you and Mr. Rogers select the date and time more than five weeks ago. I then followed up our agreement with a notice to take deposition and a subpoena. I never heard any objection from the defendant bank or any indication that the starting time needed to be delayed until we arrived five minutes ago, prior to the scheduled commencement time."

I took a breath as I decided what to say next. "It's a five- to ten-minute walk from the bank's main office to here. I suggest you get on the phone and tell Mr. Rogers that if he's not sitting in that chair at 9:00 answering my questions, I'm calling the judge and will be asking the court to find him in contempt and sanction him for failing to appear at his deposition as subpoenaed. Mr. Rogers may be the president of a bank, but he's still subject to the Rules of Civil Procedure just like the rest of us. If he wants to find that out, then let him push me. This isn't a very good way to start a deposition."

Lanier, taken aback, excused himself to make the call. The three associates growled at Addams and me. I loved it.

Fifteen minutes later Keith Rogers sat ready to answer questions. I spent the first half hour on the witness's background and education. *Impressive, for an Ivy League snob.*

Next I pulled out an organizational chart of the bank for 1996 and established that Mr. Addams as a senior vice president of international banking reported to the executive vice president, who reported directly to Rogers as president.

ORGANIZATIONAL CHART

"All senior vice presidents reported to Mr. Porter, the executive vice president?"

"Yes."

"No senior vice president reports to another senior vice president?"

"That's correct."

"In 1996 Mr. Addams and Carl Seaman, senior vice president of operations, are on the same line of this chart, right?"

"Yes."

I produced the organizational chart from a year later. Mr. Addams was the manager of the bank's main office branch reporting to Mr. Seaman.

"In 1997 Mr. Addams was transferred to manager of the main office branch?"

"Yes."

"That was a demotion?"

"No, the bank made a business decision to reorganize, and we decided to move Mr. Addams to the main office. He was still a senior vice president, and his compensation was the same."

"It was a demotion?"

Lanier softly objected, "Repetitive."

Rogers answered anyway, "No, it was a lateral move. Same title, same salary."

I pulled out the bank's policy and procedure manual. I asked Rogers to turn to the compensation section. Rogers testified that positions at the bank had salary ranges, lows and highs that could be earned.

"What is the salary range for senior vice presidents?"

"$90,000 low to $135,000 high."

"What is the salary range for managers?"

"60,000 low to $100,000 high."

"At the time of his transfer to manager of the main office, what was Mr. Addams's salary?"

"$110,000."

"He exceeded the high salary for a manager?"

"Yes."

"Have you ever heard of the term *red circled*?"

"No."

I read from the policy and procedure manual. "An employee is red circled if his salary is being paid more than the high of the salary range for his position."

I paused a moment. "Mr. Addams was red circled?"

"Yes."

As I pulled out an article from the *Tennessean,* Lanier objected.

I asked, "What are you objecting to? I haven't asked a question yet."

"Hearsay."

I smiled at Lanier, which only irritated him. That was my intent.

"I'm not offering the article into evidence for the truth of what the article says. There's a quote in the article that's attributed to Mr. Rogers. It claims that he selected Mr. Addams to run the main office branch "because he had gray around the temples."

"Experience. We moved him because he was an asset."

"But you froze his salary."

"Those were the ranges that existed at the time. Those ranges are constantly revised."

"You realize that this is an age discrimination suit, right?"

"That's what you allege, but it's not valid."

"You deny that age was a factor in your decision to transfer Mr. Addams to the main office?"

"Absolutely, it was his experience and because we felt he'd do a great job. He quit after the transfer. He wasn't fired."

"I direct your attention to that same article in the *Tennessean.* Did you tell the reporter that Mr. Addams's maturity was a factor in your decision to transfer Mr. Addams?"

"Yes, but in a positive way only."

I reached into my briefcase and pulled out *Webster's Unabridged Dictionary*. "Read the first definition of the word *maturity*."

"Wise because of age."

"So Mr. Addams's age was a factor in his transfer, wasn't it?"

Rogers looked at Lanier, who objected, but it was too late. The point was made.

"No further questions."

The deposition was adjourned. Despite the success of the Rogers deposition, Chris Addams was still discouraged because of his unemployment. He kept talking about leaving banking and leaving Nashville. I tried to encourage him but understood his resentment.

After lunch I met Morty at the Longfellow criminal battery hearing. Morty was desperately trying to save his pilot's license. If Longfellow was convicted of a felony, he could kiss it good-bye. The injured umpire Hamm had convinced DA Johnson Tory to pursue the felony conviction, and the assistant DA was just following orders.

A frustrated Morty argued, "The man lost his cool. He made a mistake. For that you're going to take away his livelihood forever. You've got to be kidding. He threw a punch. Can he help it if he has a good right cross and Mr. Hamm has a glass jaw?"

Bad argument, I thought.

Realizing he'd made a mistake, Morty changed gears, "This man flew for his country. He's a decorated combat pilot. Mr. Hamm, you served. You've got that in common with Mr. Longfellow. He should be punished, but that punishment should be reasonable. Don't clip his wings. Let him serve thirty days in jail. Let him clean up garbage on the side of the road. Make him apologize to you in front of the league. Make him pay your hospital bills and then some. You pick the punishment, but be reasonable."

Longfellow stood there looking pitiful, just as Morty had instructed him to do. His head hung as low as it possibly could. Hamm stared at him as hard as he possibly could, first with hatred, then with pity. Morty knew exactly what to do. He instructed Longfellow perfectly, and Hamm came around.

I reflected, *the man's a genius. I don't know how he does it. Hamm just needed to confront Longfellow and let his anger out, and then a deal could be cut.*

Longfellow pled guilty to the misdemeanor of simple assault, and he was sentenced to thirty days. The sentence was suspended, and he was to spend thirty hours of community service picking up trash. It was agreed that Longfellow would apologize to Hamm in front of the entire league, pay court costs, Hamm's hospital and doctor bills, and $10,000 to settle the civil lawsuit. Longfellow was ecstatic, and Morty was satisfied.

Back in the office, I found my uncle going over his to-do list and crossing off items. He made a few phone calls explaining he was going on vacation and waggled an extension on two of the matters and got released entirely from two others. There was nothing urgent about the remaining others, and he delegated them to me. Morty tried to associate him in a last-minute matter, but my uncle stood his ground and insisted that he'd be gone for more than twelve days and wanted nothing new. "If it needs quicker attention, then Sammie is your man."

Morty didn't push it and said, "Enjoy your vacation."

My uncle was determined to do so. Before he could walk out the door, Bella caught his attention and said, "Johnson Tory on line one, asking for either of you."

We walked back to the conference room, closed the door, and Morty pushed the speaker button.

"Johnson, you're on speaker. Ben's here, what can we do for you?"

"I've been working on a plea bargain in the Oscar Brand matter. I wanted to let you know we're real close. Jim Neal represents him. I thought you gentlemen might be interested."

"There's an outcome?" Davis asked, "Without any input from the victim?"

"What victim? William Taylor died as a result of a faulty elevator brake, not Brand's cover-up. Your client has no say or input in the terms and length of the sentence of any plea bargain."

"Johnson, you're wrong. That man caused Becky Taylor severe pain. She should have a right to testify at his sentencing hearing. A judge should hear what she has to say before he or she decides how long Brand serves for his crimes."

There was a long silence at the other end of the phone call. Johnson was close to a deal and didn't want to jeopardize it, even for Becky Taylor.

"Jim Neal is going to be mad as hell. I'm going to recommend two years to the judge, but Becky gets her day in court. She's got a right to tell the judge whatever the hell she wants to. It will be his decision how much time Brand should serve. I only make a recommendation that he can accept or reject as his prerogative."

The conversation ended, and Davis moved on to the next item on his to-do-list. He was whittling it down so he could leave town with a clear conscience.

CHAPTER FIFTEEN

A WELL-DESERVED REST

Wednesday, September 16, 1998

Davis spent the next five days, which included a weekend, working till one every night, leaving nothing to chance. By Tuesday midnight his yellow pad had every item crossed out, a clean slate. He was leaving town with confidence that Morty, Sammie, and Bella could handle whatever problem might arise. At least that was how he'd rationalized the situation. The thought of twelve days away from the office actually terrified him, not for the professional safety of his clients but for his own sanity. Other than his two-week honeymoon about eighteen years earlier, this trip to St. Barts would be his longest time away from the office. He knew back then he wasn't as critical to the operation of the office as he was now. He wondered if the absence now would make that much of a difference.

There was another issue: his wife and the amount of time they'd have to spend together. He had greater compassion, more physical stamina back then and could rally quicker, easily capable of three times a night. Now he was forced to fill these moments, once romantic, with his bride with idle conversation. The other saving grace was that Liza liked to read magazines and books more and had adopted other forms of entertainment.

The kids and dogs were taken care of. The purpose of the trip was to focus on each other and to forget their commitments in Nashville. His parents would shoulder part of the responsibility for one week. His in-laws would do their part. Even Morty and Sammie would pitch in and babysit.

Both Caroline and Jake had to be watched like a hawk. Neither was a bad kid, but they were curious. Davis had caught both of them in the liquor cabinet, and he was forced to be the disciplinarian. Liza insisted that someone had to remain their friend. Good cop, bad cop, and Davis was the designated bad cop. He had the voice and demeanor for it. Davis resented the role, felt a little hypocritical in light of his past, but recognized that someone had to do it. He'd forget it all on this vacation and prepared to enjoy himself.

The resort Liza had booked had no television, no telephones in the room, and no cell phone coverage. "That was part of its attraction," she explained. The allure was lost on Davis, but that was unimportant. His concern wasn't the emphasis of this vacation. It was payback for all the concessions made by a tolerant wife to a workaholic husband. Smart enough to know that, Davis went along without any argument. These eleven nights and eleven days, with one day of travel, might buy him three or four years before having to repeat a vacation like it. *Who knows? I might even like it.*

The flight to Miami left right on time. Liza's sister, Peaches, had lunch with them during their two-hour stopover. Since he was on vacation, Davis treated himself to a four-pound lobster, mashed potatoes, and apple pie. He'd promised Liza he'd use this time to eat better and take long walks on the beach as a new start toward a healthier lifestyle. A weak start.

When they landed on the island, the heat immediately struck them, but an attendant was there with ice-cold washcloths, which provided immediate relief. The Brooklynite in him was impressed by the attention to detail.

The resort provided a spacious van, which the Davises shared with one other couple, the Mendezes. Davis made the introductions. Roberto and Mia were from Miami, and like Davis, Mendez was a lawyer. Although neither had heard of the other, they played attorney geography, and each knew several of the same lawyers.

Mendez, born in Cuba ten years before the revolution, fled to Miami with his parents and lived among the Cuban American population in Miami his entire life. He went to law school at the University of Miami and practiced in a downtown firm that specialized in representing the displaced Cuban community and bridging the gap between, as he put it, "the corrupt Castro regime and his people."

He explained, "The United States has imposed an embargo on Cuba, but most of the world continues to trade with the island. My firm has acted as a bridge between those who had relatives still trapped on the island and those who wanted to conduct legitimate transactions. The government can often be a difficult partner in these transactions demanding more than its fair share of the profits. Sometimes its participation needs to be excluded."

Davis got the feeling Mendez wasn't simply a corporate lawyer, but a black marketer. He decided to test the waters for a good cause. Speaking in a low voice so as not to be overheard by his wife, he asked, "I've often wondered with the Kennedy embargo how one might arrange to obtain Monte Cristo #4 cigars for a dear friend. He often complains about how expensive his cigars are."

"It is difficult. Of course the transaction is illegal, but it can be done. A box of twenty-five could be delivered to you at the end of your trip on the other side of customs in Miami for three dollars a box, if a five-box minimum order were received. That's twelve dollars a cigar. Your friend pays a minimum of twenty dollars a cigar in the States if he can find them."

Davis knew that was true. Morty was always bitching about how difficult it was to find his Cubans. Supplying him with a gift of a hundred and twenty-five cigars would go a long way to putting Davis in his good graces.

"Done deal. You'll get your fifteen hundred when I get to the front desk or a cash machine."

Mendez laughed, and they talked about their children. The couples traveled from the airport to the resort together. Check-in went like a breeze, and while at the front desk, Davis got a cash advance of fifteen hundred dollars on his American Express card and gave the money to Mendez.

After they transacted their business, the porter took each couple in a small wooden motor launch to adjacent wooden A-frames out three hundred feet in the ocean. Two dozen similar structures stood on stilts a few hundred feet from shore. As several motor launches puttered along slowly on the bluest ocean he'd ever seen, Davis realized that their accommodations, a two-room, open-air bamboo shelter, had glass floors, with marine life constantly visible.

"This is incredible," he commented to Liza.

Equally amazed, she responded, "The brochure didn't do it justice."

After receiving his tip, the porter turned the craft around and returned to shore, leaving the Davises to explore their new abode.

Dinner was delivered by boat, served discreetly, and quickly removed after they finished the meal. The Davises made love that evening, falling asleep in each other's arms.

In the morning they went for a swim by diving off their porch directly into the blue ocean and then, soaking wet, made love again. *I could get used to this,* thought Davis. An hour later they swam to shore and had brunch at the hotel bar, consuming several mimosas. They couldn't swim back because they were too inebriated, so they took the launch.

After a long nap, they signaled the launch by using an orange flag to come to their hut. Within ten minutes they were puttering toward shore. They elected to eat in the hotel dining room rather than the bar.

The meal was superb: grilled fish caught earlier that day half a mile from where they sat, and locally grown vegetables. Liza, in heaven, loved all the attention she received from her husband, and although Davis loved being with his wife, he was beginning to be bored out of his mind.

Seated at the table next to them were Roberto and Mia Mendez. After dinner the two couples had several drinks in the bar, and the two lawyers started exchanging war stories while the two wives talked about children and other shared interests. Davis spent half an hour telling Mendez about the Plainview cases. When he got to his beating and the involvement of the two defendant doctors, Mendez had several questions.

"How did you know that the doctors sent the thugs?"

"I subpoenaed my own telephone records and both the call to my home and the call to my office came from Plainview Community Hospital."

"Amazing," commented Mendez. Davis explained how after he'd tried the first case, the other nine cases settled.

Mendez described his firm as offering unique services to its clients, former Cuban citizens who fled the Castro regime, or American businesses that indirectly did transactions through foreign governments with the Cuban government.

"Many of my clients still have family on the island, and they want to get money and other products to them. Remember, most of the world, unlike the United States, has open trade with Cuba. The United States stubbornly and impractically, only ninety miles away, has for the last forty years enforced a trade embargo that has tried to cripple and to some extent did cripple the small island nation."

Mendez's firm found ways around that embargo, often with the express knowledge of the United States government and the Cuban government. Other times one or both sovereign nations simply looked the other way, and then still other times, the efforts had to be completely covert.

"The Defense Minister, Raul, who is Castro's brother, is more of a businessman than a revolutionary and an idealist than Fidel."

Mendez's senior partner, Hermando Diaz, age eighty-four, knew the Castros as boys, and despite the embargo, he was still in communication with the two men. Mendez described two boys who grew up not in poverty seeking revolution but in a modest middle-class family. They were sent to military school and loved baseball. He claimed that Fidel was a pretty good student, but Raul was an academic failure.

Mendez complained, "I'm on the three-man management committee. We've got ten partners, forty associates, ten paralegals, twenty secretaries, and three people in bookkeeping. That's more than eighty people. You know what my biggest problems are?"

Davis understood and could certainly comment, but decided to be polite, so he just shrugged.

Mendez continued, "Egos and jealousy. The lawyers are the worst. Everybody is worried about what everybody else is doing and what everybody else is getting. Management is a thankless job. I'm thinking of telling my partners I just don't want the headache anymore. Let someone else be in charge. Who wants it?"

Mendez produced a Monte Cristo #4 from his inside sports jacket pocket and said, "A preview of things to come." Then he and his wife bid the Davises good night.

With his wife's permission, Davis lit the cigar and puffed away as the couple lay on the beach. Davis was in heaven. At some point most people reflect on their lives, and it is not unusual for them to have a life-changing aha moment. Davis was having one such moment.

He could tell Mendez was a shrewd lawyer who had been taught by the best, Hermando Diaz. Davis made a mental note of his existence if he ever needed help in Miami.

Davis considered what Mendez was saying and realized just how lucky he truly was. *Morty owns the building but charges the firm no rent. He and Sammie live in the building, making them both readily available, day or night. There are no egos among Morty, Sammie, and me, just mutual respect and admiration. Sammie and I are still learning from the old man, and nobody resents that. In fact, it is appreciated every day.*

As he thought more about his life and work, he recognized that he was taking Bella for granted. With Morty for more than thirty years, she made the office run. Unlike Sammie, neither Morty nor Davis could type or use a word processor. *All of our correspondence, pleadings, and briefs go through that amazing woman. She manages the phone, sends out all the statements, and pays all the bills. The office would come to a standstill without her. Nothing would be collected, and nothing would be paid.* He had to stop taking her for granted.

He pledged, *I'm going to be a better partner, employer, father, and especially husband. I'm going to be mindful of how I treat the people I love and treat them with the respect they deserve.*

After finishing his cigar, he turned his attention to his beautiful wife, embraced her, tried to kiss her neck, and worked his way to her lips.

"Cigar breath, you taste like an ashtray. I'm not kissing you until you gargle with some mouthwash back at the hut." They rode back in silence to the suite on the ocean.

As the vacation progressed, Davis recharged his battery and rekindled his relationship with his beautiful and loving wife, his partner in life. Everything went fine until the fifth day when they had one hell of a fight, which came out of nowhere. It started innocently with a comment by Liza, "Honey, I'm bored at home. I need something more. The kids are grown and don't need me as much. They're independent."

Davis was half asleep, listening to the sound of the ocean. "What are you talking about? They're twelve and fourteen. Neither of them can drive, and Jake's going to be Bar Mitzvah next year. They need you now more than ever."

"In March, Caroline gets her learner's permit, and in July, Jake becomes a man. I gave up my profession to have children. Now that our children are grown, I want to go back to work. I'm a nurse practitioner. My dad thinks he can get me a supervisor position at Hospital Practice Corporation."

"Are you kidding? You must be kidding. Don't you know I currently have two lawsuits pending against Hospital Practice?"

"No," she said sheepishly. "I actually spoke to the manager of one of their psychiatric hospitals, who indicated they'd work with me so I could be home by four o'clock. . ."

Davis stopped her mid-sentence. "Who did you talk to? Dr. Bill Anderson or his administrator Larry Ponders?"

"It was Wanda Sykes, the assistant administrator."

"Well, I'm sure she's aware of the Gems and Venus cases. I've deposed her boss Ponders in both cases. She was trying to hire you to conflict me out of those cases. If you became an employee, I'd have to withdraw." His voice went up several octaves, and she got very defensive.

"Well, how would I know that? You don't tell me anything. How would I know your pending caseload or who you'd sued? I live in the dark. Sykes may have tried to take advantage of me. No harm, you caught it in time. But I'm going back to work. Give me a list of who you've sued or who you're thinking of suing. Everybody else is a prospective employer. I'll wait until after Jake's Bar Mitzvah. Caroline will have her license by then and can act as his driver. This summer I'm going to work, so get used to it."

Wow, she said that with authority. Davis was flustered by Liza's new life direction, and he didn't take it well. They fought, and the rest of the vacation was less than cordial. They didn't make love the last four nights. He was very disappointed, but she was teaching him a lesson, and it worked.

Back at home, he realized that the office could exist without him, that problems could get solved in the very capable hands of Sammie and Bella, and that Morty was always there if necessary. He also realized that the world didn't end if he put his family ahead of work. The vacation reminded him of what a wise old man once told him, "To be a successful, sane lawyer, you need to learn to compartmentalize work, family, and play." Morty might have said those words, but he never really learned to live them. Again, Davis questioned whether the old man in his heart meant what he preached. No one could be that good.

CHAPTER SIXTEEN

A SHOCKING TALE

Friday, October 23, 1998

I arrived right on time, 9:00 a.m., for my appointment with Sammie Davis of Steine, Davis & Davis. I wondered if my attorney was the first or second Davis on the letterhead. I'd only made the appointment two days before.

She was lucky to get an opening on such short notice. Bella ushered her into the conference room and brought her a cup of strong coffee. It was French vanilla. The aroma could be smelled throughout the office. Steine, Davis & Davis served its clients gourmet coffee and delicious pastries from Schwartz's Deli: apple strudel, Bavarian torte, Black Forest Gateau, chocolate babka, and rugelach, among others. Several clients commented, "We don't mind the wait. The baked goods make it tolerable."

I sat there nervously munching on an apple strudel and drinking a second cup of delicious coffee. *Was that nutmeg*? The older woman made me feel quite at home. *Damn good.* As I took a big gulp of coffee, I jumped up and spilled some of it on the table when Ms. Davis walked into the room.

She walked over and, without a condemning remark, mopped up the mess with two or three napkins that bore the Steine & Davis logo.

Morty liked those special little touches. Morty hadn't yet added her name to the napkins. She'd ask him to change them when next ordered.

Ms. Davis, a few years younger than I, made me feel more comfortable, first by flashing her beautiful smile and then by revealing a few facts about herself and telling me to call her Sammie. She explained that she was born in Miami but grew up in New York with her paternal grandparents, her uncle Ben's parents. Now she practiced law with him. He brought her to Nashville as a paralegal. When she discovered that she wanted to be a lawyer, she went to Vanderbilt Law School.

Within minutes we were talking as if we'd known each other for years. Making a client feel comfortable enough to open up was an important skill that every good lawyer had to learn. Morty first taught that skill to her uncle and then to Sammie. She was a natural, warm and personable. After thirty minutes of chitchat, I told Sammie my incredible story. It did not take long for her to understand why I was seeking legal advice.

This is a two- or three-brain problem. I need the experience of Ben Davis and Morty Steine. Sammie admitted she wasn't too proud when a problem was beyond her capabilities.

I realized that was a sign of a smart lawyer, knowing one's limitations. Most struggled with fragile egos.

"Laura, would you mind if I asked my uncle and our partner, Morty Steine, to sit in and have you retell your tale?"

"Sammie, it took everything I had to tell you, I'm not sure . . ."

Sammie cut me off, "Look, you've been sued by January's law firm. What choice do you have? Your accurate recount of the facts is your only defense. If you can't tell others what happened, then you'd better be prepared to take out your checkbook and write a check for $14,000. I suspect that would be pretty painful. Far more painful than having a conversation with my uncle and Morty Steine. They won't bite."

Sammie could tell that her new friend for the first time regretted her decision to seek legal advice. Laura's face got red. *I may have come at her a little too hard. Sometimes the truth can be cruel.*

Laura, between sobs, nodded, and Sammie stood, gently put her hand on Laura's shoulder, rubbed it slightly, and left the room.

She went to her office and first buzzed Morty. Fortunately, Davis happened to be sitting in Morty's office and discussing another case.

Sammie recognized that Laura's story posed a unique problem. If she were going to represent her, Sammie would need the assistance of the experience and judgment of Morty. He brought to the table a different and experienced perspective. At seventy-eight he'd seen it all, beginning his legal career after World War II. He'd fought the Nazis and won. He truly was part of the greatest generation that saved the world from calamity. He continued fighting evil as an attorney. He was nationally known for his work in the civil rights movement and as the attorney who established publishing rights for country music artists against the big record companies. He marched alongside black leaders and bailed them out when necessary. He sued record companies for Dolly, Johnny, June, Waylon, Willie, and Kris, and bailed them out when necessary. He was an advocate for both the rich and the poor. He always tried to do the right thing. He now moved slowly, but his mind was as sharp as ever.

Sammie asked, "Can the two of you join me in the conference room? I have a new client, and I need your advice as to how best to proceed. It's a pretty sensitive matter."

Morty crushed his half-chewed cigar in the ashtray, slowly rose, and followed Davis out of his office, down the hall to the conference room.

Seated at the long walnut table were Sammie and a woman

about her age with striking blue eyes. Everyone in the room, except Morty, had blue eyes. He made a mental note. She stood when the two men entered the room. Like Sammie, she was tall, over five ten. With heels, everyone in the room was over six feet.

Sammie made the introductions. "Laura Chapman, this is Morty Steine and my uncle, Ben Davis. You need to understand that if I accept your case, you'll be represented by my entire firm, all three of us. I know how concerned you are about your husband learning about what's gone on. I want to assure you that these two gentlemen are bound by the same duty of confidentiality that I am."

Morty flashed a broad smile like a Dutch uncle or a Dutch grandfather that put Laura at ease. The man had a way about him. When he walked in a room, people turned their heads and took notice. There was almost an electromagnetic persona around the man.

"My dear, we're in your corner. We're here to help, not to judge. It's critical that you tell us the whole truth, the good and the bad. Try to remember as many details as possible. Start at the beginning, and try not to leave anything out."

I took a deep breath, almost like I was about to dive into the deep end of a swimming pool and swim under water. "Eight years ago I met my husband, Barry. We both worked at Saint Thomas Hospital. He's a physical therapist, and I'm a registered nurse. After a year I became pregnant, and we married. Our daughter Hannah is four, and after a three-month maternity leave I returned to work. Almost immediately, despite birth control, I became pregnant again, and fourteen months after Hannah, our daughter Lily was born. It was the pregnancy of our son, Matt, that broke our marriage."

I stopped, poured myself a glass of water from the Waterford pitcher, and took a long drink. Sammie was taking notes while Morty and Davis were listening intently.

"After Lily was born, I couldn't work full-time anymore, and we lost part of my income. Barry worked overtime when he could, but our finances became stretched because he couldn't make up what we lost. He resented the baby and me. We'd gotten used to having two incomes. We fell out of love, and the children demanded all of my energy. About two years ago the arguments became unbearable. We said horrible things to each other. Last March, Barry moved out, and in April he filed for divorce . . ."

Davis interrupted, "What were the grounds?"

"Cruel and inhumane treatment and irreconcilable differences."

Sammie held up the divorce complaint. "Barry's represented by Bob Sullivan. The document is pretty straightforward. It describes violent verbal exchanges in front of the children and claims that Laura, on at least two occasions, slapped him."

"I did. He deserved it or worse on both occasions. He made me angry, and I slapped the son of a bitch." Laura started crying.

After a minute Morty broke in, "A slap or two isn't the end of the world. We've become so politically correct sometimes it makes me sick. Fifty years ago that's how most sexual discrimination cases were settled. A man got fresh and overstepped moral boundaries, and he got a good slap in the puss. Back then if he really went too far and stole her virginity, the girl's father got out his shotgun and the young man had two choices. Things got settled quickly. He could get married, or he could start singing several octaves higher. Most young men elected to get married, and they stayed married. There weren't many divorces. You got used to each other. Some great marriages began that way."

Morty really was old school. He wasn't kidding. *Sometimes he fell behind the times and law,* thought Sammie. Nevertheless, his remark made Laura feel a little better about her conduct.

Davis insisted, "We need you to focus and finish your tale. I have a feeling there's more than just a divorce action involved, or Sammie wouldn't have called us in to hear your story."

I literally sucked it up. They could hear me take the air into my lungs as I continued, "Based upon the advice of our family therapist, Dr. Richards, I got my own therapist, Dr. Paula Milam. I retained Dan January of Sinclair & Sims. I paid him a $5,000 retainer and signed a contract that agreed after the retainer was exhausted, he'd be paid $250 an hour. My husband, Barry, retained Bob Sullivan as his attorney. Dan assured me that Bob Sullivan was a reasonable attorney, and that if Barry was also reasonable, a property settlement could be negotiated within the cost of my retainer paid."

Promises, promises, promises, mistake number one. Davis acknowledged, "I can't speak for your husband about whether he's a reasonable man, but Bob Sullivan is a reasonable attorney. The Sinclair & Sims law firm is solid, and $250 per hour is a more than reasonable rate. I never dealt with Dan January before. I don't specialize in divorce actions, From time to time, I represent longtime clients in their divorces and treat them like any other litigation. Divorce is January's area of practice. He has a good reputation as an attorney, and I've litigated against several of his partners in that firm, including Tyree Sinclair. I have nothing but good things to say about the firm based upon my dealing."

Davis turned to Morty, "Isn't January Tyree Sinclair's son-in-law?"

The question was directed to Morty, but Laura answered, "Yes, sir."

A strange silence fell over the room. It was the way she answered Morty's question. Morty knew the family dynamics but kept them to himself.

Sammie prompted Laura, "Continue."

"Over the summer Dan and I became close. He was reassuring

as we spent more and more time together. As we did, Barry became less and less reasonable. He started dating a nurse I knew from the hospital, Penny Sylva. The bitch just moved right in. When he started bringing her around my kids, I blew my top. That's why I slapped him twice. He didn't need to expose my kids to his lover. Dan was there for me and gave me the support I desperately needed. He had two shoulders for me to cry on."

The crying started again, and Morty could tell they weren't crocodile tears. "After Penny came into the picture, we pushed harder, and Barry and Sullivan pushed back. It got ugly. Dan tried to control me, but I wanted to hurt Barry for finding someone else. I got lonely, and Dan comforted me. He made me believe he cared about my children and me. We'd spend hours on the phone or in conference talking about Barry, my case, discovery, or trial strategy. I spent a lot of time crying on his shoulders, and unbeknownst to me he'd been billing me every minute for what seemed like very personal, not professional, time. A blur developed between our personal and professional relationship, and an outstanding balance owed accumulated to Sinclair & Sims."

Davis knew where this was going. He'd seen it before. Boundaries were crossed, and ethics were violated. He waited for the rest of the story.

Another drink of water and a long pause. I was in the home stretch. "Through an interim agreement worked out with Mr. Sullivan, Barry paid $1,200 a month in support. It wasn't enough. I complained to Dan that I was broke and that the case was moving too slowly. By July 4th of last year, the retainer long exhausted, Dan kept working on the case, but when I was $4,000 behind, he insisted that I make a payment. I had no money, so he suggested an arrangement. Remember we were friends, good friends. This man knew my darkest secrets. I'd confided in him like I would a close girlfriend; in some respects closer. I'd told him I was horny. I joked about being celibate and entering a nunnery. He knew I hadn't had sex in more than over two years. My husband had moved out sixteen months earlier."

Here it comes, thought Davis; another member of his profession taking advantage of a weak and helpless client. Davis prompted, "What did he propose?"

"Sex for legal fees. He suggested it in almost a joking way. It didn't sound sleazy at the time. I liked him. I trusted him. Quite frankly I wanted him. He was handsome, and I hadn't had sex in a long time. After the birth of Lily, Barry and I didn't have sex often. We'd had sex at least once too often anyway to have Matt. At first it was fear of a third pregnancy, and then later we had no desire. The thought of having sex again was exciting and to get paid, well that made it even better. Dan was charging $250 an hour, so I did the same. We agreed on a price list. A blow job was $100, and intercourse was the cost of a full hour of his time, $250. I didn't feel like a whore. It actually gave me a sense of power. As a nurse I made $30 an hour, and it was hard, backbreaking work. A blow job took less than ten minutes, and I was paid more than three times my hourly rate as a nurse. On an hourly basis, that's $600 per hour, not bad work if you can get it."

That's a lot of money an hour; time and a half for me, I guess our critics would claim that she provides a more satisfying service then lawyers do. For sure ours isn't always as pleasant.

Davis was amazed by the young woman's candor. There was a twisted logic to what she was saying, but there was more to life than just money. Self-respect came into play, and he assumed she was about to get to that part of her story.

"As time passed, his demands increased and became kinkier.

He wanted anal sex, and then later he insisted on the use of a black eight-inch dildo. Despite how I sound today, not long ago, despite my nursing background, I was a pretty naïve person. I knew nothing about anal sex and sex toys. Dan January opened my eyes to new possibilities, which at first were pretty painful. But with that pain came profit. I charged double my hourly rate for anal and for his use of that dildo. It hurt, and I decided if I was going to take it up the ass, then I was going to get paid $500 an hour. Fair is fair."

As she should have, thought Davis. *The market should always set the price; supply and demand.*

Déjà vu. The firm recently was involved in a case where large black dildos constituted critical evidence, and a young oral cosmetic surgeon had lost his medical license for sexual misconduct with patients. Sammie cringed, and Laura kept talking.

"I'd only had three lovers before Barry, and sex was pretty straightforward before Dan. My experience with vibrators was limited, only a few times alone for my own pleasure. My sessions with Dan began to trouble me. I started having nightmares and second thoughts. When I protested, he threatened me. He was going to expose our affair and my sexual perversion. I was going through a divorce, and I had three small kids. He tried to blackmail me. He threatened to go to Sullivan and tell him about our relationship. He said that Barry would take my children away from me and that my visitation would be restricted and supervised. That really scared me. He was convincing. He turned against me on a dime. We were in bed one minute, him inside me. The next he was yelling that I was an unfit mother. A week later, the bastard sued me for unpaid legal fees of $14,000. The funny thing is, I don't owe him a dime. In fact I'm a blow job and ass fucking up. He owes me six hundred bucks. Maybe I should countersue. What do you think? Would the judge order him to pay me $600 or refund sex acts worth $600?" Laura nervously laughed, not knowing what else to do. It was amazing how the once shy woman lost her timid nature and reserved demeanor as she told her story and her adrenaline started flowing.

The conduct of his fellow lawyers never ceased to amaze Davis. *What an asshole! He must have violated at least six disciplinary rules. The bastard had his own wife and kids, and his father-in-law was his boss. He had a lot more and therefore had a lot more to lose, including his law license. This woman figured that out, and that's why she's sitting across from us.*

Morty broke Davis's chain of thought, "How will we prove your allegations and the terms of this illicit agreement? Isn't it just he said, she said?"

Sammie held up a red planner and a file folder containing documents. "Not necessarily."

CHAPTER SEVENTEEN

A REAL CONUNDRUM

Friday, October 23, 1998

It was lunchtime when Laura Chapman left the office. Bella arranged for Mexican food to be delivered. The three lawyers sat around the conference table digesting their food and the Chapman story. There were three different suits: the divorce action, the collection action by Sinclair & Sims, and her lawsuit against January and his firm.

Between mouthfuls, Morty broke the silence, "I was impressed with Laura. She's quite a young lady. I like her. She did exactly what you asked her to do. She was an honest client. She told us the good, the bad, as well as the ugly."

With that Morty spilled refried beans on his tie. Sammie smiled, then laughed out loud. Davis retorted, "Maybe she was a little too candid. I'm not so sure a judge is going to like her. She's not so soft and fuzzy."

Sammie made a face. "I like her. She's no angel..."

Morty didn't miss a beat, "Bob Sullivan may be a nice guy, but he'd use her relationship with January to his advantage in a deposition or a courtroom. Bob's sharp, he might even be able to get her husband custody of the kids if Barry Chapman wants them. If not, he'll beat Laura up on the property settlement. No judge is going to condone her conduct. Sleeping with your lawyer is a definite no-no, and any judge is going to punish the woman client as well as the lawyer. If you get the wrong judge, then watch out."

Davis agreed. Their client had nothing to gain by making her affair with January public. Thinking out loud, Sammie asked, "Do we confront January and threaten him to defend the collection action by raising his unethical and sexual misconduct?"

Davis shook his head. "That's not going to work. He knows we don't want to respond to the lawsuit with allegations of his improper relations. Our client can't afford to lose her kids. No, he's not afraid of us, but he damn well better be afraid of Tyree Sinclair, his father-in-law and boss."

Tyree "Ty" Sinclair IV, a fourth-generation lawyer, came from one of the most prominent Nashville families. He was part of a ruling white Christian elite controlling all aspects of the city. They were members of Belle Meade Country Club, Cheekwood Botanical Garden and Art Museum, the Centennial Club, the Daughters of the Confederacy, and every other established conservative right-wing organization that meant anything in town. He looked the part: tall, thin, almost gaunt, and elegant with a full head of gray hair and white temples. He drank twenty-year-old scotch, but wouldn't turn down twelve-year-old in a pinch. Happily married, he was a true family man dedicated to his firm Sinclair & Sims.

Morty continued the thought, "Rachel is Tyree's only child. He's not going to take January two-timing his little girl quietly. I know Tyree Sinclair better than most. He's a proud man. He's going to make January's life miserable. Sinclair's got a good memory. I'm going to share something about him and his family that almost no one knows. Needless to say, I don't want this repeated. It's for my partners' ears only. In October 1929, the Sinclairs, like so many people in Nashville and elsewhere, were invested in the stock market and fell victim to the Great Depression. Not my grandfather Abe. We owned a department store. Everything my family had was in inventory: canned goods, tradable stock. Abe Steine came to the aid of this city—black, white, formerly rich, or poor. Steine's Department Store and its stock helped hundreds of families survive. One of them was the Sinclairs. Abe Steine literally prevented thousands of Nashvillians from starving and scores of businesses from closing their doors through reasonable, yet profitable loans. One of those loans was to Tyree Sinclair's grandfather. Tyree Sinclair knows, from family lore, that Abe Steine, a Jewish merchant, saved the family fortune and the law firm. He's confirmed that to me privately and by his actions and his words. He made sure that when his wife, Rita, crossed paths with my Goldie when she was alive, Rita gave her the respect she deserved. That wasn't always true of the rest of the Belle Meade crowd. Goldie, being Jewish, wasn't included in most social circles, but Rita at least always had a kind word and a smile for my wife that was always appreciated."

"That's an amazing story," commented Sammie. "Maybe you should talk to Sinclair and get him to back off his firm's suit."

Davis knew the answer to that question. "Morty's too close to Sinclair because of the kindness of his grandfather to hear the embarrassing facts about his son-in-law from him. I'm the best choice. He knows me and I think respects me, but there's no personal relationship. I'm clearly his junior, and I can approach him professionally and with deference. You're an unknown commodity and a woman to boot. He'll be embarrassed enough when I broach the subject, but he'll lose less face if it comes from me rather than from Morty presenting the ugly truth. It's hard to explain. No man wants to hear that his daughter's been made a fool of, and no senior partner wants to hear that someone who works for him has traded sex for legal fees and then convinced the firm to file suit to collect those fees."

Morty pulled out one of his black Cubans, lit it, and started puffing away. Davis gave him a dirty look but didn't dare say anything. Morty's cardiologist had preached to all three of them that the old man had to give up his passion, but neither Davis nor Sammie had the ability to enforce the doctor's demands. Only Goldie, a blessed memory, who died several years ago, could have reined him in. As he blew a perfect smoke ring, he commented, "Sinclair is probably not going to believe you. I'd suggest that when you set up the meeting under the pretext of the defense of the collection lawsuit, which must be at his office, ask him to have January's actual time tickets present. Argue that the outstanding bills and time tickets will be discoverable in the lawsuit anyway, so he might as well make them available. He won't object. He'll think they'll document that Laura owes his firm $14,000."

Sammie was confused, but Davis knew exactly where Morty was going.

"We should also get Laura to execute a medical authorization, and then Sammie should interview her therapist."

Sammie understood the importance of corroboration of the therapist as to the dates of her notes consistent with those of the dates of January's time tickets.

The three discussed what they wanted to secure from Sinclair as a result of the meeting. Most important were dismissing the collection lawsuit and avoiding the revelation of Laura's relationship with January during her divorce action.

Davis remarked, "Bob Sullivan isn't stupid. The substitution of Sammie for January has to be done just right, or Bob may start asking questions. I know Laura used bad judgment, but she shouldn't lose custody of her kids over this. January preyed on her. He's a weasel and deserves to be punished for his unethical conduct."

Morty puffed furiously, flicked an ash in the ashtray, and brought up a real concern, "What is our ethical obligation to report January to the Board of Professional Responsibility?" Morty had served two terms as president of the Disciplinary Board, and he was very sensitive to such matters.

"I hadn't thought of that," responded Sammie.

Morty looked at his young and eager to learn protégée and said, "Sammie, as members of the Bar and officers of the court, we are watchdogs of our profession. There are three sets of rules our profession deals with. The Rules of Civil Procedure and Rules of Evidence are addressed in the courtroom. We constantly challenge those rules to benefit our clients, and the judge is the final arbiter as to interpretation. The third set of rules, the Code of Professional Responsibility, is self-interpreting and self-governing, and we as officers of the court have an obligation to report unethical conduct if we discover it. January has preyed on a client and violated the rules."

Davis took a good whiff of the smoke that permeated the room. He enjoyed the smell, while Sammie could hardly breathe. Morty owned the building and was her boss. She silently prayed that Goldie would intervene, but she knew the dead woman couldn't.

After a long minute Davis interjected, "What if someone else reported January? That would relieve us of our obligation. Board complaints are confidential. Laura would be referred to as Jane Doe, not by name."

Morty smiled. "Part of our deal with Sinclair is that he reports January. He'll be angry as hell. It will partially exonerate his firm's involvement, and revenge will be part of his motivation."

Sammie argued, "January is the father of his grandchildren. At a minimum January's license will be suspended for a year. Will he want that much blood?"

Davis responded, "Once we present the facts to Sinclair, he'll have no choice but to open a complete investigation. When he starts digging, he's going to find other improper relationships and will have no choice but to tell his daughter. She's no fool. Rachel will file for divorce, and January will settle. Sinclair will use the disciplinary charges or the threat of the charges as leverage. He'll make the decision about whether to report his employee. As part of the settlement of the Chapman collection matter, our firm and Laura will get a release of our obligation to report January to the board. Our conscience will be clear. We reported January's conduct to his employer and left how best to proceed in his hands."

Although there was some uncertainty in the plan, they agreed that it was a reasonable course of action. Sammie called Laura and informed her that the firm would accept her case. She'd have to come back to the office and sign an employment agreement and medical authorization. She gave her a brief description of the general plan but no specifics. Sometimes sharing the details of a plan depended on the sophistication of the client. At the end of the business day Sammie reached Laura's new therapist, faxed her the authorization, and conducted an interview. Dr. Paula Milam wouldn't go into details over the phone so a meeting was scheduled for the following week at the doctor's convenience.

CHAPTER EIGHTEEN

CONFRONTATION

Thursday, October 29, 1998

Davis felt very uncomfortable as he sat in the Sinclair & Sims waiting room. He'd never been in the military, but he felt like he was about to sneak behind enemy lines into enemy territory on a secret mission with sensitive material hidden on his person. He felt like he was about to be interrogated by the opposing general. He'd played over and over in his mind his prospective conversation with Tyree Sinclair, and it never came out well. *The future looks bleak, to say the least. I'm not going to let this man shoot the messenger just because he doesn't like the message.*

He'd been offered coffee or a soft drink. He'd have preferred a double shot of Jack, but it was 10:00 a.m., and that option wasn't available, *despite the fact that it's five o'clock somewhere.*

By ten fifteen no word from Sinclair, and Davis was getting impatient. Sinclair may have been tied up, his nine o'clock meeting could have run long, or Sinclair may have just been playing a mind game. Some attorneys insisted on doing that. Davis had been taught differently, and quite frankly, he didn't have the time for such bullshit. It was true that the practice of law was like a war; strategy and tactics mattered. Motions and depositions were like battles to be won and lost, all leading up to a trial. The trial was the big test for each of the generals, and the victory came in the form of the verdict. In most cases there was an appeal. He'd been taught by the best general, Morty Steine, to think long term. Each battle was important, but the final outcome of the war was what really counted. Sometimes the war was actually won in the Court of Appeals because of a critical mistake made in a motion or during trial. That's why he was taught to evaluate every piece of evidence before it was introduced and each witness's testimony during trial whether it was important enough to risk on appeal. It was critical to assess because a large verdict meant an almost certain appeal, and the fewer issues, the better.

In the Chapman case, Davis was beginning the war by dropping, without warning, a nuclear bomb. Most lawsuits didn't involve the daughter and son-in-law of the other lawyer, and they certainly didn't involve the infidelity of the son-in-law. They usually started off slowly and built to a climax through discovery. The smoking gun came much later in the case or never at all.

Sinclair wasn't a litigator. He had a few dozen underlings to do his biddings. He directed his firm as a deal maker or a kingmaker. He was a power broker. He made and destroyed politicians and businessmen. He dished out favors and withheld them. It was in that capacity that he crossed paths with Morty Steine, who as an influential member of the Democratic Party did the same. The only difference was that Sinclair had no party affiliation, just power for the sake of power. He may have leaned Republican, but he was so powerful, he crossed party affiliations.

It was ten thirty when Sinclair's associate, Mary Forsythe, met him in reception and ushered Davis into a small conference room with a sixty-inch round table and five cordovan leather chairs. The message being sent was clear. The Chapman matter was of little concern to the firm. It didn't warrant one of the larger conference rooms, and it wasn't a concern of its senior partner. Sinclair & Sims saw this as a mere collection matter.

"Have you been offered coffee and/or a soft drink, Mr. Davis?"

No one could say that the firm of Sinclair& Sims wasn't cordial to guests. Old South to the end, even those who owed it $14,000.

"Mr. Sinclair is tied up. He asked that I take the meeting. I've prepared an agreed order of substitution of your firm for mine in Chapman vs. Chapman. Can we talk about a reasonable payment plan?"

Davis, who'd tried to think through every possible scenario, assumed he'd at least get to meet with Tyree Sinclair. He never envisioned being shuffled off to an associate.

"My meeting is with Mr. Sinclair. There are issues that I need to address with him personally regarding one of the firm's partners, who also happen to be his son-in-law. It wouldn't be appropriate to discuss them with an associate of the firm. Please tell Mr. Sinclair that I'll either wait or reschedule our meeting to a date and time convenient to him, but I must meet with him."

"I assure you I've been given the authority to resolve the collection matter. If it goes to court, I'll be the one trying it."

"I appreciate and respect your position, but I must talk directly with Mr. Sinclair." Davis added, "privately." He hoped that his last remark would get Sinclair's attention.

"I can't promise anything. Let me check with his secretary as to his availability."

"While you check, could I review Mr. January's time tickets? I requested that they be present at this meeting."

The young associate looked confused and then disturbed. Davis could tell that she was questioning whether she had the authority to give Davis the tickets and then leave the room.

He knew just what to say. "This is your case. Those tickets are the basis of your lawsuit. If you want to negotiate a payment plan and settle the case, I need to look at those tickets. I may be waiting for Mr. Sinclair for some time. We might as well use this time productively. I promise you as an officer of the court that every ticket will be here when you return."

That seemed to satisfy the young woman. After she left the room, Davis pulled out Laura's red diary and started pulling time tickets from the stack chronologically. The process took less than ten minutes. After he completed his review, he waited another twenty minutes, and there was a knock on the door. Without waiting for a response, Tyree Sinclair and Mary Forsythe entered and sat down.

Sinclair apologized for passing Davis off to an associate, but something had come up, and "this is a simple matter."

"This may not be as simple as you think, sir."

"Chapman has failed to pay. We've extended her $14,000 worth of credit, and she's in breach of contract. That seems pretty simple to me. We need to withdraw, and your firm needs to be substituted."

He pushed the agreed order over to Davis.

"Mr. Sinclair, would you ask Ms. Forsythe to excuse herself so we can have a private conversation?"

"This is her case, I think . . ."

Davis cut him off. He could tell that Sinclair wasn't used to that happening. "Respectfully . . ."

"I don't know who the hell you think you are, Mr. Davis. This is my office. Morty Steine, I'm sure, taught you . . ."

Davis changed his tone. He'd been very soft spoken until now, but his demeanor changed quickly and sharply. He got very loud and aggressive. Sinclair and especially Forsythe were shocked.

"Look, Morty knows I'm here. He knows *why* I'm here, and if he was here, he'd tell you to excuse your associate and sit down, shut up, and listen. I'm here to help."

Sinclair's face turned red. He was about to unleash a stormy response when Forsythe smartly and sheepishly interjected, "I'll let you gentlemen talk. Mr. Davis, I'll leave the agreed order with you for your review."

She stood and left. Sinclair gave Davis a hard look and in a serious voice announced, "I don't know what you're up to, Davis, but I'm in no mood for games. Get to the goddamn point. You've got five minutes!"

"First, this is going to take more than five minutes, but after five minutes I'm confident that you'll give me the time I need." Davis took a moment to let that sink in.

"Your son-in-law is not the man you think he is. I know he's the father of your grandchildren and your law partner, but there's a side of him that neither you nor your daughter appreciates."

"What the hell are you talking about? Dan's a good husband, a good man, and a good lawyer."

"I'm sorry to inform you that you're wrong on all three counts. He's been cheating on your daughter, he's a dishonest and manipulative son of a bitch, and he's an unethical attorney."

"Again, what the hell are you talking about? I said no games, and you're playing games. If you don't get to the point, I'm going to have security . . ."

You asked for it, so here goes. "Dan January for the last six months has been forcing Laura Chapman to have sex with him."

"If you're accusing Dan of rape, that's a matter for the police."

"No. He's been using his position as her lawyer and the fact that she owes this firm money to engage in various sex acts."

Sinclair stood, pointed to the door, and shouted, "Get the hell out of here! This is a shakedown, and I'm not going to stand here . . ."

Up until now Davis had been appropriately respectful, but there was a limit to his patience, and the line had been crossed.

"Sit down and shut the hell up! You're going to hear me out and look at my proof. Then you can call security, but I suspect you'll be thanking me instead."

Davis explained the course of the Chapman divorce. He described how January and Chapman got close and then too close. He pulled no punches. He presented Sinclair with a chart that set forth each date and time the couple engaged in oral sex, intercourse, and anal sex. There were twenty-six encounters. He then handed Sinclair the January time tickets he'd organized from the stack that Forsythe had given him. The tickets matched exactly the schedule that Davis had prepared. Each half hour time ticket reflected oral sex on the schedule. Each hour time ticket exactly coordinated with an intercourse entry in Laura's diary, and the two-hour tickets perfectly coordinated with her claims of anal sex or use of a dildo.

The blood drained from Sinclair's face. This was not a man who talked about intercourse, let alone oral or anal sex. He was a straight missionary position man with the lights off. To be confronted with a coordinated written record of his son-in-law's twenty-six acts of infidelity was infuriating, enlightening, and frightening.

Davis waited for him to say something, but he remained silent. Davis pondered what to say next. This was a proud man who looked absolutely dejected.

"Mr. Sinclair . . ."

"Just call me Ty. I'd say you know enough about my business to call me by my nickname that my friends call me. You know things they don't. What other proof do you have?"

Davis handed him an emergency room report dated June 15th of Laura Chapman's admission to Vanderbilt Hospital for rectal bleeding. Davis pointed to the two-hour time ticket for June 15th, and the two-hour diary entry that denoted use of a dildo anally.

"What else?"

Sinclair had switched from father and grandfather to lawyer mode. Davis couldn't tell if his attitude changed intentionally or automatically, but it was apparent to Davis. Sinclair, as a lawyer, wanted to weigh the evidence Davis had against January to determine the case against him, as he would any client, regardless of relationship. Davis handed Sinclair another document.

AFFIDAVIT

COUNTY OF DAVIDSON

STATE OF TENNESSEE

1. I am Dr. Paula Milam. I am a psychotherapist, licensed in the state of Tennessee.

2. I have treated Laura Chapman since June 1st. She sought treatment because of severe depression arising from a relationship with her attorney, Dan January. She'd been involved in a sexual relationship with Mr. January, a married man, since Memorial Day. She felt guilty and disgusted with herself.

3. I explained to her that Mr. January had used his position of trust to manipulate her into providing sexual favors in exchange for legal services.

4. At first she was resistant to my advice, but on June 15th

her relationship with Mr. January forced her to visit the emergency room because of a rectal tear. After that experience Ms. Chapman stood up to Mr. January and demanded that they end their personal relationship. In response Mr. January threatened to expose their sexual relationship to her husband's divorce attorney. When that duplicitous ploy failed, he threatened to sue her for his legal fees.

5. I am prepared to testify in court as to these facts and the effect Mr. January's actions have had on Ms. Chapman.

The Affiant Says Not,

Paula Milam, PhD

Davis waited for Sinclair's reaction.

The response was that of a good lawyer, "Part of this affidavit is hearsay and not admissible."

The consummate lawyer, thought Davis.

"And I say I can get it in under one of the exceptions to the hearsay rules and under expert testimony under Rule 26 of the Rules of Civil Procedure," Davis said with determination and resilience. He then added, "We both know that it will never come to that. So let's not waste time, Mr. Sinclair." He decided not to be familiar and refer to him as Ty.

"I think you have a bigger problem. I don't think this is an isolated incident. Creeps like January have an ongoing problem. They prey on the weak. I'm sure if you dig deeper, you're going to find that Laura Chapman isn't the first and only victim of Dan January. I bet if you look at his other female divorce clients, there were other fees for sex arrangements. If the Chapman collection case goes forward, your firm could be looking at several lawsuits for sexual harassment and breach of trust. Dan January should be brought before the Board of Professional Responsibility, and his law license should be taken away."

Sinclair bluntly asked Davis, "You came here for a purpose, not simply to tell me about my son-in-law's infidelity. What does your client want?"

Davis, Sammie, and Morty had discussed that question for more than an hour. There was no point to the meeting without having an end game. Davis opened his bloodstained briefcase and handed Sinclair a piece of paper, keeping a copy for himself.

PROPOSED SETTLEMENT AGREEMENT

1. Dismissal with prejudice of the lawsuit filed by Sinclair & Sims and costs assessed against the law firm.

2. Return by Sinclair & Sims of the $5,000 retainer paid by Chapman.

3. Payment by Sinclair & Sims to Chapman in the amount of $260,000.

4. Substitution of Steine, Davis, & Davis for Sinclair & Sims as counsel of record for Chapman in the divorce action. Steine, Davis, & Davis will accept as full and final payment a $5,000 retainer to represent Laura Chapman in her divorce action.

5. Confidentiality clause limiting disclosure of this settlement and its terms to the managing partners of Sinclair & Sims.

6. Sinclair & Sims acknowledges that Steine, Davis, & Davis has met its ethical obligation relating to Dan January's

unethical conduct by reporting his actions to his employer. Sinclair & Sims will investigate Dan January's conduct and determine whether he should be reported to the Disciplinary Board for unethical conduct relating to Ms. Chapman and/or others.

Sinclair just sat there contemplating the document. He forgot about his daughter and grandchildren and assumed the role of one of the three managing partners of Sinclair & Sims.

"You're out of your mind. That's $10,000 per encounter. No woman is worth that. The highest-priced call girl in Las Vegas is only $1,000 an hour."

"But prostitution is legal in Nevada, and the john doesn't have a fiduciary relationship with the hooker. That's a straight business transaction. The market determines the price of those services. This is different."

Davis had anticipated that argument and was ready with a snappy comeback. "Ty, this isn't a negotiation. Dan violated this woman. He victimized her . . ."

Sinclair cut Davis off, "So is this blackmail?"

It was about to get ugly. Davis was prepared for an extortion argument as well. "Look, your firm wrongfully filed suit. No money is owed. Your partner acted unethically and immorally. Don't accuse me of anything, Mr. Sinclair. I'll file an answer to this bogus collection action, raise some affirmative defenses, and then sue January and your firm for sexual harassment. January is your partner; the firm's responsible for him. He's your agent."

Sinclair, ever the lawyer, argued, "For business purposes, the practice of law, not to have sex with women."

Davis knew in principle he was right, but the appearance of

impropriety was enough in this case. The firm would be forced into a no-win situation defending a lawsuit. Davis responded, "I came here in good faith to work through this and save you and your firm that headache. Mr. Steine said you'd understand and appreciate that gesture."

The mention of Morty's name softened Sinclair. It was like bringing up something good and pure. You could see the change come over the man. He accepted the reality of the situation.

"You're right. Sorry, The lawyer in me took over. This is a lot to digest. I'm naturally pretty angry I didn't see this myself, and it had to be shown to me. Your settlement addresses your client's needs and concerns, but I may need your client's cooperation after her divorce is final, and the settlement agreement needs to be revised to specifically reflect that cooperation."

"What are you asking from Ms. Chapman?"

"My firm may elect to contact not only the Disciplinary Board but also the DA's office. If my daughter will allow me, I might arrange for January to be criminally charged with breach of trust, embezzlement, and whatever else my partners and I might think of. It may require her to testify at a criminal trial."

"What if the settlement agreement provided that if testimony is required at a criminal trial, I will testify under subpoena that Mr. January's conduct caused a loss of $14,000 of fees to your firm and that his conduct cost the firm $260,000 in settlement of a sexual harassment suit that I would have filed against the firm. The proof comes in, just through a different witness, one who will not get flustered on the stand."

Sinclair stood and extended his hand. "I need to get the approval of at least one of the other managing partners for a majority, but I'm confident that they'll follow my lead." They shook.

"I have to admit that this settlement stings, but I do appreciate the way you've handled this matter. You did a great job for your client, and yet I feel that you treated me and my firm with the respect we deserve. Tell Morty that the Steine family has again extended the Sinclairs help when they've needed it."

As he left Sinclair's office, Davis reveled in the settlement and Sinclair's last remark.

CHAPTER NINETEEN

A BIG SURPRISE

Thursday, October 29, 1998

Davis took the rest of the day off. He figured he deserved an afternoon away from the office. Sinclair was to prepare the settlement agreement based on the summary they'd agreed to and jotted down on a legal pad. It had been a profitable morning for the firm monetarily, and it had been a very satisfactory morning for Davis professionally. He'd helped his client, Tyree Sinclair, and Sinclair's daughter, Rachel.

He left the office with an orange Tootsie Pop in his mouth, sucking away hard, top down, picked up flowers for his wife, and pulled into the driveway for a little surprise. When he got to his front stoop he surveyed his yard, and a sense of pride rushed over him. He'd accomplished a lot in less than fifteen years. He'd built a law practice and started a family. Nashville had become his home. New York was now a distant part of his past.

He entered through the back door. Liza was in the kitchen. The family pugs, Abbott and Costello, greeted him first. The fawn-colored animals licked him as he petted them on the tops of their heads. Other than Liza, the dogs were the only living things in the house. The kids, Caroline, age fourteen, and Jake, almost age twelve, wouldn't be home for hours. Liza jumped when he walked into the room and almost fainted when she saw the flowers. He was still trying to make amends from their fight a month earlier. She'd not mentioned going back to work, but he knew the thought was still in the back of her mind, to reappear after Caroline got her learner's permit.

"What's wrong? What the hell are you doing home? And why did you bring home flowers?"

"Nothing's wrong. I'm home because I had a good morning, and I deserved the afternoon off. The flowers are for you because I love you."

She looked at him skeptically. He never came home before six o'clock, and it was common for him to miss dinner with the kids and get home at eight or nine. He tried to avoid missing the evening meal with his children, but the demands of the job were very time consuming.

"What is it, a national holiday? Did the Pope die?"

"Again, I had a good morning and thought I deserved the afternoon off. No one's dead. Let's leave the Pope out of this. I'm sure he's doing quite all right. The dogs seem to understand, why can't you?"

Both dogs were at his legs rubbing up against him, wanting attention from their master. Davis bent down and scratched Abbott under his chin and picked up the slightly overweight Costello and stroked him as Liza remarked, "As you can see, we're all a little surprised to see you home so early."

After several more minutes of bantering back and forth, he followed her upstairs to the bedroom.

"What do you think you're doing?"

"I thought you needed some friendly stimulation before your husband came home."

"Where are those damn guard dogs when you need them? My husband bought them for my protection, and they've let me down. They're worthless."

He put his arm around her waist and drew her to him. She pretended to resist.

"My husband's the jealous type, and I must warn you, he owns a gun and knows how to use it."

"I'll take my chances." He dipped her onto the bed, making sure his full weight didn't crush the poor woman. Verbal foreplay over, physical foreplay was short, and sex wasn't much longer, but both were satisfied. After seven minutes of mandatory cuddling, they went their separate ways. Davis settled into his home office but decided to read a book rather than do work. He turned off the office, determined to truly relax.

About two hours later, Caroline and Jake walked in the door. Davis in a pair of sweats and a black tee shirt was sitting in the den watching TV. It was a rerun of *I Love Lucy*. He greeted them with a big smile and a hug. He was then interrogated by both of them: "What's wrong? Why are you home?"

Davis realized that he'd been working too hard, despite the promises he made to himself while on vacation. He needed to spend more time with his family. Home only a month, he'd reverted to his old ways and was absorbed by the office.

"I had a good day and decided to take the afternoon off. I've been taking it easy." He didn't add *and having a little fun with your mother*. How much homework do you have?"

Caroline indicated she had about an hour. Jake claimed he didn't have any. "How about you get your work done and then we go out to dinner and a movie? Caroline, your choice as to the restaurant, and Jake, subject to your mother's approval, you pick the movie."

The kids disappeared into their rooms to complete their tasks. Davis found his wife and gave her a hug and kissed her on the neck. She cocked her head back and proclaimed, "Forget about seconds. We're not alone in the house, and anyway your daily limit is once. Tomorrow is another day," she said, imitating Scarlett O'Hara from *Gone with the Wind* as Rhett Butler departed from their Atlanta mansion.

In response Davis chimed back, "Frankly my dear, I don't give a damn. Tomorrow begins at midnight. I'll be lying next to you, and you can expect my seductive advances."

"You can try, but you might lose your hand."

They'd been married seventeen years. They'd gotten good at the banter back and forth. It helped when you were truly in love.

After much debate, Caroline picked Jimmy Kelly's, a famous Nashville steakhouse located on Elliston Place near her parents' beloved Vanderbilt. She made the selection with her father in mind, but she did cherish the corn cakes, a true southern delicacy. Everybody ordered steaks. Davis got the twenty-four-ounce Tomahawk Ribeye.

"That's an awful lot of meat," Liza scolded, "Why couldn't you have ordered a petit filet like Caroline and me?"

"Because we're men." Davis looked over at Jake, who'd ordered a New York strip. "Or at least we're almost men," Davis said, directing his question to his almost twelve-year-old. "How's your Haftorah coming?"

Jake was only eight months away (beginning of July) from his Jewish rite of passage, his Bar Mitzvah. He was required to read a portion of the Torah, the Jewish Bible, and then read commentary in Hebrew. In English he had to give a fifteen- or twenty-minute speech on a selected personal matter. All of this was done before the congregation and invited guests. Liza and Davis were working on the guest list. Family, friends, and business acquaintances were invited. The Davises expected more than three hundred.

They'd coordinated the happy event with their annual July 3rd party and the Hillwood Country Club fireworks display. Normally, a Bar Mitzvah would be on or about a young man's thirteenth birthday, which for Jake would have been in early November. The Davises had convinced their rabbi to move Jake's up several months so it could coincide with America's birthday weekend.

In recent years this religious ceremony had turned into a real dog and pony show with a theme to the party that followed the ceremony at Temple. Often the party portion of the evening was held at a hotel or country club. Caroline's Bat Mitzvah held two years earlier was at Hillwood Country Club, where the Davises were members. Her theme was Broadway. The waiters and waitresses were dressed in costumes as they circulated the hors d'oeuvres and served the meal. Little Orphan Annie, the Phantom of the Opera, and the Fiddler on the Roof all worked the party.

Jake suggested the movie *Caddyshack* as his theme. He wanted characters from the movie to circulate among his guests, and a cake shaped like a putting green.

"Poor Abraham, he'll be turning over in his grave, thought Davis.

After their meal, the Davis family went to the movies. Jake selected *Godzilla.* Liza agreed it was age appropriate. Davis relinquished decisions like that to his levelheaded wife. In the past he'd gotten himself in big trouble because of his failure to consult and communicate with the boss of the family. He'd learned his place and limited authority. He was constantly telling the children, "If it's okay with your mom, then . . ."

At work, with Morty's guidance, he was in charge. At home he followed orders, just like Abbott and Costello. He was right below them in the pecking order.

After the movie, on the car ride home, there was a heated discussion about Halloween just two days away. Davis asked, "Caroline, what are you going to be for Halloween?"

"Nothing, there's a party at Emily Green's house, and it's not costume. I'll just be going as myself."

"You mean you're ditching your brother and me and not going trick or treating? I could come home early, and you could go to the party a little later?"

"I'm not dressing up. I'm not a little kid anymore. You need to face facts."

Davis started to get angry, but he knew she was right. In desperation he looked to Liza for support but got none. The girl was fourteen, too old to be going out with her father for a children's celebration. There would be boys at the Green house, and they were far more interesting than a handful of Snickers or even an entire bag of candy. *Well, we'll make it a boys' night out.* The next thing he knew there was a full rebellion.

"Dad, I can't go with you either. I'm going out with Jack and Josh."

Davis almost lost it. Halloween was one of his favorite holidays, right behind Thanksgiving and Passover. It wasn't only the candy, but he certainly didn't mind that. It was the dressing up and going house to house with the kids. He couldn't believe that part of his life was over. Where did time go? He quickly realized he'd lost the war, so he sued for conditions.

"Here's the deal, I get to pick any five candies from your bag I want, no questions asked, and you can go out with your friends."

Jake hesitated a moment, and then they shook hands. Davis thought it was a bad deal for him, and he was pretty unhappy. He went into his home office to tie up a few loose ends. There was a document on the fax machine that he put in his briefcase without reading.

By midnight Liza was fast asleep, but as promised, Davis made his move with stealth. Interestingly, she gave up without a fight. She knew her husband was a man of his word. The clock had struck midnight, and it was another day.

CHAPTER TWENTY

NO JOKE

Friday, October 30, 1998

As usual, Davis was first to arrive at the office. It was about six, and he went straight for the coffee machine, which Bella set on a timer for 5:45, every day, just so that extra strong brew could be waiting for him.

She's an Italian angel, ever present, at least ever since my arrival in 1975. More accurately Bella Rosario had worked for Morty Steine since 1957, when she and her husband, Tony, arrived in Nashville. Over time she garnered more and more responsibility in the office.

Every morning, the rich aroma of the brewed concoction greeted Davis, and he would drink two cups before getting a full head of steam. That sweet smell remained in the air until Morty arrived at the office four hours later and began smoking his Cubans. Bella was constantly protesting, arguing on behalf of their clients. Her complaints fell on deaf ears.

Morty's response was always, "They need me a hell of a lot more than I need them. They can put up with some of my minor imperfections so they can win their case. I always ask if I can smoke in their presence, and if they say no, I don't."

She replied, "They wouldn't dare challenge you."

It's an arrogant attitude, Davis admitted, *but true.*

Bella, who'd been Morty's right-hand man, Davis's baby sitter, or Davis's girl Friday for more than forty years, pointed out, "The clients would never give you an honest answer anyway. They could be dying from lung cancer, coughing their heads off, turning blue, and they'd still tell you to go ahead and light up. Either they respect you too much, or they're afraid you'll withdraw as their attorney if they object. Grow up. If Goldie were here . . ."

Morty didn't like it when Bella brought his dead wife into the conversation, and he would cut her off. Obviously she was the one person who did have absolute control over Morty, and he didn't like to be reminded that she was gone.

"She's not here, and you're not her. There will never be another, so I'm going to keep on smoking until the day I die. End of story."

That argument raged every day to some extent. Usually Monday was the worst, just to get the week started. Davis stayed out of the fight and let the women fight the senseless battle. Sammie supported Bella, but she clearly took a backseat to the older woman. They argued that the smoking was not only a personal health hazard. They objected to the secondhand smoke. By Friday, they'd exhausted themselves and given up. After resting over the weekend, they were ready to begin again on Monday.

Sammie and Bella arrived at seven and began peppering Davis about his meeting with Tyree Sinclair. Davis said, "I'm only going to tell the story once, so you'll have to wait for the old man."

Sammie protested, "He doesn't get in till ten. That's three hours away."

"So you wake him. He's just two floors down."

Sammie and Morty were neighbors. She lived in the ninth floor loft, which was Abe Steine's office when the building was Steine's Department Store. It had long since been converted to an apartment for the firm. About two years ago when the sixth-floor tenant moved out, that floor was converted to two three-bedroom luxury units, 601 and 602. Morty occupied Unit 601. He spent the weekday nights there and the weekends at Squeeze Bottom, his 288-acre farm south of Nashville in Williamson County.

Sammie decided she'd let the old man sleep. He wasn't someone you woke for no good reason. Telling the others what happened at the meeting with Sinclair could wait a couple of hours.

Davis first looked at his messages from forty-one calls. He organized them and added them to his yellow pad. His list increased to three pages. He decided he would wait until nine to start returning calls. He next looked over the mail. Bella had culled the bullshit and the bills. He signed the checks, but she wrote them out and kept the books. He looked over a response to discovery in the Peterson case, a contract dispute. He highlighted and made handwritten notes on his copy. Bella had already scanned the document into the computer.

Bella buzzed in, "It's Bob Sullivan. He called yesterday on the Lopez matter."

"Mr. Davis, you're a busy man. I tried to call you yesterday."

"I took the afternoon off to be with my family."

The two men were friends and had worked with each other many times, both on the same side and as adversaries. They respected each other and could believe what the other said. There was, however, no obligation to volunteer information. Davis had no intention of telling Sullivan about the Chapman settlement with the Sinclair firm.

"So what's up in the Lopez case?"

Maria Lopez was an accounts payable clerk in the main office of a construction company, R&R Construction. Several male employees made improper sexual advances, referring to Ms. Lopez to her face "as a hot tamale and a hot pepper." Ms. Lopez, an attractive divorced mother of three, was thirty-five, with jet black hair and blue eyes. The first time she ignored the remark. The second time she made a joke in response, but the third, she told the man to keep his opinions to himself. On the fourth time, when it was apparent it wasn't going to stop, she reported the men to the company accountant, who did nothing. When the workers realized that the company wasn't going to stop their verbal harassment, they began touching her on the shoulders and arms. The harassment got so bad that Ms. Lopez quit. After her unemployment compensation was denied, she came to see Davis.

"Ben, it's a construction company. Construction workers tend to make comments and whistle. Their remarks weren't that shocking. Ms. Lopez may be a little too sensitive . . ."

"It's a changing world, Bob. Even people who wear hard hats need to be politically correct. They even began manhandling her. She found it necessary to quit, and she was denied unemployment. She's got to feed her kids. I'm willing to listen, but if we can't come to terms, we'll see you in Federal District Court."

Both men were good lawyers, and they knew they were only fencing. Sullivan became direct with his friend, "I'm calling bullshit. We both know this case needs to be settled. There's not enough meat on the bone for you to even file suit. I called to try to get this settled. You're usually a reasonable man, although I know at least Liza wouldn't agree. Maybe I should call her as a witness when you file suit in federal court."

Now Sullivan was mocking Davis's hollow threat. It was a good strategy.

"You're not going to negotiate a settlement if you keep insulting me."

Sullivan got down to business. "What do you have in mind?"

"I want a stellar letter of recommendation, which I get to write, from her immediate boss and the president of the company. I want the employees who harassed her to apologize. I want the company to institute a new sexual harassment policy that we can agree to and a promise from the president that it will be enforced. I want the company to pay Ms. Lopez $15,000 plus $5,000 in attorney fees to Steine, Davis & Davis."

"You know I've got to get approval from the client, but I'll recommend the payments. The other conditions are up to the client. I can't commit to them. An apology is not common practice. You're also asking for a change in company culture. "

"Bob, remind them how much you cost per hour. If they don't change with the times, in six months you'll be talking to another attorney, and he might not be as reasonable as I am."

"I can think of a lot of words to describe you, Davis, but reasonable isn't one of them. I'll get back to you."

Before Sullivan hung up, Davis casually remarked, "By the way, Sammie will be substituting for Dan January in the Chapman divorce."

"Good, I can't stand that guy. He's a real asshole. Sammie's much easier on the eyes and easier to work with. Her only real flaw is that she's related to you."

"Nobody's perfect. By the way, that last comment could be taken as sexually charged, Bob."

"Don't tell me you're getting politically correct also. The world's changing but not that fast."

Davis spoke deliberatively, "Let's face it, the law's changing. What once could be said at the water cooler can't be said any longer. You and I might not agree, but we don't make the law. As lawyers, we just enforce it and make sure others live within it. I suggest you explain this fact of life to your client, Bob, or I'll see them in federal court."

"You're quite the bull shitter, Ben!"

"Test me."

That ended the friendly phone call.

Davis returned four other calls. He had to leave two messages. The Bar was generally busy, and it was sometimes difficult to connect with other lawyers. Davis dictated six quick correspondences for Bella to transcribe. He looked over the yellow pad and considered what to work on next.

Morty strolled into the office about ten thirty, late for him, the benefits of his age and ownership of the building and founding of the firm.

He stuck his head into Davis's office and asked, "How'd the Sinclair meeting go?"

"Tell Bella to put the answering machine on, and let's have a firm meeting in the conference room."

Five minutes later, the entire staff was seated at the table. Davis had his game face on.

Morty spoke up, "So what the hell happened?"

Davis handed each of them a copy of the settlement agreement and just let them read it. The dollar amount of $260,000 jumped out immediately. Proud of himself, Davis asked Sammie to set up an appointment with Laura at four to review the document.

Sammie and Davis met with Laura in Davis's office. They sat at his table. He handed Laura the agreement, and she started crying. "What does this mean in plain English?"

"You signed two contracts with Steine, Davis & Davis. Sammie will substitute for January and represent you in the divorce action. We've discussed it, and Sammie will waive her fee. I think we can enter into a quick marital dissolution agreement before you take possession of the Sinclair settlement proceeds. If you don't have control of the funds, the funds do not have to be disclosed to your husband and do not have to be a part of your divorce settlement. The document will provide that you are dividing the property owned by husband and wife as of a date certain and that you are each waiving any interest in any future inheritance, future claims, or settlements. We will word that language very carefully to include the payment by the law firm to settle the January claim."

Laura started crying again. Davis waited for her to calm down.

"You signed a second contract with our firm, which provided that we'd be paid one-third of any settlement of any claim or trial against Sinclair & Sims. We've decided to modify that agreement because the matter was resolved so quickly. My firm is entitled to $83,333.33, but we're willing to accept $60,000 as full payment, leaving you an even $200,000. That payment and a divorce should put your life back on track."

Sammie took Laura into her office to discuss the divorce case. Davis called Liza and explained that he wouldn't be home for dinner.

"Order the petite filet."

"I'll order what I damn well please if I'm picking up the tab." *I think I'll order the porterhouse and onion rings.*

CHAPTER TWENTY-ONE

A GOOD PERSON

Sunday, November 1, 1998

It took my husband almost forty-eight hours before he had the nerve to tell me something that shattered what I thought was our idealistic life. *It was just an illusion. Like everyone else, we had problems. They weren't on the surface. They were waiting to bubble up and bite us on the ass.*

My initial reaction when my husband informed me of Mr. Davis's report of my son-in-law's infidelity was outrage, but then I remembered my daughter's efforts to reach out for help, and like most mothers, I felt guilt. I'd rebuked my daughter's direct efforts for help. Southern women didn't discuss those matters with their child, boy or girl, but especially a girl. I didn't ignore my daughter. I made sure I got her help, but I didn't help. I told myself it was a generational thing. Women of my generation didn't talk about sex. Maybe when we were younger, as sorority sisters, with our girl friends, but not with our children.

I'd made it clear to Tyree that I was going to be part of the solution. We were going to deal with the situation as a family.

I told him, "You're thinking like a lawyer and a businessman. I don't give a damn about legal ethics, your law firm, or the $260,000. Our first concern is our grandchildren, and the second is our daughter. Frankie and Gaby are innocent victims. They're bright, and they love their father. Have you considered how a bitter divorce and fight with their father will affect them? Right now we have unlimited access to our grandchildren. What happens to grandma and grandpa once the battle lines are drawn? Frankie and Gaby are going to need us more than ever. They've done absolutely nothing wrong. They are our number one priority. These actions you're contemplating will have consequences that will affect the people we love, so I say slow down."

Tyree did just that. He took a deep breath. His wife of almost forty years was right. They needed to proceed cautiously.

"Let's review where we are," he insisted. "Davis and his team know, which includes Chapman, her therapist, Davis, and his office. We know, and my two managing partners know of Dan's infidelity.

Amazingly he was considering that we might be able to keep it secret and preserve our good name.

"Tyree, you're worrying about the wrong thing. Focus on our family, not your good name. Several months ago Rachel came to me and told me of Dan's interest in wife swapping and questioned me about certain sexual proclivities. I pushed her away but helped get her a therapist."

"You should have told me."

"And what would you have done? Would you have had the sex talk with your daughter? This wasn't about the birds and the bees and how the flowers get pollinated. This was about anal sex. Ever had anal sex, Tyree?"

There was a long silence.

"Didn't think so. I hadn't either. You might not have had much to contribute because neither did I."

I explained to my husband what I remembered Rachel had told

me about the wife-swapping party she attended. I recalled that she had been befriended by one of the women, who'd held her hand during the ordeal. I described how she'd cried when she recalled that Dan moved from bedroom to bedroom, from one woman to another.

"And she just sat there and watched him go from room to room. How humiliating," he said.

We both felt our child's pain, and I turned to my husband, a man I loved and trusted. "She's got to leave him. It may get messy in the short term, but in the long term, it's got to be what's best for the children and Rachel. You know it's been difficult for Frankie and Gaby to live under the same roof with the two of them. The fighting must have been intense. Rachel for good reason must have been on edge and depressed. I turned her over to the therapist and then hoped the problem would go away. She never said anything further, and I just turned a blind eye. I should have mentioned something to you."

The couple hugged as a sign they were united.

Tyree had been listening to his wife, and said, "As Dan's employer, I'm in a better position than a father-in-law in the same position. He's made some very serious mistakes and bad decisions. I'll be able to use his ethical and legal breaches to benefit our child. I might look for revenge, or I might look for an advantage in resolving the divorce. A lot will depend on how Dan decides how he wants to proceed from this point forward."

Rita reminded him, "Remember our first concern is the well-being of Frankie and Gaby. We need to assure them that we love them, and we've got to protect them from the ugliness of what's about to happen."

"Rita, I hear you. Enough with the kids. I get it! We need to sit down with our daughter and develop a game plan. The first thing I've got to figure out is whether or not this Chapman woman is an isolated case or the tip of the iceberg. Davis implied he thought there'd be others. He may be right. The investigation needs to start with Dan's secretary and then the other staff members. The partners would be the last to know. I suspect Bonnie, Dan's secretary, who prepares his bills, would have noticed a discrepancy between time logged and work output."

There was a brief silence between the couple as they both envisioned their son-in-law being unfaithful to their daughter. It disgusted them.

Tyree bravely broached the subject, "How do we break the news to Rachel?"

That's a cowardly statement. We sit her down and tell her. She already knows her husband's been unfaithful. He's done so right in front of her. She's been seeking psychiatric help, for God's sake. I suspect we'll need to make an emergency appointment when we drop this bomb on her.

"We just tell her. We're her parents. We tell her that we love her and we'll support her through this difficult time and that whatever she needs we're there for her."

We met with Rachel that evening and discussed Dan's infidelity. To my surprise, Rachel seemed relieved and agreed with our plan for divorce. She objected to our suggestion that she move out of her home with the children and move in with us, but we didn't press the point. She agreed that her father was in the best position to select her lawyer and that he would investigate whether Ms. Chapman was an isolated client or if there were others. We didn't discuss Dan's proclivity to engage in group sex. That would have been too painful for all of us. We agreed that Rachel should make an appointment with her therapist, Dr. Ames, as early as possible.

CHAPTER TWENTY-TWO

A BUSY DAY

Tuesday, December 1, 1998

Davis and Sammie met Becky Taylor in front of the courthouse. She admitted she was a little nervous. They all took the elevator up to the fourth floor and went directly into courtroom #2. Within five minutes after taking their seats, Johnson Tory standing in front of the judge announced the case of State of Tennessee vs. Oscar Brand, case# 99-2341.

"If it please the court, the state and the defendant have entered into a plea agreement on one count of obstruction of justice, by compounding a criminal investigation by misleading the police in their investigation of the elevator accident, by altering the evidence, a Class E felony, which carries a maximum of six years. It is the recommendation of the state that the defendant serve two years. However, the state, as part of the plea bargain, insisted that the court hear the testimony of Mrs. Rebecca Taylor before the court makes its determination. Mrs. Taylor is the widow of William Taylor, who died in the elevator incident investigated by Mr. Brand."

Davis had bitterly fought with Tory to get Becky's testimony before the judge before the court passed sentence.

"The state calls Mrs. Rebecca Taylor."

Judge Mark Carlson smiled at Becky as she took the stand. Oscar Brand scowled at her.

"Mrs. Taylor, there's something you want to tell me before I pass judgment on Mr. Brand?"

"Judge, I'd first like you to listen to a tape."

Without waiting for a response, she played the tape of the last fifteen minutes of William's life. It was pretty powerful stuff. It was hard not to be moved by a man's dying words and sounds of his death. Becky clicked the recorder off.

"Mr. Brand didn't kill William, but he tried to prevent my children and me from collecting from his employer and its insurance company the money we were entitled to because of their defective product. He broke the law, which provides for a jail sentence of up to five years. The DA has recommended two years, less than half. That doesn't seem reasonable for a man who tried to cover up his crime and got caught. If it weren't for my lawyer, Mr. Davis, this man would have gotten away with his crime. It was Mr. Davis who brought Mr. Brand to justice, not the DA or the police. For that reason I feel I should have some say in the length of Mr. Brand's sentence. It is my recommendation to the court that Mr. Brand serve three years rather than two years, with no chance of probation. He interfered with the police investigation of my husband's death in an effort to defeat my claim for recovery on behalf of my family. My children were entitled to be compensated, and Mr. Brand lied to the police and altered evidence. Quite frankly I think a sentence of thirty-six months is not unreasonable. I'm advised that under the DA's plea agreement, Mr. Brand, with good behavior, is likely going to serve only eighteen months of his two-year sentence. I think that would be a travesty of justice. Thank you for hearing me out."

Becky returned to her seat next to Sammie in the gallery of the courtroom. She waited until she was seated until she started crying. Sammie put her arm around her client and squeezed her tightly.

Judge Carlson sat there for what seemed like a long time. He was watching Becky Taylor. He was moved by the woman's words and strength of action. Finally he spoke, "General, with all due respect, I'm rejecting your recommendation and adopting that of Mrs. Taylor. It was the efforts of Mr. Davis that uncovered Mr. Brand's wrongdoing. Therefore her opinion on sentencing is relevant and controlling. Mr. Brand, you are sentenced to three years without chance of probation."

Becky gave both Sammie and Davis a hug good-bye, and they went their separate ways. When they got back to Steine, Davis, & Davis, Sammie walked into her uncle's office, and said, "That went better than I expected. Judge Carlson certainly recognized your contribution in the conviction of Oscar Brand."

Davis pulled an orange Tootsie Pop out of his mouth. "Just another day in the life of Ben Davis," he replied modestly. "How about you?"

"Not bad. I got the Chapman divorce settled. We should be able to release her funds from escrow in a few weeks."

Hope springs eternal, thought Davis, familiar with the principle if something can go wrong, it usually will go wrong.

Sammie went on, "Sullivan was pretty easy to work with. In the end, the husband got reasonable, and visitation was worked out. I shudder to think what would have happened if her affair with January came out."

"Well, I don't think you'd be walking into my office telling me that the divorce case had been settled."

"Have you seen Morty today?"

Davis hadn't and shook his head. "I'll go down and check on him."

It was past one, and the old man usually made his appearance around ten, puttered around the office till lunch, ate with one or more of the staff, and called it a day around four. Despite these time restraints, his continued involvement in the firm was invaluable. During those few hours, several questions were posed and answered. Difficult questions, ones that required experience and extensive knowledge. His mind was still like a steel trap. He knew the law and the rules of civil procedure and evidence. He may not have moved too fast, but there was no one better to have sitting next to you in a courtroom.

He didn't drive much, so when he wasn't in the office, he was in his apartment. His trips to the farm happened less often, and he was no longer going there on weekends. Every month or so, he'd take Jake, Davis's son, fishing out there, but Liza didn't like Jake being in the car with him. His driving skill had diminished. She'd prefer that Davis join them and do the driving. She was even more concerned about Morty the pilot. He'd flown for sixty years. He hadn't flown his plane in more than a year, yet he had a local mechanic keep it maintained in tiptop shape. Liza had banned Davis from flying with him, even though his pilot license was still valid. Both Liza and Davis questioned the dubious circumstances of his last renewal. Davis strongly suspected that a bribe was involved but didn't dare ask questions. He told Sammie, "Ignorance is bliss."

Davis took the elevator down and knocked on the door. When he got no answer, he banged hard on the door. Morty had selective hearing, and if he didn't want to acknowledge someone, he played deaf. Using a key on his ring, Davis opened the door, and yelled, "Morty, Morty, Morty!"

Greeted by silence, he moved from room to room. He found his old friend unconscious on the bathroom floor. He'd left his cell phone on his desk, so he ran to the master bedroom and used the landline to call 911. He gave his name, Morty's name, the address, and blurted out, "Heart attack." Then he hung up and called his wife, who pleasantly answered, "Hi, honey . . ."

Davis abruptly shouted, "Find your father and have him meet Morty at Saint Thomas emergency room. Looks like it's another heart attack."

He didn't wait for her to answer. He opened the front door, returned to the bathroom, and lay next to his friend. He checked his pulse. It was faint. He put his hand on his chest. The man was breathing. He held his right hand and said a little prayer. *God, this man's been like a father to me. He's taught me everything I know. There's so much more I can learn from him, and he has so much more to give the world. He's been a credit to you, helping others, fighting the good fight. He's always tried to do the right thing. Don't take him yet.*

"Can you hear me, you old cuss? Give me a sign you're alive." Morty weakly squeezed his hand.

Davis kept talking, "I need you. We all need you. Hang in there."

Davis started sobbing so hard that his body shook. The old man opened his eyes and tried to speak, but nothing came out. The two men stared into each other's eyes and through their mutual love communicated with each other that it was going to be all right. If not, they'd had a good life together.

After fifteen minutes the paramedics flew into the bathroom. Davis stepped out so they could perform their magic on the dying man.

Davis kept repeating, "Saint Thomas, Dr. John Caldwell. Saint Thomas, Dr. John Caldwell. Saint Thomas, Dr. John Caldwell . . ."

He got a Diet Coke out of the fridge and drank it down in one large swig. The quick motion of forcing his head back made him dizzy, so he sat on the couch. His head pounded. He could hear the paramedics talking but couldn't understand what they were saying. He wanted to lie down, but he knew he couldn't.

He followed the gurney out the door and into the elevator. He leaned against the wall to steady himself, sweating through his suit. He rode in the back of the ambulance, claiming he was too shaken up to drive. It was no lie. Davis just sat there with his face in his hands. He wasn't recognizable. The cool, collected litigator vanished, replaced by a frightened man.

Waiting in the emergency room was Dr. John Caldwell, Morty's cardiologist and Davis's father-in-law. He met them at the door and started barking orders to the emergency room staff. He disappeared with his patient through two swinging doors, and Davis stumbled and fell into a chair. He felt all alone and completely dejected. He looked so bad, a nurse walked over and checked his pulse. She ushered him into a cubicle and took his blood pressure, 180 over 100, not good.

"Do you take medication for high blood pressure, sir?"

"Yes."

"Which medication and in what dose? Did you take your medication this morning?"

Davis, at two hundred fifty pounds, was seventy-five pounds more than he weighed when he got married. He was diabetic and had high cholesterol too. He smoked cigars and worked long hours. He blamed the man on the operating table for those last two bad habits. He learned many things from his old friend Morty, and one of them was how to live an unhealthy life. His wife was constantly on his back. He needed to slow down, eat healthy, and exercise. Those same bad habits may have caught up with Morty. Davis started to answer the RN just as Liza came into the cubicle.

She saw the nurse tending to her husband and asked, "What's

wrong with him? I'm his wife and a nurse." There was concern in her voice but a sense of strength as well.

The nurse professionally replied, "His pressure is up. He's pretty shaken up. I'd take him home and make sure he takes his medication."

"I'm not going anywhere," he defiantly said to the nurse and his wife. The nurse backed off. Liza, who was familiar with her husband's stubbornness and outbursts, told her she'd take over.

After the nurse left, Davis started sobbing. Liza held him close. Davis, almost always in control of the situation and others, on rare occasions did show emotions, particularly when it came to his kids. "Your dad is in with him. I don't think he's going to make it."

Liza tried to encourage him, "Don't count that old lion out just yet. He's strong as a bull."

They both knew that wasn't true. They had watched a once vibrant man physically deteriorate since the death of his wife of more than forty years. This was his third heart attack in seven years, and, as they say, three's the charm, and three strikes and you're out.

They sat there for two hours before it dawned on Davis that he never called the office and told Bella and Sammie what happened. He dreaded making the call.

"Steine, Davis & Davis," Bella answered pleasantly.

"Bella . . ."

Annoyed, Bella pressed him, "You need to come upstairs. Cut your visit short. It's a workday." Bella thought he was still in the building and shooting the breeze with the old man.

He got right to the point. "I'm at Saint Thomas. Morty had another heart attack. Close the office, and you and Sammie get down here."

Dead silence. Bella had worked for Morty more than forty years, twice as long as Davis had. Married to her husband, Tony, for a few years longer, she loved both men. "How bad?"

"Bad. I found him on the bathroom floor unconscious. He opened his eyes but couldn't speak. John Caldwell's been treating him for the last two hours. "I'm sorry I didn't call. It's been a mad house, and I wasn't thinking straight. There's nothing to report, but when I finally got my shit together I figured I better call and realized that you and Sammie would want to be here."

Davis could tell she was furious about the delay in his call, but ever the professional, she kept calm for the moment and would scold him like a child later privately. She was too distraught right now.

"I'll deal with you later. We'll be there in less than a half hour."

When Davis got back from his phone call, father and daughter were engaged in an intense conversation. Davis prepared himself for bad news. As he approached, Liza ran up and gave him a big hug.

"He's going to be all right. Some permanent damage to the tip of his heart, a long recovery, but he's going to make it, thank God."

Caldwell, a tall man, shook Davis's hand. Davis noted once more how large that hand was with slender fingers.

"He's lucky you found him. If you hadn't, he'd have died for sure. Surgery wasn't necessary, but it may be later. Is he still smoking those strong Cubans?"

Davis didn't want to rat on his old friend, but the truth was the truth. "He smokes at least four a day. I don't know how many he smokes at night."

"That's got to stop, or he's a dead man."

"This man's a skilled negotiator. You've got to give me something to use to compromise. How about he smokes one a day and then chews the stub the rest of the day?"

"Absolutely not. He can chew his cigars, but if a match gets within a foot, I'm blaming you."

Great, I've got to get him to break a habit that started in 1941, introduced by Winston Churchill.

"He'll be in the hospital until day after tomorrow. Then he'll need to convalesce for about three weeks. I'll write an order for him to go to Richland . . ."

Liza cut him off, "He's staying with us. You don't mind making a house call, do you, Daddy?"

Liza was Caldwell's oldest daughter. The doctor hadn't made a house call in more than twenty years, but he was about to make an exception. Caldwell looked at his daughter, smiled, and agreed.

CHAPTER TWENTY-THREE

LONG DAYS

TUESDAY, DECEMBER 1— WEDNESDAY, DECEMBER 2, 1998

Sammie arrived at Saint Thomas just before six. Liza, exhausted, was glad for the relief. She needed to get home to tend to her children. Morty took the changing of the guard in stride and continued his complaining. His throat still hurt from the breathing tube, and he wanted coffee ice cream. Of course the hospital offered only chocolate, strawberry, and vanilla. *The bastards*! Liza promised to bring his flavor tomorrow morning. *Always an angel!*

At seven there was a shift change, and Victor Browne, the night nurse, came in to introduce himself. Six feet tall, he had long brown hair pulled back into a short ponytail, brown eyes, and a nice smile. He asked Sammie, "Are you Mr. Steine's granddaughter?"

"No, I'm Sammie Davis. I'm his law partner. My Uncle Ben, who's also his partner, is married to Liza, the oldest daughter of Dr. Caldwell, Mr. Steine's cardiologist.

"He's a lucky man." Having read the patient's chart before he entered the room, Brown said, "This is his third one. I was reading his chart. It's a good thing someone found him in his apartment, or . . ."

"I don't even want to think about what might have happened.

He's so important to all of us," said Sammie. "I know you'll take good care of him and nurse him back to health so he can get back home to us as soon as possible."

Victor said, "I'll do my best" and smiled at her reassuringly. "I'll treat him like my own grandpa. How about that for service?" He smiled again. The two locked eyes. There was a connection between the two.

Real nice smile, thought Sammie. She said, "I work a lot of hours, as I'm sure you do, but at least I have my nights free to do something other than work. How do you like the night shift?"

Browne said, "It was hard to get used to at first, but I like it now."

Morty, feeling a little ignored, piped up, "I'm right here." Even as sick as he was, Morty saw what was happening and found it amusing.

The young people talked a few more minutes, but Browne had to move on. "It's shift change. I've got to introduce myself to my other patients, Ms. Davis." Sammie was a bit disappointed. She thought, *I would like to see more of this fellow. There is something about him.*

"Well, I've got to make my rounds. It was a pleasure . . ."

Sammie just replied, "Yes, it was nice to meet you."

The next day Liza reported to the hospital, and Davis reluctantly went to work. There was an empty container of Breyer's coffee ice cream next to Morty's bed, courtesy of Nurse Victor Browne. He'd somehow during the night managed to get the old man what he wanted.

When Davis arrived at the office, he wasn't in a good mood, but that would have been true if he stayed at the hospital and sat by Morty's bedside. He was worried about his friend. He was better off at the office harassing others than at the hospital harassing his poor wife. He could at least charge to harass others. He dictated a few mean letters. Under Bella's guidance, the second and final drafts softened. Her judgment was more tempered than his. He collected monies owed; the funds were more than ninety days past due. Payment terms were net ten or thirty, so Bella felt she had a right to unleash Davis on those clients. He got in a heated argument with a young lawyer about a point of law, about which he was right, although he should have been more diplomatic. Davis was frustrated and didn't have a witness to cross-examine, or a deposition to take.

Davis kept looking at his legal pad and crossing off items. Sammie kept walking into his office, checking on him. After three times, he threw her out and told her to "mind her business and get to work."

The office made its way through the day. There was no point in any of them going to the hospital. Liza's father had banned them.

"You're all in my way. Don't come here. Go home. He's out of the woods. He'll be annoying everyone soon enough. He's his own worst enemy. One of the worst patients I've ever treated. It would serve him right if he'd up and died."

Caldwell and Morty were practically family. The two men liked and respected each other, but their doctor/patient relationship was strained because Morty was so noncompliant. Although John Caldwell was a great doctor, he wasn't noted for his calming bedside manner, and Morty had pushed him to his limit.

Liza protested, "You don't mean that."

"I sure as hell do."

Caldwell was trying to impress upon Davis that he had to get control of the old man, or the next attack would finish Morty off.

"He's stubborn as can be, and he can't take many more of these attacks. The effect on his heart is cumulative. This was the third. It's those damn Cuban cigars. They're strong as hell, equal to three of anything else on the market. The things are twice as big in size alone. Every time I bring it up, he mumbles something about Winston Churchill that I don't understand, and the argument drifts to a conclusion."

Morty had unusual and life-changing encounters with Churchill when he was a young RCAF pilot and was rewarded by Churchill with the Victoria Cross and a box of Cuban cigars. The bad habit of the cigars stuck.

The next day Bella and Sammie got in at six and first converted the answering machine recordings to handwritten pink messages. There were dozens relating to the regular course of business, but later in the day, as the word got out in the legal community and the Jewish community of Morty's attack, the inquiries about Morty's health began. He was well known and well liked by friend and adversary. They were usually one and the same.

Bella handed Davis the business messages and manned the phone for the onslaught of well-wishers. Davis tried to organize his messages, but he couldn't focus. His heart was at the hospital. To get his mind off his problem, he started making calls.

"Jim Kelly, please."

"Ben, where's my contract? You promised it two days ago. I've got a customer waiting. I've called twice, and the second time, I got the damn answering machine. I told you last week this was a priority."

"Jim, Morty suffered a heart attack. Things are pretty chaotic here. I can't get it done today. As you know, it's not a straightforward transaction and will require at least two or three hours of work. I can dictate it tonight, and Bella can get it to you first thing in the morning. I'll be happy to call the client and explain the circumstances. In fact if you want to conference him in right now, I'll apologize and commit to have it delivered by the close of business tomorrow."

Kelly didn't like the answer, but the solution was reasonable. He got the customer on the phone, and after the apology, the customer agreed to the delay.

Davis's next call was to another attorney, Tom Joseph, concerning a discovery response that was due in two days. The case was highly contested. Davis had butted heads with Joseph over the discovery, and the judge had ordered Davis's client to answer the questions. The client had been scheduled to come in today at three to prepare the response. Bella had already canceled his appointment and rescheduled it for Friday. Joseph, who knew Morty for more than twenty years, completely understood and agreed to a week extension and offered to prepare and sign both their names on the order. Davis thanked him profusely.

Bella buzzed in, "It's Tyree Sinclair. Should I take a message?"

"No, let him through."

Sinclair started the conversation without a greeting, "How's he doing?"

"He'll survive, but he's got a long recovery ahead of him. Ty, It's a madhouse here. Can I call you in a day or two?"

"Can I see you and your niece at three on Friday?"

Davis looked at his calendar. He had a client at three. "How about four?"

"See you then. Hang in there. I'll say a prayer for our friend."

"Thanks, see you Friday." *What could Tyree Sinclair want?*

He moved to the next call. His investigator, George Hopper, called five times over the last two days. *It must be important.*

"George, what's up?" Davis didn't identify himself. His New York accent did that for him.

"Davis, I found O'Hara. He's in Tahiti. I've got eyes on him right now. I've got video and pictures. It's definitely him. I don't know how long I can keep him under surveillance. You know what a slippery bastard he can be. My local investigator is well connected with the provincial police. We need to act right now. It will cost us, though. He can make the arrangements with the local authorities to detain him and create the necessary documentation of his presence here on the island."

"What would you estimate the cost?"

"Maybe a thousand U.S. dollars."

"George, do it. Gloria O'Hara's future is at stake, literally her freedom."

Dr. Bobby O'Hara, the husband of Davis's client, Gloria, disappeared six months ago. He worked the graveyard shift at the hospital as an emergency room doctor. He never returned home after his shift and hadn't been heard from since. Gloria, a real estate agent and longtime client of Davis, was the prime suspect. The Franklin police had questioned her four times since the disappearance, and they didn't believe she was innocent. The spouse is always the prime suspect in a disappearance. Davis told the attractive real estate agent, "Don't watch so much television."

"We need to document his presence on the island. Video, pictures, and the testimony of your investigator are solid, but an official record would be even better. Have him arrested."

"What charge?"

"Who cares? He's probably traveling under a false passport. He'll have to be fingerprinted, and that will be definitive. Good job, George. Gloria and I thank you."

Next Davis called Gloria O'Hara. News like that couldn't wait. She cried with relief; her ordeal was over. *There'd been a murder charge hanging over her head. What a bastard,* thought Davis. *He left his wife holding the bag while he started a new life and tried to destroy hers. Wouldn't a divorce have been a lot simpler? Sammie will have a field day with the divorce action for abandonment, fraud, and cruel and inhumane treatment.*

Davis buzzed Bella and asked her to order his lunch: a double cheeseburger with blue cheese and grilled onions, fries and onion rings. *I won't be kissing anyone in the near future.*

Sammie walked into his office, and he said, "I just asked Bella to order me lunch. If you want to add to the order, buzz her."

"Great. Do you want to read the Foreman appellate brief? I made the changes you suggested."

"Not a good use of my time. I trust you got it right. Read through it one more time, and if you're satisfied, sign both our names and file it."

"Have you heard from Liza?"

"No, I'll call her next. Guess who called me?"

Annoyed, Sammie replied, "I don't have time for guessing."

"Tyree Sinclair. He's made an appointment with us for Friday. Put it in your book at four."

"I bet he wants us to represent his daughter in her divorce action against January."

"Don't be ridiculous. We're conflicted out because of Chapman."

"Not necessarily."

"You're daffy. Why would he want us?"

"Because we've proven to him that we're the best."

"Well, we'll have to just wait since you don't like guessing."

Childishly, Sammie stuck out her tongue.

"Very professional," Davis chided her.

She just smiled at him and went back to her office.

Davis dialed Liza's cell. "How's he doing?"

"Conscious and complaining. Someone did bring him Breyer's coffee ice cream. Was that you on your way into work?"

"No, I haven't been in. Maybe he has a guardian angel. I'll ask Sammie if she stopped by and took his beloved treat."

Davis could hear her say, "No, you can't have a cigar. Yes, I'm sure every room in the hospital is a no smoking room. Stop pestering me. I'm on the phone."

She turned her attention back to Davis and the phone. "Can someone relieve me? I'd like to be home when the kids get there. They were more affected than you realize. Jake cried on my shoulder this morning."

Davis recognized that Liza needed to be relieved, but he couldn't do it. He needed a plan. "I've got to work late. I'll ask Sammie to leave early and sit with him until he falls asleep. Love you, really got to go. Can I wake you when I get home?"

"Just to let me know you're home safe. Don't expect anything more than that."

"We'll see. Love you."

"Don't think your sweet talk will do you any good." She hung up.

Lunch arrived, and Davis devoured it. The meal took no more than five minutes, and he got ketchup on his tie. Morty always claimed that was "why the French invented the damn things, to catch food as you eat."

Davis decided his next call would be a selfish one.

"Mr. Larry Davenport's office."

"It's Ben Davis. Put me through to your boss."

"He's on the phone. Can I have him call you back?"

"No, I'll hold."

"He may be quite a while."

"Just tell him I'm holding."

Davis wasn't usually so abrupt with staff, but Davenport's secretary had been screening his calls for more than a week. He understood the ploy. The insurance man spent his day on the phone moving from one client to another. The last person he wanted to talk to was someone he owed money. Davis had represented Davenport in a breach of contract case involving the sale of a policy, had won, and was owed his fee for hours expended in excess of his small retainer. Davenport hadn't paid a dime since the retainer was paid.

Davis put the phone on speaker and started reading a document in preparation for his next call. He then started highlighting some cases he needed to read for a brief that Sammie would take a stab at later in the day. Twenty minutes later he was still holding and reading.

The secretary broke in, "He's still on the phone."

"Unless he's talking to his dying mother, tell him to have the person on the phone call back later. He needs to get on the phone with his lawyer, or not only will I resign as his lawyer, but I'll be suing him for breach of contract. He does understand that I know how to sue someone."

Davenport owed Steine, Davis & Davis $24,000. The receivable was more than ninety days old. The firm's contract with Davenport was net ten after the retainer was exhausted. Bella called after thirty and sixty days. Over the last month Davis had three calls with Davenport, who promised partial payment. Under the terms of the contract, Davenport was entitled to payment of $300,000 a year after the contract was executed. Davis's total fee was less than ten percent of the total commission he collected for Davenport. A job well done, yet he hadn't been paid, and what made matters worse was that he'd been lied to three times.

Ten minutes later, Davenport was on the line. "Ben, how the hell are you?"

"Pissed. I don't let anyone lie to me more than once, and you've done it three times . . ."

"Ben . . ."

"Shut up and listen. I'm sending a messenger to your office. He'll be there before close of business. He'll be picking up a check for fifty percent of what you owe this firm, $12,000. Next Tuesday by close of business, that same messenger will be at your office to pick up the balance owed of $12,180. And Larry, those checks better be good."

Davenport asked, "Why's the second check $180 more?"

"Because I'm charging you for the half hour I just spent on hold."

"What happens if I refuse and tell your messenger to hit the road?"

"Good question. You've seen me in court. I'm very comfortable there, and I'm sure I'll know the judge. First payment today at five."

After he hung up, he told Bella, "Send a messenger service to Larry Davenport's office to arrive at 4:45 to pick up an envelope and bring it back here. I'm working late."

That felt good; that lying sack of shit.

Davis made three other calls, looked at his watch, and buzzed Sammie. "Can you relieve Liza at the hospital? She's been there all day and needs to get home to the kids."

"Sure. I'll stay until he falls asleep."

Davis decided he'd try to get a jump on the Kelly contract. He dictated for an hour and gave the tape to Bella. While she was typing, he dictated the second part of the contract. At 5:30 the messenger arrived with the check and a letter of apology from Larry Davenport. Davis made a mental note to call him and try to smooth things out. He reminded himself he'd been lied to three times. By 6:30 the first draft was completed. He placed it in his briefcase and drove home to be with his family.

It had been a long day. He knew Liza's day had been even longer. He stopped and got her two dozen roses. It was a nice gesture. He remembered St. Barts and the promises he made to himself. When he walked in the door, he was greeted by a kiss and take-out. The family, even Caroline, piled onto the bed, and they watched *Play It Again, Sam* by Woody Allen. It was a family favorite, guaranteed to get laughs. It didn't quite do the job. Everybody's thoughts were with Morty, even though nobody mentioned him. The four just lay in the king-sized bed and cuddled as a family, thinking about their missing member in the hospital. They all knew he was in trouble, and they were sad that none of them could do anything to help him.

CHAPTER TWENTY-FOUR

A STRANGE REQUEST

Friday, December 4, 1998

The day began with a call from Jim Kelly informing Davis that the contract was executed and thanking him for his help. Davis, still playing catch-up, pressed through the morning. At noon Davis met Liza at the hospital. Dr. Caldwell had reluctantly released the patient to the care of his daughter. She was a nurse, and he was disruptive to the hospital's operation. Better Liza and her husband deal with Morty Steine than his poor staff.

As Davis wheeled the old man out of the hospital's front door, Caldwell yelled out, "Those Cubans are going to kill you. Mark my words. I don't give a damn what Churchill said, or even if he did live to ninety-one. You're not Churchill. You're Morty Steine, and the next time it's going to kill you."

Harsh words from an old doctor; I might just surprise you, Caldwell, and outlive you. Wouldn't that be a kicker?

"*Maybe not,* but old habits die hard," and he waved good-bye in a defiant way. It was a short ride to Davis's house. The Davises' four-bedroom home more than accommodated their guest, but the guest room was on the third floor. They figured once Morty made it to the third-floor bedroom, they'd serve his meals in the room.

It was a herculean task to get him up the stairs, but the room had an easy chair, TV, and a motorized queen-sized bed that worked exactly like a hospital bed without railings. Once he was in bed, they figured he wouldn't fall out. After Morty settled in, Davis excused himself to return to the office for meetings at three and four. Liza didn't appreciate his exit, but the meetings weren't fabricated and were necessary and scheduled.

As Davis walked past Bella's desk, she handed him two documents. "Maria Lopez called. She got four heartfelt apologies. She seemed very satisfied. She already had two interviews lined up, one as a bookkeeper for a gun range, and she felt very good about her future. She said, 'Thank you, she'll keep in touch.'"

Davis grabbed a cup of coffee, and as he gulped it down, he read the two letters of recommendation he'd drafted for the accountant by her immediate supervisor and the president of R&R Construction. *I hope Elliot Richardson, the president of R&R, chokes when he signs his letters and the two payment checks.* He called Maria, congratulated her, and wished her good hunting for a new job. He was sure she'd have no difficulty finding one.

The booking photo and the fingerprints of Dr. O'Hara arrived by Federal Express. *Nice picture. The police report nailed him for vagrancy and lewd and suggestive conduct. Good luck trying to apply for a new medical license with those arrest charges. You got a lot of splaining to do, Lucy, as Ricky Ricardo would say.*

Davis had a weird sense of humor, often referencing TV shows from his childhood that only his contemporaries or older people might understand if they were TV nostalgia nuts like him. His kids were the exceptions. They understood all of their father's obscure references to the past because they knew him and loved him. Like their mother, they'd come to accept him for who he was and stopped trying to explain or change him.

Thank God Gloria faced the music and didn't run, or I would have had another Sam Sheppard on my hands, like in The Fugitive. *How dare you leave your wife of over ten years high and dry, facing a possible murder charge? Shame on you!*

At three sharp, Karl Moore walked into Davis's office to review his discovery responses. Moore, a security consultant, formerly a DEA agent from Miami, moved to Nashville about ten years ago when he retired from government work. His wife, DeAnn a would-be country music singer/waitress, soon thereafter divorced him, and they'd been in a bitter custody post-divorce battle ever since. They had identical twin boys, Rick and Nick, age sixteen. Karl's work required him to travel, but he made an effort to stay close with his sons and teach them good values. As a security consultant, he hired a team of men or women to protect celebrities or corporate executives from threats by their fans or even threats as serious as assassinations.

"Karl, the judge has ordered that we answer questions 12, 13, and 14."

"I don't want to, and I shouldn't have to."

"I told him that. I also argued that the questions weren't relevant, nor would they lead to discovery of admissible evidence. That's the test under Rule 26 of the Tennessee Rules of Civil Procedure."

"That's right."

"I know that's right, but he overruled my objection and directed you to answer."

"What happens if I refuse to answer?"

"You'll be held in contempt, and he'll order the sheriff's office to arrest you and lock you up in the county jail."

"For how long?"

"Indefinitely. Civil contempt is coercive, not punitive."

"I don't understand. What the hell does that mean?"

"The judge can't lock you up to punish you. He can only lock you up long enough to make you answer the questions. How long depends on you. It depends on how stubborn you are. The longer you refuse, the longer you stay. So answer the damn questions."

Moore sat across from his lawyer and contemplated the consequences. Those two minutes seemed like an eternity to Davis. "I won't do it, and you can't make me."

A very frustrated Davis commented, "He's not asking you whether you're a member of the Communist Party. These are simple questions." Davis repeated them: "12. Have you ever used cocaine? 13. Have you ever used any other scheduled I, II or III controlled substance without a doctor's prescription? 14. Have you ever used any type of controlled substance as defined when your children were present in the house?"

"What about the Fifth Amendment?"

"It's not applicable. The judge in his order makes it clear that he's granting you testimonial immunity, and therefore you're not subject to criminal prosecution."

"Why do I need to answer these questions?"

"Because the judge claims drug use is evidence of lack of moral turpitude, but more important, because he's the judge and he says so."

"I won't do it, end of story. I could lose my security clearance as a bonded security bodyguard. At the very least I could jeopardize a closed undercover operation. People hire me as a bodyguard because I'm trustworthy and clearheaded to protect them and their families. If it came out I've used drugs in the past, even pot, that could cause a big problem for me professionally. If my ex-wife had sworn answers admitting use, she'd leak them to the general public or prospective employers and hurt me somehow. As a former DEA agent, I worked cases on both sides of the law. I had to be in character, which required drug use and drug purchase. It was just part of the game in catching the bad guys. I'm not going to disclose any details of my job under oath, and that's the position my bitch of an ex-wife is trying to put me in, and she knows it. She knows I won't breach that trust."

"Let me at least tell the judge that you're former DEA."

"I can't let you do that. I could be putting others at risk, either current or former agents, or witnesses in the program. I'm not going to be responsible for somebody being exposed."

"He's a judge. Disclosure of information to him isn't like leaking it to the press or someone out in the community. He knows how to keep a secret."

"But he has clerks and they have girlfriends and they have sisters and so on and so on."

"What if I asked for a gag order to be imposed on your ex-wife or that the answers be placed under seal?"

Moore looked at Davis and gave him a hard stare. This was a man who had faced down drug dealers and death. "Ben, this is a matter of principle. This is the right thing to do. You need to convince the judge. You're a convincing guy."

Not convincing enough. I'm not doing very well with my own client, thought Davis. "Let me tell the other lawyer. He's not a bad guy. He'd back off, and this whole thing would go away."

"No way. We're going to ride it out."

"You're a stubborn son of a bitch. Think about that jail cell." Davis finally conceded and said, "I'll call you tomorrow."

The meeting ended badly, and Davis wished he never accepted Karl Moore as a client. He was seriously thinking of passing him off to

Sammie and giving her a learning experience. *Everybody deserves a difficult client once in a while, but not every week.* Davis wished the old man was available to discuss this one. It could wait till he got home.

At four Tyree Sinclair was sitting in the conference room. Sammie and Davis walked in together. They almost didn't fit through the door because Davis had gotten so big. Greetings were exchanged, and Sinclair asked about Morty.

"He's recovering at my house the next month. Liza, my wife, is a nurse, so my home was the perfect solution."

"You're a good partner. That's one of the reasons I'm here."

Davis asked the million-dollar question, "Why are you here, Ty?"

"I want both you and Sammie to represent Rachel in her divorce action."

You think you're so smart, don't you? He looked hard at his niece.

I am so smart! She stared right back.

Davis answered quickly and firmly, "That can't happen. We have a clear conflict of interest. We represented Laura Chapman in her divorce action."

Sammie, who'd been quiet up until now, except for her personal thoughts, just nodded her head.

Sinclair was ready for the objection and answered immediately, "How's it a conflict? Dan January's name didn't come up in the Chapman divorce. It's over. Where's the conflict?"

Davis smiled to himself. *A father's love for his daughter is blinding. Tyree Sinclair is a better lawyer than this. He has a plan.*

"Ty, we specifically agreed in the Chapman settlement that her affair with January would remain confidential and that if necessary I would testify in your daughter's divorce action, not Chapman. That was our deal. Well, how am I going to testify in the January divorce action if Sammie and I represent Rachel? Do I crawl on the furniture and ask questions of myself? I think I'd look pretty absurd. I think I saw Woody Allen do that in one of his first movies, *Bananas*. I don't think I want to use him as a role model."

Again, Sinclair was ready, "No, you're Rachel's attorney, and Ms. Chapman gives a deposition under seal. Confidentiality is preserved. Dan already knows about the affair. His lawyer will be held to secrecy while the case is pending. If it settles, which is exactly what will happen specifically because of Laura Chapman's testimony, then the world remains ignorant of the affair."

Davis thought a long minute, and the silence was deafening. Sammie sat there thinking. She hadn't said anything because she was mulling it all over.

Davis responded, "That's a lot of ifs. You don't have a crystal ball. Your little plan may not work. What happens if the case doesn't settle, and we have to go to trial and Laura has to testify in an open court and her testimony is a matter of public record?"

"Then the truth is told, and Dan January gets what he deserves. Chapman and my daughter are both victims."

Davis objected, "That may be true, Ty, but Chapman's put her life back together. She's not interested in getting involved in your daughter's divorce action. That's why she hired me in the first place. She has her life back and a good settlement. She is functioning reasonably smoothly. Her relationship with her ex isn't perfect, but it's at least civil. I have an obligation not to rock that boat. That's my conflict. How can I represent your daughter and give the recommendation to Laura Chapman that she risk all that? There is no upside for her, only a downside. Why would she do it?"

Sammie had been keeping her opinions to herself. Finally Sinclair turned to her and asked, "Cat got your tongue? Is there a conflict?"

"Most definitely, but I was taught by both my uncle and Morty that there is a solution to every problem and that any conflict can be waived by a written document that identifies the conflict with full disclosure and is waived with informed consent. All it takes is willing parties."

Sinclair jumped on Sammie's position. "Let's call a meeting, and I'll explain to her . . ."

Davis erupted and much too loudly said, "You're not meeting with my client. Sammie and I will sit down and explain the conflict and . . ."

"You need me there. I can sell this."

"I don't want to sell this. She needs to understand the risk that the January divorce case might not settle, and her ass will wind up on the witness stand."

"You meet with her first, ask her if she'll meet with me, and then leave the rest to me."

Sinclair was too aggressive, trying to protect his daughter and destroy January. He didn't give a rat's ass about Davis's client. *I can't lose sight that my fiduciary obligation is to protect Laura Chapman.* Despite the old man's heart attack, Davis wanted to run this problem by Morty, whose clear thinking he still felt would agree with him and insist there was a glaring conflict. When he got home, he conferred with Morty. As expected, Morty's inclination was the same as Davis's: This is a bad idea.

CHAPTER TWENTY-FIVE

A BIG DECISION

Tuesday, December15, 1998

Sammie walked into Davis's office with two cups of coffee and started the conversation by saying, "You'll never believe who called this morning."

"I remind you, I don't like to guess. Neither Davis nor his protégée liked wasting time playing guessing games with each other, and they thought the other was acting ridiculous when the suggestion was made. They were very much alike in many ways and would argue, "Just spit it out."

"Brad Littleton."

"You're kidding. Don't make me sick. I'm going to throw up. What did that pansy want?"

"Believe it or not he wanted to talk to you. I think he wanted to associate the firm in a medical malpractice case."

Davis shuddered at the thought of the Plainview cases. "That idiot has a short memory, but I don't. Tell him to drop dead. In fact I'll return the call."

Davis picked up the phone. He hated Littleton. Turning him down would be a real pleasure. He dialed the number. He'd spent almost five years as his co-counsel in the Plainview cases and hated every minute of it.

"Brad Littleton."

"Brad, answering your own phone, how quaint. Ben Davis."

"Hi, Ben . . ."

Davis interrupted, "Look, Brad, I don't give a shit what the case is about. I'd never work with you again. You're a liar, lazy, and stupid."

"Tell me how you really feel." Littleton was just baiting him.

"I pity your clients. Lose my number. Never call me again."

Davis hung up and smiled at Sammie.

She smiled back and said, "I bet that felt good. Wow!"

Seven years earlier, Littleton brought Davis ten medical malpractice cases with the promise that he'd do thirty-three percent of the work and pay one-third of the expenses. He did none of the work and advanced none of the expenses. In fact he was so counterproductive that Davis spent most of his time looking over his shoulder making sure Littleton wasn't stabbing him in the back. He was by far the worst co-counsel Davis ever associated with. It felt good to slam the phone down in his ear.

Sammie reminded him, "Laura will be coming in at eleven, and if she's willing to meet with Sinclair, then we call him and he shoots right over. Any thoughts?"

"I still think this is a bad idea. Morty agrees. That's over sixty years of experience saying, "This is a bad idea."

Sammie didn't want to take no for an answer. Despite her lack of experience, she had spunk. "My gut tells me this is the right move professionally. Call it woman's intuition, but I've got a good feeling about the case."

Davis was skeptical and didn't want to back down. "I call it inexperience and cockiness, but let's see how the meeting goes. I'm willing to be proved wrong. Make your argument."

"I'd like to represent Rachel January. Good fee, good experience, and great publicity to build my reputation."

Davis didn't like Sammie's last remark. "Remember your primary obligation is Laura Chapman. She's already our client."

Bella brought Laura into the conference room. First, Sammie reviewed the terms of her marital dissolution agreement with her husband. He paid $2,400 a month, $800 each kid, and $1,000 in support. If she went back to work, support was reduced to $500 the first five years after employment and then disappeared. Child support was paid until eighteen.

Any funds acquired after the execution of the document were the sole and exclusive property of the recipient, such as inheritance or the $260,000 payment by Sinclair. Sammie had suggested that specific language, and Sullivan and his client had agreed. The wording was crafted to protect the fact that even though the deal was cut with Sullivan before the execution of the document, the payment was excluded because it was made after execution. Barry Chapman was just out of luck. He couldn't get to the money.

The husband had the children every other weekend. Except in June, he got them for two weeks. Holidays, including birthdays, were alternated.

She got the house, which had little equity, and they divided everything else fifty-fifty. The $260,000 meant she could bide her time and wait to go to work and suffer the reduction in support.

As Laura signed, she thanked Sammie for her hard work.

"Before you thank me, I have a favor to ask."

"Ask away."

"I'd like you to meet with Rachel January's father, Mr. Sinclair. If you're willing, he asked that we call him and he'd come over."

"For what purpose?"

"He wants you to allow his daughter's lawyer to identify you as a witness and if necessary request that you give a deposition under seal in his daughter's divorce action. Your name would be known only by those persons directly involved in his daughter's divorce action: the lawyers, the judge, and their staffs."

Davis sat there quietly. He planned on sabotaging this fiasco, but he wanted Laura to reach her own conclusion first so he wouldn't have to.

"Why would I agree to testify? We just negotiated a settlement where my identity was kept secret. This is crazy. This could put everything I just negotiated at risk."

Davis sighed with relief. *She got it. I'll keep quiet.*

"Why would I agree to meet with the father? And who is Rachel January's lawyer?"

Sammie started squirming. "That's the other favor. She wants to hire my uncle and me . . ."

Laura turned to Davis and asked in a somewhat angry tone, "Have you agreed to represent Rachel January? Do you think this is a good idea?"

Perfect, she asked me a direct question, and my client is entitled to a direct answer.

"No, I think this is an absurd idea. I strongly recommend against meeting with Sinclair. I have not agreed to represent Rachel January and would not do so without your express written agreement allowing me to do so. It is my recommendation to simply proceed with your settlement and move on with your life."

"Why wouldn't you get involved?"

Davis was prepared to answer that question. *Smart girl.* "Sammie and Sinclair's plan counts on January caring that the affair is revealed. He has lost his job and family regardless of whether you testify. He probably won't care. My concern is if he calls their bluff, they have a worthless sealed deposition, or you'll have to testify. It could, but probably won't, affect your property settlement. But you've never testified either by deposition or in court. It isn't a pleasant experience. Why subject yourself to all that? We've gotten you a great settlement against the law firm and fair property settlement in the divorce. Why jeopardize either? Move on for the benefit of your children."

"That's a compelling argument, Mr. Davis, but I'm willing to hear Mr. Sinclair. Call him and have him come over."

Sinclair must have run over. It was four blocks away. Intro-ductions were made.

Surprisingly, Laura spoke first, "My lawyers have explained what you want of me. They seem to be divided as to whether I should testify on behalf of your daughter. Say what you want to say, sir."

Sinclair bowed his head and truly looked apologetic. "First, I want to apologize on behalf of my firm for what Dan January did to you, and the fact that my firm sued you. Dan deceived my firm, my daughter, and me, just the way you were. He's lied to me on many matters, and I trusted him not only because he was my partner, but worse my son-in-law, the father of my grandchildren."

Sinclair paused. His eyes were watering but not yet crying.

What a performance! opined Davis.

"Second, I hope you feel once I learned of Dan's conduct, my firm made fair restitution. Mr. Davis will confirm that I accepted his terms as presented and didn't try to nickel and dime you."

Davis acknowledged the truth of the statement.

"Third, my daughter, Rachel, and my two grandchildren are victims, just like you. They're innocent of any wrongdoing whatsoever."

Beautiful, unlike Laura, who knowingly had sex with a married man, Rachel and her kids were completely blameless. This guy's good. Laura Chapman doesn't have a chance.

Both Laura and Sinclair got emotional. She turned to Sammie and asked, "What do you think?"

"I've been told by two very smart men that you should always try to do the right thing."

That cinched the deal. Laura agreed.

Sammie had already prepared written waivers. The first provided that despite the Sinclair settlement agreement, she'd give a deposition under seal. The second allowed her attorneys Steine, Davis, & Davis to represent Rachel January in her divorce action against Dan January. Despite the documents, Davis was uneasy about the afternoon's events.

CHAPTER TWENTY-SIX

DISAPPOINTING CLIENT

Monday, December 28, 1998

Morty, on the road to recovery, felt better and better every day. As he improved, rather than becoming easier to care for, he became more difficult. The healthier he got, the more he got on Liza's nerves. Even a saint has so much patience.

Jake was a big help. He played chess and gin rummy with the old man every day. His biggest contribution and distraction came from getting Morty's help as the twelve-year-old prepared for his Bar Mitzvah.

The boy, in the tradition of Abraham, Isaac, and Jacob, was scheduled to read his weekly portion of the Torah and address the entire congregation over the July 4th weekend.

Morty had nothing but time on his hands, and he was by profession a great orator. *Lucky boy.* They practiced his Torah portion and his speech two hours every day. Jake, off from school because of the Christmas holiday, had nothing but time on his hands. The Jewish Davises didn't celebrate Christmas and because of their houseguest had not planned a family vacation. For these reasons and Morty's availability, Jake's practice schedule was daily. Jake kept insisting, "I don't want to be over-rehearsed. We're six months away." His Bar Mitzvah wasn't until July 3rd, so Morty was getting a real jump on the project. His protests fell on deaf ears, and neither his father nor his mother had the guts to back up the poor kid. Jake didn't mind too much. He liked being with the old man, and he saw how much pleasure Morty derived from teaching and guiding him.

"Again. Do it again. Try not to let your voice squeak at the end of the sentence."

The boy would do as told. Morty was relentless, full of energy. "Don't slouch. Stand up and be proud of who you are. You're reading the Torah, the word of God. Say it with authority. These aren't your words. They have meaning beyond you. These words have lessons for all men to pass on to each other and follow. You're just the messenger, but do it proudly and loudly."

Morty was teaching the boy more than just words on a page. In a way Davis was glad that Morty was an extended guest in his house and that his son was spending quality time with the man he came to know and love. *What an opportunity for the kid!*

The responsibility of Morty couldn't be left to just Jake and Liza. For the benefit of his wife, Davis kept Morty up late watching television in his room so that he'd sleep till ten. Liza would then serve him breakfast and bring him the local paper, *New York Times,* and the *Wall Street Journal.* During his break, Jake took over until Davis came home.

Today, for the first time Davis took him to work. As they drove in, they talked. "We meet with Rachel January today at two. Do you know her?"

Morty knew almost everybody in town. "Rachel must be thirty-five or so. Tyree married later in life. I went to her wedding. Goldie was alive and not yet sick so it must have been about ten years ago. She went to one of the Ivy League schools, Columbia or Brown. She's some kind of artist. I'm sure she's smart, but that's about all I know."

The two men played gin last night for a few hours. Morty won even though Davis tried his best. His competitive streak would allow nothing else. Jake and Caroline joined them, and the four played a game of Risk. Davis started out in Australia, with an outpost in North America, and won in record time. The kids excused themselves, and the two men watched a movie on cable, *Young Frankenstein* directed by Mel Brooks, a very funny man. Morty fell asleep with his bed elevated.

Davis left him in the upright position and joined Liza in their bed. She was fast asleep. He thought about waking her, but figured she'd just get mad and he wouldn't get any sugar anyway.

Davis deposited Morty on the sixth floor, took the elevator to the eighth floor, and got a cup of Joe. He looked over his yellow pad. Everything was under control. The document was just short of a page long, and no one project would take more than an hour. He began opening the mail left on his desk by Bella. She'd already culled the bills and the things he didn't need to see. She missed one. A letter from Brad Littleton went right into the garbage can without him even opening it. *I don't want to read anything from that son of a bitch.* The rest of the correspondence was pretty vanilla. He made a few calls to clients. He looked over his yellow pad again and reorganized the order of how he might attack the work to be completed. He noted that the deposition of Chris Addams was coming up. He debated in his mind whether he should attend. Sammie would prep him. He'd only be window dressing. If he failed to appear, it might send an interesting message to the other side: complete confidence in his niece. If his client did a good job, the case would probably settle. Sammie certainly had hit a home run at the deposition of Keith Rogers. Davis didn't really understand the continued depression of the client, who kept talking about leaving town. Davis realized that money wasn't the solution to every problem. Chris Addams had lost his sense of self-worth, and no dollar amount of recovery was going to restore that. Sammie reported a similar conversation. She'd become close to her client.

Sammie popped in and suggested lunch at the Gerst Haus, a German-style deli that had been on the courthouse square but moved to the other side of the river. They got in Davis's new navy blue Bentley convertible. He loved that car with rosewood dashboard and fine leather tan interior. The sound system was incredible. Liza hated the car, an unnecessary expense and not very practical. Davis went overboard at lunch. He ordered three bratwursts, spatzle, and two beers, topping the meal off with apple strudel. He was so full, he let Sammie drive back to the office, and he rarely let anyone drive that machine.

When they got back, Tyree Sinclair and his daughter were in the waiting room. Sinclair made the introductions and then started back to the conference room.

Davis stopped Sinclair when they got to the door by putting his hand on his chest. He gently pulled him aside and said, "Ty, you know you can't sit in on this interview. It will destroy the attorney-client privilege. You're a witness in this case, an important one."

What Davis was pointing out was explained to first-year law students in their first semester. This was basic stuff. Sinclair knew Davis was right, but he protested anyway, "She's my little girl."

Davis assured him, "You know she's in good hands. I'll be in there with her, and Sammie will relate to her as her peer. Your presence will only complicate matters. She will have greater difficulty talking in front of you."

Surprised that Sinclair would make such a basic mistake, Davis walked in the room and closed the door. He heard Sammie offer Rachel water, coffee, or a soft drink. She declined.

The three made small talk. They let her talk about her kids. They sounded pretty normal. Franklin, known as Frankie, age eight, and Gaby, age six, attended school. They asked her what she did during the day, and she told them about her paintings and her sculptures. That kept her busy.

"I have a separate specific studio on the other side of the pool. It's quiet, and it's easy to get my work done. I don't want to give up my studio."

"We don't need to get specific right off the bat. I want to talk generally first, and then we can address specific items.

Davis smiled in an effort to make the young woman feel more comfortable.

"Aren't you going to offer me something to drink?"

Davis looked at Sammie, who asked, "What would you like?"

"A drink of water would be nice."

Sammie went to the credenza and poured a glass of water from the Waterford pitcher.

"Could I have a Diet Coke instead?"

"Sure." She buzzed Bella, who quickly brought in the drink.

Rachel, age thirty-four, physically fit, five-five, a hundred fifteen pounds, with brown curly almost shoulder-length hair, had a detached look about her. She took a sip of her Diet Coke and hummed.

Davis looked at Sammie and let her take the lead. She asked, "Rachel, are you on any medication?"

"Yes," and she emptied her bag on the table. The contents spilled out: wallet, compact, can of mace, and medicine bottles.

Davis examined the mace while Sammie examined the medicine bottles.

"Valium, Percocet, Ambien and Lipitor." Sammie questioned her about each medication. The answers were inconsistent, and the side effects of the medications were contra-indicated.

Davis asked her about the mace.

"Protection. Better safe than sorry." It was the way she said it. *Weird.*

Sammie gently asked, "Rachel, when was the last time you had intercourse with your husband?"

"I don't remember."

"Well, has it been in the last month?"

"No, I've known about that Chapman bitch . . ."

Sammie stopped her. "You know Laura Chapman is helping you and testifying on your behalf."

"She seduced my husband. I hate her guts."

Sammie started to correct her, but her uncle held up his hand like a cop behind Rachel. So Sammie started over, "When did you last have intercourse with your husband?"

"That's none of your fucking business."

They were surprised by her cursing. The rest of the interview didn't go well. Most of the time Rachel didn't answer their questions. They independently decided she wouldn't be a good witness and wondered whether she was properly taking her medication. Several of her answers didn't make sense, and as the interview progressed, Davis questioned Rachel's judgment and possibly her competency. Dan January was a sleazeball, but at least he was sane. They thanked Rachel for her time and sent her on her way.

They looked at each other, knowing what had happened. Tyree Sinclair had hoodwinked them into representing his daughter. He'd wanted to attend the interview in an effort to control it or minimize and mask his daughter's incompetency.

What a fool. He should have warned us that she wasn't competent. This is a mess. Even worse, we've gotten Laura Chapman involved with this poor woman. Davis felt professionally violated by Sinclair, and Sammie felt responsible for pushing to accept employment.

Davis, angry with Sammie, didn't hide his feelings, and he sulked in his office and devoured a box of Entenmann's chocolate donuts he found in the kitchen. Steine, Davis, & Davis always had something sweet for their clients to munch on. At least that was Davis's excuse for having baked goods around the office. In reality, Davis ate when he was angry. Six donuts made him feel a little better.

Bella told Sammie on her way back to her office, "There's a Victor Browne on line two for you."

Pleasantly surprised, Sammie told her she'd take it in her office.

"Nurse Browne, I hope there's no medical emergency?" Her tone was playful, and she knew the call wasn't medical related.

"No, Attorney Davis, it's not medical or legal related. It's personal. I find you very attractive and want to take you to dinner and get to know you better."

Sammie liked the fact he was direct and got right to the point. She didn't waste time either. "When did you have in mind?"

"As you know I work the graveyard shift, seven to seven. So we could do lunch any day, but dinner would have to be on one of my nights off. I happen to be off the night of January 1st if you're not too hung over."

"That sounds perfect, but I make no promises as to my condition. I went to the University of Florida, and once a party girl, always a party girl. I'll see you then. I live in the same building as my office on the sixth floor. The back door is on Printer's Alley. Call and I'll come down and get you. Shall we say seven?"

"I'll look forward to the new year," he said.

"Until then," she ended their conversation.

The evening of January 1st may be more fun than New Year's Eve this year, thought Sammy as she hung up.

CHAPTER TWENTY-SEVEN

CONFRONTATION

Monday, December 28, 1998

(SAME DAY)

Bella answered the call from the judge's court officer, Winnie Bray, and put her through to Davis.

"Are you suicidal? I just got a motion to compel and a motion for contempt in the Moore case. The judge's order was very specific: answer the questions. I've got to put this motion on his desk. He's going to issue a capias, and the sheriff is going to arrest Karl Moore at his work or his home."

Davis rubbed his forehead. He just got a splitting headache. He needed an aspirin, possibly two or three, but the court officer needed an answer. "I've not seen the motions yet, but I suspect you're right. I've explained all this to my client. He says he's willing to bear the consequences."

Winnie Bray, a woman in her mid-fifties, had been around the courthouse for thirty years and had seen more than a few stubborn litigants. She knew the difference between tough talk and reality.

"That's big talk. He's never been in a jail cell before."

Davis wasn't sure that Moore in his former DEA days hadn't done some time, but he couldn't mention that to Bray. He was sworn to secrecy. Bray and Davis had a solid relationship, and she made the call out of friendship.

"I appreciate the heads-up. I don't want you to get in any trouble. Tell the judge that I called you and told you that a capias won't be necessary. My client will surrender himself at the court's convenience and will appear when directed to address my client's contempt."

"Smart move. At least the taxpayers get to save the cost of sending the sheriff's deputy out. I'll call you back with a date and time. I suspect it will be pretty quickly."

Davis tried to call Sinclair to schedule an appointment to discuss his daughter's severe depression and her inability to participate in a defense. He wasn't available. Davis decided not to leave a detailed voice message but asked that Sinclair schedule an appointment through Bella.

When he hung up, Ms. Bray was on the other line. "You'd better get down here right now. He's pissed. Your tactic to surrender your client backfired. He considered the maneuver as your attempt to usurp his authority and control the situation. He said, and I quote, 'tell Davis to get his ass down here,' and then he issued the warrant for Mr. Moore's arrest. Do you know where your client is? I could pass that information along to the sheriff's office and report to the judge that you cooperated. Be prepared for a rough time when you get in front of him. He's looking to chew someone up, and it looks like you've been elected. I wouldn't resist, or you might just join your client in the county jail."

Davis became concerned that Moore might complicate matters by resisting arrest. He was trained in martial arts and other forms of defense and had access to weapons. If he was confronted by sheriff's deputies, the situation could turn violent quickly. He needed to find Karl Moore immediately and take control of his client and surrender him to the court. Bray didn't understand Davis's silence. She mistook his contemplation as trying to circumvent the court. Bray was trying to help her friend. She knew Davis could be defiant and was giving fair warning. She'd probably stuck her neck out too far already. This was her last piece of advice.

"Moore works out of his home. I'll transfer you to Bella, who can give you his home address."

I'm doing this for Moore's own good. If I have to make the judge find him, it will only go worse for him.

"You'd better be prepared for this storm."

"Thanks, I'm prepared to grovel."

As Davis ran toward the door, he warned Bella she'd be hearing from Tyree Sinclair. "Set him up when Sammie can attend," and he was out the door.

A short walk to the courthouse, up to the Sixth Circuit Court, he took a seat in the back row. The man who started it all, Tom Joseph, Moore's ex-wife's attorney, soon joined him.

"Fancy meeting you here."

Even though Joseph wasn't to blame, Davis did anyway.

"Your client's making this easier than it should be. Why piss the judge off?"

Davis knew Joseph was right, but it would be bad form to agree. "Maybe he'll respect my client for his principles?"

Joseph laughed and said, "He'd better agree to answer the questions, or he's not going to be laughing. Strange thing about principles, they're fine in the abstract, but hard to live with, even harder from a jail cell."

"Tom, back off. Withdraw the questions, and I'll owe you, plus we'll get this settled. I'll lean on my guy. Who cares if he smoked pot? The twins are sixteen. Both of them smoke pot. One has even been arrested for possession. Truth is your client has done drugs too. I've just never asked. It's a non-issue."

Joseph knew that his client had smoked pot and that one of the twins had been arrested for pot. The questions were posed as more of an annoyance than anything else. Joseph's client had suggested the tack, and Joseph adopted it. She claimed it would annoy her husband, and, boy, was she right. He never thought it would come to this. At first, he was ecstatic that Karl Moore made an issue out of a non-issue. But now, the thought of Ben Davis owing him one and also leaning on his client to settle the case favorably was awfully appealing.

"Quite frankly, I was just pushing your client's button. If he'll agree to pay for my time to prepare the motions and to be here today, I'll withdraw the questions. Davis, you owe me one. Let's just call it a big one."

"Thanks, Tom, I won't forget it."

Fifteen minutes later Karl Moore in handcuffs came through the courtroom door, ushered by a sheriff's deputy.

As Judge Paul Billingsly came through the back door, everyone rose, and he took his seat behind the bench. Ms. Bray made her opening remarks, ". . . the Sixth Circuit Court of Davidson County is now in session. God save the state of Tennessee and these United States of America."

Joseph stood, and Billingsly barked, "Sit down, Mr. Joseph."

Then Davis stood, and the judge loudly stated, "Sit down, Mr. Davis. We'll get to you in good time. Don't be so anxious."

Davis looked at Joseph, who shrugged. He wasn't going to risk Billingsly's wrath. He silently communicated, *All bets are off,* and Davis silently communicated back, *I don't blame you.*

"Hello, Mr. Moore. Do you know why you're here as my invited guest?"

"Yes, sir, you've ordered me to answer questions about my alleged use of cocaine, and I've continued to refuse to answer those questions."

At least he's acting respectfully, thought Davis.

"Has Mr. Davis explained that I have the authority to order you to answer those questions, and that I can hold you in civil contempt and have you held in the county jail until you cure that contempt?"

"Yes, sir, and he's done everything in his power to try to convince me to answer the questions, but under the Fifth Amendment of the Constitution I don't have to incriminate myself."

"You're not facing criminal charges, Mr. Moore. The Fifth Amendment applies only if you're at risk of criminal prosecution. This is a civil matter, and the answers to these questions are relevant to the issues of the case."

Bravely, Joseph stood.

"I told you to sit down, Mr. Joseph. I'm addressing Mr. Moore right now."

"Mr. Moore, do you recognize that this is my court because I was elected by the people?"

"It's your court, but your power is not absolute. That's why there are appellate courts to review your decisions. I'm sure most of the time you're right and upheld, but there are occasions that the higher court reverses you. In my opinion, this will be one of those times."

"Are you willing to sit in jail until my order holding you in contempt is reviewed by the Court of Appeals?"

"I don't want to go to jail, but if necessary, I guess I'll have to."

"Deputy, take Mr. Moore into custody. Mr. Moore, I find you in civil contempt of my order. You can end your incarceration on any day between the hours of nine and five by agreeing to answer questions 12, 13 and 14. Until then you're denied visitation and telephone privileges, with the exception of Mr. Davis."

Davis stood, and the judge recognized him. "You're lucky, Mr. Davis. Your client exonerated you. As an officer of this court, it appears you did everything you could to encourage Mr. Moore to comply with my order. He also understood the consequences of his failure not to comply with my order, so you cannot be found guilty of any fault. What do you have to say? I suggest you stay in my good graces."

"I'd like to make an oral motion, to be followed by a written motion, under Rule 9 for the court's order, the motion for contempt and the transcript of this hearing to be transmitted to the Court of Appeals for Middle Tennessee, with a request by this court that it be ruled upon expeditiously."

A trial judge used Rule 9 to request that the appellate court consider an immediate review of one of his or her rulings. Often used right before a trial, it was to avoid a mistrial because the judge was uncertain of his or her ruling and wanted to get it right. The Court of Appeals almost always agreed to consider the issue. Most judges didn't grant Rule 9 motions because it was an admission of uncertainty. If denied, Davis could file the same motion under Rule 10. The only difference was that a Rule 10 meant that the trial judge denied the Rule 9 and that the Court of Appeals almost never agreed to hear a Rule 10. Davis, in his twenty-year career, had tried four times and had one Rule 10 granted, and the trial judge was reversed. His twenty-five percent was better than most.

There was no uncertainty in Billingsly's mind that he was right, or for that matter in Davis's mind. But Davis added, "A man's liberty is at stake. If my Rule 9 motion is denied, Mr. Moore could remain in jail for months simply because of the Court of Appeals' docket. He's clearly in contempt, but he conducted himself during this hearing with respect to both you and the court."

Billingsly pondered Davis's last argument and granted the motion. As Davis turned to leave, he whispered to Joseph, "I still owe you. You tried. I'm not sure I would have stood that second time."

Back at the office Davis had trouble focusing on work. He dictated short Rule 9 motions and called Ms. Bray and ordered that the court reporter transcribe the hearing. She promised it would be available by the end of the business day. Davis was worried about Karl Moore. Davis didn't know whether Moore had been in jail before. He might have. Regardless, Davis figured it was a very unpleasant place.

CHAPTER TWENTY-EIGHT

A FATHER'S LOVE

Wednesday, December 30, 1998

It had been two days since the Moore hearing, and Karl Moore had been going stir-crazy. He'd been desperately hoping that Davis would bring good news. The weekend was approaching, and so was New Year's Eve. He didn't look forward to spending them in jail and missing his weekend with his kids.

Davis came by at eight when visiting hours opened. "I haven't heard anything from either the Court of Appeals or the judge. He's not going to budge. Bella has been checking in with the appellate clerk's office twice a day. They're tired of her calling. They've promised to call her the moment a decision comes down. You know I'm confident that the appellate court is going to affirm the judge. Look, man, you don't want to stay here. Please let me call the judge. I can get you out by the new year. I know he'll take my call and let you out. All you have to do is answer the damn questions, probably over the phone under oath. He's not a bad guy, just stubborn like you."

Moore softened a bit and said, "If we lose the appeal, I won't go further. I'll answer the questions, but I have to hear it from the Court of Appeals that Billingsly is right."

"Listen to me, I went to law school for three years. I've been doing this for almost twenty years, and I spent several hours specifically researching this shit. He's right. He's going to win the appeal. Answer the damn questions."

"I want to hear it from the higher court. Then I'll answer them."

"You mean you won't make me file a writ of certiorari (an appeal) to the Tennessee Supreme Court," Davis said sarcastically. "Tell you what. How about you write the answers to 12, 13, and 14 on a piece of paper, and I just give it to Ms. Bray. That would probably get you the hell out of here."

Davis suspected he knew the answers to the questions, but he'd never heard them from Moore. *Moore dealt with drug addicts and drug dealers. Of course he used drugs to maintain his cover. That should not count against him in a divorce case ten years later. He was only doing his job and protecting his country. Billingsly's a reasonable man and a reasonable judge. I wish I could share this information with the court and just make this problem go away, but attorney-client privilege prevents me from taking that course of action.*

"I'll take my chances with the appeal."

Davis shook his head. "Stubborn bastard. See you next year."

They said their good-byes.

A florist delivered a dozen roses to Attorney Davis with the simple note, "Looking forward to our dinner." Bella buzzed Sammie, "I'm not sure, but I think a delivery just came for you. Or it could be for your uncle?" When she walked out to reception, she exchanged a knowing smile with the other woman, took the flowers, and went back to her office.

Tyree Sinclair's appointment at nine, moments away, wouldn't be a fun experience for anyone. Davis and Sammie felt betrayed. Rachel January wasn't competent or coherent, and she was abusing prescription drugs. How could they argue that she was competent to care for her children? Over the last couple of days Davis and Sammie had more than one conversation about whether Sinclair's grandchildren would be better off with Dan January, liar and cheater, rather than their client.

Bella brought Sinclair into the conference room, and Davis took charge. "Ty, you should have warned us about your daughter's mental health problems. Her depression will impact on her ability to mount a successful prosecution of the divorce action. She can't withstand cross-examination by the other side. We were ambushed by you. She did nothing wrong. She's just a victim, with post-traumatic stress disorder from a bad marriage. Nonetheless we won't be able to do our jobs correctly to the best of our abilities because of lack of client support. We accepted employment, and even worse, against my better judgment, we put an existing client at risk without knowing all the facts. Chapman deserved better than that; I deserved better than that. There was an implied level of trust in our discussions that our client would have a certain level of competency. As her surrogate, you misled us. I learned a very valuable lesson. I hope my niece did too. I'm very disappointed in you. You're better than that."

Sammie sat there. Pushing for the January case put her on thin ice. Silence prevailed. She rarely disappointed her uncle. Usually it was very small things, but this was big. *Hey, nobody's perfect, not even the great Ben Davis or the greatest Morty Steine. We all make mistakes. The key is not to repeat them, but Uncle Ben is going to take a few moments to rub this one in. I deserve it!*

"You're right. I should have come clean, but you were already on the edge. I didn't want to spook you. If you knew how badly off she was, I might still be shopping for a lawyer. I made a mistake. Everybody makes them."

"Here's the deal. You lie or withhold information from us again, we're gone, and your daughter can find alternate representation. I won't tolerate a repeat performance and find us in the dark again. This was no way to start a relationship. The truth, good or bad, is a must."

Sammie was holding her breath. This disaster might be straightened out after all. Sinclair seemed sincere. Her uncle, although upset with Sinclair and her, seemed willing to let things go and move forward. Always forgiving with family and friends, Davis usually put aside professional differences at the end of a trial and shook hands with his adversaries. On very few occasions the contests were so bitter, the tactics so brutal, and the victory so sweet that he just couldn't extend his hand across the battlefield.

"Agreed. She wasn't always like this. She was always a little artsy, but she was a good wife and mother. Now she's so depressed that she's a mess. She's taking those pills like candy. It's that bastard's fault. She can't handle the fact that her husband cheated on her. Rita and I think she and the grandchildren should move in with us. Rachel refuses because she claims she'll lose rights to the house. I'm the lawyer, and she's telling me about the law. I hate that I'm suggesting that she should give up possession of the house, but there is no way they can live together. It's the kids' home, but that bastard's not moving out voluntarily."

Davis didn't give any credence to the traditional legal proverb that whoever stayed in the marital home gained a tactical advantage. He'd seen couples, upon advice of counsel, stay in the residence, become even more miserable, and almost kill each other.

"Rita and I have taken almost full responsibility for the kids. Luckily Dan hasn't pressed her to spend too much time with the kids. Rachel claims that he's working hard to keep his solo practice going. He's come by our house three times. I've had to bite my tongue whenever he walks in the door."

Davis pointed out that Rachel could move from the house and still use the garage studio to paint in during the day. "Dan's at work during the a.m. I'm sure we can negotiate access to the studio, have all the art moved there, and let her and the children live with you and Rita. That makes the most sense."

Sammie finally interjected, "Do your grandchildren appreciate how distraught their mother is?"

Davis would have described her condition differently, but Sammie was being diplomatic.

"They know something is up. Frankie's eight. He's got a better grasp of what's going on than Gaby does. They've had such limited contact with their father. Despite Rita's and my best efforts, we can't hide what's going on. Rachel spends very little time with them. You've met her. She wears her problems on her sleeves."

Davis knew from the prescription bottles that she recently had two medications prescribed by Dr. Virginia Ames.

"What has Dr. Ames told you?"

"Not much. Rachel saw her three times a week last month, but Rachel has not signed an authorization for the doctor to speak to either Rita or me. I've asked Rachel to do so, but she gives me double-talk about protecting her privacy and being an adult, not a child."

Legally Rachel was absolutely right. Anyone over eighteen controlled her own destiny and was entitled to absolute confidentiality, even if her parents were paying for the services provided.

"Look, Ty, you've been dealing with this situation like a loving father, and you have forgotten how to address this problem like a lawyer. You need information about your daughter's mental status, and so will Sammie and I as her attorneys if we're going to competently represent her. Dr. Ames is Rachel's treating physician, but she's also got to be a resource for us in this divorce action. If we don't get control of this situation immediately, January is going to get custody of your grandchildren. I know that's not what Rachel wants. She needs to come in tomorrow and sign a medical authorization that provides for her parents and her lawyers to confer with Dr. Ames, so we can figure out what's going on."

"You're absolutely right. This is not a problem that I can solve as a father, and I can't think like a lawyer about it. I'm going to let you and Sammie take charge. Just tell me what I need to do."

Davis liked the sound of that. Sinclair rarely let someone else take charge, but he was a smart and reasonable man.

"Let's discuss your fee. You've not mentioned it, and I want to get it settled."

"Sammie's hourly rate is $250. She'll be doing most of the heavy lifting. What do you charge an hour?"

Sinclair hesitated. He was expensive. "It's $400."

"Then that's my hourly rate too. Does Rachel have her own money? If not, you can loan her the $15,000 retainer." *That seems like a reasonable retainer. I'm sure his firm would charge at least $25,000 under the same circumstances.*

Sinclair said, "Actually, that's another problem. Rachel and my grandchildren are named as beneficiaries in three separate irrevocable trusts, each with a total of more than $5 million. I'm the trustee, the first substitute trustee is Rachel, and Dan is the second backup trustee. If I were to die and Rachel was held incompetent, Dan as the trustee would control more than $5 million of my grandchildren's funds."

Davis grimaced. *Holy shit! What a damn mess! What the hell did I get myself into? I should have gone with my gut and passed on this one.* He said, "As trustee, transfer $15,000 from Rachel's trust to my escrow account. Bella can give you the routing and account numbers."

"Ben, I know what you're thinking. What the hell did I get myself into? I promise you this, you've made a friend for life."

I already have plenty friends. I didn't really need another friend. I should have asked for $25,000. Sinclair & Sims is smarter than I am, for sure.

"Do everybody a favor and talk to Rachel about moving out of the house."

Sinclair gave Davis a hard look. "She doesn't want to give up the house. She claims it's her kids' home. It sits on the highest hill in Forest Hills overlooking Radnor Lake. It's a very modern structure that is breathtaking. Nothing else is like it in Nashville."

In a calm voice, Davis said, "It's just a thing, and I bet the bank really owns it."

"True, there's less than seventy-five thousand dollars of equity."

Davis smiled and said, "Let him have the house and the debt."

Sinclair explained, "It will take time to convince her to move out of the house, and she won't be willing to lose her art."

"I'll protect her interest in her art. She created it. I can get a judge to understand that her art should be hers. Let's focus on getting her and the kids out of the house. Have Rita call me. If you think getting Sammie involved would help, let us know."

Sammie had been quietly sitting there and finally spoke up, "Rachel might be more willing to listen to me than to her parents. I'd be happy to stop by over the weekend and wish her a happy new year. I might need the morning to recover, but late afternoon would work."

Sinclair stood up, shook hands with the Davises, and left the conference room.

The Davises had a quiet New Year's Eve with their house-guest and their children. Liza cooked a lobster boil, with clams, Maine lobster, corn on the cob, boiled potatoes, and melted butter. Davis was in heaven. Caroline screamed bloody murder when she had to spend New Year's Eve with the family. Morty begged Davis for a cigar but was refused.

Sammie's date, her friend Billy's trainer, wasn't much of a gentleman, but she didn't care. They toasted the new year at Billy's house and took a cab back to Sammie's loft, where she had her way with him twice. He was quite acrobatic, and then at two fifteen she put the young man out on the street. *Not easy to get a cab in downtown Nashville at that hour even on New Year's Eve. At least he was properly dressed for the weather.* Sammie rationalized that she needed one last fling before she began a possible relationship with Nurse Victor Browne. She decided she'd take things slower with him, more traditional. Do things more like her Nana Shelly would want her to.

Sammie woke up the next morning with a slight hangover but no regrets. She had no intentions of seeing Ray again, and she suspected that Raymond, after freezing his balls off last night, wanted no further part of her. After two cups of coffee, she dialed Rachel January at her home, and Dan answered. After an unpleasant exchange, Dan got Rachel.

"That was a bit awkward," Sammie began.

"He was pissed. You should have seen his face. I thought he was going to explode."

"Happy New Year."

"I don't think so. I think this year's going to suck."

Sammie knew she needed to take control of this conversation if Rachel was going to get her ass out of that house.

"You're looking at this all wrong. Last year was a shitty year. You caught your husband cheating. This year you're divorcing his sorry ass, getting your life back, and starting over. The first step, and I know it's a big one, is leaving him. You're not alone. You'll have your kids. You'll have your parents. You'll have me. I'll be with you every step of the way. Ironically, he'll be the one alone."

"I can't leave my house, my art."

Sammie cut her off, "The house is just a house. The bank really owns the house, not you. Look, we can talk about this down the road. We don't have to settle this today. Just think about it. *The seeds were planted. I've got a splitting headache, and I've got to make a quick recovery for my date with Nurse Browne tonight.*

Mission accomplished, Sammie took four aspirins and went back to bed.

That night Victor Browne picked Sammie up at the back entrance of Steine's Department Store. Dinner was at Houston's on West End, and it lasted four hours, a good sign. The couple talked and talked about everything and about nothing.

He talked about his family and his love of medicine. He truly cared about his patients and helping people. He had no desire to be a doctor. It took too long, and he didn't want to accumulate all that debt.

Victor came from a prominent Nashville family on his mother's side, the Robertsons. In fact, they were one of the founding families of Nashville, having arrived in the late 1700s. At one time the Robertsons held large tracts of land, but lost most of their wealth in the Civil War. Victor's grandparents abandoned what remained of the family homestead during the Depression.

She talked about her family. She grew up living with her Nana Shelly and Grandfather Larry in New York, who owned dry cleaners. Her mom lived in Miami, and they didn't get along. Her parents divorced when she was six, and her grandparents raised her.

She talked a lot about her aunt and uncle. Her aunt Liza was a nurse like him. Her uncle shaped her life, as did his patient Morty

Steine. She was dedicated to the law and to trying to do the right thing. They drank, but they became intoxicated more on each other than on the liquor. They stopped in Centennial Park, necked like two teenagers, and fogged up the windows.

He parked in Printer's Alley, gave her one last goodnight kiss, and said good night.

CHAPTER TWENTY-NINE

NO SURPRISE

Monday, January 4, 1999

On the way out the door, Davis stopped at the guest bedroom. The old man, who was usually sleeping when Davis left for the day, was sitting up in bed reading.

"What's got you up so early?" Davis asked.

"*The Glory* by Herman Wouk. It's the story of Israel's fight for independence. It might be the best book I've ever read by the author of *The Winds of War* and *War and Remembrance*."

Davis was impressed. He'd read both books about World War II, and they'd been two of his all-time favorites also.

Morty squirmed a little, probably from slight embarrassment. The Davises had been incredibly kind to their friend and partner, but Morty was a man who said what he meant.

"After I finish this great book, I want to get back to my place. I've got to get the hell out of here. I've been an incredible burden to Liza, I can live in the sixth-floor apartment. I won't be isolated there. The office is only two flights up, so during the day I can spend part of the day in the office, and when I get tired, the rest of the day one of you can check on me every so often."

Davis saw where this was going. The two men were capable of completing each other's thoughts.

"Sammie lives only three floors up, so she'll be there at night. I'm a big boy, and she's only a phone call and an elevator ride away. It's time to set your wife free. I'll never forget her kindness, but enough is enough."

Davis decided not to argue. What would be the point? For the last seventy-nine years Morty Steine did exactly as he pleased except when his wife, Goldie, told him otherwise, and she was long gone, a blessed memory.

Although Morty was still weak, spreading his care among three rather than placing the burden solely on Liza, with Jake back in school, made good sense. She could still provide nursing care when needed. At this point, all the old man really needed was companionship. Besides, the firm needed his mind and good common sense. Davis wasn't too proud to admit it. Sammie was coming along fine, but she needed the guidance of Morty to finish her education. During the day, Davis was generally too busy putting out fires and didn't have the time and attention he'd like to give to her. Also over the last few weeks, there were several times Davis wished he could have run a question or two in front of his old friend just for reassurance. *We always want to hear we're right.*

Morty, an emotional person, remarked, "I'll miss the kids. Jake's developed into quite a gin player and chess master."

"How about we compromise and you spend the weekdays downtown, but weekends here? I think splitting your time will be best."

Morty had negotiated his freedom, and once back downtown, he'd weasel his way back into the office. Nobody's fooling anybody, Davis said to himself. He'd watched Morty win many an argument before he knew exactly what was happening.

Davis took the stairs two at a time and stopped at the kitchen table to kiss Liza good-bye. As he downed his coffee, he shared his most recent conversation with their departing houseguest. She had no objection and remarked, "It's time to let our little bird fly. He's been itching to get back to the office."

Davis heard her last word and was out the door, in the Vette, and on his way, music blasting, to work. "Sweet Melissa" by the Allman Brothers was his song of choice as he barreled down West End Avenue to the Commerce Street garage. He popped out of the car and rushed down the Alley, past the Rainbow Lounge, and into the back door of the old Steine's Department Store. At the eighth floor, he opened the front door to be confronted by Bella. In an unusually excited manner, she handed him the decision of the Court of Appeals in the Moore case. No surprise. Motion denied. The appellate court agreed with Judge Billingsly. The questions were discoverable under Rule 26. Joseph had the right to ask the questions, and Moore was compelled to answer them.

Bella asked, "Do you think you can get him to answer the questions now?"

If Moore were a man of his word, he'd give the answers now. Davis was damn well going to give it his best shot. *Karl Moore can't be that stubborn, can he?*

He looked at his messages, decided he didn't want to get sidetracked, made an about-face, and walked over to the jail behind the courthouse to visit his client. *I'm going to talk some sense into that son of a bitch.*

The guard took him directly to Moore's cell and let Davis in. Davis had never been in a jail cell before. The few times he'd come over, he'd met his clients in a visitation room. The accommodations were Spartan: two cots with worn gray woolen blankets, a wooden shelf with four paperbacks, including *Winds of War*, which Davis had brought Moore, and a toilet. Moore jumped to attention when his lawyer walked in.

He looked pretty rough. He'd been muscular to begin with, but he'd lost some of his six-pack.

Davis got straight to the point, "Motion denied. You've either got to answer the questions or appeal to the Tennessee Supreme Court, and its affirmation of the Court of Appeals is inevitable. You've fought the good fight, but it's over."

"I want to get the hell out of here. What do I have to do?"

"Let me call Judge Billingsly's court officer, Ms. Bray, and find out what needs to be done. I think I can have you home before the end of the day."

Davis used his cell phone to arrange for Moore to be taken to the Sixth Circuit Court and appear before the judge at noon. Both he and Tom Joseph were directed to be present.

Davis went back to the office to get some work done before the Moore hearing. He called several clients and adversary counsel. He reviewed some pleadings that he needed to file with various courts. Two hours flew by, and it was time to get to court. Bella wished him good luck.

"Don't wish me luck. It all depends on Moore. He better answer those damn questions."

Davis rushed to court. When he got there, Joseph was already waiting. Not long ago, Joseph had been willing to pull the plug on this whole fiasco. He spoke first, "You know we lost control of this situation. I can't believe your client has spent several days in jail. I'm not sure who is more stubborn, Moore or Billingsly? Although you're a close third."

"What the hell did I do?"

"How did you let this situation go so far? It's drugs. In today's world, who really cares?"

"Wait a minute! You asked the questions. You obviously cared. If not, then why did you ask the questions?"

"To provoke your client."

Davis said, "I guess you succeeded."

"In retrospect, I'm sorry I did."

Davis looked at Joseph. He believed him. Davis decided he still owed the other lawyer one for trying to avoid the disaster that neither of them could avoid.

Just then Moore in an orange jumpsuit was brought in. His hands were cuffed. Davis grit his teeth and hoped Moore would behave.

Billingsly took the bench, and the hearing began. "Mr. Moore, good to see you. Have you enjoyed your stay in our jail?"

Davis thought, *the judge could be a little more gracious.*

Moore decided to play nice, "You were right. The Court of Appeals backed you up. You win. I'll answer the questions."

The judge directed Ms. Bray to swear the witness and to read the questions to him.

Ms. Bray read from the interrogatories prepared by Joseph, "#12, Have you ever used cocaine?"

"Yes, ma'am. Last time was about ten years ago. I first snorted it as a DEA agent. About five years later, as an agent, I smoked it as crack. It was necessary for me to smoke it as part of my undercover work. It was dangerous and put me in contact with people who could potentially put my family at risk, so I resigned five years ago. The last time I did crack was five years ago. I realized, as my kids got older, that smoking crack and being around the people who were selling it and distributing were unhealthy and placed my family and me at risk. I could have asked for a desk job and gotten out of the field, but the excitement and action were in my bloodstream. I just couldn't sit behind a desk. It probably would have been the smart move to just bide my time another ten years and earn my pension, but I decided to go into protection and security instead. It kept me active, away from drugs. It was a good move for me and my kids."

Ms. Bray asked question #13 about other scheduled drugs. Moore's answer surprised everyone. "I've never used any other scheduled drugs. As a DEA agent, I've been around tons of the stuff, but I've personally never used any scheduled drugs other than cocaine. I've never even smoked pot. I had to use cocaine as part of my job to infiltrate certain gangs. It was ten years of undercover work that I didn't want to talk about, that I shouldn't have had to talk about in this divorce action. I resent that I had to spend those days in jail trying to preserve the confidentiality of my work history that I swore would remain confidential."

Davis was shocked. He thought, *If Moore was drug tested, he would have showed up positive for at least pot, maybe worse. Why the hell wouldn't that stubborn son of a bitch have answered that question? Joseph would have taken that answer and had nowhere to go. I don't understand.*

Ms. Bray read from the interrogatories, "#14, Have you ever smoked marijuana while your kids were in the house?"

"Absolutely not!"

In a loud, almost angry voice, Judge Billingsly asked, "Mr. Moore, why the hell didn't you just answer the questions? Are you insane?"

"I didn't answer those questions because it was none of your damn business. I also wanted to set an example for my children that one's principles are worth sacrificing for. Before I appeared before you, I did some research into you as a jurist. I read several of your opinions and talked to several community leaders about you. I was told you were a fair man, who understood that a man's principles were important and should be protected and were worth fighting for. I really didn't think you'd make me spend those days in jail. "

The judge's expression completely changed. He went from hard to mush. Billingsly took a deep breath. Davis could tell he was going to say something important.

"Mr. Moore, I want to extend to you my deepest apology. I was technically right but morally wrong. You failed to follow my order, but you weren't defiant about it. You argued your principles, but I didn't hear you, blinded and deaf to why you didn't answer. You never were in contempt of this court. I'm reversing my own finding and will be sending a letter to the Court of Appeals explaining my actions."

Both Davis and Joseph were stunned. Neither knew what to say.

After about a minute, Billingsly said, "Since the cat's got both of your tongues, I'll draw my own order. My order will not only reverse my finding of contempt but will also include an apology from the court to Mr. Moore and acknowledge that I was legally within the law and acted within my discretion as a trial judge. However, upon reflection, I realized that Mr. Moore, who stood on his principles, was right and as a responsible seasoned jurist, I should have recognized that fact and acted differently. Mr. Moore should not have been jailed for a week. I've learned from this experience. I hope that Mr. Moore gets some solace from my remarks."

That's a first. I've never seen or heard anything like that from any judge. Davis couldn't believe it. *I can't wait to tell Morty about this one. I don't think he'll believe it either.*

"I just insisted that I was right because I knew the law was on my side. The law's important, but as lawyers, Mr. Joseph and Mr. Davis, we should always remember it's not the only consideration. Humanity is complex, and the law is only one of many aspects of social morality."

CHAPTER THIRTY

A GIRL UNDER A MICROSCOPE

Monday, February 1, 1999

After a month of dating, four dinners, six lunches, and some heavy petting, I figured this breakfast date might be the morning that Nurse Victor Browne and I would consummate our relationship. The man was the complete southern gentleman letting me control the pace of our relationship. He'd reached second base and had vigorously massaged my breasts. I felt like I was in junior high. I hadn't waited this long for a man since high school. I desired more, and since I was in control, I knew my time had come. Nurse Browne was getting some delicious dessert.

We brunched at ten and then returned to my loft apartment. As we were saying good-bye, I raised my knee and began using it to rub hard against his member. He became aroused. I'd done this once before, but for the first time, I brought my hand down and placed my thumb on one side of his penis and my other four fingers on the other side of his excited fellow. I moved my hand up and down his shaft first slowly back and forth. His penis grew larger within my grip. As he became more and more excited, I moved quicker and quicker, up and down in a fast, steady stroke. I opened his pants and unzipped his fly. I reached inside and grabbed his swollen penis while his pants fell to the floor.

I'd done this many times before with other men: college students, young adult males, older men, single ones, and married ones. Although I was very busy learning my profession, first as a paralegal and then as a lawyer, I still made time for my sex life. I'd had many casual relationships; I was an experienced woman. I intended to proceed more cautiously with Victor. He was special, and I intended to treat him as such.

Victor, on the other hand, had limited his love life to serious girlfriends. His first relationship began in his sophomore year of high school and went all the way through his third year at Memphis State. It was a difficult breakup that left him devastated. He'd had three other relationships since then, each lasting more than two years. He didn't believe in casual relationships or sex. He'd wanted something more from all of his women, and he wanted more from Sammie.

He was very tender and sweet as he entered me. Finally in a mutual groan we both orgasmed and fell to the bed, exhausted from our effort. I was truly satisfied. It was a beautiful experience, unlike many of my earlier trysts. We lay there together taking in the moment. He placed his arm across my chest to cuddle me to reinforce just how important what had just transpired was to him. I had to stop him.

"I've got two meetings. Stay here until you've got to be at work."

Victor had the luxury of being able to take a nap. He didn't have to be at work until seven. I had to quickly shower, dress, and go downstairs to prepare Chris Addams for his deposition. He was waiting for me.

"Sorry I'm late. I had pressing business." *A small white lie.*

We first reviewed the written discovery and how defense counsel might use the documents during the deposition.

"Keep your answers short, yes, no, with an explanation including solid facts. The facts are on our side. Your salary was frozen. Before the demotion, you reported to an executive vice president and were a senior vice president. Lanier can't change those facts. If you don't know an answer, don't be afraid to say, 'I don't know.'"

Davis stuck his head in the door and asked, "How's it going?"

Addams responded, "She's getting me ready. I'm getting comfortable with the idea of testifying, but I still don't know where I'm going to work when this is all over."

"I'm working on that, Chris. Good luck."

Davis walked on, and I continued to work with the client. We worked together about two hours, but I noticed his mind seemed to drift.

"What's wrong?"

"I've got no future. My wife's dead. I have no children. All I have is this lawsuit. All I can be awarded is money, and that won't solve my problems. I really don't have anything to live for."

That was disturbing, particularly the way he said it. My radar went up. There was something really bothering my client, and it wasn't his lawsuit against the bank. I tried to get him to focus on something positive in his life.

"You don't mean that, Chris. What about Troop 34? The boys are very important to you, and they need you."

"They'll grow up and move on with their lives, just you wait and see. Once they're men, they'll forget about me. They'll get married and have children, and their families will become their priority. It's happened before. Remember I've been involved in scouting thirty years. My troopers have come and gone. I lose them all the time. That's life, they move on."

I hated to end our conversation on such a depressing note, but I had to get to my next appointment with Davis, so we said our good-byes. I remained concerned about Addams.

Davis and I had an appointment with Dr. Virginia Ames. We were a few minutes early for our two o'clock appointment. A woman in her mid-seventies walked out of the inner office. Davis stood, and the woman walked straight out the door without a word. *I guess that wasn't Dr. Ames.*

A moment later another woman, tall, statuesque, in her mid-thirties, emerged from the rear private office. She wore a midnight blue dress that hugged her body tightly, exhibiting her exquisite form. Davis, quite happily married, wasn't dead. He noticed and was aroused by the woman's body. Immediately attracted to her, he noted to himself, *This woman knows how to dress for success, and midnight blue is my favorite color.*

He extended his hand. There was a shock from the electromagnetification of the plush carpeting.

"Wow, that's quite the handshake you've got, sir," she said as she jumped back. "Let's try that again." She offered her right hand again. The second time there was no shock. Their blue eyes met, and their second handshake lasted longer than it should have.

"Dr. Virginia Ames. I'd be concerned if you could repeat that shocking experience twice in a row."

"Ben Davis. One is my limit. This is my partner, Sammie Davis."

"Brother and sister?"

"No, Sammie's my niece."

My radar shot up. I didn't like this bullshit banter back and forth. The age difference between us was apparent. Davis was more likely to be mistaken as my father than my brother. I took a deep breath and paused. *This little cutie's act isn't fooling me, but what's her game? What does Dr. Virginia Ames have to gain by buttering him up? Is she playing for herself or for Rachel January?*

Regardless, I didn't care for this woman. An inviting smile and a shapely oversized C cup may have taken in my uncle, but something didn't feel right, and I told myself to be guarded.

The doctor offered us seats. We sat on the couch while the doctor took the dark blue leather chair across from us. I thought her dress blended right into the chair.

Davis joked, referring to the couch, "I guess this is where your clients tell you all their secrets?"

Still flirting. Wake the hell up, I mentally scolded.

"Most patients just need someone to talk to. We've all got problems. I'm a good listener, and I'm trained to help patients understand and, if possible, solve their problems. Of course some problems can't be solved, so I help them recognize them, face them, and then finally address them as best they can. Dealing with a problem is often the only solution and often the most difficult and requires the most intense help and skill."

I wasn't buying any of this bullshit. *Smug bitch. I bet she's got a few problems* of *her own.*

I was a good judge of character, learned from two of the best. I saw some deep flaw in this health care professional. After this meeting, I would conduct an extensive background check and put the good doctor's professional and personal lives under the microscope.

While I was deep in thought, Davis got down to business. "Doctor, thank you for sending us your resumé. We've had an opportunity to examine it. Impressive." Trying to be more diplomatic, Davis said, "Good academics, undergraduate Boston College, Medical School Tufts, residency at Johns Hopkins . . ."

Ames broke in, "I'm glad you approve. I . . ."

Now it was Davis's turn to interrupt. "You've never published, you've got no fellowship, and your resumé is only one page long."

"What the hell does that matter?"

"Have you ever acted as an expert witness before?"

"No, but I'm Rachel Sinclair's treating physician. That makes me qualified to testify in this case, and by the way, you might not like what I have to say. I understand this is a custody issue, and I have pretty strong opinions that neither of these parents is a good role model for these children. That might not be what you want the judge to hear."

Good point. We jumped the gun. Rookie mistake. I just assumed her testimony would be helpful. I knew that Morty would ride us hard about misjudging the situation.

I asked, "Tell us about Rachel."

Dr. Ames confirmed that Rachel, severely depressed, sought treatment after being told that her husband had an affair. She resented the person who revealed the ugly truth, her father.

"She's always had a difficult relationship with both parents. Her father, born not with a silver spoon, but a golden one, has taken his advantages and made the most of them, becoming a pillar of the community. He's active in the West End Methodist Church and most of the prominent charities and organizations. The pressures on Rachel to be a model citizen and southern lady were unbearable. She was expected to become part of the social elite of Nashville society and had no desire to do so. She wanted no part of it. She's always been more of a free spirit, artistic, less interested in the social graces. She likes the finer things in life but not the trappings. Her father is also one of the most successful lawyers in the state, fourth-generation lawyer, managing partner of Sinclair & Sims. He wields power and influence in every aspect of state and federal governments and in most industries. He's a deal maker with political influence behind both parties."

Davis acknowledged that they were familiar with Tyree Sinclair's political background and power he wielded.

"She despises politics, thinks it's corrupt, and hates all lawyers. So guess what? She'll hate both of you for sure."

Great, by profession, my client hates me.

Ames kept talking, "Her mother, Rita, well respected in the community, worked tirelessly for about a dozen charities, alternating from president to co-chair of each one."

Ames talked about Rachel's childhood, "Sheltered all her life, spoiled by her parents, ill equipped for life. She attended a private all-girls high school and then Tulane in New Orleans, but unlike most college students, she avoided drugs and casual sex. She was kind of a nerd. She wasn't unattractive. Boys pursued her, but she showed no interest. She got lost in her art and avoided most human contact."

I asked, "I always thought that Tulane was a real party school and that its students spent most of their time drinking in the streets, doing drugs, and having a good time. How did she spend four years in that carnival atmosphere and not get swept up by it?"

People from the University of Florida like to think that there's a school with a worse reputation for partying. Tulane and UF were neck and neck.

"Dr. Ames didn't answer right away. She knew the answer, but she was searching for the right words. Finally she replied, "Her upbringing, the morality she was taught by her parents. Drinking, using drugs, and having casual sex just weren't part of who she was taught to be."

"How did her upbringing prevent her from sexually being engaged?" I asked.

"She saw sex as something dirty. She was looking for Mr. Perfect and didn't want to even consider anyone else until the right man came around. So she spent her high school and college years alone, waiting.

She continued, "Enter Dan January, good-looking Vanderbilt law student, just what daddy and mommy wanted. January wasn't a missionary position kind of guy. He had some, shall we say, fetishes. For the first time Rachel became sexually active. She reached climax, but it took work. Rachel wasn't easily satisfied, and January convinced her to experiment with various alternatives."

In graphic detail Ames described how January tried to get Rachel to engage in wife swapping and how Rachel rejected the concept. "I'm paid not to judge others."

I inquired. "Why would the affair with Laura Chapman bother Rachel so, if she knew that her husband had been trying to engage in a swinger lifestyle?"

"Good question. After six months of Dan engaging in a swinging lifestyle, with Rachel being a spectator, Rachel became pregnant with Franklin. Even though she remained monogamist, January insisted on a blood test. It confirmed that the baby was Dan's, but Rachel became concerned about what impact their family would have on their sexual promiscuity. January argued that there should be no change to his lifestyle during the pregnancy, that he should continue to be sexually active. Rachel became furious and threatened to leave him."

Sinclair never mentioned that his daughter had prior marital problems and thought of divorce. Did Sinclair know?

"So what happened?"

Ames handed Davis a piece of paper from her file. "A compromise was negotiated by January. He agreed to be faithful during the pregnancy, but after the birth of Franklin, the couple would abide by the Ten Commandments."

Davis and I read together. Davis looked at me. Without saying a word, he communicated, *What a mess! We can't let Dr. Ames near a courtroom.*

Then it dawned on him. "Do you have a professional opinion as to whether either Rachel January or Dan January is competent to raise two children, ages six and eight?"

"I wouldn't let Dan January dog sit. Rachel is currently heavily medicated. If she were to divorce January, recover from the trauma of that divorce, and through medication achieve balance in her life, I am confident she could raise her children. She'd have the support and love of her parents to help and guide her. I suspect that would take time and succeed over several stages. Her parents would be an integral part of her recovery from the divorce."

"Based upon what you know about Rachel's parents, do you have a professional opinion as to whether they'd be good candidates to raise their grandchildren?"

"I would like to see Rachel and her children move in permanently with her parents. She doesn't have to give up her parental rights, but the Sinclairs need to protect their grandchildren and provide a stable environment."

"If you feel that way, why didn't you share your opinions with the Sinclairs?"

Davis knew the answer but wanted to hear it from Ames.

"I couldn't get Rachel to sign the medical authorization. I didn't think she was a threat to herself or others, so I couldn't go to the police. It's critical that I have her trust, and if I went to her parents without her permission, she'd fire me. I believe I'm her lifeline to reality."

Davis asked, "Why did you get angry earlier?"

"Sorry, that wasn't very professional, but despite the authorization, I felt like I was betraying Rachel."

In a twisted way that made sense. I asked, "Do you have a professional opinion as to whether Dan January is competent to raise two children ages six and eight?"

"Absolutely not, he's . . ."

In his commanding courtroom voice Davis said, "Objection, hearsay. Dr., you've never met or spoken to Dan January?"

"No, but . . ."

"Any information you have comes from Rachel, who you've admitted isn't competent and is deceptive to authority figures?"

"Yes, but I'm trained . . ."

"Dr. Ames, trust me. You're not qualified to testify about Dan January's competency as a parent. We'd need an independent psychiatrist or psychotherapist to examine him and form independent opinions from the biased information provided by Rachel."

I knew he was right. Dr. Ames was slightly offended by his rebuke. "Dr. Ames, in your professional opinion what, from a parental standpoint, would be in the best interest of the January children?"

"For custody to be granted to Mr. and Mrs. Sinclair and visitation by Rachel and Dan January to be restricted and supervised."

Davis stood, and I followed.

When we got in the car, Davis put the tan top down and an orange Tootsie Pop in his mouth. He looked at me and said, "We've got to have Rachel January fire us or resign."

"You're not a quitter."

"We have to convince Rita and Tyree Sinclair to allow us to represent them in a custody battle with their daughter and son-in-law. I need to talk to Morty. I don't know how to tell the Sinclairs. This is another fine mess you've gotten me into, Sammie."

CHAPTER THIRTY-ONE

AN OLD MAN'S TALE

Thursday, February 4, 1999

I'd done the best I could to prepare my client for the onslaught of his deposition. Despite these efforts, he was nervous, and that made me nervous. Kurt Lanier had deposed many witnesses. He'd have that advantage for sure over his witness, but we had the facts and the law, and those were good things to have on our side. It was a fact that Chris Addams was demoted, and it was a fact that his age was a factor in that decision. I had that on the record. The bank had admitted that fact to a newspaper, and I used that article to get the bank's president to admit it in his deposition. The bank's board was in quite a pickle. He admitted the bank violated the Age Discrimination Act, a federal statute passed by Congress to protect older citizens. That meant my client was entitled to sworn testimony of its president. My client's testimony couldn't change those facts, and the law was clear. Age, by law, couldn't play a factor.

A paralegal ushered Chris and me into a large conference room. She offered us refreshments, but we just wanted water. Lanier and his entourage of one partner and three associates joined us. It was important to bill the bank as much as possible.

"Ms. Davis, are we ready to go? Can I get you anything else?"

"No, sir. My client and I are ready to start. Fire away."

Chris was put under oath, and Lanier spent the next half hour delving into his background and education. It wasn't very impressive. He graduated from high school in Nashville and then went to Western Kentucky. He started with the bank as a teller and rose through the ranks. He took night courses at David Lipscomb University and Belmont University in finance and international banking to better himself. It was clear from his testimony he was a self-made man.

"What are your hobbies?"

"I play golf and tennis. I'm also very active in the Boy Scouts."

"How often do you play golf and tennis?"

I wondered where this was going. My client's golf game seemed irrelevant. Rule 26 of the Tennessee Rules of Civil Procedure allowed Lanier to ask Chris any question that might lead to the discovery of admissible evidence. I decided to give Lanier some leeway and not object.

"If I'm lucky, I play once a week on Saturday. I usually have a seven or eight o'clock tee time."

"What about tennis?"

"I play indoors in the winter when I can't play golf. I rarely play in the summertime. Most of my spare time is devoted to scouting."

"You're a scout leader, aren't you?"

"Yes, Troop 34."

"What does being a scout leader entail?"

I decided we were getting a little far afield.

"Mr. Lanier, how will this line of questioning lead to admissible evidence?"

"Are you objecting, counselor? Are you asserting some kind of privilege? Does your client have something to hide?"

"No, but you know the scope of Rule 26. I've been very tolerant sitting here, waiting for you to ask a question relevant to this case, and quite frankly you haven't asked one. Where my client went to high school may be discoverable, but it has no bearing on whether the bank violated the Age Discrimination Act. Why don't you get to the relevant questions about the case?"

"Look, young lady, I've been taking depositions longer than you've been alive, and I don't need you telling me how to conduct a deposition."

Lanier was angry. His face was beet red. His posse glared at me as if I had dethroned their king. Lanier ignored me and had the court reporter read the question back to Chris, who was noticeably shaken.

"You set an example for the boys. You teach them good values. We work on projects together. Most of them don't have a father figure in their lives because of death, divorce, or abandonment."

"How many boys in the troop?"

"It varies from eight to ten, depending on circumstances."

"How old are the boys?"

"They're eleven or twelve."

"What are the names of the boys currently in Troop 34?"

Chris turned to me with panic on his face. I knew I had to step in.

"He's not going to answer that question. We can stop this deposition right now and call the judge. Those boys are minors, and without the express permission of their parents, Mr. Addams will not identify them. Now move on to relevant questioning about this case. This deposition is a farce. If it continues, I will seek sanctions."

I looked at Chris, who seemed about to have a nervous breakdown. "We're going to take a fifteen-minute comfort break, and when we return, this deposition needs to address the issues raised in the complaint and the defenses raised in the answer. If not, it will be adjourned, and I will file the appropriate motion with the court. We came here to move this case forward to trial. You are entitled to depose my client. I suggest you do so and not waste everyone's time."

Chris and I walked out of the conference room, and he went straight into the men's room. Standing outside the door, I could hear him throwing up. I knocked and asked, "Chris, are you okay?"

I repeated, "Chris, are you okay?"

No answer. I knocked again. "Is anyone in there?" I heard no response, so I entered. I hadn't been in a men's room since my University of Florida days. Truth be told, I wasn't very proud of what I did on that occasion; better to let sleeping dogs lie.

I found Chris in a stall and helped him to his feet. He was pretty wobbly, so I assisted him to the sinks. For the first time I noticed my surroundings. Although I had been in a men's room only once before, I realized how ornate the men's room of Bone, Lanier & Bass really was. All of the stalls were made of mahogany, the floor was terrazzo tile, the vanities were the finest granite, and the sinks were ivory porcelain. In the corner was a massive wooden shine chair with a picture of a stately black gentleman in a white dinner jacket and the name Solomon and the dates 1932-1979. A short paragraph explained that he was the bathroom attendant for forty-seven years.

I needed to rally my client. "Chris, you've let Lanier get to you. He's upset you over nothing. The court will not require you to discuss the identity of your boys. Don't worry. I need you to go in there and answer his questions about bank business and how the bank demoted you. You need to get the truth on the table. He can't trip you up. All you have to do is tell the truth. It's that simple. Keep your answers short. Most questions can be answered yes or no. Don't be afraid to say. 'I don't know' if you don't know. It's a valid answer if you just don't know. You can always answer, 'I don't remember.' That leaves you the option later on to remember, particularly if you're shown a document later on."

Chris washed his face, and we left the restroom. Back in the conference room, Lanier was all business. He asked relevant questions about the case. Chris was a little shaky at first, but as the deposition progressed, he improved. All in all, I was satisfied with his testimony, but I had to admit being concerned that Lanier was able to send him fleeing to the bathroom, sick to his stomach. I worried: *Could Chris stand the rigors of a trial?*

CHAPTER THIRTY-TWO

DAMN FOOL

Friday, February 12, and Friday, February 19, 1999

Davis reread Littleton's board complaint for the third time and then picked up the phone. On the second ring, the receptionist answered, "Tennessee Board of Professional Responsibility, how may I direct your call?"

"Ms. Ziegler, Chief Disciplinary Counsel, please."

A moment later Davis heard, "Pamela Ziegler."

"Pam, Ben Davis, I'm calling . . ."

"I know why you're calling, Mr. Davis. Before you say one word I want to put you on notice that I'm recording this conversation. I suspect this phone call is your attempt through an ex parte communication to get this office to pull back our efforts to discipline your misconduct toward a fellow member of the Bar. You can't just talk your way out of this one, and Morty Steine won't be able to bail you out either."

Davis didn't particularly like Ziegler. They'd butted heads when Ziegler was in private practice, an associate with one of the bigger firms before the governor as Chief Disciplinary Counsel appointed her.

"So you've read Littleton's complaint."

"Yes, I have. Your answer's due Monday, the 15th. I suggest you file before that deadline expires. You should have returned his phone calls. You shouldn't have admitted to him that you didn't read his letters and you threw them in the trash can. That was stupid. Let's start with you filing an answer. There's going to be a hearing. You're going to have to defend your actions. I suggest you get a good lawyer."

"I'll be represented by Morty Steine. He's the best lawyer I know."

For eight years Morty had been the president of the Tennessee Board of Professional Responsibility, and for two of those years he was Ziegler's boss. He'd retired from the position three years earlier. He may have been hard on Ziegler on occasion, and Davis as Steine's protégé was now in her sights. Revenge could be sweet, although she respected at least Steine and probably Davis's ability. Ziegler admitted, "He'd be the lawyer I'd want defending me. He understands procedure, and he knows every member on the board. Despite those advantages, I doubt that will help you. I think you disrespected a member of the Bar, and at the very least you're going to be censured. I'll be prosecuting the case myself."

Usually a minor case like this would be handed off to a low-level assistant disciplinary counsel.

"Isn't that a bit unusual for the chief to be prosecuting a case like this rather than delegating a minor infraction to an associate counsel?"

"I don't want to pass up an opportunity to censure the great Benjamin Davis for misconduct."

The phone call ended. Davis made a mental note to subpoena the telephone tape for the hearing. That last remark by Ziegler would make her appear petty before the board. Her role was to seek justice, not to embarrass or to prosecute other members of the Bar.

Davis asked Bella to pull a specific file from Malone vs. Plainview Community Hospital et al, a case in which Brad Littleton was

Davis's co-counsel between 1992 and 1994. That case filed in state court was one of ten medical malpractice cases against two doctors and Plainview Community Hospital for performing unnecessary gallbladder surgeries.

Davis explained in his answer that Littleton had brought the cases to him contracting to advance one-third of the expenses and perform one-third of the work. Davis attached a copy of the two-page contract to his answer.

Davis described in detail how hard he fought in the Plainview malpractice cases and how little support he received from Littleton. Davis attached the time tickets of Steine & Davis and the time tickets of Brad Littleton evidencing the amount of work each attorney had performed in the Plainview cases. Davis explained that the Malone trial lasted thirteen trial days, and the jury deliberated three for a verdict of $2,250,000, of which $2,000,000 was punitive damages. Davis attached a copy of the verdict form in the Malone case.

During the sixteen-day Malone trial, Littleton cross-examined one witness. Davis attached a copy of the transcript of that examination by Littleton.

Without providing details because he was bound by a confidentiality agreement, Davis explained that after the Malone trial, the other nine Plainview cases settled. However, before the settlement proceeds could be disbursed to the clients, an IRS federal lawsuit was filed because of an IRS lien owed by Littleton. Littleton's and Davis's clients were deprived of their funds for months because of Littleton's lien, which Davis never disclosed, and which Davis only learned of when served with the federal summons as he was leaving the settlement conference. Davis attached a copy of the federal lawsuit filed by the IRS and the lien. He also filed a copy of Judge Thomas Wise's November 14, 1994, order in that federal lawsuit.

The last thing that Davis added to his answer was a subpoena for the telephone call between Ziegler and him. Davis filed the answer on time, and a hearing was set for that Friday.

The hearing was open to the general public, and the hearing room, which held about one hundred, was filled to capacity. There were three cases on the docket. One lawyer had stolen money from his escrow account. His license was sure to be suspended. Another prosecutor had been accused of being racially motivated in jury selection. That would be addressed last and would be hotly contested. The NAACP, ACLU, and several other groups had brought the charges and were prepared to back them up statistically. Davis thought it would be difficult to prove. Many factors went into selecting a juror, and race was at times a legitimate consideration.

"Benjamin Abraham Davis, TBA # 7132, disrespecting another member of the Bar. How do you plead?"

"I'm Morty Steine. I represent Mr. Davis. He pleads no contest, with an explanation."

Pam Ziegler responded, "Mr. Davis is neither admitting nor denying his guilt but is wanting to explain his conduct. Is that correct?"

"Yes, Chief Counsel."

"Under these circumstances, it's appropriate to let the complainant, Mr. Littleton, present his case first before hearing from Mr. Davis."

Morty's ploy worked. Under the no contest rule, Littleton rather than Ziegler presented the facts of the complaint. The putz wasn't smart enough to hire counsel. Ziegler, although a mean bitch, was a more than competent prosecutor. Littleton, on the other hand, was a bungling idiot, and because he was unrepresented, he would have to proceed on his own.

"May it please the court."

"This is not a court, Mr. Littleton. It's a professional board of your peers."

"Right, I'm Bradley Littleton, and I'm a member of the Tennessee Bar. Mr. Davis is a member of the Tennessee Bar . . ."

Impatiently one board member broke in, "That's why we're here."

Littleton had already sweated through his shirt. He was nervous, and in a high, shaky voice, he began, "I called Mr. Davis three times. He refused to take my calls. I also wrote Mr. Davis twice. On the fourth time I called, Mr. Davis rudely told me that he wouldn't take my calls and that he threw my letters in the trash can without reading them."

Littleton was out of breath. His whole body was noticeably shaking, not from anger, but from fear.

Ziegler came to his rescue, "Thank you, Mr. Littleton, for your account of the facts. Mr. Steine, Mr. Davis's explanation."

Morty stood. These were old friends. He'd been their leader for eight years. Smiles were exchanged like secret handshakes.

"Before I begin, I'd like to request that we play a copy of the audiotape of Chief Counsel Ziegler's telephone conversation with Mr. Davis, of a week ago, before Mr. Davis filed his answer."

Ziegler broke in, "Unfortunately that tape is unavailable. It's inaudible."

"It can still be produced, inaudible or not?"

"What's the purpose if it's inaudible?"

"Are you a sound engineer? Maybe I can retain an expert who can retrieve the sound and provide this board with an audible tape. It's been subpoenaed. Comply with the subpoena."

The president of the board ordered Ziegler to "comply with the subpoena."

Morty moved on. "Having served on this body, I know that you've read the attachments to Mr. Davis's answer. So I can summarize. In the Plainview cases, Ben Davis spent 2,420 hours on them. Our firm spent 6,700 hours in more than thirty-one months on those cases. Our firm had more than $70,000 advanced in expenses out of pocket in the Malone case and over $284,000 total out of pocket in the Plainview cases.

"Mr. Littleton, under contract, should have advanced $93,720 in expenses, and he failed to advance one penny, despite the fact he was requested to do so thirteen times in writing. Mr. Davis has attached those thirteen letters to his response. Mr. Littleton, under their contract, should have performed one-third of the work in the Plainview cases or 2,233 hours. He originated no pleading; there were more than a thousand filed in the ten cases. He attended five depositions and took none of the more than two hundred depositions. During the sixteen days of the Malone trial, Mr. Littleton cross-examined one witness, the ambulance driver. A copy of that cross-examination has been provided to the board. As the board can read, Mr. Littleton's examination was so incompetent that the entire courtroom, including the judge, laughed at him because he kept asking leading questions, and the judge had no choice but to keep sustaining the defense's objections. He was a laughingstock, and he detracted from the plaintiff's case.

"What's probably the most important and damaging factor of Mr. Littleton's misconduct in the Malone case was his failure to disclose his indebtedness to the IRS, which resulted in an IRS lien on the file for several months. That hurt not only Steine & Davis, which is forgivable, but it hurt our clients, who were delayed in collecting their settlement proceeds of more than five million dollars. Greedy doctors, who they'd trusted, had already injured these people. Their unnecessary surgeries took place in 1990 or 1991. This was August 1994, so they'd been patient, and they'd trusted their lawyers who'd worked out a settlement. Then out of nowhere Mr. Littleton's IRS lien holds off payment for months. Six of those plaintiffs are here to testify on behalf of Mr. Davis if the board will hear them. They wouldn't take Mr. Littleton's calls either. He broke their trust. If it wasn't for Mr. Davis's efforts, their settlement proceeds could have been tied up a lot longer because of Mr. Littleton's negligence, breach of trust, and failure to disclose.

"I direct the board's attention to the fact that Judge Wise judicially amended the contract between Mr. Littleton and Steine & Davis from a division of attorney fees of 66 2/3% and 33 1/3% to 95% and 5%. The court found that this was consistent with how the work was actually performed in the Plainview cases. I cannot disclose the actual dollar amount of the settlements because of the confidentiality clause, but it exceeded five million dollars. The IRS seized Mr. Littleton's 5% fee. I am not in a position to disclose the exact dollar amount of the fee, but the total fee exceeded $3 million, and the IRS received more than $50,000. In conclusion, Mr. Davis would like to make a statement."

"I recognize that I should return the phone calls of members of the Bar and that I should read and respond to letters sent to me from members of the Bar. Those are obligations that I owe, and I promise the board that in the future I will meet those obligations. The board has never sanctioned me, and I take my reputation seriously. Please consider that in making your determination. I respect the law. My law license is an integral part of who I am as a person. Thank you for listening to my explanation."

The board called a recess. They invited the parties into chambers. The president directed his first question to Littleton. "Mr. Littleton, what was your purpose in contacting Mr. Davis?"

Littleton wasn't prepared for the question, so he hesitated, "It was a probate matter, concerning a will."

The president pressed Littleton. "What was it? Don't you want to get an answer? Don't you need the information?"

"I represent a former client of Davis. Davis still represents the mother, and I wanted Davis to give me a copy of the mother's will so I could see if the son was still a beneficiary under the will. He's the only child."

Davis jumped to his feet. "Do you see what I'm dealing with? You have no right to see the will. A child has no right to inherit from a parent. A child has no right to see a parent's will. How did you ever pass the Bar?"

Davis's anger was apparent. This was the type of overreaction that could get you in trouble. And it did.

Now it was the president of the board's turn to get angry. "Sit down, Davis. You can't talk to him like that. He's a member of the Bar. His license is the same size as yours. Littleton, if you insist, I'm going to publicly censure Davis for disrespecting you, and I'll return to the hearing room and do it right now. Every lawyer is entitled to have his phone calls returned and his letters answered. Davis will be embarrassed, and then he'll move on with a slight blemish on his record. However, your conduct in the Plainview cases was outrageously unethical as to Davis, your co-counsel, and even worse as to your clients. I'm sure Mr. Davis can get one or more of those six plaintiffs sitting out there to file charges against you for your misconduct, and I can promise you those charges will end in a suspension of your license for at least three months, possibly a year. Let's say you withdraw your complaint, we call it a day, and I simply recite your withdrawal and the obligation that an attorney should treat his fellow member of the Bar with respect. I'd like this matter closed. It's all up to you, Mr. Littleton."

Littleton had no choice. A suspension would have disrupted

his practice and his life. Ziegler was mad as hell. Davis narrowly escaped, and Morty as usual was the hero. They all went out to the Captain's Table and had a few too many to celebrate. Hopefully Davis learned a valuable lesson from the experience. Even the lowest member of the Bar deserves to be treated with a certain degree of respect. Davis would try to be less arrogant, and he gave Sammie and Bella permission to remind him of the Littleton fiasco if he forgot and his ego got ahead of him again.

CHAPTER THIRTY-THREE

A TOUGH TALK

Monday, February 22, 1999

Davis thought about playing hooky. It was sleeting hard, and Nashville was under an ice storm warning that threatened to cripple the city. He couldn't duck work. He had a nine o'clock meeting with Tyree Sinclair.

He took a couple of laps around the Parthenon in Centennial Park, just to clear his head and enjoy the scenery. The snow on the ground gave the building a postcard appearance. He stopped at the dog park, where he often took his two pugs. They hated the rain, snow, and ice and refused to leave the comfort of the house during inclement weather. The lazy animals had to be forced from the house into the yard where they were contained by the invisible fence. Despite the weather, several other owners were with their braver pets, who were off the leash. A gray pit bull challenged a golden retriever, which held its own. The two soaking wet animals playfully fought in the snow. The humans in their rain/snow gear rushed in to separate the animals. His dogs, overweight, and peace loving, would have been no match for either animal.

He parked his beloved Bentley convertible in the Commerce Street garage just off Printer's Alley. His silver Vette was safely parked in his own garage back home. He'd never risk Albert Wilson's gift to an ice storm or even when snow was on the ground. That vehicle was his fair-weather automobile. After parking the car, he carefully walked down the slippery cobblestone street of the Alley, passing the still open all-night colorful clubs and strip joints to the back door of old Steine's Department Store. He was dripping wet by the time he got to the freight elevator. His suit felt like lead and was freezing cold from the icy rain. Davis didn't believe in umbrellas, which would have been of little help with the sleet pelting him. Both Sammie and Liza thought his aversion to umbrellas was idiotic, and they never lost an opportunity to reinforce their point. However, this morning, because of the consistency of the precipitation, they didn't raise their argument. It made for a bad start of the day. Fortunately, he kept a complete change of clothes at the office for just such a problem.

He stopped at the sixth floor to check on Morty. He used his key instead of knocking. He figured the old man would still be sleeping, but when he peeked in, he woke him.

"Who do you think you are, the tooth fairy?"

"Hell no, I'm the bogyman. I've got a meeting at nine. I thought you might want to tag along. You might learn something."

Morty practically jumped out of bed. The only thing better would be if Davis asked him to lead the meeting. That would have been difficult since he knew nothing about the subject, but Davis suspected, *The old bastard could fake it without knowing anything, just on sheer determination and chutzpah.*

Davis filled him in on the meeting with Dr. Ames. Morty at almost eighty was shocked. *It's become a weird world.*

Morty pulled out of his inside pocket two Cubans and handed one to Davis.

Davis frowned and protested, "Awfully nice of you, but all you can do is chew. If that's acceptable, I'll light up."

Morty made a sour face, but then shook his head and said, "Okay."

Midway through his cigar, Davis started blowing smoke in Morty's face out of pity. *It's eight thirty in the morning. I can't believe we are starting the day off with a cigar. If Liza finds out, I'm a dead man. Sammie better not turn me in.*

Sammie stuck her head in.

Speak of the devil.

"Are you ready for this?"

Davis shook his head. "Are you kidding? There's no good way to do this. We've delayed this meeting too long. Sinclair knows his daughter is severely depressed, but because of a father's love, he refuses to admit all of the underlying reasons for her depression. January's a pig. He put that girl through hell, and she's not ready to be a witness in a divorce action or any other court proceeding. The pressure of testifying would be too much for her. He came to us for advice and guidance. He may not have fully disclosed all the facts to us, but we have an obligation to be truthful to him. He has a right to know. I worry because of his love, he won't be able to fairly assess her competency. I just hope he doesn't shoot the messenger."

Sammie nervously asked, "What do you want me to do?"

"Sit there and be invisible."

"That I can do. I don't envy you."

Morty wondered out loud, "Do you think my being there makes things better or worse?"

Davis thought for a minute before answering. "Quite frankly, I can't see how your being there can make matters worse. Your friendship may lend support. He's going to be embarrassed with or without you being there. I want you there for your experience, and so will he."

Sinclair arrived right on time. It was part of his type A personality. Bella greeted him with a sympathetic smile. Everybody in the office knew what was coming, except Sinclair. She ushered him into the conference room. Davis rose, stuck out his hand, and shook it vigorously. Davis took the lead, and Sammie and Morty for the time being hung back.

The two men exchanged small talk about wives and Davis's children. Jake would be Bar Mitzvah the end of the year. Morty asked about Rita, and the two older men discussed several of Sinclair's partners. The conversation was light, and they avoided the reason for the meeting.

Sammie just sat there, keeping her promise to remain quiet, making mental notes, observing her uncle as he performed a difficult task. This was a learning experience for her. How to communicate disappointing news to a client, not an easy task. She hoped she'd never have to tell a father that his daughter had abandoned his and society's sense of morality and values.

It was Sinclair who got down to business. "What did Ames say? Do I get to talk to her directly, or would that compromise her as a witness?"

Fortunately for Davis, Sinclair began the meeting with a softball question about the law. This question could be easily answered.

"You know the answer to that one. Any conversation between you and Ames would be discoverable. I can't let that happen. To suit their purposes, January's attorney could twist any discussion between the two of you. For example, I'd argue that you've bought and paid for Dr. Ames's testimony. We want to control what Ames might say in court. Her testimony is already tricky. Your contact would only make it worse."

"Look, Davis, we made a promise to be fully honest with each other. I expect the two of you to live up to what you said. I can tell by the look on Sammie's face that something is really wrong. You've got a better poker face than she does. You two need to come clean. I'm a big boy. I can take it, whatever it is."

Davis had made that promise and was going to keep it. "We started speaking to Dr. Ames about ninety days ago. I got a detailed report from Dr. Ames, which I filed with the court. I've waited this long to talk to you because it's taken this long to get Rachel to sign a waiver to release information to you."

Davis looked at Sinclair sympathetically. *Sinclair's quite a tough guy. I'm not so sure I could be so detached if we were talking about either Caroline or Jake.*

Disappointed by her transparency, Sammie remained silent.

Easier said than done, but here goes. Davis took a deep breath and began, "The most difficult job we all have is being a parent. It is much harder than being a lawyer. If you don't know the law, you can conduct research on an issue of law. You can't do that as a parent. There aren't black and white answers. You can teach your children morality and your values, but it might not stick."

Sinclair's face puckered as he said, "Let me make this easier. I know Rachel's messed up. I know her marriage with January was not made in heaven. I'm sure she's done things that I wouldn't approve of, but I'm her father. I want to help. Without information I can't do that. The only person who has that valuable commodity is Dr. Ames. What the hell did she tell you?"

Sinclair was right. He needed to know, and no matter what, he'd do his part to support his daughter.

Davis opened up, "Your daughter's relationship with her husband was complicated. She knew he was sexually active and agreed to his infidelity in writing. She denies that she engaged in any outside sexual activity. At least that's what she told Dr. Ames."

Although he was apparently uncomfortable with the topic, Tyree Sinclair related to the Davises what his wife, Rita, had told him about the swingers party and the young woman who held

Rachel's hand as January moved from bedroom to bedroom having sex with different women. I don't know if she's been faithful, but she swears she's only watched."

Sammie tried to put a name to it, "So, they had an open marriage."

Sinclair, acting the lawyer, tried to clarify, "They had permission to sleep with other people?"

"Not exactly. They engaged in group sex and selected their spouse's partner. They even promulgated rules to outline how they'd do this."

Davis pulled a folded single piece of paper from his inside jacket pocket. He handed it to Sinclair, who read it aloud,

TEN COMMANDMENTS

1. We shall consider the well-being of our children first; they are the most important people in our lives.

2. We shall pray to God so he will understand our relationship and our need to have sexual contact with others.

3. We shall have sexual contact only with a partner approved by our spouse.

4. We shall engage in sexual contact with another, each time, only with the full prior disclosure to our spouse.

5. We shall agree that all potential sexual partners be tested for disease within one month of proposed sexual contact and provide written evidence of such testing.

6. We shall agree that either spouse may require testing of any sexual partner at any time or that the other spouse shall refrain from further sexual contact until such written testing is provided.

7. We shall each use two forms of birth control to minimize the possibility of an unwanted pregnancy. Female sexual partners shall provide written evidence of prescribed birth control.

8. We shall endeavor to find other couples who share our sexual viewpoint, and we agree that we all share a bed or engage in sexual contact in separate rooms in the same house, simultaneously.

9. We shall accept a spouse's decision to terminate sexual contact with a partner or another couple or a request to terminate such sexual contact.

10. We shall not be jealous of our spouse's sexual contact with another because we recognize each other's need for such sexual contact.

For the purposes of these commandments, we define the term *sexual contact* as any form of affection with another: kissing, fondling, oral sex, vaginal or anal intercourse, any use of sexual devices.

On the couple's second anniversary, August 4, 1981, Dan and Rachel signed the document.

Sinclair let the declaration slip from his hand. In a whimper he remarked, "You're right. This is not my morality, and it's nothing like anything I've ever heard of. What's Dr. Ames's perspective on all this?

"She says it's complex but explainable. This was the compromise that January negotiated after the birth of Franklin in order to have sex with other women."

Sinclair was disgusted. He didn't know how he'd explain all this to his wife or face his daughter.

"According to Dr. Ames, Rachel exercised her right to terminate January's relationship with several women under the document. He'd agree and then find another to engage in his perverted acts. Finding women was not difficult for Daniel January."

"Rachel ended those relationships because of this belief system?"

"Commandment 9 and probably others."

"So Rachel's pissed at Dan because by having sex with Chapman, he violated the Ten Commandments?"

"At least Commandments 3, 4, 5, and 8."

"Okay, what do we do? My grandchildren appreciate that their lives are in turmoil. They're starting to act out. The six-year-old is wetting her bed. The eight-year-old is getting in fights at school. My daughter's weird behavior is impacting her children. Dan has leverage over Rachel..."

Davis broke in, "He only thinks he has leverage. His control is only momentary. He's going to make a mistake. According to Dr. Ames, to quote her, 'Swingers have to swing, once they've tasted the forbidden fruit.' He'll engage in some sordid behavior, and we'll be there to document it. Ames is also convinced that despite all his shortcomings, the First Commandment is the most important. Both January and Rachel love and care about your grandchildren and will place them first."

Davis decided he'd raise the possibility of the worst-case scenario, "If neither of the parents will see reason, I'm sure we can convince the court to strip them of their parental rights and name you and Rita as guardians."

"January would never agree, first out of principle, and second because I do believe he loves his children. He hates me. I fired him and forced him into solo practice. I thought I let him exit the firm gracefully, but I'm sure he doesn't see it that way."

Sammie spoke for the first time, "Ames was right. This is a complex problem."

Morty went into Davis's office and flopped into the chair opposite his desk, and they talked about the Sinclair meeting. The fitness of the Januarys came up, and Morty opined, "Quite frankly depending on the judge and his or her morality, a court may find them unfit on religious grounds. There are several Puritans on the bench."

Davis listened carefully to the old man's remarks and digested them. His response was equally measured. "Terminating parental rights is a pretty drastic step. Trial judges don't order it lightly. They weigh the facts carefully."

Morty feverishly chewed on his cigar, rolling it between his thumb and third finger. "What would it take to make Dan January agree to a non-contested divorce and give sole custody of his children to Rachel?"

Davis thought a moment and then answered, "A shit load of money, transfer of her interest in the house, no alimony, reasonable child support, and reasonable visitation for January."

Morty agreed those were the right issues. "Our clients have plenty of funds to satisfy those goals. Right now January is struggling to keep the doors open to his law office. We have an advantage."

Morty paused, "Go dark. It will drive him crazy. We send Rachel to an intensive rehab to get emotionally stable to deal with her depression. We find a secluded place nearby and have Dr. Ames slowly work with her to help her cope with her divorce. At first January will do nothing. We'll document his inaction. The kids will live with the Sinclairs, and his failure to act will work against him. Over time the silence will bug him, and he'll demand answers but get none. Rachel's continued treatment can be on an outpatient basis. She can live with her parents, and we'll negotiate a settlement."

Davis saw where Morty was going and agreed.

CHAPTER THIRTY-FOUR

SETTLEMENT AGREEMENT

Thursday, JUNE 24, 1999

Davis waited more than a hundred days to let the tension build and then called January, who answered his own telephone, "Dan January, can I help you?"

"Dan, Ben Davis. My partner Sammie and I represent your wife. Before I go any further, are you represented by counsel?"

"I'm not. Do I need to hire one?"

"At some point probably so, but you are an attorney, and I don't think I can push you around too much. What do you think?" *I played to his ego, always a good play.*

"Let me assure you, Davis, you can't push me around at all."

"Good, I don't see why this has to be painful for any of the parties. Look, I called to see if we could come to terms and get you a divorce without scandal. That's in everyone's best interest."

"Yeah, you were a big help in the Chapman matter. You got me fired."

"I didn't fire you. Sinclair, your boss, did, and do you really blame him? I'd have fired you for bartering sex for legal fees with a client. You've devastated his daughter."

"I didn't do something I hadn't done in front of her fifty times."

"I've read the Ten Commandments. That was your problem. You should have had your relationship with Laura Chapman right in front of her. Why was that so hard?" *This is quite a candid conversation. Maybe I can get a settlement yet.*

January didn't answer. Davis couldn't see him but suspected, *He doesn't know the answer to the question. In retrospect, I bet he wishes he did have sex with Chapman in front of Rachel. Live and learn.*

"I wish I knew. Maybe I knew Laura wouldn't commit to an open relationship like that. If I had, we wouldn't be having this conversation. Make your first offer, and I'll counter."

Davis moved in for the kill. He had the authority and the ammunition. "Let's not quibble. Let's avoid dancing with each other. You're living in the house. It's worth $400,000, and there's $75,000 in equity. It's yours. The house is fully furnished. She wants six paintings and her jewelry. The rest is yours. Your pension and IRA have $270,000. It's yours. The checking account has $62,000. It's yours."

"I'm impressed you've got my financials down. Get to the point. You want Rachel to have sole custody. That won't come cheap, both in time with the children and in cash. What's Sinclair willing to do?"

I guess we're not going to play games. Davis almost choked as he finished his offer: "$500,000, every other weekend, three weeks in the summer, alternating holidays, and she gets sole custody of the kids. No alimony, and $1,000 monthly in child support for both children until eighteen."

"Great opening offer. I'll make a serious counter. All terms acceptable, but make it a million two."

Davis's authority was $1million. He wanted to save his client as much as he could. "Maybe I can go $600,000."

"A million is a nice round number. Let's cut a deal. Neither one of us wants our lifestyle included in legal pleading."

No kidding, it would be interesting reading!

Davis could end it right now, but he wanted to squeeze every dime from January. Besides, they'd come so far. January wasn't backing out now. "We're at my authority. This offer is subject to Sinclair's approval at two thirds of a million."

"If you can get him up to $800,000, we have an agreement."

Over the phone January symbolically extended his hand, and Davis took it. A savings of $200,000 was quite an accomplishment. Sinclair would be satisfied.

That was easier than it should have been. Maybe I should have been a little tougher in my negotiations, thought Davis. January immediately had the same thought. That's the problem with compromise. On reflection, no one's happy. But then after reflection, each man realized the ordeal was over. January realized he'd have access to a boatload of money, and Davis realized that his client and her father would avoid the embarrassment of a trial.

Davis dialed Tyree Sinclair. He'd bought January off. It wasn't cheap, but it was over. Rachel January would be spared the trauma of a messy divorce, and the Sinclairs avoided humiliation.

"Ty, Ben Davis. Good news, it's done. The terms are as we discussed, except . . ."

Tyree didn't want to hear, but he braced himself.

"I agreed to $800,000. Do I get my bonus?"

"Tomorrow night, you and your lovely wife will have dinner with Rita and me at the Palm. I'll get a five-pound lobster as our appetizer and then steaks for all."

Davis loved the Palm. He'd get a cowboy rib eye, with three of its delicious sides: Lyonnais potatoes, creamed spinach, and sautéed mushrooms. Davis liked his steak covered in grilled onions. He already knew Liza would scold him for gorging, but saving $200,000 deserved a good bonus. He'd earned it.

"I don't want to put a damper on our celebration, but I've got to get approval of my client, and that's not you. It's Rachel. You may be funding this settlement, but she's got to live with the visitation, no alimony, and limited child support. When can I meet with my actual client?"

Sinclair knew Davis was right, but he dreaded presenting the deal he and Davis had masterminded. She hated lawyers, so that put Davis in hot water, and she hated him as a lawyer and her father. Davis knew what Sinclair was struggling with, so he broke Sinclair's train of thought and his silence. "Look, this is unavoidable. Let me handle this. Let me earn my dinner at the Palm. Let's put our dinner date off until I've earned my bonus. We're going to have to sell this to Rachel. I made the deal, so I'm the one who better sell the deal. It's a good deal. It's in her best interest, but more important, it's in the kids' best interest."

"Can she see you tomorrow at eleven? And we'll have dinner at seven."

"Have her come alone. Sammie will sit in on the meeting. If things turn sour, I'll turn her over to Sammie, who can take another tack of girl with girl. Look, Ty, we might as well tackle this problem head-on. Rachel needs to get a divorce, and January will have to get bought off. The most important considerations to Rachel should be her kids. This deal gives her sole custody. Between you and me, I don't think a judge would award her sole custody. In a dogfight she'd probably lose custody. If my meeting turns nasty, she's going to hear that. I hope it doesn't come to that, but the truth is the truth. The second most important thing to Rachel is her art. This deal gets her all of her most precious pieces, and the others are divided equally. In a court fight some of her coveted pieces might go to him. The deal does give him the house. But there's only $75,000 in equity. Technically the bank owns the house. She should be pretty satisfied with the deal. I'll sell her on it."

As soon as Davis hung up, Bella buzzed in. "Richard Sasser has called three times. It's an emergency."

Richard Sasser was one of the firm's best clients, the sole shareholder of Sasser Industries, which had projects all over the country. His company required constant contract work, and both Davis and Morty had represented him in four complex litigations. The company had applied for so many patents and copyrights that they had an in-house patent lawyer, Ned Simmons. Davis liked Simmons and worked closely with him. All of the lawsuits had been patent related, and Ned had been a key witness in several lawsuits.

Sasser's company developed cutting-edge software and did highly sensitive work for the U.S. government. Sasser's son, Dickie, age twenty-three, a boy genius with a Yale doctorate, was the heart of the company. The government wanted Dickie real bad, so it wanted the company real bad.

"Dick, sorry. I've been tied up. What can I do for you?"

"It's Richard Jr. He's been arrested."

Sasser was sobbing and muttering. Davis tried to calm him down, "Dick, slow down. What's he charged with?"

"It's a mess. Leaving the scene of an accident, assault with a deadly weapon, an automobile, reckless driving, and DUI."

"Where are you?"

"I'm at the jail. They won't let me see him. He's scheduled for an arraignment tomorrow at nine."

Richard Sasser Sr. also had several battles with the U.S. government, including the IRS. Sometimes over the last twenty or so years, legal specialists had to be hired, but Morty and Davis were always by his side. He trusted them, and he needed them now more than ever.

"Is he smart enough to keep his mouth shut?"

"He's plenty book smart, but he'll be lost in a jailhouse. I love him, but lately I've questioned his common sense."

"The immediate problem is best addressed by Morty. He knows everyone in the courthouse. I'll bring him up to speed and send him over. There's nothing you can do. Go home and figure out how we're going to make bail."

"How much?"

"Morty would have a better idea, but your son isn't a flight risk. Bail is only a guarantee he'll show up for his court appearances and trial. Somewhere between $250,000 and $750,000. You can put up cash, securities, or property or put down ten percent and work through a bondsman."

"I've got the money in cash if your dollar amount is correct."

"I'll see you with Morty at court at eight, and we'll figure this out."

He asked Bella to call Tyree Sinclair and move Rachel's appointment to one and tell him dinner was still on. He stuck his head in Sammie's office and asked her to join him on a trip to the sixth floor. Morty was in his chair reading a Tom Clancy novel and chewing on a cigar. Davis quickly filled in both Morty and Sammie on the progress of his conversation with Dan January and Richard Sasser's unfortunate problem.

Morty stood and announced, "It's good to be needed. I'll call in some favors and give the father a call after I do my thing." With that he walked out the door, went down the elevator, out the back door, and up Printer's Alley toward the courthouse.

Davis turned to Sammie, "The old man's back."

"He's the right man for this job. Now, what do you want me to do tomorrow at our meeting with Rachel January?"

"I'm going to try to handle it, but she doesn't like lawyers."

"Do I need to remind you that I'm a lawyer too?"

"Yes, but to her, I'm nothing but a lawyer. You're also a woman and a contemporary. You have a chance to approach her from another angle. Plus I'm the one who cut the deal. You can blame me if you have to."

"This is more complicated than it should be."

They sat in the sixth-floor apartment and discussed strategy in the January case for another hour. He went upstairs and took a seat in reception. Davis glanced at and ran through his legal pad. It was two pages long, filled mostly with short, easy to complete tasks. He quickly stopped in his office and dictated three letters and dropped the tape on Bella's desk. She was paying bills.

"Thanks for doing that."

"Our creditors thank me too."

"Where's the other Davis?"

"She left early. Mr. Browne showed up at the office about four, and they exited to the sixth floor. I would go down there, but a sock may be on the doorknob."

Davis laughed and said, "They're both over twenty-one, and he seems like a pretty nice guy. Does he own a flower shop? I see flowers around here all the time."

"Bullshit, I know you've checked him out. What does Dr. Caldwell say about him?"

"John claims he's the real deal. He's a genuine good guy who cares about his patients and is a good nurse. He says she'd be lucky to have him. I think the world of John. He's a good judge of character. He approved of me. She has my approval if she so desires."

It had been a long day. Davis decided to go home. He was doing better and spending more time with his family. He called Liza from the car and suggested that the family go out for a pizza. She agreed and told him she loved him.

The kids already had their homework done, so the family jumped in the car, and it was off to Pizza Perfect near Vanderbilt. The pizza joint filled with college students was loud, and several tables were over served, probably with fake IDs. The pizza was well done and crisp, thin crusted, just the way Davis liked it, New York style, with just a little olive oil dripping when he held it upside down. Liza, a true southerner, ate her pizza with a knife and fork. Their cultures clashed, but their lives meshed, and their children were the best of both worlds.

CHAPTER THIRTY-FIVE

BOYS WILL BE BOYS

Friday, June 25, 1999

Dickie Sasser had recently been awarded his second doctorate in computer science from Yale University, where he graduated magna cum laude in complex mathematics four years earlier at the age of nineteen. He earned his first doctorate a year early in quantum physics at the same university. An extremely good-looking young man, he was the type of kid who almost always made his parents proud. Not today. His father, frowning in disgust, sat in the front row, flanked by Morty and Davis. His wife was home in bed, too ashamed and afraid to come to court and see her only child a criminal.

Dickie smiled at Morty, his new best friend. They'd met last night and then again this morning. Court was called to order, and the clerk quickly read through the docket. Richard Sasser Jr. was the first name read.

"Is it good or bad to be the first name?" asked the father.

"Good, you get to go first and not spend all morning while the court deals with fifty other defendants. I got him moved up from thirty-one to the top of the list. We would have been here until almost noon otherwise."

Davis thought, *I couldn't have done that.*

After the entire docket was read through once, all one hundred and eleven names, the court took a ten-minute comfort break and then resumed.

"Richard Sasser Jr. 99-8134."

Ushered by a deputy to the front of the courtroom, Dickie went forward.

Morty leaped to his feet with the energy of a sixteen-year-old. "Morty Steine for the defendant, Dr. Richard Sasser Jr., Your Honor."

"Mr. Steine, a pleasure to see you up and back in court. We've missed you."

I'm not sure any of the judges would have missed me.

Judge Randall Small, a longtime political ally of Morty, followed his recovery and recently attended his welcome home party. Last night Morty arranged with a jailer acquaintance to move Dickie's case from Judge Barnes's docket to Judge Small's docket.

"Have you had an opportunity to consult with your client, Mr. Steine?"

"Yes, sir."

"Are you prepared to issue a plea?"

"Yes, sir. Not guilty on all charges."

"Mr. Sasser, do you understand the implications of your plea, that you will be tried by a jury of your peers as to your guilt or innocence?"

In his most polite tone, Morty corrected the court. "If Your Honor please, it's Dr. Sasser. I know he's young, but he recently obtained his doctorate from Yale. We ask, despite these circumstances, that he be addressed accordingly."

Davis thought it was a ballsy move, but he trusted the old man.

"Dr. Sasser, do you understand the process?"

"Yes, sir, Mr. Steine provided me with a full explanation."

Dickey's tone was respectful and yet clear and confident. He did exactly what Morty wanted from him.

From the back of the courtroom, a voice boomed, "Like hell, he's innocent. That little bastard totaled my truck, and my little brother Bobby's got a broken wing."

The two men, Caleb and Bobby Dean, walked quickly and defiantly to the front of the courtroom. Bobby had a cast on his right arm. Caleb kept talking as they moved forward.

"We've got no truck to get to our construction site, and Bobby's got one arm. You can't hang drywall with one arm."

Judge Small didn't like his courtroom being disrupted, but he controlled his anger. "Sir, you have no standing or right to speak at this hearing. You should present your concerns to Assistant DA Beck. She works for the Metropolitan Government of Nashville. She speaks for all citizens, including you, who may have been affected by these alleged crimes. You can call her or make an appointment, or after this hearing I'm sure if she has time she'll talk with you outside in the hallway to discuss this matter. Now sit down and be quiet and stop disrupting my court."

The Dean boys nudged their way into the fourth row, forcing others in the gallery to scoot over and be crowded.

Judge Small resumed, "Let's talk about a bond. What do you have to say, General?"

All district attorneys are referred to as "General." General Sue Beck was twenty-seven years old. This was her first job out of law school, and she was six months into her government job. As low man on the totem pole in the district attorney's office, she pulled the assignment of the arraignment docket. Beck began, "These are serious charges. Mr. Sasser's blood alcohol . . ."

Morty interrupted, "Ms. Beck."

Small corrected him, "That's General Beck, Mr. Steine."

Davis now understood why Morty interjected Dickie's title, so he could break up the DA's argument. She immediately got flustered and off track. She stalled and hesitated for a minute and then resumed her argument.

"His blood alcohol was two and a half times the legal limit at 2.5. That speaks for itself. He injured two members of the community and fled from the scene. Police stopped him half a mile from the collision site. He's an out-of-state student who will be leaving our jurisdiction in two months. The state asks for $500,000 bond."

In a louder than necessary voice, Morty proclaimed, "That's absurd. The state obviously doesn't understand or has forgotten from criminal procedure class the purpose of a bond."

That was an intentional elbow in the ribs at Beck because of her age and inexperience. Davis loved watching the old man in court.

"This young man has finished two doctorates at Yale University and is now gainfully employed locally. He's employed by a Nashville-based company, Sasser Industries, which is owned by his father, Richard Sasser Sr. His family has lived and been a part of this community for more than seventy-five years, three generations. My point is that Richard Sasser Jr. will be back here in court whenever requested to do so. In the courtroom is the defendant's father. He's here to support his son and post whatever dollar amount of money this court requires. Mr. Sasser has been my client for more than twenty-five years. He'll vouch for his son's appearance in this court. That is the test for the dollar amount of bond, not as the general contends the seriousness of the crime. This court needs to focus on the proper criteria in making its decision. I submit to you that Richard Sasser's word and good name are worth a hell of a lot more than a half million dollars suggested by General Beck."

"Mr. Sasser Sr., do you stand for your son and promise this court he will appear when directed?"

Sasser stood and answered, "Absolutely, Your Honor, you have my word."

Beck protested, "This man left the scene of an accident..."

The judge cut her off. "General, whether the defendant is guilty of the crimes charged is a different issue. Do you have any information that this father will be unable to live up to his promise he'll get the defendant here when necessary?"

Beck remained silent.

"I hereby release Richard Sasser Jr. into the custody of his father, Richard Sasser Sr."

Wow! Davis thought, *I couldn't have done that.*

From the fourth row, "What a bunch of bullshit."

Judge Small responded, "Who said that?" He was looking at Caleb Dean.

"How'd you like to be held in contempt, sir, and spend the next ten days in jail? Don't you dare disrespect my court."

Morty jumped in, "I don't think that's necessary, Your Honor. Mr. Dean's upset, he's lost his transportation, his brother can't work, and he doesn't understand the process. Let me meet with him following this hearing. I'm sure he'll apologize to the court. "Mr. Dean," Morty urged.

Caleb Dean stood, hung his head, and said, "I meant no disrespect to the court."

The judge directed the dejected man to meet with Mr. Steine outside the courtroom after this matter was concluded. The judge continued, "I'm setting the pre-trial conference for September 30th at nine in my chambers. Any objection?"

Dead silence. The judge marked the case in his calendar. All the lawyers understood that by law a criminal defendant's trial had to begin less than 180 days from his arraignment, unless a defendant waived that right. It was commonly referred to as the "speedy trial act."

Son and father were reunited in the back of the courtroom.

"Dad, I'm so sorry. Mom couldn't bring herself to come, could she?"

"Never mind. You're coming home. That's all that counts. How was last night? Pretty scary?"

"I was petrified until Mr. Steine showed up. They'd locked me up in a holding cell with six guys, and two of them were pretty rough looking. Five of us grouped together for protection, but it was a weak alliance. Then Morty showed up. He knew the jailer and got me my own cell. I probably wouldn't have slept if I hadn't been moved. He was a lifesaver."

The older Sasser turned to Morty. "I won't forget this. Dickie screwed up, but he's not a criminal. Please keep him out of jail."

With confidence, knowing that Small owed him several favors, Morty assured father and son, "I'll do my best, and I'm pretty sure that will be good enough. I need you to follow my instructions to the letter, no questions asked. I need to take care of the Dean boys. They can make trouble with the DA. I can't have them screaming bloody murder to the DA or, more important, to the judge."

"Whatever you say, it shall be done."

"Who owns the car that Dickie was driving last night?"

"One of my companies."

"Who insures the car?"

"Allstate."

"Give me your insurance card and authorize Davis to rent the Dean boys a truck."

Sasser handed Morty his insurance card, and Morty walked over to the Deans standing twenty feet away.

"Gentlemen, let me get to the point. The state brings criminal charges, but you have a right to sue both father and son. I don't want that to happen, but you've seen me in court. I could tie up your case for more than a year. See that man standing with the Sassers? That's my partner, Ben Davis. He'll drive you over to Avis and rent you a truck. Give me seventy-two hours, and I'll work through Mr. Sasser's insurance company to get you a settlement. I can't undo what the kid did, but I'll get you a fair amount of money to compensate you for the loss of your truck and Bobby's injuries and lost wages. The alternative is to hire a lawyer, wait sixteen months, and pay your lawyer one-third. This is, to use your words, no bullshit."

Caleb looked skeptically at Morty.

Morty's response was simple: "Just give me the seventy-two hours. I'm not asking for much. Your truck will still be totaled and Bobby's arm will still be broken, and during that time you'll be driving around in my rental car."

The brothers looked at each other, and Bobby extended his good hand. Morty shook it.

Morty walked back over to Davis and said, "Rent these boys a truck at Avis. I'll take care of the rest."

Davis smiled, shook his head, and smiled again. Under his breath, he said, "You're amazing. I continue to learn from you."

CHAPTER THIRTY-SIX

A MASTER AT WORK

Thursday, JULY 1, 1999

The Dean boys were coming in at noon, and important groundwork needed to be laid so the ultimate goal could be achieved. Morty, who'd been placed in charge of the Dean settlement, called Elaine Godwin, senior claims adjuster, at Allstate Insurance Company. Elaine had worked for Allstate at least thirty years; she was close to retirement. Morty knew her when she started as a young woman and had always treated her with respect and kindness. That was one of the keys to his success. He followed the golden rule. He always said, "Treat others the way you'd want to be treated." He'd taught that to Davis and then to Sammie. His basic kindness was in sharp contrast to most lawyers, who thought they were better than everybody else, especially an insurance claims adjuster who was a woman. It was fair to say that most lawyers were arrogant assholes. Morty's equal opportunity attitude was evident not only as a civil rights leader, but also as a true feminist, and that set him apart from the rest of the pack. He grew up in Middle Tennessee in the thirties and as a Jew experienced prejudice and fought against it as a victim and then later as an adult white man during the fifties and sixties.

The day of the Sasser hearing, Morty called Elaine and gave her a heads-up that the Sasser claim was coming. As a courtesy to an old friend, she assigned the claim to herself. After a few pleasantries, Elaine started right in, "I've reviewed the police report. You have real problems with this case. The kid was stinking drunk and left the scene of the accident."

"Elaine, let me worry about the criminal case. I need your help on the Deans' possible civil suit."

"Well, you have a problem there too. Have you read the policy?"

"No, but I'm confident you're going to read to me the relevant clause."

"The insured's coverage is voided if there is an intervening cause that proximately causes the property damage and personal injury. It's Allstate's position that the boy's drinking was an intervening cause, and therefore there's no coverage. When he's convicted of DUI and reckless driving, the state will have proved our defense."

"First, there's not going to be a conviction, and second, it will cost $20,000 to $30,000 to lose that argument. I've got a better idea. Allstate buys the Deans a new truck. Maybe it will cost $20,000 and contributes $20,000 toward a personal injury settlement, and Richard Sasser Sr. picks up the rest of whatever settlement that I'm able to negotiate. "

"Forty grand seems a little rich for a defendable verdict. You're pushing way too hard. Steine, you need to lighten up. I'll buy the vehicle, and the father gives us a full release."

"Elaine, how many vehicles does Sasser's computer security company insure with you? How much is the premium on his building, both liability and contents? Doesn't it insure ancillary policies like patents and copyrights with you? Isn't there an umbrella policy of $25,000,000?"

Morty knew the answers to all of these questions were yes. Elaine knew the answers to all of these questions were yes. The two were just sparring with each other.

"He insures fourteen company cars and trucks for an annual cost of $28,000. His companies have sixteen other policies with Allstate ranging from comprehensive liability to copyright infringement. The total premiums for all those policies are just under $110,000 a year. He hasn't made any claims in the four years he's been with your company. He's paid you about $440,000, and I'm asking you to give back $40,000 on this claim. Seems reasonable to me."

"There's no coverage on company grounds. The car was a company vehicle, and the son wasn't an employee."

"Nice try. The kid was a summer intern, employed by the company at the time of the accident and about to start full-time employment. Look, Richard Sasser Sr. is a good customer. A new truck and twenty grand aren't too much to ask."

There was a long pause. Morty could hear Elaine thinking. *Sasser could move his business to another company. This claim involved his son. Blood was thicker than loyalty to one's insurance company.*

These two adversaries had fought dozens of battles over the years. Almost all of them were settled, which required compromise on both of their parts. Sometimes one had to give a little more than the other; this time, Morty needed Elaine to bend slightly more to get the deal done. She knew he was a dangerous man in a courtroom, and she wasn't anxious to find out if his half joking threats could be made good.

"Okay, only because I like you. I've always liked you. What's an extra twenty grand among friends? The truck and $20,000 toward settlement. Make sure that Allstate's on the release you get the Deans to sign."

Two hours later, Bobby and Caleb Dean were in the conference room of Steine, Davis, & Davis. Morty addressed the brothers, "Hello gentlemen, how's that rental truck working out for you? Pretty nice ride?"

"It's pretty fine, but Bobby here can't work, and every day he can't work we lose money. It's all because of your drunk client. He's a spoiled snot-nosed brat."

"Let's put him aside. I want to work this out so you're satisfied. How old was your truck, and how many miles did it have on it?"

"It was a 1995 and had over seventy thousand miles."

"How about I replace it with a fully equipped Ford 150, and you get to pick out the color?"

"How about black on black?"

"You weren't injured in the wreck, were you?"

"No, but Bobby was, and he can't work."

"Hold on. Let's talk about you. No injuries?"

"No injuries for me, but I've been worried sick how we're going to pay our bills with just me working."

"Let's put Bobby aside for a second, okay? How about a new Ford 150 and $5,000 for you to release the boy, the dad, and the insurance company?"

"That would be fair if you were also fair with Bobby."

Morty turned to Bobby and asked, "How long does the doctor say you'll be in a cast?"

"Eight weeks, and then light work, no lifting for another eight weeks."

"So you're out of commission four months, right?"

"Yeah, at least."

"What's your hourly rate, and do you get much overtime?"

"Twelve dollars an hour and four or five hours a week at time and a half."

Morty did the math on a legal pad in front of the Deans. "$12 per hour x 40 hours= $480 per week; $16 per hour for overtime x 5 hours=$80 per week. That is $560 per week x 52 weeks per year=$$29,120."

Morty, still using a pen and paper, said, "Let's make it an even $30,000, a year's wages."

A new truck and $35,000 were more than they'd hoped for. Morty had the paperwork prepared by Bella right then and there. It was less than two pages in length. He told them, "Go pick out the truck, and let me know who to pay. After a few days, you can pick up your money."

They seemed satisfied and signed the documents.

"Let's say we celebrate. You boys like good cigars?"

Bobby spoke up, "Not sure we've ever had a good cigar."

Morty handed each one a Cuban, offered his clipper and lighter, and they both lit up.

"Say, how about blowing a little smoke in my direction."

The Dean boys obliged, and Morty was in heaven. After about fifteen minutes, the Dean boys left. The air in the room was filled with the smell of the cigars. Morty had a big smile on his face for more than one reason.

Bella went in and cleaned the ashtray and dusted the table. One or both of the brothers got ashes everywhere, and the room stunk.

Dan January arrived right on time. Davis had faxed him the signed document earlier in the day. Pleased to have avoided a long, dragged out fight, he told Davis he was ready to move on with his life.

Under Tennessee law, a divorce decree was not final for ninety days if the divorcing couple had children. Any other order under Tennessee law was final, depending on the nature of the order, in either ten or thirty days. The logic behind the longer time period of the ninety-day rule for a divorce decree was to give the parents of children ninety days to reconcile and request that the court rescind the order. On rare occasions couples had reconciled, and marriages had been saved.

Both Davis and January knew this marital dissolution agreement wouldn't be rescinded. Neither January nor Rachel was willing to take the other one back. During the ninety days, January would continue to live in the house, and he'd maintain the visitation as the order provided. Getting the title to the property and receiving payment of the $800,000 would occur on the ninety-first day.

In an effort to make small talk, Davis asked, "How do you like solo practice?" Bad question. He hit a nerve.

"It's hard. You've got to get the business, and if you don't collect, you don't eat. I preferred a firm where I was fed work, and if I got a new client, it was a bonus."

Davis appreciated what he was saying. Twenty years ago, fresh out of law school, he started to build his own practice, but fortunately for him, he had the crutch of Morty, who could feed him work and provide Davis with credibility by association. January, divorced from Rachel, fired by Tyree Sinclair, had an uphill battle. The promise of $800,000 made life and the practice of law a lot easier.

After January left, Morty came in and told Davis his success in resolving the civil case against young Mr. Sasser. While they were together, they called Sr. and broke the good news.

"Total cost to you is $15,000, the cost of a rental car, and our fee. Your insurance company is picking up the rest. More important we won't have the Dean boys complaining to the DA's office that justice wasn't served."

Sasser was obviously pleased, but he was still concerned about the criminal charges. "What about that young DA? She seemed pretty pissed off the other day."

"Don't worry about General Sue Beck. I plan on going over her head to one or more of the senior DAs to cut Dickie's deal."

"Do you think he'll get any jail time?" the older Sasser asked in a shaky voice.

"Dick, I'll do my best, and most of the time, that's good enough."

"Morty, you need to understand something about Dickie. He's not your average twenty-three-year-old. His IQ is 178. That's high genius level. He's writing software that is scaring people. He's scaring certain people in our government. Most people don't understand what he's capable of doing, but the NSA is concerned that foreign governments will kidnap him and turn him against our vital national interests. I don't know whom to trust. I've been talking to Bill Gates. He doesn't trust the NSA either.

"I don't think you realize what the NSA really is. It's the largest of the U.S. intelligence agencies. It was formed in 1953 by Truman, and its mission is to defeat terrorism at home and abroad. It's under the jurisdiction of the Defense Department. It has unlimited power and resources."

Sasser assured them that every one of his calls was being listened to and recorded. "I want the NSA to know that I trust you and Ben. I may need your counsel to deal with it at a later date."

"Ben and I will be there if you need us, and in case they're listening, we're not afraid of them."

"Morty, thanks a million."

Davis was surprised that Sasser would speak so openly about the NSA not being afraid of Steine, Davis, & Davis, ignoring the need for a warrant, and being quite willing to invade Sasser's privacy. Several years ago Steine, Davis, & Davis had defeated the U.S. government in a highly publicized litigation involving Sasser Industries and the Israeli government. Criminal charges were brought against the company and Sasser individually and then later dropped. Bad feelings still existed on both sides, and Sasser didn't want his son working for the Feds in any capacity.

Davis commented, "Morty Steine never ceases to amaze me. I learn something from him almost every day. I look forward to seeing you on Saturday at my son Jake's Bar Mitzvah. I'm leaving the office in just a few to pick up my parents at the airport. They're coming in for the festivities."

Sasser had been so preoccupied with his own son's predicament that he'd forgotten this was a big weekend for his attorney and his family.

"A rite of passage to manhood. What do you people say? Mazel Tov?"

"We'll make a good Jew out of you yet, Dick."

With that the call ended.

Davis turned to Morty and said, "Sammie's going with me to the airport. She can't wait to see her grandparents. She's staying at the house this weekend. I'd offer to have you stay, but with three extra people in the house, it's bound to get crowded."

"Quite frankly, the last few days have been exciting, but I'm a bit worn out. I think I'll go back to the sixth floor, have a Jack, and finish my book. I've only got sixty or so pages left. Tomorrow I'll go out to Squeeze Bottom and spend the night and then join the family at Temple on Saturday. If I drink too much at the party Saturday night, Sammie can drive us back downtown."

"You've had a busy week. Take it easy. If you need anything else, give me a call. I'm only a car ride away."

"Enjoy the time with your parents. I'm sure next week will be full of surprises."

Davis thought, *I bet you're right, as usual.*

CHAPTER THIRTY-SEVEN

FRIDAY NIGHT DINNER

July 2, 1999

Larry and Shelly Davis flew into Nashville on a rainy Thursday night from Islip, New York, a small airport near their home on Long Island. It wasn't easy for Davis to convince his father to leave his three dry cleaning stores for several days. The elder Davis's other son, George, Sammie's father, accompanied his parents on the flight so he could attend his nephew's Bar Mitzvah. The businesses were left in the hands of three very capable managers for the duration. Nevertheless, Davis's father still worried. He called the shops multiple times each day, driving the poor women managers crazy.

Friday night Sabbath dinner was usually a special night at the Davis house because the family would light candles and say the blessings over the wine and bread. When she was alive, Goldie hosted the dinners at the Steines' home. After her death, Morty frequently ate at the Davises. Sammie tended to have a date or plans with friends most Friday nights.

This Friday was especially important because it was the eve of Jake's Bar Mitzvah and because of the presence of extended family, Larry, Shelly, and George Davis. Liza cooked an early dinner so the family could attend services at the Temple. The family had been asked to participate in the service, and the rabbi planned on introducing Jake to the congregation, since the next day by tradition he was becoming a man and thereby becoming a member of the Temple, no longer just a youth member through his parents.

It could not have been a more delicious meal. Liza made her mother-in-law's famous Swedish meatballs, creamy mashed potatoes, and honey-glazed carrots with large plump raisins. The compliments just kept on coming from the guests. The food was actually very good and the compliments genuine, but even if they weren't, the Davises would have complimented her anyway. The Davises loved their converted Gentile daughter-in-law, who without hesitation raised their two grandchildren Jewish. To them, she was a real mensch.

Despite his loud protests "that he really wasn't family," Morty was there for such an important life cycle event because he was family. Larry and Shelly weren't threatened by his relationship with their son. They saw it for what it was: very much like father and son but not quite. It actually had several dimensions, including that of parental.

Sammie and her father sat next to each other and caught up. They rarely saw each other, and with the others at the table, their conversation was limited to superficial matters. Their relationship had always been a little strained because of the divorce and George's drug use and alcoholism. Sammie's grandparents raised her, and she loved them dearly.

George was grateful that his parents were there for Sammie, as they were there for him. The four of them had a complex relationship, with George going in and out of rehabs, Sammie growing up with his parents, and George working in the family business when sober. George had been clean and sober almost ten years, and no one was more proud of him than his father. George would remind him that it was one day at a time.

There was a new addition at the table, Victor Browne. Sammie felt comfortable enough exposing the young man to her family. She hoped she hadn't made a mistake. The Davises were a lot to take in all at once, but Vic had already met everyone except her father and grandparents. Her aunt, uncle, and Morty were already big fans.

Liza had done quite a sales job on Nana Shelly. She said, "He's handsome and a true southern gentleman. He's a nurse, like me. He can take care of her when she's sick, and when they have children, he'll know exactly what to do to take care of them as well. He's a keeper."

At dinner Vic felt right at home and jumped in at every opportunity. He and Morty had an extensive conversation about the founding of Nashville. Larry Davis was impressed that Vic's distant relatives were part of the founding members of the city.

Vic wasn't a timid man, and he knew how to turn a woman's head and make a compliment. He said, "These meatballs are so pungent, how do you get them so sweet?"

Shelly answered for Liza, "That's a family secret, and you're not in the family yet."

Liza, as a supportive and respectful daughter-in-law, remarked, "I learned everything I know from Nana Shelly."

The grandfather turned to his oldest granddaughter, Sammie, and asked, "How about you? Have you inherited any of your Nana's talents? Can you cook?"

"Not a lick. I can't even boil water."

Everybody at the table laughed, much to the annoyance of the older Davis. "I wouldn't laugh. If you want to land a nice guy, you'll need to be able to cook."

Browne came to her defense, "I think she's perfect just the way she is. I wouldn't change a thing."

Shelly actually ruled the roost. She just let Larry think he was in charge. "Hush. What the heck do you know? Men will line up to marry this beauty," she said with the pride of a nana. "Her ability to cook is unimportant. That's why they invented restaurants and take-out."

Everybody laughed even harder.

After dinner, the family went to Temple, and the rabbi presented Jake to the congregation as the young man to be Bar Mitzvah at services tomorrow. Browne, who was raised with no religious affiliation, found the ceremony interesting. He whispered in Sammie's ear, "Fortunately for me, I'm already circumcised. I'm not sure you're worth that kind of sacrifice."

Sammie smiled at him and kissed his cheek.

The family sat in the first row. They were the center of attention for the evening. Vic whispered, "How often does your family go to services?"

Sammie didn't answer right away. She wasn't certain how she wanted to answer that question. She didn't want to appear too religious, nor did she want to appear irreligious. She and Vic had been going out six months and hadn't discussed religion once. He knew she was Jewish, and she knew he was Christian, but that was the extent of their exchange of information. They hadn't had a serious conversation about God or their other spiritual beliefs.

She finally answered, "We go less than six times a year. A few weekly services like this one, which we go to randomly, and then there are the two big holidays: Rosh Hashanah, the Jewish New Year, and Yom Kippur, the Day of Atonement. Those two we go to every year. Every Jew does. They're like the Super Bowl. We just can't miss those two. The crowd increases tenfold. We ask for forgiveness so we can start off the new year guilt free."

The rabbi's sermon was about mitzvots, helping others, asking the question of his flock, "Are you doing enough for your fellow man?" On reflection, Sammie felt good about herself. She and her uncle did quite a bit of pro bono work at Steine Davis, & Davis. Vic as a nurse also could positively consider the rabbi's challenge because he devoted his life to helping others.

After Temple there was a reception in the foyer where coffee, iced tea, soft drinks, cookies, and cake were served by the Temple Sisterhood. The members chatted before scattering.

Fifteen minutes later, George, Morty, Vic, and Sammie left the Temple for the ride downtown to their separate loft apartments. Vic went back to Sammie's apartment and had a serious talk with her about their future. He was willing to make a commitment, live together, and discuss marriage and a possible family.

He said, "I'd like to get married and have children. I'd consider converting to Judaism. I'd have to understand what's involved. I certainly wouldn't object to you raising our children Jewish. I love you. We don't have to answer these questions right away. I say we live together and see if we can get along. I've got some bad habits; you've got some bad habits, I'm sure. Those might be too much for both of us to handle, and we may have to go our separate ways. Then again we might find we can't live without each other. Shouldn't we find out? I think we should give it a try. We can live right here. You wouldn't even have to change your commute."

Sammie was unsure, but she did admit she loved him. "I've never felt like this about anyone else before. You've captured my heart, but marriage is for life. That's a long time. I don't want to wind up like my parents or so many of my clients, divorced and miserable. Fifty percent of people who marry get divorced. I know. I see them in court."

Vic wasn't discouraged because Sammie was thinking like a lawyer.

"Yeah, and the other fifty percent wind up like your grandparents and your uncle and aunt in love for their entire lives raising their families and making a good future for themselves and others. That's who'd we'd be. I'm sure of it deep in my heart. If you'd look down deep in yours, you'd see it too."

They hugged and agreed to continue the conversation. They had the entire weekend off, filled with family and festivities.

Back at the Davis house that night, no one could sleep. Jake kept practicing his Torah reading and his speech in front of the mirror. The older Davises stayed in the guest bedroom at the house. Davis and his father stayed up most of the night playing gin rummy, and the women went to bed. Everybody was up at dawn ready for the big day. Jake, calm as could be, tried to keep his mother under control. "What's the worst thing they can do? Drum you out of the religion? Remember, you're one of the chosen people."

The convert Liza didn't think that was funny.

Jake assured his mother, "It's going to be fine. I've got this. Don't worry. Morty drilled this stuff into me."

The twelve-year-old, soon to be thirteen-year-old, had the benefit of studying with a man who instilled such pride and confidence that whoever he touched moved forward with the heart of a lion, unafraid.

CHAPTER THIRTY-EIGHT

TAKE ME OUT TO THE BALL GAME

Saturday, July 3, 1999

Dan January came riding up the hill, just before eight, on a red Harley with Gaby in the sidecar on his right and Frankie in the sidecar on his left. The vehicle was a thing of beauty, and the sound of the Harley brought Rachel out of her studio. The bike perturbed her as it roared up the drive to a stop. Frankie removed his helmet, revealing a big smile on his face.

Gaby did the same and was giggling as she jumped from the sidecar and said, "Morning, Mommy, what do you think of Daddy's new motorcycle? Isn't it cool?"

"Very cool, honey. I like the color. Frankie, take your sister inside. I need to talk to your dad."

Frankie grabbed Gaby's hand and led his little sister inside the house. The two children skipped from the bike to the house. They obviously had a good morning with their dad.

When the children were out of earshot, Rachel turned on January, "Where do you come off letting our children ride on a motorcycle? I would think that would be something we'd agree to beforehand, not unilaterally."

The morning quiet was broken not by the roar of the motorcycle but by the tension of a bad marriage. The Januarys had more rematches than any two fighters in the history of the fight game, and they always went the distance and were bloody.

"You thought wrong. I don't need your permission for anything I do anymore. I'm a free man. Read the divorce papers. We're not married anymore. Besides they were riding in a sidecar, not on a motorcycle. Look, the kids are fine. We're fighting over nothing."

"What possessed you to purchase that thing?"

"I didn't purchase it. I got it in barter as part of a fee."

"What do you mean?"

"The client didn't have enough cash, so I took the bike in lieu of cash. When you're in solo practice, that happens. Seventy years ago, during the Depression, they'd pay a lawyer or a doctor with a chicken or a few potatoes. Now it's something a little fancier, but it's still barter."

"Who is the client?"

"None of your business."

January didn't want to share with Rachel that the bike was a partial retainer from the Wild Cats, a biker gang, for three members who'd been arrested for drug trafficking and were facing fifteen to twenty-five years. January got $9,999 in cash and the bike as a fee. He wouldn't be reporting either the cash or the bike on his tax return.

"I'm taking in the Sounds' doubleheader today with a client. What are your plans with the kids?" January's reference to a client was a little misleading. He was going to the game with the Wild Cats. The group planned on having a drunken brawl.

"No plans this morning. Tomorrow I'm taking them up to my father's office to watch the fireworks that will be shot off downtown."

"I get them tomorrow during the day. You do whatever the hell you want during your time with them. I don't give a rat's ass what you do. We're going to follow the decree to the letter. I'm off. I'll pick up the kids in the morning." He got on the bike and roared away.

Four hours later January and fifteen members of the Wild Cats were seated on the third base line of the Sounds stadium. They chugged beers two at a time. It was hot as hell, and with each beer, January complained louder and louder about Rachel to Chet, the leader of the Wild Cats. "She hated that beautiful machine you gave me."

"You're kidding me. What a bitch. How could she not love that beautiful machine?"

"She criticized me for letting my kids ride in those sidecars. My kids loved them."

"Those sidecars are as safe as baby carriages, man."

"I can't stand that woman. She needs to be taught respect for machinery."

January was beyond drunk. He'd reached the level of his drinking companions.

Chet stopped a young girl carrying a tray of large cups filled with beer. "I'll take the tray." He handed her a fifty. The pretty vendor started handing the Wild Cats their beers, including the three female Cats, who would later be passed around by the members. As the cups were being distributed, Chet turned to January, "She's not a reasonable person. You're lucky you're getting out of that marriage. Do you want me to set you up with some female companionship? That could be easily arranged."

January thanked him for his offer but assured him that he had that aspect of his life more than adequately covered. He wasn't going to be lonely tonight or any other night.

January finished his fifth beer, and Chet had the Sounds girl bring him another. The Wild Cats were living up to their reputation.

"I'll be rid of her soon enough." January gave Chet a hard stare, confirming his certainty.

Chet stared right back. He had been in prison twice. He knew how to return a hard stare. "It's good to have a plan."

January didn't know what he meant, but it sounded pretty good, so he let it slide.

In the box next to Chet, January, and two other Wild Cats sat Brad Littleton and his client Tommy Hamilton. Tommy did not sound any happier than January, "My mother isn't going to give me the money. These guys are going to kill me. I can't borrow the money from anywhere. I've got nothing left of value to sell or pawn. I'm desperate."

Littleton quietly said, "You owe them the money. If you go to the police, it's your word against theirs that they've threatened your life. "

"Well, we can wait until they kill me, and we'll have a good case against them. Then you can go to the police."

"I could draw up a note."

"These people aren't interested in partial payment."

Tommy was quiet a few moments. He was listening to January complain about how much he hated Rachel. He hated his mother as much or even more. "Maybe I need to skip town. I could get my allowance forwarded to another city. What if I played in smaller games, started winning, and built up a nest egg. Say only in five-dollar, ten-dollar games?"

Littleton started laughing. "Tommy, you crack me up. You think you could really start playing in nickel and dime games? Get real. Part of the thrill that you seek is that you can lose more than you can afford. In your case, your monthly allowance is $10,000. That means to live dangerously, you have to lose thousands, even tens of thousands, for you to get hurt. No, you couldn't go back to playing small time."

Tommy took a different approach, "Maybe, I could start winning?"

Littleton started laughing uncontrollably. "Tommy, you are not only a degenerative gambler but a bad gambler. I'm told you have so many tells that even the worst gambler can beat you. Forget it. Your luck will never change."

Dan January was now listening to Littleton's and Tommy's conversation. He finished his sixth beer and ordered another.

Tommy excused himself to go to the restroom. A minute later, January turned to Chet and did the same. The two men stood next to each other and shared their problems as they relieved themselves in the urinals. Then they returned together to their respective parties.

CHAPTER THIRTY-NINE

A BEAUTIFUL SERVICE AND A HELL OF A PARTY

Saturday, JULY 3, 1999

The Saturday morning service began with the rabbi greeting the congregation and announcing that today Jacob Albert Davis would be reading from the Torah and become a Bar Mitzvah. His grandparents Larry and Shelly Davis were invited up from their place in the audience to the bema, where the immediate family sat with the rabbi and the cantor in front of the congregation to recite the traditional blessing.

After Larry nervously said the prayer, the two New Yorkers returned to their front-row seats next to Morty, Sammie, Victor, and George. George as Jake's uncle was next up and presented the young man with his tallit, his traditional prayer shawl. The garment was white with blue stripes at the ends with fringes. George returned to his seat, and Jake was now prepared to begin his journey to manhood.

Jake, who studied for more than six months under first the careful eyes of the cantor and then the additional guidance of Morty, was magnificent. His Hebrew chanting was far from flawless in either pronunciation or tone, but his delivery was poised. It took about twenty minutes for him to complete that portion of his presentation. After he delivered his Torah portion and the Holy Scriptures were put back in the ark, he addressed the congregation in English. He thanked the congregation for witnessing his becoming a man.

"When I woke up this morning, and I took a shower, I looked down and noticed I didn't have any more hairs on my chest than the day before nor did I have any more hairs anywhere else on my body."

That got big laughs from the crowd. Jake's mother, slightly embarrassed, looked over at his father, who just smiled. Morty had added that line to the speech.

The young man talked about the responsibility of becoming a man and a member of the Temple and the responsibility of being a member of the community. He tied his speech to the rabbi's sermon as to the importance of mitzvot, helping others.

"As part of our tradition, I will be receiving gifts from my guests today in celebration of my Bar Mitzvah. I want to thank those guests ahead of time for their generosity. Those gifts will come in the form of cash, checks, and other material things. If any of you gave me a sports car . . ."

Jake paused for effect. "I hate to inform you I'm not even thirteen years old, and I won't be getting my learner's permit for another two years. But if anyone has elected to give me a sports car as a wonderful gift, I will accept it and park it in my dad's garage until I'm old enough to drive. I prefer blue, but any color except green will be acceptable. Seriously, as an act of mitzvot, I plan on donating all of the money I receive to the Jewish National Fund. I hope you recognize that this action in no way is in disrespect of my guests, but honors their generosity to me."

Jake returned to the theme that this life cycle event coincided with his becoming a man. "I'm only a few hours older, yet in the eyes of my religion and my God, today I went from a boy to a man. I actually feel different. To my parents I'm still their little boy. Let's face it, there hasn't been a miracle. The Red Sea hasn't parted or anything."

Big laugh from the crowd; another line provided by Morty. Jake looked over at his parents, and he could see the pride on their faces. He smiled and continued his speech for another fifteen minutes.

"I'd also like to thank the rabbi and cantor for their guidance through this process. Sure I've been coming here for years, Sunday school, Hebrew school, and family services, but I was part of the Davis family. Now Jacob Albert Davis is a member of the Temple that accepts me as a man."

Jake looked over at the rabbi and the cantor, each of whom gave him an approving nod.

"I want to acknowledge that I'm named after a gentleman, Albert Wilson, whom I never met, but I'm told he was a great man respected by my parents and by a family friend Morty Steine. I wish he could be here today to see me and share this day. I know his wife, Mary, is in the audience."

Mary Wilson was sitting next to Morty and squeezed his hand at the mention of Albert's name.

"I'd like to thank my Uncle Morty Steine, who drilled me on my Torah portion. Without him I'd still be stumbling around up here trying to finish. He kept pushing me, giving me confidence, and telling me that not only I would get through this day but that I would shine."

Morty whispered to Mary, "The boy's a natural. He's got his father's innate abilities. We'll make a lawyer of him yet."

"I'd also like to mention my sister, Caroline. My parents said I had to say something nice about her, and I always listen to my parents." Jake made a contorted face, and the audience went wild.

"Well, maybe not all of the time, but they are throwing me a lavish party after this service, so I'm no idiot. I have the sweetest sister God ever put here on earth. Actually, we get along pretty well. We like the same music, the same movies, and the same television shows. That allows us to spend a lot of time together late at night after we finish our homework. Well, I might not always have gotten my homework finished."

Jake looked at his parents for a sign of support, and then he looked up toward the heavens. "That should satisfy them, right? It has a touch of honesty."

Caroline didn't look very happy. She obviously felt the brunt of the joke.

Again the crowd broke up. He had them.

"I'm a very lucky guy. My parents have given my sister and me everything two children could want. We live in a beautiful house and have been given an excellent education in a loving home. My mother, a nurse, and my father, a lawyer, have spent their lives helping others. They have set an example for my sister and me of how to treat others. If my father has taught me one thing, which he attributes to his old friend and mentor Morty Steine, and I intend to follow as my guiding creed for the rest of my life, it is to try to do the right thing."

"Immediately following the service my parents invite you to a luncheon here at the Temple. Later tonight at seven, my parents invite you to our home at 23 Robin Lane to celebrate my becoming a Bar Mitzvah. There will be food, and I'm told an open bar. We'll have live music, and at approximately ten o'clock courtesy of Hillwood Country Club, there will be fireworks. Please join us and share this important day with us."

On that note Jake sat down. The service ended quickly.

The luncheon consisted of an assortment of bagels, various cream cheeses, lox, chicken, tuna, and egg salads. There were all sorts of baked goods and a coffee bar.

Later that evening the guests began to arrive at the Davis home. The parking attendants shuttled the cars to a nearby community tennis parking area. The men were dressed in tuxedos and the women in evening dresses, all in their Sunday best. The Davis family greeted their guests at the door.

"Hello, Your Honor." Davis shook the hand of Judge Paul Billingsly and then his wife.

Next in line were his court officer Winnie Bray and her husband. "Hello, Ben, you must be so proud of Jake."

There wasn't time for much conversation between guests.

"Couldn't be more proud."

Howard Longfellow and his wife, Denise, followed. Longfellow was the commercial pilot whose license Davis had saved.

Caroline felt out of place. It wasn't her party. She asked, "Can I get out of this line and blend into the crowd with the other guests?"

Davis answered before his wife could, "No, the last time I checked, you were still part of this family, and if I'm not mistaken, you still want to be. You'll remain and continue to greet our guests."

After all three hundred guests had arrived, the family started to mingle as the hors d'oeuvres were served. There were pigs in a blanket, little potato pancakes, smoked salmon with cream cheese on crackers, and shrimp served by waiters.

An eight-piece band with two female singers played all types of music: rock and roll, Motown, hip hop, and pop. The Davises had tented the part of their backyard near the swimming pool, and dozens of tables were set up there.

It was one helluva of a party. The food was served in stations. There were three carving stations: turkey, roast beef, and tenderloin. There was a station of sushi, one of poached salmon, and one of varied side dishes including squash casserole, stuffed potatoes, glazed carrots, and several others. A keg of beer and an open bar were set up.

Most guests overate, and some got drunk. Everybody had a good time.

At Jake's insistence, Morty was forced on stage and sang the Rolling Stone classic, "Under My Thumb," which he dedicated to Albert Wilson. He sang two other songs: "Bell Bottom Blues" and "Yesterday," which he dedicated to Peter Nichols, the other member of his band, Third Coast, and the last to his beloved Goldie. The old man could sing the blues.

"Hello, Rita," said Davis as he grasped her hands between his two large paws. "How's Rachel doing?"

"Not good. She may have signed all the documents you asked, but she's not right in the head. I tried to get her to come tonight. I thought it would be a good thing for her to be around people. She's very paranoid. She doesn't trust me." Between sobs, "I had hoped that Sammie might talk to her. Rachel seems to like and respect her."

It was hard to look at this loving mother in so much pain. Davis assured her that Sammie would do what she could, but Rachel needed psychiatric help. "What does Dr. Ames say?"

"I've never spoken to her. All my information comes from Tyree. He talks in generalities, not specifics."

"Maybe you should sit down with Dr. Ames . . ." Davis stopped mid-sentence when his father interrupted the conversation.

"Larry Davis. I'm this reprobate's father."

Davis completed the introduction. Rita took the older Davis

by the arm and said, "Mr. Davis, we don't know each other, but I admire both you and your wife. You've raised an incredible son. Not only is he a great lawyer. I suspect I need to give Morty Steine credit for that virtue. Your son has compassion, and that comes from you. He's a great person."

The New Yorker, momentarily lost for words, finally said, "Thank you, you're too kind. I suspect my wife, Shelly, deserves more of the credit than I do."

It was an awkward exchange. Davis moved the conversation along by saying, "Rita and I have worked on several charitable committees, and she's married to a prominent attorney, Tyree Sinclair."

The father excused himself, and Davis turned to Rita. "I'll have Sammie call Rachel tomorrow."

They parted company, and Davis rejoined his father. "You know, son, I have appreciative clients when I remove a difficult stain, but none of them talk about me like that. You should be proud of yourself, and I suspect Morty deserves more of the credit than your mother and me."

Davis didn't know what to say. "Sammie will exceed me in ability and character. Morty's got the time to spend with her that he didn't have for me."

Larry's response was quiet. "I guess I owe Morty Steine more than I realized."

The younger Davis quickly responded, "I guess we all do."

The fireworks exploded in the sky. Father and son stood there looking up, mesmerized by the color, listening to the loud booms of thunder. Sparks landed near and around them. One landed on top of the older Davis's balding head, singeing his scalp, "Holy shit!" he yelped.

"It's a problem every year. We've got to keep an eye on the kids and the tree line."

During the big finale, the father commented, "It's beautiful. You're a lucky man. What a great place to raise your family. I couldn't be more proud of you, son."

The two men hugged and then kissed. It was a Kodak moment.

Victor put his arm around Sammie and drew her close. "This has been a glorious night. I love you and want to spend the rest of my life with you."

"You sound pretty sure of yourself. I can be pretty stubborn and pigheaded."

"That may be one of your more endearing qualities, according to your aunt."

"So you've been talking to my aunt Liza about me, have you?"

"You bet. We've become allies. She's rooting for me. She wants love to prevail. She's a smart lady."

Then the couple joined the rest of the family on the dance floor. The party lasted until 2:00 a.m. It was a night to remember. A photographer and a videographer preserved it all, including the fireworks. Davis would cherish that video for the rest of his life.

CHAPTER FORTY

A FAMILY GATHERING

Sunday, July 4, 1999

The Davis family woke slightly hung over but happy. The party had been an enormous success, and now all Liza wanted to do was rest. She'd been an entertaining relative for the last three days, and she was tired. But Sunday morning came, and they were still here.

"Morning, Larry," she said as she stumbled down to get her first cup of coffee. She looked out her kitchen window and saw the fifteen workmen preparing to tear down the tent and removing the tables and chairs. Her backyard looked like a war zone, and it looked like the Davises had lost the war.

Nana Shelly clumped down the stairs followed by the Bar Mitzvah boy. "What's for breakfast?"

Liza, normally calm, was about to lose it. The stress of her in-laws, Jake's life cycle event and a few glasses of champagne had caught up with her. She said, "How about you grab a glass of milk and a donut? I'll wake your father and sister, and we'll all go out for brunch. I think I'd prefer to go out rather than cook breakfast." She wasn't kidding.

She quickly went upstairs and kicked Davis out of bed. "Rise and shine and give God his glory," she sang in his ear.

Davis got up slowly, and a short, but direct conversation transpired, which resulted in his calling the beverage manager of the Opryland Hotel, a client, who arranged for a table for ten at ten thirty for its famous and extensive brunch. Davis then called Sammie, woke her and Victor, asked her to wake her father and Morty, and meet them at the hotel for brunch.

"Victor and I had planned a quiet day alone."

"Well, unplan your quiet day together. Your family is in town, and you'll be entertaining them. You have an obligation. Your father and grandparents are in town. They leave tomorrow, you and Vic will have plenty of time to talk about your future together, but right now your aunt needs your help entertaining these relatives. Any ideas?"

Sammie paused a moment and then responded, "How about taking them up to the roof tonight and watching the fireworks?"

"I think we've had enough fireworks after last night."

Sammie came right back, "I've got it, a fish fry. After the brunch, let's go out to Squeeze Bottom and try our luck on Lake Dear. If we catch something, we'll cook them. If we have no luck, Vic and I will run out and buy hamburgers and hot dogs, and we'll grill out."

Sammie was suggesting that the group go out to Morty's farm and try to catch their dinner and then fry up the catfish. The lake was well stocked. Jake on a fairly regular basis accompanied the old man on such expeditions, but it would be a first for the New Yorkers, Larry and George Davis.

The brunch was delicious. As usual Davis overate. The meal, like the Bar Mitzvah party, was served by stations. The ones in the hotel were broken down ethnically. There were an Italian station, a Chinese station, a Greek station, a French station, and a seafood station. During the meal, the beverage manager visited the table to make sure that everything was satisfactory.

After the meal, the family toured the hotel, which was the second largest hotel in the United States. After forty minutes, Morty announced, "The fish aren't going to wait. Let's get going."

George and his father weren't as keen as Morty about the idea of catching their dinner. These men were used to ordering their lunch in and having one of their employees bring it to them during the day and having dinner served to them at night. The thought of having to catch supper was alien.

"Are you sure this is a good idea?" asked George.

"Come on, Dad," urged Sammie. "It will be fun. Give it a chance. Worst case, you'll catch nothing and eat a hot dog."

They left the hotel and all drove out to Squeeze Bottom.

Funny thing they had a great time. Morty had on hand plenty of beer, and Larry elected to overindulge. Not wanting to be left behind, Morty joined him. As a group, they caught four fish, not enough to feed all of them. The menu changed to hamburgers and hot dogs.

After the meal they made a big bonfire and roasted marshmallows and made s'mores. Morty pulled out his guitar and started leading them in song. He had a strong voice, but Larry Davis sounded like a bullfrog. Morty led the group, his ties to the Third Coast shining through. Sammie, Jake, Liza, and Morty sang an old Mamas and Papas song, "California Dreaming." A tear rolled down Davis's face. He wiped it away before anyone could see. He was very proud of his family, and they knew it. They didn't have to see him cry to know that.

Davis's cell phone rang, interrupting the intimate exchange. It was Maureen Wagner, Martha Keller's stepdaughter. "Mr. Davis, I hate to disturb you on a holiday, but I don't want to beat around the bush. Martha's dead."

Talk about getting right to the point. This lady doesn't mess around. Shocked, he'd seen her less than a week ago. He choked out, "How?"

"We don't know. We found her at the bottom of the stairs. Her neck was broken. She was supposed to meet us for dinner. We came over to check on her and found her dead. The police are here at the house. They want to take our statements. What should we do?"

Davis's client was dead. Reluctantly, but realizing his services might be needed, he offered, "If you don't have your own attorney and want my help, I can be there in thirty minutes."

As the words came out of his mouth, he realized he'd made a mistake. *Liza will kill me for leaving her high and dry with the family.* It wouldn't be the first or the last time he'd be in trouble. Trouble was his middle name. Well, actually, Abraham was his middle name, but trouble sounded more exciting.

He returned to reality and digested Maureen's response. "I know Martha trusted you. We're pretty shaken up. Your help would be greatly appreciated."

Davis explained to Liza he'd have to leave and asked Sammie to accompany him. Morty had a little too much beer to be of much help. Surprisingly Liza understood. That may have been a result of her being a doctor's daughter and accepting the concept of a professional emergency. Victor also was very understanding. Larry was too drunk to appreciate what was happening.

Davis explained to Sammie what happened as they drove to Martha Keller's house. When they arrived, they found several police cars and an ambulance. Two uniformed officers met them at the door.

"We're Mrs. Keller's lawyers."

"Who's Mrs. Keller?"

Annoyed, Davis blurted out, "The deceased."

They entered the dining room where the family was seated around the table: Martha Keller's son, Tommy, her stepdaughter Maureen Wagner and her husband, Robert, and her sister Betty Andrews and her husband, Sam. Davis knew all of them. He'd represented Martha Keller's second husband, Stanley Keller. The group looked somber.

"You'd be the lawyers?" The question came from the female detective, Sharon Duncan. Over six feet in heels, the thirty-something female lawman was taller than Davis. She had an Amazon quality to her. "Names."

"I'm Ben Davis, and this is my partner, Sammie Davis. What's the timeline?"

"911 called 9:45 by Maureen Wagner, who reported finding the dead body. The first officers arrived on the scene at 9:58. I arrived at 10:09. You two arrived at 10:18. I was told that you were on your way and that the family wanted to wait for you before they were questioned. So sit down and let me do my job."

Davis and Sammie joined the others at the table.

Maureen explained that the family had made plans to eat dinner at Sperry's, a local steakhouse. Reservations were for 8:00. Everybody arrived on time, except Martha. By 8:30, they became concerned and tried to reach her by telephone. When she failed to answer, they assumed she fell asleep or forgot about the dinner.

It was obvious that Tommy was drunk. They could smell the beer from ten feet away. When he spoke, his speech was slurred. The Wagners and Andrews had driven together, and the four of them discovered the body. Maureen's second call after 911 was to Tommy, who rushed over in a cab, or Duncan would have arrested him for DUI.

Duncan looked at the other members of the family, and asked, "Anybody have anything to add?"

Everybody remained silent, so Davis asked a question, "Any evidence of forced entry?"

Duncan looked at Davis hard. She didn't want to share any details with the family yet. "We're checking on it."

Tommy, who'd moved away from the table and was sitting by himself away from the others, slumped into an armchair. He commented, "She never locked the door. You just walked in the house, day or night."

The others confirmed the lack of security. Concerned about what Tommy might say or do next in his drunken state, Davis offered, "Detective Duncan, I think the family has shared their knowledge of what they know about the events of tonight, may I suggest . . ."

"Sir, this is my investigation, and I'm going to conduct it the way I see fit. I don't need any help."

Davis's patience had been tested. He was going home, and the Keller family wasn't going to be questioned any further. What was the point? Martha was dead. Either her killer was out there, or she fell down the stairs and broke her neck. Either way, this asshole was wasting everyone's time and annoying the hell out of him.

"You're welcome to conduct whatever investigation you want. Since Mrs. Keller never locked her door, you can leave the door unlocked on your way out. These people lost a mother and stepmother tonight. They're tired and grief stricken. They're going home. If you'd like their addresses and telephone numbers, they'd be happy to supply them. Here's my card. You really need to work on your people skills."

Davis rose. Sammie followed as well as the family, and without another word, the group walked out, leaving Duncan sitting at the table. Davis had to support Tommy as they left the room. Since Tommy came in a cab, the stepsisters and their husbands had to give him a ride. Davis certainly wasn't going to give the drunk a ride home. He was pissed at Tommy, he was pissed at Duncan, and he was pissed at himself.

Sammie whispered to Davis, "I don't think you made a friend."

Davis responded, I already have enough friends."

CHAPTER FORTY-ONE

THE COPS DO THEIR JOB

Monday, July 5, 1999

The problem with a long weekend is that you pay for it on the back end. Davis was late into the office after taking his parents and George to the airport. He passed Bella's desk, and as he did, he squeaked out a "hello." Although she and her family had been at the Bar Mitzvah, Davis, because of his commitments, had barely acknowledged her at the party while he mingled with his other guests. He knew she'd understand. Like Morty, she was family, and they'd have a lifetime to relive and talk about the big day when they got back to the office.

"Jake was magnificent. I couldn't have been more proud of him if he'd been my own flesh and blood. You must be exhausted, entertaining your parents and brother all weekend. How'd Victor hold up? Did he make the cut with Nana Shelly? Sammie was so worried. I told her not to, but I know she did."

"He was a resounding success. We all spent the entire weekend together, and he didn't blink, and neither did they. If he'd have her and she'd have him, there will be no objection from New York."

Bella was relieved. Although the Davises had completely accepted their southern daughter-in-law, she didn't know if lightning would strike twice without a fire. But obviously those Yankees learned that a little southern charm was more than a good thing.

Davis looked at his longtime secretary, trying to figure out what the hell she was thinking. Apparently she and Sammie, prior to the holiday weekend, spent considerable time discussing his family dynamics and trying to figure out whether Victor Browne would fit in.

It was hard to describe Davis's relationship with Bella Rosario. When they met, she knew the ropes, and he knew nothing. A first-year Vandy law student fresh off the boat from New York, he practically spoke a foreign language. He certainly knew nothing about the law. She, along with Morty, trained him. Over time Davis, a quick learner, earned her respect, and she provided guidance and helped hone his skills. Now they were true colleagues, and Davis didn't lord over her his license and his name on the letterhead. He emphasized that they were a team that needed to get the job done.

"Jake was amazing again."

"He takes after his mother."

"Baloney. There's more of you in that kid than you'd like to admit. He looked very natural up there. Maybe we've got another Davis to add to the firm name."

"The old man deserves most of the credit. He schooled Jake in Hebrew and English. Our houseguest was relentless, and a real bond developed between them."

"It paid off. The kid was poised."

She handed him his messages, and he asked her to bring him a cup of black coffee.

Standing behind his desk, he started sorting the message slips. He gave up trying to organize and just picked one. Bella handed him his coffee, and he dialed. He burned his lip and let out a curse just as Bill O'Mara answered his phone.

"I know I'm not your best client, but I don't deserve being cursed at."

"Sorry, burned my lip on coffee."

"Great party. I couldn't find you to say good-bye. My grandkids loved the fireworks."

"Glad to hear that. We were so pleased to see the people who came. Life has been busy with the Bar Mitzvah and relatives in town. Then yesterday, I had an emergency. Martha Keller died Sunday night."

Davis didn't feel compelled by confidentiality. The news would be in the paper today or tomorrow at the latest.

"How'd she die?"

"Not sure, found at the bottom of the stairs."

"I'm sure the kids are broken up, but at least Tommy will be able to pay his gambling debts. Boy, he's a bad poker player."

Davis's antenna went up. Tommy Hamilton had been a screw-up his entire life. Davis wasn't surprised that he'd racked up gambling debts. He subtly started cross-examining his friend and client. How do you know Tommy owes money?"

"I play in two games a week with him: one at my club and the other at the marina. There are at least five guys holding paper on him in those two games, and I'm one of them. He really has one of the worst poker faces I've ever played with. His nervous tick gives him away every time."

Davis hesitated before asking, "How much does he owe you?"

"Five grand to me. He must owe at least another twenty-five among four or five other guys. It's impacted on his reputation; he's not well liked. Everybody knows he's on a pretty hearty allowance paid on the first, so those holding his markers collect as much as they can on the first, and then extend him more credit causing Tommy to go further into debt. I think the allowance is ten grand a month. Now his allowance can't cover half his debt, so at this point he can't sit down in our games because he's exhausted his credit. No one will play with him until he pays off all of his debts. People are looking for him. He needs to start making payments. I understand because the country club set has refused to play with him that he's taken to playing with a rougher crowd. They see his monthly allowance and his tick as an easy mark. When he gets behind with them, they'll be a lot less understanding than some dentist from the country club."

That little shit. Maybe Martha knew about his gambling problem and didn't want the inheritance to go for that. Maybe I should have just done the codicil when she asked me.

Davis started feeling guilty for several reasons. First, he did not change Martha Keller's will immediately when she asked. Second, he interfered with the police investigation of the family, including Tommy Hamilton, who had a real motive, the need to pay off his gambling debts. *Holly shit.*

Changing the subject, he asked, "Bill, what can I do for you? I'm jammed after the holiday."

"I've got to go in for laparoscopic gallbladder surgery, and from what I remember, you know something about that surgery."

He sure did. He'd sued two doctors and a hospital in ten different suits for performing that surgery unnecessarily in Plainview, Tennessee. He spent three years of his life litigating those cases. The mere mention of them sent a shiver down his spine.

"Where and by whom are you having the surgery?"

"Dr. Petersen at Vanderbilt."

"Good doctor, good hospital. You'll be in the hospital one day and back at work, doing light duties in three days. Make sure you have it done before the 15th. That's the start of the new rotations, and everybody at a teaching hospital, like Vanderbilt, is new in the job and inexperienced. Good luck."

O'Mara's surgery was scheduled for the 11th. He should be all right.

As soon as Davis hung up, Bella buzzed in, "I've got Rita Sinclair on the phone. She sounds real upset."

"Okay, put her through." Davis took a sip of coffee. *Cold, goddamnit.* "Hi, Rita." Those were the only two words he got out.

Rita released a torrent of words: "She didn't come home last night, or maybe she did and she left early this morning. It's hard to tell. Her bed was made, but it always is. The window was open, but she does that sometimes."

Rita was rambling, and Davis was having trouble following. Using his courtroom voice, he said, "Take a deep breath and start from the beginning. Take your time and give me as much detail as possible."

"She didn't go with us to see the fireworks last night because she had a bad headache. When we picked up the kids at Dan's house, she decided to stay there, take a nap, and we were supposed to pick her up after the fireworks and all drive back to our house afterward. We returned to the January house just before eleven. No Rachel to greet us. We figured she went to bed, so we checked all the bedrooms. No Rachel. Dan got home a few minutes later. He had no idea of her whereabouts either. We brought the children back to our house for the night. She hadn't come home. I stuck my head in her room, and she wasn't in bed. I didn't look at the pillow. Dan remained at his house and reported around twelve that she had not returned. He swung by this morning and said he went to bed around one. I don't know whether she came home or not."

"What do you mean?"

"Well, there was a note left on Rachel's pillow. It said, 'I'm leaving, take care of Frankie and Gaby.'"

Davis didn't know what to say. What he said next could shatter the fragile state of Rita Sinclair, and that would do nobody any good.

"Rita, Rachel rightfully is depressed because of Dan's conduct and the divorce. It's a lot for a young mother to handle. She knows she can rely on you and Ty to take care of her children. She needs a break away from all this. She'll come back to reality and to her responsibilities. You and Ty brought her up right. "

The truth seemed to ease the poor woman.

Davis started acting like a lawyer and asked, "Are you sure that the handwriting is Rachel's?"

"I can't tell. It was block printed. Rachel has such beautiful handwriting. Why would she block print? I don't believe she wrote the note. She just wouldn't get up and leave. She loves her children."

"Who has the note?"

"Dan does."

Why the hell would Dan have the note? They should have left it on the pillow undisturbed.

Davis thought about that a moment and then advised, "Rita, there's not much we can do until Rachel's been gone twenty-four hours. It takes that long before the police will declare her a missing person. I suggest you call some of her friends and maybe check the hospitals."

Davis regretted that remark the moment he said it. "I'm sure everything's fine." The mother was sobbing.

Trying to ease her pain, Davis suggested, "I'll call Dr. Ames to see if Rachel called her."

"Would you?"

"After I've spoken to her, I'll report back."

Davis walked out of his office into Sammie's. "Have you spoken to Rachel January?"

Sammie looked up. She was reading a brief. "I'm struggling with this Redman brief. Bob Sullivan's a really smart man, who knows how to think outside the box."

Davis interrupted. He didn't care about the Redman brief. "Did you call Rachel January like I asked you to do?"

"I've been playing catch-up all morning. I planned on calling at the end of the day . . ."

"She's gone."

"What do you mean gone?"

"She didn't come home last night or maybe she did."

He went through the tale, providing as much detail as he had.

"She left a note, or at least Rita thinks that someone left a note for her."

Sammie hesitated and then asked, "What did the note say?"

"I've not read it, but it sounded like she'd had enough and was saying good-bye to the kids."

"Who has the note?"

"According to Rita, conveniently, Dan January. "What do you think happened?"

Sammie speculated, "She's depressed, had a few drinks, met someone, lost track of time and forgot about her kids and her problems for a short time. Everybody has to escape from problems. Can you really blame her? The kids are safe. She's blowing off a little steam. Give her a day or two. She'll be back. She's a mother first."

That's certainly a possibility, Davis conceded.

Davis went back to his office and called Dr. Ames. He had to leave a message. "Please call me back, 373-2047."

Davis convinced himself that Sammie was probably right. Rachel slipped into her old habits. He went back to work. He made call after call without giving Rachel another thought.

Sammie dropped her first draft of the Redman brief on his desk. "It still needs a lot of work. Tell me what you think."

Ignoring the phone, Davis read Sullivan's brief first and then

Sammie's response. He liked the other side's position better. He put his feet up on his desk and leaned back in his chair. He actually took a moment to think. The practice of law moved so quickly that he rarely took the time he should have to think through the problems he faced every day.

While he sat there, it came to him, the flaw in Sullivan's brief. It wasn't obvious, but it was there. He took Sammie's response and wrote feverishly. As he did, he recognized another issue that needed to be raised. He was pretty excited and proud. *It's amazing what you're capable of if you just stop and take a breath.*

He stood there while Sammie read his notes. A big smile came across her face. It was contagious. He smiled too. She came from around her desk and gave him a hug.

"Brilliant. Sullivan won't know what hit him. Good move."

Back in his office Davis took a mental victory lap.

Bella buzzing in startled him. "I've got Tyree Sinclair on line two."

"Ty, is she back?"

Silence and then Sinclair choked out, "Not even a phone call. She's not this irresponsible. Something's wrong. Help me."

"You last saw her at seven last night. Meet me at the main police station behind the courthouse at seven. The police won't do anything for twenty-four hours, so let's make our report one minute after that deadline expires."

Davis hadn't seen Morty all day, so he walked down the stairs to the sixth floor. He knocked and then used his key. The old man was asleep in his chair. Davis lovingly nudged his shoulder.

Morty woke slowly. "I was dreaming that the Third Coast was jamming with B.B. and Albert King. It was fantastic. Peter and Albert were there."

Morty was the last surviving member of a memorable blues trio, Third Coast. Morty missed the music, and he certainly missed his old friends, both deceased.

Davis filled him in on the disappearance of Rachel January.

He suggested, "You might call Dan January to see if he's seen her. He'll be the first person the police contact. Remember the order's not final. Technically Dan is still her husband."

Davis pulled his cell phone out and called January. He hadn't heard from Rachel. Davis asked for a list of people she might have contacted if she left of her own volition. Davis told January that they were meeting Sinclair at the police station, and that he could expect a call or a visit.

The two men walked up Printer's Alley and five minutes later were standing in front of the duty sergeant's desk and making their report.

There was an exchange of information, and Sinclair provided a picture of Rachel. Questions about the divorce, her relationship with Dan January, and her therapy with Dr. Ames were discussed in confidence. These old friends knew how to keep secrets and had buried a few political bodies together. Did she have access to money? Had she made a large withdrawal recently? Did she have a boyfriend? The officer implied by his questions that Rachel disappeared because she wanted to disappear.

The report made, Morty turned to Sinclair and Davis and said, "I'm not sure we just accomplished a great deal. The police believe she ran away. We better be proactive."

CHAPTER FORTY-TWO

STRAIGHT TO THE TOP

Tuesday, July 6, 1999

Morty waited till morning before he began his quest. He was a man on a mission, not like Don Quixote. More like President Kennedy's race to the moon. Unfortunately he had to work within the limitations of the system. The politicians he was calling didn't like to work at night. *Come to think of it, they didn't like working at all. It was a foreign concept unless there was some self-interest to gain.*

When seeking political favors, Morty knew he needed to use finesse. The first person he phoned was the chief of police. They played poker together for years, even though gambling in Tennessee was illegal. The chief was usually one of the big winners, so he was happy to participate in the game and usually didn't threaten to shut it down. He rationalized that gambling was a victimless crime, except for the big losers. Besides, two judges and the DA rotated in and out of the game, so, if charges were ever brought, you could always find a friendly ear to get them dismissed.

"Gerry, I need your help."

"Who's been arrested and needs to get out of jail?"

"Nothing like that. You know Tyree Sinclair?"

"Solid guy. I like him. Has always been supportive of law enforcement."

Morty described the situation. He shared with the chief the sordid details of Rachel's marriage to Dan January and her mental status. You told the entire story to Police Chief Gerry Neenan if you wanted his help. Half-truths were a bad idea, as bad as a lie. He wanted the facts, just the facts. He was a straight shooter.

"You've made your report. There's no evidence of a crime. It sounds like she ran away. She sounds like she's confused and depressed and in need of seeing her therapist, not the victim of any crime."

"Come on, Gerry. A mother is missing. She's going through a divorce. She's had several complex sexual problems with her husband. I want your department to open an investigation. Both Sinclair and I would be in your debt. We need you to light a fire under a couple of detectives and start looking for the woman. We don't want the trail to go cold. If she's run away, we'll figure that out pretty quickly, but if it's foul play, let's not lose time. Even if she's a runaway, her family needs her back. She's got two kids and parents who love her."

Neenan agreed he'd send two detectives to interview Dan January. Sinclair would organize volunteers to search the woods near Radnor Lake in the Forest Hills subdivision. Morty ended the call dissatisfied.

He called Sinclair, "Ty, it's time for you and Rita to call in every favor you've got. You've been pillars of the community for the last thirty years. Rita has been involved in fifteen charities. She's got to mobilize those different organizations. Employ a telephone tree system to get the word out. Give each person five names to call, and then let them call five other friends. It will stay light till about nine, so let's meet at the Granny White Market at two. We'll start again tomorrow at seven. Rachel likes to run around the lake. We need to start searching there."

"What exactly are we looking for?"

Morty didn't want to say Rachel's body, so he said, "Any evidence of Rachel's existence, a piece of her clothing or a witness who saw her that night. We need to flash around her picture."

Morty and Davis arrived at Granny White Market a bit late, having stopped off at the printer, which had donated a thousand color copies of Rachel's photograph, with the notation "Rachel January, Missing Since 7/4/99, Age 34, Call 424-9999." It was Rita's cell phone. She agreed to field calls. It was a good likeness. She was smiling, happier days.

Morty was amazed at the turnout. More than four hundred people were willing to look for Rachel. Morty assigned fifty volunteers to post the photos at local retailers and then on whatever they could in the residential neighborhoods. Fifty of the volunteers were sent to the Sinclairs' neighborhood in Green Hills. The team was still uncertain as to whether Rachel disappeared from the January house in Forest Hills or the Sinclairs' home in Green Hills. Even though the two neighborhoods were adjacent, that complicated the search. The balance of the force began looking in the woods around the lake. It was tedious work as they looked in the underbrush for the body of the young woman.

The Parks Service provided fifty maps that divided the area into grids. Teams of five began walking the eleven paths, triple checking the grids for clues. Other teams of five walked across the grids off the paths looking for any signs of Rachel. Seven searched the entire area. They found nothing. The search was very methodical.

Morty turned to a ranger and asked, "What's involved in searching the lake?"

"That would depend on the extent of the investigation. This is a federally preserved area, so it's not going to be dredged up to look for a body. If we're talking about a few divers, then I guess with permission from the Army Corps of Engineers a couple of divers could go looking. But you better get permission first."

Davis noticed Dan January in the crowd and walked over. "Dan, how are the kids doing?"

"They were confused first by the separation, then the divorce, and now this."

Trying to size him up, Davis stared at the man. He was difficult to read. He was a lawyer and knew how to cover his emotions. Davis broke the silence, trying to gauge his reaction. "The police think she split town."

"You wouldn't have thought that based upon my questioning last night. Detective Duncan came at me real hard. I told her what I knew, which wasn't much. I ate dinner with a friend, finished about eight thirty, and then I went home with my date. We drank too much and went to bed. We had sex. I gave the detective the name of the woman I was with. She verified I was with her. Whatever happened to Rachel, I was having sex with another woman when it occurred. I've got a solid alibi. No matter how much you'd like me to be responsible, you can't prove I had anything to do with Rachel's disappearance. I hated her, but you freed me from that bitch, so what's my motive?"

"If you hated Rachel, why are you here?"

"Because it would look bad if I wasn't. I'm strictly here for appearances. I think she split. I bet she's been planning this a long time. She's not much of a mother, and she knew the kids would be taken care of by her parents and their trust."

Honest, coldhearted bastard. "So, who's your rock solid alibi?"

"That's none of your fucking business."

Davis didn't like January before Rachel became his client. He tolerated him so that he could cut a deal with the bastard because it was in the best interest of his client, but now Rachel was missing, and he wasn't going to take any shit from this jerk.

"You're pretty stupid. I represent the missing person, and I filed the report. Don't you think the police are going to share with me the alibi of their primary suspect?"

"Why am I the primary suspect?"

"Because the spouse is always the primary suspect."

"I'm the ex-husband, not the husband."

"You're not only stupid, you're a bad lawyer. That order isn't final. It's not final for ninety days. In light of Rachel's disappearance, I can ask the court to void the order. If that motion's granted, then all those assets that Rachel agreed to transfer to you will be tied up until her whereabouts or death is determined. If she's dead, half of those assets will be a part of her estate. One thing is certain. If I set aside the order, the $800,000 payment from her trust to you won't happen. Rachel's trust, including that $800,000, will roll over into the children's trusts, and Tyree Sinclair controls those trusts. You might be tied up in litigation for years."

January's expression noticeably changed from smug to anger. Trying to push his buttons, Davis pointed out, "You might want to find Rachel more than anyone else does."

January walked away, unhappy.

Davis found Morty and Sinclair and recounted his conversation with January. They agreed that Morty would call the chief of police and discover the identity of January's alibi.

Davis lent Morty his cell phone. He had one, a gift from Sammie, but the old man was stubborn and refused to carry it.

"Gerry, Morty, I'm out here in Forest Hills. We had a great turnout, more than four hundred volunteers. If she's in Forest Hills or Green Hills, we'll find her or her body."

The chief acknowledged that the number of volunteers was impressive.

"Ben Davis just had a confrontation with Dan January. He admitted he's out here for appearance's sake only. Claims to have a solid alibi: dinner and at home having sex with a woman."

Police Chief Neenan didn't answer right away. He was weighing the substance and then the confidentiality of the information and how he could use it while still preserving the confidential nature of what he'd heard. "We interviewed his date. It's a little sensitive. January may have been going through a divorce, but his alibi is a married woman. She doesn't want any trouble, and I have no reason to make trouble for her. It's not a crime to be unfaithful to your husband. My only concern was whether she confirmed where January was from seven till ten on July 4th."

"What's her name, Gerry?"

"Robin Gaines."

Morty turned to Davis, "Does the name Robin Gaines mean anything?"

Davis looked at Sinclair, who looked back at Davis. "Robin Gaines and her husband, Robert, from 1996 until 1998, were lovers of Dan January, and they ended their relationship at the insistence of Rachel in June 1998, according to Dr. Ames, her therapist."

Morty repeated the information to the police chief, who commented, "That's very interesting. Neither January nor Gaines volunteered that information. I'd say we need to interview them again. In light of Robert Gaines's past involvement with January, we should have a few questions for him as well."

Morty handed the phone back to Davis and in a concerned voice said, "In light of these half-truths, we may have a real problem. Rachel may not have disappeared voluntarily. It's possible she may be dead."

CHAPTER FORTY-THREE

A ONE-SIDED NEGOTIATION

Wednesday, July 7, 1999

Davis got to the office early, before seven, just like he did every morning. He checked his calendar, nothing until noon, so he figured he'd get some dictation in and get the day rolling. He visited the kitchen where there was a cup of Joe waiting, courtesy of the ever-faithful Bella. He didn't expect anything unusual during the morning, but he was wrong. Bella arrived a few minutes after seven, and right behind her were Richard Sasser, Dickie, and four gentlemen in identical dark blue suits and sunglasses. Bella silently led them all into the conference room.

The oldest man identified himself, "I'm agent in charge Brian Greene, and these are agents Smith, Potts, and Lamb. We're all licensed attorneys in the District of Columbia and at least one state Bar. Mr. Sasser Sr. has identified this office as his attorneys, and the government has agreed to meet with you before we charge him under the Espionage Act of 1996 for selling classified software to a foreign government. Last year, Sasser Industries sold Neptune software to Sweden. You did that without the permission of the U.S. government in violation of the act."

Sasser turned to Davis and angrily said, "This is pure bullshit. These are trumped-up charges..."

"Shut up, Richard," Davis blasted back. Then Davis turned to Agent Greene. He looked at the agent and smiled. "I'm from New York, so I'm used to people being in kind of a rush, but I've lived here in Nashville for almost twenty years, so I've learned to slow it down a little. Let's all get to know each other just a bit first. Let me call Mr. Steine and give him an opportunity to join us. That might take some time so I'm going to have juice, coffee, and pastries brought in here. While that's happening, my clients and I are going to excuse ourselves and confer. Enjoy the amenities."

Davis buzzed Bella and told her to wake Morty up and get him upstairs immediately. He and Richard Sasser left the group for his private office. As he was leaving, he pulled Dickie by the arm and deposited him in Sammie's office. She was still putting on her make-up on the ninth floor.

When alone, Davis asked, "What the hell is going on? These people don't just show up on your doorstep for no reason."

Davis's words were forceful, almost angry. He wanted information, not denials. He had four government agents in his conference room, and they had a warrant for Richard Sasser Sr., his client.

A knock at the door, and Sammie joined them in the midst of Sasser's explanation.

"I sold the Neptune software to Sweden, and their techs figured a way to piggyback our military satellites. The feds want me to eliminate the product and destroy all research. I might agree to do so if I thought that would solve the problem. We've got an even more sensitive issue. They want the designer."

Sammie asked, "What do you mean 'want'? Isn't it a design team?"

"No, it's one person, my son, Dickie. They want him to become one of them."

Again Sammie asked, "One of them"?

"My answer was that I wanted to see my lawyer, and here we are."

Morty arrived, was briefed as best they could, and they retrieved Dickie from Sammie's office. The five of them joined the agents in the room. There was room for twelve at the table so the ends were unoccupied. There was silence for a three full minutes before anyone spoke. Three hundred and sixty seconds is a long time for people to stare at each other and not speak, almost an eternity. Morty had taught them in a situation like this to let the other side open the conversation.

Agent Greene finally did. "We're here to negotiate the sale of certain assets of Sasser Industries and the employment contract of Richard Sasser Jr. We understand that you and Mr. Steine represent the company and Messrs. Sasser Sr. and Jr. individually. We'd like to begin those negotiations immediately."

Forgetting Morty's strategy, Davis got right to the point and asked for details. Agent Greene proceeded like a steamroller. There was no stopping Greene. He warned that the Neptune code could fall into the hands of a foreign government less friendly than Sweden. He informed them that the secretary of state was currently in Sweden trying to negotiate back the code. He informed the group that the U.S. government was confident it would accomplish that mission.

Greene argued, "He'll get it back, but it will cost us. I'm here to tie up loose ends. I'm prepared to buy the code. That's easy. The problem is I need to tie up Richard Sasser Jr. What's in his head can be duplicated. He could be kidnapped by an unfriendly, and then where would we be? His loyalty needs to be guaranteed to this country, and that knowledge needs to work for us, and by us I mean the U.S. Eventually, the code will be obsolete, but that's way into the future."

Ignoring Greene's concerns, Morty said, "We were talking about what assets of the company might be included in the sale."

Davis waited for the answer, and Morty rather than Greene responded, "We're taking a different approach. Richard's going to list the assets to be excluded, and then we'll set a price. He's going to be allowed to keep any software, copyrights, or assets he wants. The NSA's main interest is Dickie. It just wants Richard satisfied financially because he is losing Dickie's services."

So the purchase of the company is just a ruse to compensate the father for the loss of the son. Don't lose sight of that fact, Davis reminded himself.

Richard sat there and wrote on a yellow pad the fifteen top products of the company and titled the document "Excluded Assets." He also included his office furniture and computers.

The government didn't give a damn about the company. All it wanted were the Neptune code and Dickie. Greene looked at the pad and announced, "The government will pay you $2 million for the rest of the assets."

Davis interrupted, "This is an all-in-one deal, asset purchase and employment contract. Let's talk about a global deal. You say you want Dickie too. I assume you mean some sort of protected employment, like the witness protection approach. He'd be restricted as to travel and with whom he could communicate?"

Greene looked at Davis and assured him that Mr. Sasser would be a valuable asset to the government. He'd be guarded while he performed his duties for his country. He'd be given a comfortable place to work and live.

That was Davis's cue to begin negotiations. He rattled off, "He'll need the following:

1. Annual salary of $250,000
2. A contract term of three years with confidentiality clause
3. Three-bedroom home free and clear
4. Warm climate
5. Two security guards
6. Four weeks protected vacation
7. Fifty-hour work week
8. Commencement date after Dickie completes certain work for Steine, Davis, & Davis
9. Life insurance of $5,000,000, health, and other benefits."

Greene laughed at Davis and said, "I don't think you understand how badly we want this boy. We're offering our highest clearance, two levels above top secret. We want a fifteen-year contract. We'll start the boy at a GS 15 and pay him $300,000 a year. The president only makes $400,000. The house wherever he wants is no problem, and we'll provide a security team of at least two men, maybe more. Work hours and vacations will depend on the demands of national security. He'll be worked hard and treated well. He'd be a valuable asset. If the work with Steine, Davis, & Davis doesn't create a conflict or issue with the government, I'll request that he be allowed to work on your project from our location with whatever restrictions we deem necessary to protect our asset."

Davis didn't like that last answer. "No, we're going to work out his work hours and vacation time. He's not signing any fifteen-year contract. That's unheard of. You're not committing this young man to a lifetime of indentured servitude. This young man is twenty-three. I'm not letting him sign away his life to you."

Greene decided to flex his muscles. "What damn choice do you have?"

"I could go to the press. The *New York Times* would love to report how the NSA impresses U.S. citizens into service of their country and what happens if they refuse."

"How'd you like an IRS audit, Mr. Davis? I make one call, and it's at your front door tomorrow."

"Admittedly an inconvenience, but all part of a bigger story for my reporter friend at the *New York Times*."

Davis didn't scare easily, but Greene could make good on his threat. An IRS audit was nothing to laugh about, and the government had other inconveniences in its arsenal. Morty and Davis did a fair amount of work in federal court, and as they knew, federal judges could be influenced for good as well as for evil. Davis and Morty both reported all income, but every tax return was subject to scrutiny. Yet Davis had to show strength and determination.

"I'm going to do the right thing by this client, no matter what shit you throw at me, so you might as well get real."

Prior to their meeting Greene had done his research on the Steine Davis, & Davis law firm. He knew the kind of lawyers he'd be dealing with. He pushed hard, but it didn't work. Now he was losing his nerve and suggested, "Let's make it seven years, and young Mr. Sasser gets to restart his new life at the ripe old age of thirty. That seems reasonable, doesn't it? By then we should be able to work around the Neptune Code to protect national security."

The father jumped in, "$3 million for the company, seven years employment at $400,000 per year, the same as the president, fifty hours a week, and four weeks protected vacation."

Greene was still staring hard at Davis. He corrected Sasser Sr.,

"That was $2 million on the table."

Davis responded, "$3 million sounds better, and he may be more important right now than the president."

Greene hesitated, "You've forgotten about the Espionage Act?"

Davis smirked, "That would have been a long, painful, and embarrassing prosecution."

Greene announced, "Deal."

Bella came in, and with everyone sitting right there, Davis dictated both contracts. They were short and sweet. The Excluded Assets List was attached to the sale of the company. The government had purchased all of Sasser's liabilities including all of the company's debts. Richard Sasser Sr. would form a new company using the excluded assets. Dickie would begin full-time work for the NSA, but he'd have the ability to start his job for Steine Davis, & Davis. He would begin his life with the NSA as soon as the contracts were signed and money transferred. However, his first priority had to be the Sinclair case.

Davis outlined the scope of the job as it existed today but indicated that he anticipated it would expand over time as new facts were discovered and actions taken. The primary current objective was finding Rachel Sinclair. Davis speculated that surveillance of Dan January would be necessary and demanded that Sasser be given access to whatever NSA assets he needed. Greene had no objection. Dickie Sasser had sold his soul to the United States of America. He had no choice. His lawyer felt very uncomfortable, probably for good reason.

CHAPTER FORTY-FOUR

A MISSING GIRL

Thursday, July 8, 1999

Dr. Jackie Samuels, PhD had a confident air about her, which one might attribute to pedigree or her height. She'd been an FBI agent for more than twenty years, and she was more than six feet tall in her stocking feet. She'd been the leading handwriting expert for the Chicago FBI office until her retirement three years earlier. Last year she testified on behalf of Steine Davis, & Davis at trial that a contract had been forged and a judgment was rendered for false notarization of a document in the amount of half a million dollars.

Morty made the introductions, "Tyree Sinclair and Rita Sinclair, Dr. Jackie Samuels, former agent of the FBI, handwriting expert. It's their daughter, Rachel, who's missing and who allegedly wrote this note. This is a photocopy. The police have the original." Morty handed the three-by-five sheet of paper to the expert.

Samuels studied it carefully. "It is critical that I see the original document. But I can give you some general impressions just from a glance. Unless your daughter is very masculine, it's highly unlikely that she wrote this note. Whoever did was very masculine in style. Does your daughter have unusually large hands or fat fingers? I'd say there's an eighty percent chance this note was written by a man.

The other twenty percent chance is that it's a woman, who has man-like size and mannerisms."

Morty looked at Davis and Sinclair and smiled. "I wonder who wrote the note?" Morty said sarcastically. "If we obtain Dan January's handwriting sample, can you compare it to the note and render an opinion as to whether he wrote it?"

"Of course."

"What if the sample is not printed like the note, but cursive?"

"I can still offer an opinion, but it is more difficult to render. It requires more analysis."

Morty said, "Tyree, I want you to find evidence at your office of January's printed handwriting. What about Rachel's? Do you have any examples of her printed handwriting?"

The mother spoke up, "I've got dozens of her printed work from elementary school somewhere in the basement. I can look for them when we get home."

The meeting adjourned. The men left the office, and Davis, Morty, and the Sinclairs went to the Granny White Market to resume the search for Rachel.

The search revealed nothing. It extended the evening of the sixth through the evening of the eighth, two full days. More than a thousand persons, devoting more than five thousand man-hours, covered twenty-two square miles. Every blade of Forest Hills and neighboring Greens Hills and Brentwood (Williamson County) was scoured. No one saw or heard anything. The three communities were picked clean. The Sinclairs thanked the volunteers for their efforts, but they were in vain. The grid was explored completely, and there was no evidence of Rachel.

Law enforcement did its part. Each local sheriff office, the Metro Police Department, and the Tennessee Bureau of Investigation (TBI) were out in force. The lake was dredged, and the divers exhausted the possibilities of where they might discover a body.

The police couldn't figure out if Rachel left the January house the night of the 4th. No one saw her walking down Granny White Pike in either a northern or a southern direction. Whether she was abducted or left under her own steam, she was gone. The volunteers canvassed Green Hills, where the Sinclairs lived, and found nothing. If Rachel did go to her parents' house and sleep in her bed, then she left early the morning of the 5th. All the family cars, including Rachel's, were accounted for. The police scrutinized the records of every cab company. No fares were picked up during that three-hour window within ten miles of the January house. Even if Rachel had left the house a minute after the family was out the door and started walking at a brisk rate of 3.3 miles an hour, she still didn't fit the physical descriptions of the fares. The nearest bus stop more than ten miles away posed a similar problem. There were no records of a car rental in the last week by anyone matching her description.

The informed conclusion was an unknown person, either friend or abductor, drove her from either place, uncertain as to which. That person could be male or female, age fifteen through eighty-five. That left a wide berth of suspects or co-conspirators. The answer could be as simple as Rachel Sinclair, under tremendous stress, temporarily flew the coop with the help of a friend. She could be sipping a drink somewhere until she was ready to come home, or maybe she didn't want to come home.

Rita Sinclair took charge of her grandchildren. Frankie had a much greater understanding of the situation than Gaby did. Frankie tried to explain it to his sister, "Mommy disappeared, and no one seems to know where."

Rita explained that many people were trying to find their mommy, and with all that help, they'd find her. She assured them that she and Grandpa loved them. Both wanted to see and talk to their father, who'd yet to reach out to them. Rita made the excuse that he was out desperately looking with Grandpa for Mommy. She couldn't understand why Dan was staying away and hated him for his lapse of parental responsibility.

Rita was most worried about Gaby. The divorce, the absence of her father, and now the disappearance of her mother were more than the six-year-old could cope with and digest. Rita kept her close, never leaving her side.

Morty and Davis left the Granny White Market with sufficient time to get to their three o'clock meeting with Police Chief Gerry Neenan. It was time to come clean with the police. Damn Rachel's reputation. Her life could well be in jeopardy. Even worse, she could be dead.

When they arrived at the chief's office, seated on the couch was Detective Sharon Duncan, who stood when they entered the room. Everyone knew each other, so introductions were skipped. Davis wondered how angry Duncan remained because of his harsh words the other night.

Davis shared with the two lawmen the Ten Commandments. The lawmen, who were churchgoers, but not puritans, were shocked as they went down the list.

Duncan shared with Davis January's alibi that he spent the July 4th evening in the January home having intimate relations with Robin Gaines. She told Davis that January gave a detailed statement about his evening and that Ms. Gaines corroborated his statement. The gist was that the two had been together from before the time that the Sinclairs had dropped Rachel off at the January house until about ten thirty, just before the Sinclairs' arrival back at the home. "According to Gaines, 'He was in me almost the entire time.' I'd say that's a pretty good alibi if you ask me. It's pretty hard to kill another woman if you're inside another. Not impossible I'll grant you, but difficult."

Davis didn't think Duncan was very funny.

Duncan still didn't like Davis. She thought he was an arrogant ass. Despite his personal feeling about Duncan, Davis felt obligated to cooperate with the police investigation. Davis produced a memo that Sammie created based upon their very personal conversation with Dr. Ames. The memo provided names and dates. The names of the three couples engaged in the group relationships were identified. Rachel had refused to have intercourse with any of the other males. She watched as January had sex with her female counterpart or with the other couple. She did have enough curiosity to watch. That was well within the purview of the Ten Commandments.

The couples involved were the Coopers, first, the Kings followed, and then the Gaineses topped the list. Ames had provided a few strays who participated in threesomes, both male and female. This information created the possibility of at least ten new suspects and additional unknown sex partners. The Januarys' lifestyle complicated the investigation by creating multiple leads to be followed.

Davis suggested that Duncan might interview Dr. Ames. He soon learned that the detective still held a grudge from the Keller home incident.

"Mr. Davis, I know how to do my job. I'll be creating my own memo based upon my interview of the good doctor. Thanks, but no thanks."

Morty and Sinclair added their two cents in order to break the tension between Davis and Duncan. They all speculated that January was still their prime suspect.

Duncan argued that there was strong evidence that Rachel may have left because of the pressures of life. Leaving January under the shadow of her disappearance would have been a bonus to her.

Davis and Morty said their good-byes and promised to keep in touch. When they were out of the building and across the street, Morty asked, "What the hell was that all about? Duncan must really dislike you to show her colors like that in front of the chief."

"Apparently so. She must be sensitive. I stomped on her foot at the Keller home the other night, and it looks like I broke something."

"Yeah, goodwill."

Davis shrugged. "I was just protecting the family of my client."

Morty shook his head and pointed out, "That should have been accomplished without pissing her off. As you see, in only days, now you need her help, and your smart mouth got you in trouble."

Even though Davis knew Morty was right, he argued, "You weren't there. The family, tired and in shock, pressed by Duncan could have implicated themselves in the death."

"I thought it was an accident."

"Probably, but nothing in life is a hundred percent."

Morty didn't know about Tommy's gambling debts or that Martha wanted to disinherit him only a few days before. Those were pretty strong motives to kill somebody. Davis, lost in thought, was disturbed by his partner's criticism.

"We're standing in the back of the courthouse. Let's visit my old friend the DA and see if we can cut a good deal for young Dickie Sasser."

They took the stairs to the fourth floor. Morty almost had a stroke on the way up. He pulled out his linen handkerchief and dabbed at his brow. He stopped at the water fountain to get a drink. Refreshed, they walked into the DA's office.

"General Carpenter, congratulations on the Murphy securities fraud conviction. Your office got the maximum sentence, and he's been put where he belongs in a prison. Being in a county jail, while he fights his appeal, is much too good for him."

"What's this transformation? What happened to Morty Steine defense lawyer?"

Morty spent the next ten minutes telling General Larry Carpenter about the Sasser case. "He's just a kid. He's got a bright future, and you have the power to give him a pass. This boy is doing important work." Morty opened his briefcase and handed Carpenter an affidavit from the director of the NSA. As Carpenter read the document, his eyes widened. It concluded by stating, "the work of Dr. Richard Sasser Jr. is vital to the national security of the United States of America and Dr. Sasser's incarceration would be contrary to national interests."

Carpenter put the document down and asked, "What the hell does this kid do?"

Morty didn't exactly know. "It's hush, hush; something to do with national security. You know the old saying if I told you, I'd have to kill you. Well, I didn't ask, and I suggest that you don't either. I value my life, and I suspect so do you. It has something to do with computer security. He writes software. It has to do with firewalls and protecting our computers from other governments hacking in. He's a genius. His father owns the company. He earned a doctorate at twenty-three. The kid made a mistake."

Carpenter was listening intently. This wasn't the run-of-the-mill defendant who came through his office. "I can't help you on the civil matter."

Morty smiled internally. He knew he'd just turned the corner. "I've smoothed out the problem with the other party. There won't be a civil action."

Carpenter frowned and said, "If I give him a complete pass, then he's more likely to become a Murphy. I know we don't have the poor black robbing the convenience mart to feed his family. This young man left the scene of an accident. That shows he has no moral compass. He needs to be taught a good lesson. Ninety days in county jail might be just the right thing. He may be smart, but it appears he has no common sense."

Morty decided to take a different tack since Carpenter was backtracking and being harder than he thought. He proposed, "General, I've always supported you, haven't I, both financially and politically?"

"Yes."

"You know who Dickie Sasser's father is, don't you?"

Carpenter just shook his head. He didn't want to commit until he heard the offer.

"Give the kid pre-trial diversion, and his father, Richard, will get two of his friends to host a luncheon for your next campaign, no matter what position."

Carpenter was listening, greedy and ambitious. Morty threw the line in the water, "Where do you want to go next?"

"I've been thinking state attorney general."

"That will take a lot of money and help."

There it was, the prize to be had and what needed to be achieved for poor Dickie to go free. Over the years Morty had made many backroom deals. All that was necessary was clarity of purpose, and now he had it.

Carpenter inquired, "I know you've got the political connections in the party, but who else will be vying for that position?"

Morty honestly didn't know but could find out. "I'll do some checking and let you know. How about helping me out with the kid? It will be a win-win."

Fifteen minutes later the deal cut for Dickie Sasser would be permitted: pre-trial diversion.

Davis, impressed, learned from the master how to cut a deal without getting anyone angry. A lesson learned.

Back at the office, the work piled up. Davis called Maureen Wagner back, "Maureen, how are you and the family doing?"

"We're struggling. The police have released Martha's body, and we'd like to have her funeral on Monday. Would you please give the eulogy?"

Davis was surprised. He didn't know Martha that well, but he agreed.

"After the funeral, we'd like you to come back to the house and share the terms of Martha's will."

Davis thought of poor Martha, their last conversation, his advice, and the unwanted outcome of how her estate would be divided among her family.

Davis spent the remainder of his day cleaning up his desk. He kept ticking off items on his yellow pad. He continued to play telephone tag with several clients and adversary counsel. It was a brutal game, nobody's fault, just a product of the times.

After he felt he'd tormented himself enough, he left for the day to go home to his loving family to share a good home-cooked meal and an evening together.

CHAPTER FORTY-FIVE

READING OF THE WILL

Monday, July 12, 1999

Davis spent the weekend with his family. He played a round of golf with Jake. The week before he became a man, he cried like a little boy when his father taught him a good lesson on the golf course. Davis chastised him for being a poor loser.

The family lay in bed late Saturday afternoon eating popcorn and watching a movie. Caroline complained the entire time. Davis relished days like these. He knew that they would happen less often. Soon Caroline would be off at college, and Jake would be out drinking with the guys. He wanted to cherish these last few special Saturdays together as a family.

Saturday night the kids went out with their friends, so when the parents had the house to themselves Davis thought it might be an opportunity for romance. He crawled into bed with his wife of almost two decades, but before he knew it, Abbott and Costello were wildly licking his face.

"What the hell?"

Liza, in a teddy, joined them. "You've met my friends."

Looking at his wife seductively, Davis pleaded, "Why are they in the bed? I thought we might . . ."

"And I thought I might read and enjoy my evening alone. I thought they could run interference for me tonight. You win some; you lose some. Tonight isn't your night."

Frustrated, Davis knew when he'd been outmaneuvered and dramatically left the bedroom, cursing at his four-legged friends, "traitors."

Once outside the bedroom, Davis hit the refrigerator hard. He made a second dinner with all the fixings. He then retreated to his home office, went to his briefcase, pulled out and reviewed his yellow legal pad to see what matters were left to be completed. He did no work, just fretted over what had to be done. He lay on the couch and watched two old movies until he fell asleep, snoring loudly.

Sunday was a better family day beginning with a big breakfast consisting of lox, eggs, and onions on bagels, and good conversation. Jake kept everybody laughing. Late afternoon, Sammie and Nurse Browne, together with Morty, came over for a barbecue. Jake pulled out the karaoke machine, and everyone performed. Liza and Davis sang the Sonny and Cher song "I Got You Babe." Davis was terrible. Caroline and Liza had beautiful voices; they sang in the choir during the Jewish holidays. Morty was incredible, the only professional, but even Jake wasn't half bad. The only frog in the group was Davis. He couldn't carry a tune, but he participated just the same. It was a fun, late evening. Victor, Sammie, and Morty drove downtown after midnight.

Davis was deep in thought as he drove to the office Monday morning. When he sat behind his desk, he quickly reviewed his yellow pad and started adding things that he conveniently forgot about Saturday night as he pouted. He soon recognized that his work plate was more full than he realized and that he needed to delegate to others.

The funeral at ten meant he needed to meet first with Sammie and then with Morty. Both assignments related to the January case. Sammie's task was more immediate.

Bella, old faithful, was at her desk. She produced only the more important messages. Davis asked her to call each of those clients, and he promised he'd return phone calls in the afternoon.

Davis made notes on a legal pad regarding the motion and brief he'd be asking Sammie to draft; she'd done a very good job. His notes were superfluous.

Sammie entered his office without knocking. "Bella said you needed to talk to me immediately. What's up?"

"The other day I threatened January with filing a motion to set aside the marital dissolution agreement and property settlement. I told him that I was confident he still might get most of the marital assets, but the $800,000 payment would most certainly be in jeopardy because it came from the trust. January has no legal right to invade either Rachel's or the children's trusts. Only Ty can access any of the trusts as the trustee. The house and the marital funds might be January's after probate, but Rachel would have to be declared dead first. I suspect the divorce court would give him reasonable access to funds while we determine her missing status."

Sammie would be the one to appear before the judge. She asked, "What about custody of the kids? Even a bad father trumps the greatest grandparents. I suspect with Rachel gone, January as the only parent has absolute right to custody of the children, no ifs, ands, or buts."

Davis said, "That's what I want you to research. How bad does the surviving parent have to be for the court to award custody to the grandparents? What if the father is arrested for murder of the mother? Wouldn't the court award the children temporarily to the grandparents even if the father is out on bond? Find out about other family members of January, parents and siblings."

Sammie asked with concern in her voice, "Have you spoken to Tyree Sinclair yet about a custody battle?"

"No, I thought we'd do the research before I spoke to him about this matter. I doubt we will have many options since we have no evidence of foul play. Right now, the police are treating Rachel's disappearance as a runaway. My gut tells me otherwise. I've got a strong suspicion that Rachel's dead and that January was somehow involved."

"You may be right, but proving murder without a body is nearly impossible. It's what they taught us in law school. Maybe it was different in the olden days."

Davis didn't like to be reminded of his age, forty-five. While Liza at age forty-two aged well, the overweight Davis had lost his boyish charm. But with age came experience.

He took the elevator to the sixth floor, not wanting to be bothered with the stairs. He used his key because at eight thirty, Morty would still be in bed. He stuck his head in, coughed loudly, and the old lion woke up.

He was in a grumpy mood. "What the hell do you want so early?"

"Working people have been at their jobs almost two hours, or are you retired?"

"I'm semi-retired. I've earned the right to work when I want to and . . ."

"I need your advice and help."

He explained Sammie's assignment in detail.

"You're playing a dangerous game with the lives of those children. If January gets his $800,000, he'll leave the kids with the Sinclairs and probably won't exercise his entire visitation. If you set aside that order, it will be an all-out war. Fighting over children is the hardest of all lawsuits because they're living and breathing assets, not things."

"Right now, all we're doing is the research to get information and understand the law."

"I've got no problem with that." Morty got to the point, "What do you want me to do?"

Davis's answer was equally direct, "If we don't like the law, I want you to get the law changed."

Ask a simple question, get a simple answer. Who does he think I am?

"You've got friends in the legislature. Start with the appropriate committee and then start getting votes for the proposed bill. After we have the research, we'll decide what we want this law to proclaim."

"Boy, when you wake up a guy, you drop a bomb in his lap."

"Stop complaining and get started by putting your pants on."

Davis waved good-bye and left for Martha Keller's funeral. He drove to Oaks & Nichols funeral home in Columbia, Tennessee, where Martha Keller was born and raised. It was about twenty miles south of Nashville. The turnout was light, but seated in the front row were Tommy Hamilton, the Andrews, and the Wagners. Davis sat next to the family, and when introduced by the minister, he took his place behind the podium.

Davis felt comfortable behind the wooden triangle. He'd tried dozens of jury and bench trials and argued more than a hundred motions. Crowds didn't bother him. He spoke without notes. "We're here today to remember my good friend and client Martha Keller, who survived two husbands and the memories of two loving and happy marriages. Born and raised in Columbia, she attended this church until she left for George Peabody College for Teachers in 1963. After school and during her marriage to Tommy's father, Harold, she taught elementary school in Nashville. Two of her students are in the audience today, saying good-bye to their favorite teacher."

That's a white lie, but sometimes a white lie is the right thing to do.

He talked about Martha's marriage to Stanley Keller and her

support of his publishing empire. "Martha helped raise Stanley's two daughters, Maureen and Betty, who continue to run his company and his good work."

Davis kept it short, about fifteen minutes. He really didn't know Martha Keller that well. The graveside ceremony was equally brief. He then followed the family in the limos back to the Keller home. Top down in his Bentley, sucking on a cherry Tootsie Pop, he tried to anticipate the family's questions.

A maid brought tea punch and little pimento cheese sandwiches. Present were Maureen and her husband, Robert, Betty and her husband, Sam, and Tommy.

Davis took charge, "Before I read the will, I want you all to know that Martha over the course of the last five years had several wills. Each time she prepared a will, I directed her to destroy the previous one. Martha also directed me over the last year to prepare three codicils or amendments to her last will. The only amendment that counts is the last one because each new codicil recites that it voids or cancels the previous codicil."

Davis handed everyone a copy of Martha's last will and a document entitled third codicil. The will was dated February 5th, 1997, and the last codicil was dated April 23rd, 1999.

Maureen was named the executor, and the will directed that Steine Davis, & Davis probate the will. There were a specific bequest to Martha's sister, Deborah, of $450,000, and a specific bequest to the church where the service was held of $150,000. There was a provision that if any of the beneficiaries challenged the last will or any codicil, the challenging party by doing so was disinherited. Davis commonly referred to this provision as a "drop dead clause." It tended to avoid probate litigation.

Davis then explained that the third codicil controlled the balance of the last will of February 5th, 1997. He read from the third codicil, "I revoke paragraph 9 of my last will dated February 5th, 1997, and any earlier codicils replace the provisions of those documents with the following: I give, devise, and bequeath to my stepdaughter Maureen Wagner one-third of the residue and remainder of my estate in fee; I give, devise, and bequeath to my stepdaughter Betty Andrews one-third of the residue and remainder of my estate in fee; I give, devise and bequeath to Maureen Wagner, trustee, one-third of the residue and remainder of my estate in trust for my son, Tommy Hamilton. I direct that on a monthly basis on the first of each month, Maureen shall distribute to Tommy $12,000 for an annual distribution of $144,000. The balance of the trust, which totals approximately $8 million, shall be under her control. I direct that Maureen, who is a smart businesswoman, shall seek the advice of my attorney, Benjamin Davis, as she deems necessary concerning not only legal matters but distributions to her stepbrother as well. This trust shall last for twenty years, and Maureen in her sole and exclusive discretion may distribute to Tommy as much of the principle and interest of such trust for his necessary expenses. At the end of the twenty years, the trust shall dissolve, and the remainder of the funds in the trust shall be distributed. If Tommy should die before the trust dissolves, then what remains shall go equally to Maureen and Betty. If either of them should die before the expiration of this trust, then their one-half interest shall be divided equally among their children and held in trust until they reach the age of twenty-one. If Maureen shall die or refuse to serve as trustee during this trust, Betty shall serve as substitute trustee. If Betty shall die or refuse to serve as trustee, Benjamin Davis shall serve as second substitute trustee."

Davis put down the two documents.

"What the hell! I've got to go to Maureen for my money?" shouted Tommy.

Before Davis could answer, Maureen blurted out, "Martha told me she'd cut you out of her will. I don't want to be your nursemaid. I'll tell you right now, as trustee, I'm not staking your gambling." Her volume got louder with each word.

"You're not controlling my money, you stupid bitch."

"Who the hell do you think you're calling a bitch?"

Things were getting out of hand quickly. Davis decided he'd better take charge, but that was easier said than done. He reminded Tommy of the drop dead clause and what impact it could have if he elected to challenge the will. He also pointed out that he'd have to hire a lawyer and pay him a retainer and pay him legal fees during an ongoing lawsuit.

"I guess the retainer and those fees would have to come out of your $12,000 monthly allowance. What are you going to live on in the meantime? A court battle would take at least a year, maybe longer. You're better off just taking the allowance and moving on with your life, Tommy."

Maureen pointed out, "Under this will, you got a $2,000 a month raise. Your allowance was ten thousand a month. You lazy son of a bitch. You were supposed to get nothing. Martha told me she was tired of funding your gambling."

Davis couldn't take it any longer. He said sternly, "All of you be quiet and listen. Neither a child nor a stepchild has any right to inherit. Martha could have given her money to any one of you or none of you. I remind you that Martha specifically provided that anyone who challenges her wishes is cut out completely. Let me assure you that under Tennessee law, that's an enforceable provision."

Davis let those points sink in. "Tommy, Maureen's in charge of your trust. I suggest you be real nice to her, or you better live twenty years before you see a penny."

"But I'm a grown man. My lawyer . . ."

"Your lawyer, Brad Littleton, is an idiot, and that's an insult to the other idiots."

Davis knew he shouldn't have said that, but it felt good, and it wasn't slander because truth was an absolute defense to slander. Technically it probably was slander because the medical definition of an idiot was someone with an IQ of less than fifty, and Littleton if tested might have tested slightly higher. *Oh well.*

Davis continued to explain, "Under the last codicil the estate is divided three ways. The first codicil took Tommy out of the will. The second put him back in, and the third put his money in trust. She recently talked to me about kicking Tommy out of the will completely, but she never finalized that decision."

Davis picked up his briefcase with his initials, BAD, and said, "Try not to kill each other." He walked out without another word.

CHAPTER FORTY-SIX

A CALL FROM AN OLD FRIEND

Tuesday, July 20, 1999

Davis slept in and ate breakfast with the family. He had everything bagels with scallion cream cheese, nova lox, a slice of red onion, and a slice of tomato. He'd re-brush his teeth and swig some Scope after breakfast.

Jake, age twelve, going on thirty, planned on swimming in the Davises' pool, eating lunch with friends at Hillwood Country Club, and then getting on the course for a tee time at two.

Davis thought about asking whether the golfers in Jake's foursome were members of the club, or were they going to be Jake's guests, or more correctly his guests? *Oh, what the hell, it doesn't matter. I'll let the kid have fun on my dime.*

"How about you try to get us the first tee time tomorrow at seven, and we play a quick nine? If I shower and bring my suit to the club, I can get to the office before ten."

Jake's eyes lit up. He'd been playing a lot of golf this summer, and he thought on a good day with some luck, he might just beat the old man.

"You've got a date," he responded excitedly.

Davis ran up the stairs. Liza was still in bed with Abbott and Costello. He kissed her on the lips and reached for her breast. Abbott barked, and he retreated.

"Will resume later tonight when you are not protected by your vicious guard dogs."

Costello rolled on his back, and Davis scratched his stomach. The dog's leg moved back and forth quickly.

Down the stairs and out the door, Davis jumped in the Bentley, and lowered the top as he backed up. He reached for his Yankees ball cap sitting in the passenger's seat. Even at this hour the Nashville sun beat down on Davis's thinning hairline. His sandy hair, once lush and long, was receding, so he kept what he had left cut short. He missed his lush longish hair. In the seventies when he first met Morty, it was shoulder length.

In the office he stopped to have a brief but meaningful conversation with Bella. "How are Tony and the family?"

"Running the market with the help of Tony Jr. Angela's fifteen now and a handful. Has Caroline discovered boys yet?"

"If she has, no one's told me yet. Ignorance is bliss."

"You'd better pay closer attention because teenagers are stupid enough without any help from their parents."

"That's a cheery thought to begin the day."

"Reality is the best way to start the day."

"Type something. I don't pay you to be a philosopher."

Davis walked back to Sammie's office. Hard at work, she looked up, but before she could say anything, Bella buzzed in and said, "You'll never believe who's on the phone."

Sammie put her on speaker. "Mickey Mouse?"

"No, Amy Pierce. She wants to talk to the Davis handling the January divorce."

"Give us thirty seconds and then put her through."

Davis suggested, "You take the lead, but let's keep her on speaker."

"Amy, what can I do for you?"

"I'm on speaker. Is your uncle there?"

"We both represent Rachel January. Can we keep you on speaker?"

"No problem. The more, the merrier. I find it amusing that you need two lawyers to represent a non-existing client, who no one can find. Hello, Ben."

"Amy, so you represent Dan January in what capacity? Divorce, criminal, civil?"

"His divorce and for whatever other matter he may require my services."

There was an awkward silence until Pierce spoke again. "I've been waiting for your motion."

Innocently Davis responded, "What motion?"

Sarcastically Pierce complained, "Come on. I've called so we can discuss this matter like adults. Your motion to void the marital dissolution agreement and property settlement in January vs. January. Proof isn't developing the way you'd hoped."

Davis didn't like this bitch before this conversation, and he certainly wasn't warming up to her as they talked. He spit out, "What's the purpose of this call?"

"I figure since Chapman and the good Dr. Ames can't carry the day, you might want to settle this matter. I've been waiting to hear from you."

"How would I know to call you? Last conversation I had with your client, he wasn't represented by counsel, and my client was alive and well."

There was a lull in the conversation. Pierce waited for Davis to say something else, but he didn't. He was waiting for her to respond.

"As far as my client knows, Rachel is alive and well. She walked out of the January home before he arrived the night of the fourth. Do you want to try to work this out or not?"

Another lull in the conversation; the two were having a little game of cat and mouse with each other.

"What do you have in mind?"

"First is confidentiality and strict compliance to Rule 408 of the Tennessee Rules of Civil Procedure. Nothing we discuss from this point on is admissible. No crossing your fingers. Second, you let the police conduct its own investigation, and you back off."

Sammie, who'd remained quiet up till now, jumped in and stated the obvious, "Let me start by telling you that I don't trust you or your word. Second, we won't agree to anything that's illegal or unethical."

Pierce didn't answer right away. "I understand the law. It's usually black and white, but ethics are gray."

Sammie snapped back, "Your ethics are gray. Ours are clear.

Pierce barked back, "Don't be such a Girl Scout. It's all semantics. Your uncle understands the world, little girl, grow up. Do we have an understanding?"

"Amy, we don't have any understanding. Anything you say may be held against you in a court of law, so with that understanding, if you want to go ahead and proceed with your pitch, go ahead. Let's hear what you've got to say. We'll listen, but no promises, and I mean no promises. You proceed at your own risk. Like the Girl Scout says, we don't trust you, and we all know you don't have any ethics." Then Davis hit the record button on the micro recording device next to the phone.

"As I see it, you have two options: The first is a version of the original deal with $800,000 and the property division as agreed, but with Rachel gone, Dan as the father gets sole custody. The Sinclairs get the visitation that Dan was to be awarded: every other weekend, three weeks in the summer, and alternate holidays. If we go to court, he'll get the order enforced, and the money promised him. I seriously doubt the court will give them that much visitation. You've done the research. Tennessee doesn't recognize the visitation rights of grandparents."

Both Davises knew she was right. She had them and the Sinclairs over a barrel.

Sammie asked, "What's the other option?"

"The Sinclairs get custody, and January gets the agreed upon property settlement, except $800,000 is now $2 million."

Davis got angry. "Your client is selling his children for a million each?"

Pierce laughed and said, "That's ridiculous. He sold custody for $800,000. He's selling custody a second time for an additional $1,200,000. Get your math right, darling."

So the bastard was willing to admit exactly what's going on without any hesitation. Sammie needed to test the waters. "The court isn't going to invade the trust. You can forget about the $800,000. We'll tie you up in court for two years. The lawyers will make money, but your client will be broke in the end. Your client will get the house, the couple's savings, his pension, and the art. That's a total value of less than a quarter of a million dollars. The art only had value to Rachel."

Pierce knew Sammie was right. She was waiting for a reasonable counteroffer.

Davis said, "I have no authority without first discussing this matter with my client, but if I can get you an even million, then January also needs to withdraw as substitute trustee."

Davis knew he had authority for a million because Sinclair had originally given that amount to him to settle the matter.

Pierce said, "I don't have authority to make that deal. He's not agreeing to terminate his parental rights. He's allowing the Sinclairs to have custody of the children until they reach majority. After that, the kids can legally do whatever they want as to where they live and as to how much time they spend with any party."

Davis said, "The decision is up to the Sinclairs. Those are their grandchildren, and it's their money. Just so you know, I'm going to recommend that they reject both of your options. January's trying to sell the custody of his children and then hopes he's going to outlive Tyree Sinclair, who is almost forty years his senior. Put both of your offers in writing, set a deadline, and we'll respond."

Pierce snarled, "You haven't changed, still pigheaded and arrogant."

Davis quickly responded, "Those are two of my best characteristics" and hung up.

CHAPTER FORTY-SEVEN

NO SALE

Wednesday, July 21, 1999

The Davis boys had donuts and coffee for breakfast and were on the first tee precisely at seven. They agreed on the rules of the round, match play. The golfer who won more of the nine holes was victorious. No carryovers.

Jake asked, "Do we need a written contract signed by both parties?"

Davis stuck out his hand, they shook, and Davis said, "Gentleman's agreement. Neither of us has a pen or paper so a handshake will have to do. May the best man win."

Jake smugly responded, "He certainly will." Father and son laughed. They did that a lot. A twosome, they parred the first two holes. Jake started talking trash. Davis kept his head down and ignored the young whippersnapper. Jake's strategy backfired, and he lost focus, double bogeying the third and fourth holes, putting Davis two up. The lost holes rattled the young man. Golf is a game of confidence, and Ben Davis had plenty of that. The younger man's came and went on the golf course. In general, Jacob Albert Davis had more confidence than most young men of his age.

Davis pulled his micro recorder out of his golf bag and recounted the match to date. The younger man knew exactly what his father was doing and decided not to argue but play along. As each one hit shots, the other provided commentary, handing the recorder back and forth.

On the fifth tee, Jake remarked, "We're halfway through the match, and Ben Davis is facing his nemesis hole, the dreaded fifth, where he consistently hits his drive into the lake and must take penalty strokes. The crowd takes a deep breath awaiting his next shot."

Davis put his first drive and the second in the water. He glared at his son and conceded the hole. Both of them parred the next hole and bogeyed the seventh. Davis had Jake boxed out going into the eighth. Jake couldn't win; his best result was a tie. The younger Davis birdied the eighth. Davis, a tough competitor, debated whether to throw the match on the last hole so they'd tie. He didn't get the chance. He unintentionally double bogeyed, putting a big smile on Jake's face.

Jake argued that they needed to play sudden death: first one to win a hole won the match. Davis begged off, using work as his excuse. In reality he was satisfied with the tie and didn't want to risk the loss.

Jake grabbed the recorder and started making chicken sounds. Davis wouldn't be goaded into sudden death and delivered into the recorder, in a high-pitched female southern voice, the famous Vivian Leigh line from the last scene of *Gone with the Wind:* "Tomorrow is another day." Jake, who'd watched the movie with his father at least a dozen times, crisply delivered Clark Gable's response, "Frankly, my dear, I don't give a damn." The exchange ended the dispute. No sudden death. Davis showered and drove to work, while Jake stomped off mad and walked home from the club.

On the way into work Davis pondered his two bad holes. *I can't believe the kid tied me. I'd better practice more.*

As soon as he walked in the door, Sammie handed him a fax from Amy Pierce. "She gave us twenty-four hours."

"Or what?"

"The offer expires."

"Bullshit. We can always settle with the bastard. I'm not going to be rushed into a bad decision."

The fun of his morning golf match with his son faded as work took over. Davis had the ability to compartmentalize his family life from work. Morty taught him that it was critical to his sanity. Davis quickly switched to work mode and realized he needed the wisdom of Morty. He barked at Sammie, "Call Ty. See if he and Rita can come in at five. I want you to do research on what constitutes an illegal contract. If you can find a case involving custody, that should give us some guidance."

Sammie reminded him, "I don't make the law. I only find what case law is out there. Tennessee law is pretty scarce in general and even more so on something specific like this."

Of course she was right, but Davis was desperate to find precedent so he could rely upon it to recommend rejecting Pierce's options.

"Look, New York City and Chicago are pretty wild places. Weird things happen there. Check the laws of New York and Illinois. Maybe problems like this came up in New York City or Chicago."

"I can check several other states with big cities as well. You never know where something might happen. We might find what we need in Omaha, Nebraska. "

Davis just wasn't comfortable with the selling of the January children's custody by their father since he believed the man murdered their mother. The concept was fine when their mother was alive and it was for the children's benefit. That was done all the time. It was accepted practice. What Pierce was proposing had a certain stink to it.

"This proposal doesn't feel right. Do me a favor. Take a copy of the letter down to the sixth floor and transcribe the conversation with

Pierce from the tape from yesterday, and ask Morty to be here for the meeting with the Sinclairs at five. Do you think I'm overreacting?"

"I agree with you that January and Pierce are sleazeballs, but I don't think we can win the motion to set aside the order. If we try to set the order aside based on what we've got, January will probably be awarded custody of those children. I truly believe that would kill Rita Sinclair. I don't see how we can advise the Sinclairs to take that risk."

Davis tried to get some work done. He reviewed correspondence, but his mind kept slipping back to the January offer. Bella buzzed in, "I've got Richard Sasser on line two.

"Dick, how are you? How's Dickie doing? Is he on the straight and narrow?"

"I owe you and Morty. He's going to AA meetings three times a week. He stopped seeing certain friends because they party." The NSA has assigned Dickie five full-time agents. He's been working with George Hopper on the Sinclair case, trying to find Rachel. He doesn't tell me much, just that there have been some dead ends."

Davis was sorry to hear there wasn't any significant progress.

Sasser continued, "Sammie and I have set up a new company and transferred all the patents and copyrights to it. I'm starting to solicit new clients and hire new employees. She's been a big help. She's smart and much better looking than you. Thanks for recommending her to me."

Davis was proud of Sammie. He knew she was up to the task, and with that compliment, he ended the conversation.

At four, the three partners met in the conference room. Sammie handed each of them six cases with the important parts highlighted in yellow. There were two extra copies for Tyree and Rita Sinclair. The purpose of the meeting was to discuss strategy, but

Davis intentionally withheld an important piece of the puzzle. He didn't make that disclosure so opinions would be revealed without preconceived notions.

The Sinclairs arrived precisely at five. No time was wasted on small talk. Davis had been elected spokesperson to initiate the meeting. Sammie would present the law, and Morty, because of his experience and reputation, would present the firm's recommendation.

Davis began, "This isn't going to be an easy meeting. We have to deal with several difficult issues. The first, is Rachel alive? She's been gone more than two weeks. Can you concede that if she could, by now she'd make an effort to contact her children?"

Rita answered, "What if she's been kidnapped?"

Davis anticipated the possibility. "There's been no ransom demand. She's not being held for money or any political demand. No one has taken credit for her disappearance."

Those were harsh words for the Sinclairs to digest. Davis's next statement would be even tougher: "I think we need to face the reality that Rachel is dead."

Rita started crying, and tears welled up in the eyes of everyone else in the room.

Ty said quietly, "Let's assume that's true. Who thinks Dan January either killed or had Rachel killed?"

They all sat there a long minute. Rita raised her hand first, then the father, then Davis, Sammie, and Morty followed.

Davis continued, "If we all believe that, then how can we let that coldhearted bastard get custody of your grandchildren?"

Sammie jumped in, "Before you answer, I must point out that the law is not on our side. Our best legal arguments are by implication of the law rather than directly on point."

She handed the highlighted cases that allegedly supported that what Amy Pierce proposed was an illegal contract. "I haven't finished researching this issue, but . . ."

Davis apologized for his surreptitious behavior, and he pulled out his micro recorder and replayed the entire telephone call of yesterday that was on speakerphone between Pierce, Sammie, and Davis. When he got to the commentary of his golf match earlier in the day, he clicked it off.

Rita spoke first, "Is that tape legal?"

All four lawyers in the room assured her it was legal and admissible because one party to the conversation knew that it was being recorded.

Rita asked. "Pierce knew it was being recorded?"

Sinclair answered, "No, dear, Ben did. He was a party to the call. He counts."

Davis had already thought this through, but he let Morty take the lead, since Morty wasn't present and was in a better position to explain. Even his position was one of conflict since he was the Davises' partner. Another lawyer would have to introduce the tape into evidence.

"This tape and January's offer to sell the custody of his children prove his immorality and his unfitness to be awarded sole custody of the children. Sammie and Ben become critical witnesses in the case. We'll have to withdraw as counsel for Rachel, but she's not going to be at the hearing anyway. We'll need to find a great lawyer for Tyree and Rita, who will request that they be awarded custody of the children." Morty took a deep breath. He was overly excited. He didn't look good.

Davis took over, "We can win this and get you custody. Pierce sounds despicable on that tape, and she was January's agent. A judge will be shocked by their conduct."

Morty reminded Davis to preserve the custody of the tape. Davis put the micro tape in an envelope, sealed it, signed, and dated it with the time.

Morty asked, "What else is on that tape?"

"An exciting golf match with my son. I guess that's just part of the record in this case."

Sammie asked, "Do we respond to Pierce's offer? The deadline expires at nine tomorrow."

Morty answered, "Our response is 'Nuts.'"

Everyone in the room except Sammie was familiar with American General Anthony McAuliffe's response to the Nazis at the battle of Bastogne in Belgium. It had to be explained to Sammie, and they all had a good laugh, but everybody in the room knew they were about to engage in a war, not over land or a country's freedom, but children.

CHAPTER FORTY-EIGHT

NO EASY WAY OUT

Thursday, July 22, 1999

The day began like any other, I looked over my computer and studied my to-do list. It was pretty long, much longer than I wanted. *Where to begin, that's the question? As Julie Andrews would say, "Let's start at the very beginning, a very good place to start."*

With no further mental gymnastics I plowed down the list. Phone call after phone call. If I connected, I solved or at least moved a problem forward. I kept it moving. Friend and foe, always pleasant, never nasty, no reason to be. That wasn't my style. I could be tough and hard, but never nasty. Morty told me, "Never leave a bad taste in anyone's mouth." You'll have to work with them again. Let them remember that you beat the hell out of them and that you didn't rub it in. You just walked away a winner."

It was about three o'clock when Kurt Lanier called about the Addams case. "Hello, Ms. Davis..."

"Sammie, please."

"Sammie, then. How are things?"

"Fine." I didn't want to give him much, so I waited.

"You represented the January girl. Any leads on finding her? How's Tyree doing? I've sent him a personal note. I can't even begin to imagine how he's feeling. We've all got children. They're the most important things in our lives. Are you married?"

"No."

I didn't want to go any further with Lanier. He wasn't someone I wanted to know much about my personal life. *Let him do his own research. I bet he knew the answer to that question.*

I didn't particularly like Lanier. Whether he was sincere or not, I couldn't tell over the phone. I could if I could look him in the eye. I guesstimated it was 50/50, but I'd accept it graciously. Why not?

"Nobody knows how he's feeling. It's unimaginable. At first you hope she's run away. But with time you realize that's probably not true. There's no ransom note so you start thinking the worst. It's been three weeks. You try not to give up hope, but it's hard to hold on."

After a moment of awkward silence, Lanier said, "I've got an offer in the Addams case."

"I'm listening." I really wanted to settle Chris's case. The man was very depressed. I didn't think he'd make it to trial. It would also be a big win for me. My uncle turned this one over to me, and I'd gotten the job done with almost no supervision. That would be something. With my voice under complete control, I asked, "What do you have for me?"

"Try this:

1. Addams is made president of Franklin National Bank.
2. Addams is on the board of directors of the bank.
3. Salary: $125,000.
4. Performance bonus: $0-$125,000.
5. Vacation: four weeks.
6. Settlement payment: $100,000.

7. No admission of liability. A standard contract with a confidentiality clause, non-compete for one year and a morals clause, etc."

I didn't answer right away. It was a very fair first offer. I figured there was more on the table if Lanier wouldn't make his best offer right out of the box.

"I'll take it to my client and get back to you."

"Sammie, I need to know fairly quickly. They need to fill that position at the bank starting next Monday. They need to have someone steering the ship."

That was a fair request. It was the top operating position. The ship needed its captain. Either we were going to settle or not. There was no point in a delayed negotiation.

"I'll get right back to you."

Before I could call Chris Addams, I got called into Davis's office. Brad Littleton was on the line, and he didn't want to have a conversation with him without a witness.

Why the hell am I being dragged into this? What's wrong with the great Morty Steine? He seems pretty credible to me. Or the lovely Bella Rosario; she seems pretty believable.

"I'd be nice to him. You can get more with sugar...."

"Thanks for the ethical advice."

"Hello, Brad. What can I do for you?"

"Glad you took my call."

"Look, Brad, you know why I took your call. Get to the point. There's nothing in that finding that says I have to be cordial to you. I'm really busy. I'm in the middle of settlement negotiations. What can I do for you?"

Littleton cleared his throat. He seemed nervous because he was nervous.

"Spit it out, Brad. Whatever it is, it's not going to get any better by delaying telling me."

"Tommy's got gambling debts he can't pay."

"Everybody knows that. I've been told he owes more than $25,000 to five or six guys at the country club."

"Forget about them. They don't count. They might hire a lawyer to sue Tommy. I'm not worried about their collection methods. Yesterday two gorillas came to see me on behalf of Mr. Tony Rosa. They showed me Tommy's markers for $115,000 and told me with the vig, the total was now $186,000. They broke my finger. I told them that Tommy's trust was controlled by his stepsister Maureen and that you were authorized to advise her. I thought about not warning you and letting them jump you and use their physical influence to persuade you to convince Maureen to give Tommy the money to pay them off. But I figured even though you hated me, you'd warn me because it would be the right thing to do, so I better do the same. Watch your ass." Littleton hung up without waiting for a response.

Davis immediately called Maureen Wagner and then Betty Andrews. Both women were very upset and feared for their safety. Davis suggested that they come in at three to discuss options. Davis called down to the sixth floor and asked Morty to join them so they could call Gerry Neenan together.

Before they made the call, Morty pointed out, "Tommy Hamilton is a degenerate gambler. His gambling won't stop and break this debt cycle unless you can teach him to gamble within his means. From experience, that's not possible. Whatever the limit we set, a gambler will exceed it. Tommy Hamilton was fine when he traveled in the country club set. They tolerated him and let him pay off debt at the beginning of the month and then let him continue to gamble the rest of the month until he exceeded an acceptable limit. Then they cut him off. At that point, no matter what point it was in the month, he had nowhere to play. He traveled within his own group, and it was a safe environment. At worst he was cursed at or blackballed from a dinner party. He now moves in a much rougher crowd that carries guns and doesn't use finger bowls. He's now dealing with a new element that is tacking on a vig to his debt every week so he never gets out of debt. His only salvation is to stop gambling. Convince him to go to rehab."

The call to Police Chief Neenan wasn't very productive. They learned that Tony Rosa owned a gun range called the OK Corral out on Old Hickory Boulevard. He had no priors, and there was nothing the police could do unless Littleton filed a complaint for battery for his broken finger. Admittedly he did not know the identity of his attackers.

My uncle called Littleton and asked if he'd file assault and battery charges against Rosa and his two henchmen.

Littleton declined. "Are you crazy? I'm not as out of my mind as you were in those Plainview cases. You risked your life for a bunch of strangers. I'm not risking my life for Tommy Hamilton and his evil stepsisters."

My uncle hated to be reminded about the Plainview cases, particularly by Littleton.

I'm playing it safe. You and Tommy's sisters can face Rosa and his men, not me. I'll let you catch a bullet."

Davis slammed down the phone, ending the call.

I decided to change the focus of the gathering. My uncle's blood pressure was soaring. I told him and Morty about the proposed

Addams settlement. Morty thought that in light of Addams's mood, it was a great deal, and a counteroffer should be made.

"At least it keeps your client in the banking business, and he gets to end his career running a bank."

I responded, "I think we'd win the age discrimination case but Chris's heart is not in it, and you can't go to trial with a client who is not one hundred percent behind the case."

I invited Addams to come in rather than try to explain the settlement proposal on the phone. I was surprised by his reaction. He was less than excited. He didn't complain about the money; he didn't complain about the new job; he complained that the settlement didn't admit he was discriminated against and that it didn't admit liability.

"They broke the law. They should have to admit that. I think our counteroffer should require an apology."

What the hell is he talking about? A bank isn't going to apologize. No way.

I tried to explain, "Chris, the premise of every settlement is to resolve the dispute and put the dispute behind the parties. You know that the bank has a board of directors, and it's not going to approve an apology. How would it explain an apology to its stockholders?"

"I need an apology."

"That's not customary, and it's not going to happen."

"I don't care what's customary. These people discriminated against me in violation of the law and then flatly tried to deny it."

"You're not going to get an apology. Take the deal, please, Chris."

Addams started to cry. He was a proud man who managed other men. I put my arm around my client as he wept. The man started to shake, which caused me to start to shake as well.

In a soft voice Addams said, “Prepare the documents. I’ll sign. Thank you for your help.”

When Addams left the office, he was still crying. As he walked out, Maureen Wagner and Betty Andrews walked in the office.

Bella ushered the two sisters into the conference room. Morty, Davis, and I joined them.

Betty, who tended to be quiet, began, “I’m not going to expose my family to some thugs because of Tommy’s gambling problems. He’s an animal, and now he’s brought the jungle into our lives. It’s not right.”

Davis decided he needed to get ahead of these two frantic women. “Look, Tommy is who he is. He’s been this way for a long time. Unless he changes, we can expect these problems for the next twenty years or until someone kills him.”

“That’s a thought,” Betty added.

Davis retorted angrily, “Shut up, Betty. Do you want to try to solve this problem or not?”

Davis pushed a paper in front of them.

PROPOSED ORDER

1. Payment to Sam Reed: $4,320
2. Payment to Louis Dean: $5,123
3. Payment to George Kelp: $8,769
4. Payment to Wendell Sands: $3,245
5. Payment to Robert Cooper: $5,673
6. Payment to Tony Rosa: $186,349
7. One hundred twenty days in voluntary committal to Whispering Pines, a gambling twelve steps program

8. Trust pays for Whispering Pines.

9. A monthly allowance of $12,000 ($48,000) will be paid upon graduation.

"This cleans the slate of monies owed and may stop Tommy from gambling. If it doesn't work, you've done what you could and Tommy's on his own. Then I suggest we turn it over to the police."

Morty nodded his head in agreement. The two women looked at each other and begrudgingly agreed. There was no right answer. Davis faxed the order to Brad Littleton. Littleton called within five minutes.

"Hello, Brad."

"Tommy is kicking and screaming about four months in rehab. Why can't we make it thirty days?"

"No dice. This has to be a serious rehab. Whispering Pines is a serious place. He won't be able to check himself out. Once he checks himself in, he's there for the entire four months. We're paying off more than $225,000. We're going to get our money's worth. This kid has a chance to live a great, full life, but he's got to stop gambling. If he doesn't, he's going to die in an alley somewhere. Maureen's not going to bail him out again. Let us know."

Davis hung up. Five minutes later, Littleton called back, "We've got a deal."

CHAPTER FORTY-NINE

SELECTING THE RIGHT MAN

Friday, July 23, 1999

Davis drew up the Whispering Pines order not a moment too soon. When he arrived at his office, he found two guests waiting. Bella had already given Mr. Bruno and Mr. Domino cups of coffee. Davis led them into his private office and closed the door. He had the two men sit across from him at his desk.

"Gentlemen, before you commit a felony, I suggest you say nothing." Davis handed them a copy of the Whispering Pines order. "This will be a public document by the end of the day. I direct your attention to the payment to Mr. Rosa of more than $186,000. I suggest your employer declares that dollar amount on his income tax return because this document is going to be a matter of public record. I also direct your attention to the fact that Tommy's stepsister will not be bailing him out again in the event Tommy becomes indebted to Mr. Rosa again. She will not be bailing him out on any other gambling debts owed to anyone. Pass it along. If anyone gambles with Tommy and his losses exceed his money allowance of twelve grand a month, don't come here or to the sisters for payment.

"If your employer lets him run gambling debts above his monthly allowance, his ability to collect falls on his shoulders. I expect you to spread the word about Tommy's limited resources on the street. You can all race for the same twelve grand, or you can stay away from Tommy Hamilton because he's a known risk. You see, if anything happens to Tommy Hamilton, whether he's injured or a piano falls on his head and he dies, the investigation begins with your boss. In a way Mr. Rosa just became responsible for the life of Tommy Hamilton."

Bruno responded, "We don't want that responsibility. It would be easier to get rid of him than babysit him."

"That's not my clients' problem. They're going to supply the allowance. I suggest you have a good talk with Tommy to live within those parameters. Do not contact me again. If you do, I will be contacting Chief of Police Gerry Neenan and prosecuting you and Mr. Rosa to the full extent of the law for extortion."

Davis paused for effect as he removed a .357 from his top desk drawer and placed it on the desk with the muzzle pointed at the two men.

"I am an officer of the court, but I'm also a father and a husband first. For that reason, I'm not going to mince words with you gentlemen. You see, I was born and raised in Brooklyn, New York, not Nashville, Tennessee. I own several guns and won't hesitate to use them if you boys decide that somehow my continued involvement is necessary to solve your problem with Hamilton. Leave mine alone."

Davis made sure his accent was pronounced as he said the word *Brooklyn*.

"I don't care how fucking big you are. That doesn't impress me because this .357 can cut through your bones and stop both of you just as fast as some poor slob who's five foot five. If either of you comes through the threshold of my office door again, I will put a bullet in your fucking head. If you come around my house or my family, I will blow your heads off with a shotgun, which I keep nearby at all times. I shit you not. I'm from New York. This is over."

Davis believed that these thugs only respected strength, a willingness to fight. Davis told them in his commanding voice that he was willing to do just that.

"You'll have your funds delivered to the OK Corral by eleven. It's the last payment you'll see from this office. Now get the hell out of here."

After they left, Davis went to the bathroom, took a good leak, and washed his face. His hands were shaking. He'd held it together, but he really wasn't a tough guy. He had the voice and could be momentarily tough in a courtroom setting, but he wasn't street hardened. He'd held it together long enough to send the right message.

Steine, Davis, & Davis debated for almost a week about which attorney should succeed the firm in the January case. More precisely, the firm's client Rachel January had disappeared, and unless she reappeared, she had no real need to be represented. The newly retained counsel would represent Tyree and Rita Sinclair, who would be seeking custody of their grandchildren Franklin and Gabriela January over the objection of their father, Daniel January.

Bob Sullivan was one of the proposed alternatives, but he was eliminated because he'd represented Laura Chapman's husband, and she'd be an important witness. Sinclair suggested two members of his firm, but after considerable discussion, it was agreed that would be a conflict. Davis and Morty urged Sinclair to select a litigator who wasn't necessarily a member of the divorce Bar. Morty argued that Sinclair should select Jack Henry, who was neither a divorce lawyer nor a Nashville lawyer. Henry practiced in Franklin and Williamson County, south of Nashville and hadn't appeared before either of the female judges who might hear the case.

Sinclair's objection to Henry had nothing to do with his reputation but with his age. Sinclair thought the old warrior at seventy-four might be past his prime.

Morty at age seventy-eight was slightly offended by Sinclair's prejudice. "Don't confuse age with experience. This man has almost fifty years of practicing law and thinking on his feet."

Sinclair's insensitive response was, "How long can he stand on those feet?"

That pissed Morty off. It made him think about the Addams age discrimination case and the fact that even good men like Tyree Sinclair, a good lawyer, discriminated based on age. *Jack Henry deserves better than that.* Morty kept arguing, and with time Sinclair's heart softened.

The deciding factor convinced Sinclair when he learned that Henry was instrumental in 1994 of bringing charges against Amy Pierce that resulted in the suspension of her law license for three months.

Morty argued, "Henry is one of the few lawyers who has not only gotten the better of Amy Pierce, but hurt her where it really counts. He convinced Judge Thomas Wise to take Pierce's law license away for violating the confidentiality clause of a settlement agreement by contacting the IRS. Pierce will remember Henry for taking away what she cherished most, her law license. She not only dislikes Henry. She fears him."

Sinclair admitted that counted for something.

"Remember, Ty, Pierce may start the case by representing January, but I promise you in short order she will either voluntarily resign or be forced from the case. That tape and her settlement offer are at the heart of the motion, and the court will quickly recognize that she's a witness in the case and therefore is conflicted out from acting as January's counsel."

Sinclair admitted, "I'm kinda looking forward to Henry cross-examining Pierce and that bastard January. Morty, you've got Rita's and my best interests in mind, and if you think Henry's the right man for the job, then he is."

Davis and Sammie stayed out of the selection process because they were critical witnesses, and that wouldn't have been appropriate. They figured whoever Morty and Sinclair selected, they'd be working closely with that professional. They trusted that Morty would make a good choice. In fact, whoever that attorney was, that attorney would be directing them throughout the litigation. Davis could take orders from Morty, but he wasn't used to following anyone else's lead. He'd have to learn.

Sammie polished her brief and the motion. Davis prepared a draft affidavit, which provided:

AFFIDAVIT
State of Tennessee
County of Davidson

Comes now the affiant and makes oath as follows:

1. I am Benjamin Abraham Davis, a citizen and resident of Davidson County, Tennessee.

2. I am licensed to practice law in this state, my bar #7342.

3. I am a partner in the law firm of Steine, Davis, & Davis, and my firm represented Rachel January, who mysteriously disappeared on July 4th, 1999.

4. In connection with my representation of Ms. January, I had a telephone conversation on July 20, 1999, with Amy Pierce, Esq. who represented Daniel January, the husband of Rachel January.

5. I recorded my July 20, 1999, telephone conversation with Ms. Pierce. I was aware I was recording the conversation; to the best of my knowledge, Ms. Pierce was unaware she was being recorded.

6. Attached as Exhibit A is a micro cassette that preserved my telephone conversation with Ms. Pierce.

7. Attached as Exhibit B is a true and exact transcript of the recording.

8. The last eleven minutes of the recording are an unrelated conversation between my son, Jacob Davis, and me. I didn't erase that portion of the tape to preserve its integrity. As an officer of the court familiar with the Tennessee Rules of Evidence, I can state under oath that I preserved the chain of evidence of the recording.

9. Further the affiant sayeth not,
   Benjamin Abraham Davis

The recording was the key to the motion. Davis would make whatever changes Henry directed. He'd be deposed, and one of the first documents he'd be questioned about would be his affidavit.

He'd be attacked for taping Pierce without her knowledge. He'd be challenged that what he did was unethical, but it wasn't. It was within the bounds of Tennessee law and the Code of Professional Responsibility. Davis refused to agree to keep the conversation confidential. In many states, the tape would be not only inadmissible, but also criminal. Davis knew the law. He was confident he'd conducted himself appropriately.

He'd be asked about whether he taped all of his telephone conversations, and the response would be no.

"Then why did you tape this conversation?"

"Because I've dealt with Ms. Pierce before. She's unethical and has a conveniently poor memory. She's not truthful. I knew that she was going to address issues in the January case, and I wanted there to be an accurate record of what was said in the conversation. I didn't know what she was going to say. I suspected that what she was going to say would be important and decided it should be memorialized. I didn't know she was going to propose that the Sinclairs purchase the custody of their grandchildren. But that's what she did, and as the agent of Dan January, he's bound by her conduct."

That's what January's new counsel would have to face.

"I pity the fool," Davis promised.

The firm put together a tight package of the law and the facts and sent it to Jack Henry with a request that he represent Rita and Tyree Sinclair.

In several phone conversations Morty prepped his old friend, and it was a given that he'd accept employment. A meeting was scheduled at Steine, Davis, & Davis for Henry to meet the Sinclairs and share his opinion.

Henry was the man for the job. There was a lot at stake not in money but in the lives of two young people.

CHAPTER FIFTY

NUCLEAR EXPLOSION AND ANOTHER AVOIDED

Friday, July 30, 1999

I was glad when the Addams paperwork was signed. Chris had buyer's remorse for several days before execution. I couldn't put my finger on it, but he seemed nervous. Lanier reviewed the contract with us paragraph by paragraph. Chris's start date was Monday, August 2nd, 1999.

Bella buzzed me at ten, "I've got Kurt Lanier on the line."

"Hello, Kurt." After our settlement, we were on a first name basis.

"We've got a big problem, Sammie. Have you seen the morning news?"

"No."

"Your client Addams made it. He's been charged with molesting a minor, a twelve-year-old boy. The boy's identity has been withheld, but he's a member of his Boy Scout troop 34. The boy's father has been giving interviews with his voice garbled and his face masked. The father's divorced from the mother and really hasn't played any role in the kid's life, but he's surfaced now. He's screaming bloody murder. If you ask me, the whole thing seems pretty unjust. A man should have a right to face his accuser."

I was floored. I didn't know what to say. I counted to ten and then counted to ten again. I choked out, "What channel? When was it aired?"

Lanier gleefully responded, "Every local channel. It might even make national news. It's been on all morning. I'm sure they'll carry it in the evening as well. It's a disaster. You can tear up that contract. The bank is evoking the morals clause of our contract."

Without thinking, I argued, "We've got a settlement..."

"We *had* a settlement. That's history, young lady."

I didn't like the way Lanier slipped back into disrespecting me. What happened to his good friend Sammie? I guess we never were friends. No kidding.

I was devastated. I sat at my desk and cried, not a very professional thing to do, but I didn't really care. It felt good. I needed to talk to Chris and get his side of the story. I wanted to hear what my client and friend had to say.

When I got him on the phone, there was a deafening silence, and I was forced to directly ask, "Is it true?"

"Does it matter?"

"Of course it matters. If you're innocent, the world needs to know that."

"I've been charged. There will always be those whispers, always those doubts. I'll never work in banking again. I'll have to go through a trial and be judged by my peers. That will take time and money. These charges won't help my lawsuit against the bank."

"Lanier is screaming bloody murder, asserting the deal is void because of your alleged illegal actions. I'm not supposed to ask this question, but did you do it?"

"No, but I don't see what the fucking difference that makes."

After that, Chris hung up.

I went to the bathroom and wiped away my tears. I had to report the latest development to my uncle and Morty without the passion I was feeling. It was bad enough that the settlement had fallen apart and our client was facing criminal prosecution. I could not be seen as an additional liability.

Neither my uncle nor Morty blinked. They took the news in a professional manner and began brainstorming what to do. After fifteen minutes Morty pointed out, "We've got to meet with Jack Henry this morning as a possible substitute counsel in the Sinclair case."

I greeted the older litigator, "Good morning, Mr. Henry."

Jack Henry sat in the conference room. He was distinguished with a full head of snow-white hair. Short of stature, Henry was soft spoken but changed in a courtroom, where judges and juries carefully listened to his well-chosen words. He was a man to be heard.

"Excuse me, Mr. Henry, my uncle is on the phone. I'll get him."

When I walked into his office he was on the speakerphone with George Hopper, private investigator.

"George, I need you to find out everything you can on the Gaineses, Kings, and Coopers. January has something on each of them, or he's bribed them, or he's promised them something. These people wouldn't give Sammie and me the time of day."

"Maybe they just didn't want their sexual exploits exposed?"

"No, it was more than that. I realize that would be embarrassing, but people have short memories, and besides, a third of the women and most of the men on a jury would envy them."

"Has our source provided you with any good leads?"

"What that kid can do with a computer is amazing. I never realized what you could learn remotely and how much information is just floating around out there. These people are talking to each other on e-mails and on cell phones, and they don't know we're listening. This kid can listen in real time. He can record it. He can even distort it. He can change a single word and change the entire meaning of a conversation. He's very dangerous. He can do this to my conversation; he can do this to your conversation. He could start a war; he could end a war. He's very dangerous, and we certainly don't want anyone but us controlling him.

"As to January and his friends, he's going to force them to make a mistake, and when they do, we'll be there. Just hold your breath. I promise you, he's putting together a game plan; laying pitfalls, bait, which they'll take and then fall into his trap. Trust him."

Hooper was a crack investigator, the best, even though he'd been doing it only five years. He'd been a middleweight contender until he broke his right hand in a bar fight defending the honor of his girlfriend, Kelly. That ended his dreams of a championship. Davis was the one who convinced him he'd be good at his new profession. Hopper was grateful and wanted to help with the case.

"What about finding Rachel?"

"Dickie has set up a methodical way to look for her. It's a complex computer model he designed. He divided the country into ten regions, and we hired ten large detective firms in ten big cities, like New York, Miami, Houston, Chicago, Vegas, Seattle, Los Angeles, etc. Let them look for Rachel. I don't think they're going to find her, but we've got to try. I'm the central rallying point for information. Quite frankly I think you're more likely to find her through Sasser's eavesdropping and computer hacking than door-to-door police work. I think she's buried somewhere, and we're not going to find the body. I think Dan January knows exactly where that body is."

Davis hung up, joined Henry in the conference room, and fixed himself an everything bagel with scallion cream cheese lox, red onion, and tomato. *I'm not kissing anyone.*

A minute later Morty and I, and a tall, lanky, completely bald man, who introduced himself as Dr. Peeler, joined them.

The meeting began with a review of the agreement between the Januarys, and then the tape between Davis and Pierce was played. Morty, Davis, and I shared with the doctor our suspicions about why we feel that January killed his wife. Our opinions were consistent and not imaginary.

I got a little emotional, "After the deal was cut, something happened. There was an argument. Rachel may even have verbally provoked him because she knew she'd bought her way out of the marriage. Her taunting may have been too much for him. I'm not sure he intended to kill her, but once she was dead, he covered it up. He may even have had help getting rid of the body. He certainly got help with his alibi. What better one than I was screwing a married woman, and the woman and her husband confirm his whereabouts?"

My uncle had to explain that one to Peeler, who was rightfully confused. Davis gave a fairly detailed explanation of the Januarys' relationship with the Kings and Coopers and Gaineses and provided him with a copy of the Ten Commandments.

Peeler spent several minutes reading the document, and when he was finished, all he said was, "Exceptional. I've never seen anything like that in my thirty years of practice." The group waited for more, but there was nothing else.

Peeler moved on and commented, "I've never met the man, don't know the man. He's innocent until proven guilty beyond a reasonable doubt in my book, and that has not happened yet."

The lawyers knew that Peeler was right, but because of their investigation to date, they reached the conclusion based on the circumstantial evidence that the son of a bitch was guilty.

The real purpose of the meeting was to rethink lighting the fuse.

They knew the monetary cost of making a deal with January. It cost $1 million. Should they fight, or sell their souls and get the children back?

Henry asked the important question, "What will the money be used for?" He then rhetorically answered his own question. "I don't mind if the money is used to make Dan January's life easier and Franklin's and Gaby's lives easier. But what if January uses that money to cover up the murder of Rachel? What if we're giving him the very money he needs to do that? Or worse, what if he uses that money to flee the jurisdiction of the court with the children? You can go pretty far on $1 million. How will we feel then? That would be quite a nightmare, wouldn't it?"

Henry wanted to discuss the emotional impact of such a deal on the Sinclairs. That was why Henry invited Dr. Thomas Peeler, MD and PhD, to sit in on the meeting. The lawyers agreed that Peeler, a psychotherapist and a behavioral scientist, would be a consulting expert. Therefore his identity and opinions under Rule 26 of the Tennessee Rules of Civil Procedure were confidential and not discoverable by the other side. *He'll be our little secret,* thought Davis.

I was ethically concerned. If the motion was filed, my uncle and I were going to testify. Morty, Henry, and Davis argued that the members of the Stein, Davis, & Davis firm were permitted to sit in on the meeting with Dr. Peeler and not testify as to his existence as witnesses because they still represented Rachel January, who was still a party in the case since she had not been declared legally dead. Therefore, the attorneys could agree as co-parties to assert a co-party privilege of confidentiality. The Davises were not obligated to disclose their knowledge of Peeler's identity or opinions. The whole line of reasoning was shaky, but since Morty as past president of the Board of Professional Responsibility blessed it, I accepted his judgment.

Henry handed everyone a summary of the motion, which described the eight key points to be presented to the court:

1. That in January vs. January, initially Daniel January, a licensed attorney, was pro se, and Benjamin Davis and Sammie Davis represented Rachel January. They negotiated a marital dissolution, child custody, and settlement agreement ("Agreement");

2. That under the agreement, Rachel received sole custody of Gabriela and Franklin, the couple's minor children;

3. That under terms of the agreement, Dan January was paid $800,000, received title to the house, title to most of the marital assets except certain art, his 401K, no alimony, and $1,000 a month child support, alternate weekend visitation, and three weeks visitation in the summer;

4. That under the terms of the agreement, Rachel had planned to live with her parents, the petitioners Tyree and Rita Sinclair, in their home and that the petitioners would have played an instrumental role in the raising of Franklin and Gabriela;

5. That since July 4th at 7:00 p. m., Rachel January has not been heard from by any known person and that it is feared and presumed by the petitioners that she is dead;

6. That the disappearance and presumed death of Rachel January are of suspicious circumstances and the petitioners fear for the safety of their grandchildren;

7. That Daniel January, by and through his agent and attorney, Amy Pierce, Esquire, did illegally and unethically try to sell two human beings, his children, Franklin and

Gabriela January, for $2 million to the petitioners. A copy of this taped conversation has been filed with the court;

8. That the petitioners reasonably suspect that Daniel January has knowledge about the disappearance and possible death of Rachel January and therefore suspect that the respondent has failed to provide relevant information to the police in connection with the disappearance and presumed death of their daughter, Rachel, and that this suspicious behavior renders him unfit to act as guardian for his minor children, the petitioners' grandchildren.

Peeler took charge of the conversation. "Let's assume for purposes of argument that January killed Rachel. Then he'd do anything to cover it up, including kill again. That's a real problem because that means we're dealing with a desperate individual, willing to do anything to protect himself. Accordingly the more pressure you exert on such a person, the more reaction you can expect from such a person. These reactions can include, but need not be limited to, violence, flight, and/or suicide."

"Could that violence be against the children?" I asked.

"Not likely, especially if you accept the notion that January still believes in the Ten Commandments. Remember the First Commandment that puts his children first ahead of everything else. He may stray but not from that core principle."

I was relieved.

Peeler continued, "No, it's more likely he'd go after you, your uncle, Mr. Steine, or Mr. Sinclair."

I looked at my uncle a little nervously. We'd had trouble with adversary parties before who didn't play by the Rules of Civil Procedure. "That's cheery news" was all I could say.

Henry looked hard at everyone in the room and asked the critical question, "Do we recommend to Tyree Sinclair that we cut the deal or file the motion? I want each of you to give an opinion, but the call is mine. He hired me, but I value your advice."

Morty, the senior one in the room, spoke first, "I say file the motion. I think it's a loser. I think January will get pissed. I think he'll withhold the kids, and I think the court will eventually grant Tyree and Rita visitation and will make new law establishing grandparent visitation rights in the state of Tennessee. I think it will be painful, and I think it will be expensive, but I think it will work. I'll double my effort in the state legislature to get a law passed as well. If you think that bastard killed Rachel, I can't see paying him a dime."

I went next. I got to the same place but for different reasons. "If you pay January $1 million, you provide him unlimited resources. He can leave Nashville with flawless fake identification to a country with no extradition, and then where are we? I don't think we'll win the motion, so why poke him in the eye? Let's not allege foul play. Let's assume disappearance. Let's argue Rachel's gone and assume she's coming back. Let's ask for the order to be suspended until she returns, not set aside."

Davis hadn't thought about that. Neither had Morty. *Brains and beauty, a dangerous combination.* Davis smiled. He liked where I was going.

I kept going, "The kids live with January, but visit with their grandparents as often as January will permit, at least every other weekend. January, the lazy son of a bitch, might just concede a substantial amount of time to avoid the responsibility. It's not perfect, but at least it gives the Sinclairs access to Frankie and Gaby while we try to figure out this mess, and we keep looking for proof to implicate the bastard in the murder of Rachel. When we find it, we pounce.

They reached a consensus and agreed to a plan. A new motion would be prepared. It would be short and sweet.

MOTION

The petitioners Tyree and Rita Sinclair move for the court to suspend the entry of the marital dissolution and property settlement agreement in the divorce action of their daughter, Rachel January, in January vs. January docket # 99-2343 because on July 4th, 1999, their daughter disappeared and her whereabouts are not yet known. The petitioners, the maternal grandparents of Franklin and Gabriela January, during the unknown whereabouts of their daughter, ask for reasonable visitation of their grandchildren every other weekend.

Respectfully Submitted
Jack Henry, Esquire

Amy Pierce, on behalf of Dan January, objected, but she had no compelling argument. She couldn't deny the disappearance. She certainly couldn't deny that Rachel might be coming back or that she was dead. The judge granted the requested visitation. They might have asked for more. Davis suspected that January would concede more after he got tired of playing daddy. The judge set a hearing in one hundred twenty days and suspended entry of the order.

Davis called George Hopper and told him to get to work.

CHAPTER FIFTY-ONE

ALIBI DESTROYED

Monday, August 23, 1999

It took more than a month for George Hopper to waggle his way into Robert Gaines's regular poker game. He first became friends with Larry Davenport, an insurance agent, by purchasing a $1 million term life policy and naming his brother as the beneficiary. The purchase of the policy was a big surprise. George's brother suddenly remembered his birthday by sending a present for the first time in thirty years, since George's eleventh birthday.

Because of the recent policy sale, George and Larry became immediate friends. As they bonded, George told Larry a few Vegas stories involving voluptuous showgirls and big losses at the poker tables, which made him sound like a real mark. With those qualifications and his actual fight stories, which were pretty exciting, there was no problem getting George invited to the next poker night.

It was a friendly game of five, ten, twenty dollars. A man could lose five, six hundred dollars pretty easily. If hot, a player could win or lose a few thousand. George decided not to alter his identity. If he had to testify, it would look better by giving his correct name and background. He simply failed to mention he was currently employed as an investigator for the Steine Davis, & Davis law firm.

His story focused more on his military service and boxing careers. He'd been a marine as a young man, where he learned his craft as a boxer. The fact he had been a fighter made him colorful and made him sound tough.

For some reason it opened up the other players and got them sharing about themselves. These men knew each other pretty well. They played together for years. As the conversation progressed, it was also apparent that several of the men were swingers and had exchanged wives and girlfriends.

George just listened and kept his mouth shut. He had come to the game prepared. His recorder was taped to his chest and was of the newest technology from East Germany. Dickie Sasser was monitoring every word from his car parked a short distance away. He was also listening to the conversations to help him crack the passwords of each of the players. Most people used words, a regular part of their lives, such as pet names or some form of a family member's birthday.

The men started showing pictures of their wives and talking about them. George was prepared with a topless picture of a twenty-something model that he'd never met. "I'm divorced, but I've got one hell of a girlfriend." He passed around her photo that was admired by all.

Albert King stared at the picture for quite some time and then handed it to Robert Gaines as he quietly said, "I wish George and this young lady could have joined us on the 4th this year. She would have been quite a nice addition to our foursome, don't you think?"

"Shut up, Albert."

The conversation ended there, but King's remark may have been enough.

Bingo, alibi destroyed.

Hopper intentionally lost the next five hands big. He had no more chips and pretended to be a sore loser so he could leave the game. In the car, Hopper listened to the tape and confirmed he'd captured the confession. The alibi was revoked. January had lied. Robert and Robin Gaines had lied.

The game broke up at four, and Hopper was so excited that he called Davis before five at home. He was surprised that the lawyer was already up, getting ready to go to the office. Hopper played the tape into the phone. They agreed to meet at the office at seven. Morty and Sammie were already on site in their apartments.

Morty protested that the meeting was scheduled so early. "I need my beauty sleep. Can't this wait? Whatever is on that tape will be there at ten o'clock, just the same."

But when the tape was played, all Morty could say was, "Wow!"

Thinking out loud, Davis said, "We need to play this for Duncan. She can then charge Robert and Robin Gaines with obstruction of justice and . . ."

Morty interrupted. "Slow down. We need to think about this. Let's not rush into anything. This is great evidence, but I think we should meet with Duncan and convince her not to pull the trigger yet. Let's use George to gather more evidence before we show our hand."

It wasn't lost on anyone that Morty was using a poker analogy in light of the fact that the tape was secured through a poker game.

Morty continued, "First thing I think we need to do is bring Jack Henry, Tyree and Rita Sinclair into the loop and get their input. I don't think the Sinclairs should attend the meeting with Duncan, but they're entitled to a status report."

Three hours later Detective Duncan was sitting in the conference room of Steine, Davis, & Davis on one side of the table, and

Davis, Hopper, Morty, and Henry were on the other. Each had a cup of coffee and a plate of donuts between them. Sammie was delayed because she had to attend a previous court appearance. She resolved the issue before court and ran back to the office, breaking the heel on her right shoe on the cobblestones of Printer's Alley.

Sammie walked in, saw the seating arrangement, and sat next to Duncan. As she slipped off her shoes, she said, "Looks like you could use a friend; a female friend at that."

"I was kinda feeling lonely on my side of the table, being all alone, with all those penises over there pointed at me."

Sammie in the spirit of solidarity turned to Duncan, in an effort to make a lifelong friend and ally said, "Don't mind these dinosaurs. It's an old lawyer trick to try to intimidate adversaries by isolating them in a room."

"Are the donuts a joke because my last name is Duncan and sounds like the donut company name?"

"No, my uncle likes donuts and anything else he can put in his mouth. It's not personal. It's an eating disorder."

Duncan got down to business. "It's not that I don't enjoy the company, but what's so earth shattering that we had to meet here at your office?"

Sammie introduced George Hopper and Jack Henry. She explained each of their roles in the January case. She then recounted Hopper's contact with Davenport and inclusion in the poker game.

Hopper explained that he'd preserved the chain of evidence, which was critical to Duncan if it was to be useful in her criminal investigation. Hopper played the tape.

Duncan sat there without a word for a good minute. "Up until a minute ago, I was eighty-five percent sure that Rachel January voluntarily left her home with someone she knew. I wasn't sure whether she was alive. She may have met with foul play after she left, but I thought that January's alibi was solid. Now that his story has crumbled, murder is a real possibility. Mr. Hopper, I'll need you to surrender that tape and give me an affidavit to document the chain of evidence how you obtained it and who you've played it for. Do you think you can get back in that poker game?"

"I left pretty abruptly, but it was four o'clock. I don't think I'll have to apologize. I was one of the big losers, about six hundred dollars. I told some good stories. Big losers who tell good stories are usually welcome."

A big smile came over Duncan's face. Do you think you could get the game to let you host?"

Henry leaped up from his chair like a Mexican jumping bean and said, "I have a fifty-four-foot cruiser docked at Rock Harbor Marina. What if you offered your friend's boat as the spot for the game? You could get a court order to have it wired for both sound and video. George could suggest that there'd be room for two tables, and maybe Gaines would invite King or Cooper to the game. We might get lucky."

Duncan thought it was a great idea. She already intended to bring criminal charges against Dan January, Robin Gaines, and Robert Gaines for obstruction of justice and filing a false police statement, both felonies. The question was, were they involved in a murder? Duncan had no problem securing the necessary warrants. The plan was set in motion.

CHAPTER FIFTY-TWO

THE GOOD SHIP LOLLIPOP

Wednesday, September 1, 1999

Jack Henry's *The Good Ship Lollipop* was tied up at slip thirty-one at the Rock Harbor Marina, and it had been rigged for both video and audio by a warrant signed, sealed, and delivered by Judge William Barnes based upon the affidavit of George Hopper. District Attorney Johnson Tory was prepared to present to the grand jury indictment against Robert Gaines, Robin Gaines, Albert King, and Helen Cooper, but he wanted to see what additional charges might be brought based upon the cruise down the Cumberland River. He was going to hold back on Dan January, and his older brother, Phillip, hoping to use the small fish to catch the big fish.

The crew was comprised of police officers, including a female hostess in a tight silver jumpsuit serving drinks, snacks, and sandwiches to the players. The rest of the crew of officers had strict instructions to remain above deck so that the players would feel free to talk openly.

Everyone began arriving at 2:00 p.m. By three the boat left the dock. There were twelve players in all, including George Hopper, Robert Gaines, Albert King, Dan January, Phillip January, and

Tommy Hamilton. Hamilton was a friend of Albert King, and Hopper learned he had recently become one of January's boys.

The players broke into two games. Hopper, Hamilton, and the two Januarys were at one table. King and Gaines were at the other. Under each table were sophisticated bugs capable of separating the conversation of each person. The games progressed a few hands with mindless chatter back and forth between the players. Nothing personal was exchanged. King and Gaines at their table made a few sexual remarks about each other's wife that the other players at the tables didn't hear, and if they did, they wouldn't understand. Then Phillip January asked Hopper, "What line of work are you in?"

"I'm a retired boxer, middleweight. I was pretty good. I had a 24-4 record. My four losses were to Sugar Ray Leonard and Thomas Hearns, each twice. One of my fights against Sugar Ray was a title shot."

The table was impressed. Hopper was more than a minor celebrity.

Hamilton asked, "Do you miss the limelight?"

"No, remember, I got punched hard in the face for a living. After a fight, I hurt for weeks. After fighting someone like Sugar Ray, a little bit of me was gone forever. I could have kept on fighting for a few more years, but there would have been nothing left of me, so I stopped."

Never shy, Dan January asked, "Did you save any money? Most fighters wind up broke without a penny to their names."

"I was pretty lucky. I had a good manager. He looked out for me. I invested my money wisely. I'm not rich, but I'm comfortable. I own a car wash, a Laundromat, and one-half of a dry cleaner's business. The car wash and Laundromat run themselves. I have an excellent operating partner at the cleaners. I'm basically retired."

It was all a lie. Hopper would be attacked on cross-examination for telling them, but they were white lies to preserve his cover.

He couldn't admit he was a private investigator working for Steine Davis, & Davis on behalf of Rachel January. That just wouldn't fly. In every lawsuit, both criminal and civil, the trial was like a boxing match. Each side landed punches. The key to the fight was to win rounds, but the ultimate goal was to be standing at the end of the fight and not be knocked out and to win the decision. In a civil case, it was a judgment. In a criminal case, it was guilt or innocence.

As the day progressed and the whiskey flowed, tongues loosened. Hopper talked about his two nasty divorces. Again white lies, but he hoped he might get January talking about Rachel. It didn't work. "My manager had each of those bitches sign pre-nups. They got practically nothing. Their lawyers tried to break them, but they were iron clad. One thing I learned is that a good contract is important. Once you get something signed on the bottom line in black and white, it's like it's in cement."

All of a sudden, Dan January became really angry. It was as if the liquor got to him. "Don't be so sure of that. I had a contract. In fact I had a signed court order, and it's not worth the paper it's written on."

There was a long pause. Hopper didn't want to interrupt because he wanted January to keep talking of his own volition. But he didn't, so Hopper prodded him, "What the hell are you mumbling about?"

"I entered into a divorce settlement. It was all agreed to. The property divided, custody worked out, but Tennessee law has a ninety-day cooling off period before the order becomes final, and my ex-wife disappears."

Hopper needed to word his next question very carefully, and January, if he was smart, needed to answer even more carefully. "What do you mean disappeared?"

"Quite frankly, I don't know. I think she just split. She was a little flaky. We had sexual problems."

Phillip broke in, "That's one way to describe it. He liked sex, and she didn't. As a result my brother had to seek sex elsewhere. She was a watcher rather than a doer. He's better off without her. Good riddance."

Hopper was a little surprised by the brother's candor. He lost his poker face for just a minute, which prompted the husband to add, "I think she met some guy and took off. Some people think she's dead. She may be. Some people think that I killed her. I didn't. I just wanted to be rid of her. The divorce accomplished that, so I had no reason to kill her."

That was a pretty good answer, Hopper thought. *January must have been practicing that one in case he thought he was going to be questioned by the DA.* That ended his answer and the conversation on that issue. Hopper didn't want to push it any further.

After about three hours, the boat turned around for the return voyage to the marina. The players switched tables, and Albert King, Larry Davenport, and Robert Gaines joined Hopper, and Hamilton and January went to the other table.

Hopper saw this as an opportunity to gossip. Hopper directed his question to Davenport: "Larry, what's the story on January's wife's disappearance?"

There was an awkward silence at the table. Davenport didn't answer.

"Is it a trade secret or something? I don't mean to pry, but it sounded so mysterious, and he got so angry. I'm curious, that's all."

Albert King answered, "It's a sore subject. Under the deal, Dan was supposed to get almost $1 million. With his wife's disappearance, the money is tied up. Dan was counting on that money. He doesn't think Rachel's disappearance or even death should prevent its disbursement."

"Not unless he killed her," Hopper added.

"Why would you say something like that?" Albert asked in defense of his friend. Hamilton broke in, "She may have been murdered, but it wasn't Dan. I think she was murdered on the road after she ran away from home. She was a weird bitch."

What a strange thing to say.

The boat docked, and all of the players thanked Hopper for an excellent afternoon and evening.

After the players disembarked, the police and Detective Duncan met in the cabin and congratulated Hopper. Duncan commented, "You're quite the junior G-man, aren't you? We may have to make you a special deputy. You will be a star witness in the criminal trial. That is certain."

"Lucky me. I'll have to thank Ben Davis for that honor," replied Hopper.

"Look on the bright side. You got to ride on *The Good Ship Lollipop*."

Hopper smiled and said, "I'll write a fan letter to Shirley Temple.

CHAPTER FIFTY-THREE

A SHORT RIDE HOME

Monday, September 13, 1999

Tyree Sinclair ruled Sinclair & Sims with an iron fist, yet he was a benevolent dictator. September 30 was fiscal year end, and 1999 had been a good one. Only the three managing partners, Tyree Sinclair, Harold Sims, and John Timmons and the firm's auditors knew the details of footnote sixty-four, the January/Chapman confidential litigation settlement of $260,000. If pressed by one of the non-managing partners, Sinclair had convinced himself that he would direct him to the confidential reference to the footnote and hope that would satisfy the curiosity. If not he'd then argue that the partner's bonus of up to $600,000 should be explanation enough.

The end of year meeting successfully chaired by Sinclair resulted in three junior partners becoming full partners; five senior associates becoming junior partners; fifteen associates becoming senior associates; and six of the fifteen summer law clerks being offered jobs as associates with the firm. It was a very competitive place to work, and the firm paid very well. The starting salary for an associate was $75,000 a year, and the firm had its choice from the best schools in the country. It preferred Harvard and Vandy grads. Firm philosophy required one to work up the ranks, but after seven years, a junior partner made more than $300,000 plus perks. If you didn't move up the ladder, it became apparent to those staffers, and you got the message loud and clear and moved on. If you didn't, you were shoved out the door.

At the top of the ladder was Tyree Sinclair, and he and the other two managing partners decided who moved up the other rungs. Satisfied with the status of this year, Tyree called the meeting adjourned and left his downtown office, got in the elevator, pushed B, and went to the underground garage.

As he pulled out of the garage, he stopped in front of the automatic gate, opened and leaned out the window to insert his security card. Without warning, a figure emerged from the shadows. Presumably, a he, because he was tall, dressed all in black, with black racing gloves, and a black ski mask. There were three flashes, and Sinclair slumped over the steering wheel with three .32 caliber bullet holes in his brain. His left arm was hanging out the window. He mumbled something, but there was no one to hear his last words and try to help him.

Using a seven-inch knife, the attacker cut Sinclair's seat belt, opened the driver front door, and the body fell from the car to the ground. With the body clear from the car, the assailant jumped into the driver's seat, put the car into drive, and drove through the barricade, shattering the wood, into traffic.

Sinclair lay there brain dead, but his heart was still pumping. If someone were to check, he still had a pulse. A security camera at the gate preserved the shooting, carjacking, and Sinclair's death on video.

Peter Mitchell, one of the new associates, heard the shots and came running down the ramp. He'd been parked on the second floor. He saw the assailant, but his description would later be of no help to the police because of the nature of the clothing. He did tell the police that on the person's belt was a Bowie knife, and he saw him cut the seat belt and drive away. Mitchell's description added nothing that wasn't already on video.

Peter Mitchell called 911 as he ran toward his fallen employer and checked his pulse. Nothing.

The 911 operator got on the line. "911. State your emergency."

"I'd like to report a shooting. He's taken a car. He's on the ground... a black Caddy... hurry, hurry. Oh, my God!" The young man yelled into his cell phone.

Harold Sims volunteered to tell poor Rita Sinclair what happened to her husband. He just couldn't let her find out through the police department. Before he did, he required a little courage from three double scotches. When he arrived at Sinclair's home, he had to sit in the driveway for fifteen minutes and have a good cry before he could go in. He'd been Tyree's partner for more than thirty years and would miss him. He dreaded telling Rita, but he mustered the courage and knocked. A maid answered the door. He saw Gaby out of the corner of his blurred eye.

"Hi, Gaby. Is your grandmother home?"

"Hello, Mr. Sims. She's upstairs, I'll go get her."

The six-year-old ran up, two steps at a time. Unlike her granddaughter, Rita Sinclair, a lady, gracefully came down the stairs and held out her hand, which Harold kissed.

Playfully, Rita began, "To what do I owe this . . ."

"Stop!" He took her by the shoulders and forced her to the couch. He brought her close to him, closer than he would have under normal circumstances, and then he gently whispered in her ear, "Tyree's dead. I'm so sorry. He's dead." He squeezed her hard.

He did not anticipate her reaction. He thought she might cry or become hysterical, but not so. Maybe it was shock, or maybe out of strength, Rita turned to Harold and asked him to call Morty Steine, Ben Davis, Sammie Davis, and Jack Henry. "Tyree wouldn't want us to make a move without their advice."

Morty and Davis went to the Sinclair home while Sammie went to the crime scene. Henry remained at his office in Franklin in charge of contemplating what pleading should be filed in the divorce action prior to the October 20th hearing.

When Sammie arrived two hours after the shooting, Tyree's body was still on the scene. It was covered by a blanket but hadn't been moved. It lay in the same position where it fell to the pavement in a pool of blood. DNA samples and photos galore were taken for evidence. Police detectives and forensic personnel were everywhere. The crime scene looked like a zoo.

Sammie saw Duncan and got her attention. "What do you think?"

"We've got a witness, some young lawyer from his firm. He describes a carjacking. His name is Peter Mitchell, a new associate with Sinclair's firm. He didn't see the shooting. His story doesn't make sense. Sinclair was shot execution style, three to the head. Why do that if you're just hijacking a car? Usually the victim is forced from the vehicle. Why add violence and an additional twenty-five years to the crime? The lifting of the car is a Class D felony with a loaded gun. That's two years, out in eighteen months. If you fire the gun, add another two years, and serve another year or so. Why shoot the victim and add fifteen to twenty-five if all you want is the car? He didn't even stop to rob Sinclair. He wore a gold watch and had six hundred dollars in his wallet. This was more than a jacking. He just wanted us to think it was a jacking."

Sammie thought Duncan was right. Duncan didn't say it, but

both women thought that Dan January was behind Sinclair's death. Proving it would be difficult.

Harold Sims rather than the maid answered the door at the Sinclairs' house. The maid had put the children to bed. They'd become inconsolable upon learning of the death of their grandfather. Rita knew she needed to address legal matters so she sent them to their rooms to regain control of themselves as well as give her some breathing room. She recognized that she and these children would need individual as well as family counseling.

Rita stood as she greeted Morty and Davis, who followed Sims into the den. Henry would arrive later because his office was in another county.

"You all know each other?"

Morty assured her, "We're old friends. To preserve confidentiality, Harold, will you accept a twenty-dollar retainer for your consultation in this matter?"

Rita handed Sims a twenty-dollar bill. Sims put it in his pocket. A dollar would have done, but Morty didn't want to insult the man by suggesting a mere dollar.

Morty began, "We've got a big problem. Dan January under the trust documents is the substitute trustee under all three trusts and now has absolute control of more than five million dollars for the benefit of Rachel, Frankie, and Gaby."

Morty let everyone absorb that before he continued, "He can spend Rachel's money to try to find her. We think that would be a waste of time and money, but it would take pressure and suspicion off him. He can spend the children's funds for their benefit, which is broadly defined, and he's the one who gets to define it. Most important, he has the ability to travel and to take the kids with him. He could disappear. That's what scares me. Amy Pierce is about to file a motion in Probate Court, and we better file first or have a pretty good response planned."

Rita didn't know what to say. Harold Sims didn't know what to say. Morty turned to Davis and asked, "What's our next move, genius?"

Davis didn't like being put on the spot. He figured the old man could have at least warned him of his intent to throw him in the deep end of the pool. But he did the best he could and outlined a plan, "The petitioner Rita Sinclair should move to continue the freeze on Rachel January's trust for another ninety days, since the status of the beneficiary is unknown."

He paused slightly and then argued, "In support of the motion the petitioner files a brief citing legal authorities and the documentation evidencing our search for Rachel and hiring ten detective agencies trying to find Ms. January. The Sinclairs have expended a total of a hundred and fourteen thousand dollars of their own funds attempting to locate their daughter, Rachel. If Rachel is not found, then Rita Sinclair's grandchildren, Franklin and Gaby, are the ultimate beneficiaries of this trust. We see no reason to expend any more funds from the trust for this purpose at this time."

Morty thought that the motion made sense. One of its primary advantages was that the judge would be comfortable with the short-term nature, only ninety days, on the effects of his ruling. His decision wouldn't be subject to criticism by anyone.

As to the other two trusts, Davis suggested that they wait and see what Pierce filed with the court. The children were primarily living with their Nana Rita. She was feeding them and providing their living expenses. There was no need for the trusts to spend large sums of money. If January started spending large sums, he'd have to justify those expenses. The statements were still going to go to the Sinclairs' home unless January made a concerted effort to have them stopped. That red flag would require the filing of a motion. Davis urged Rita as to the children's trusts just to sit tight and to watch January and let him make the first move.

"Why make this an issue within days of the death of the trustee unless Dan January was up to no good? This was not a natural death but a murder investigation. Why appoint a new trustee so fast?"

Davis would come at January hard and raise suspicion and implication. He wanted to see Pierce's petition first and react to it.

Morty and Sims liked the strategy. Rita was numb. She trusted Davis and just nodded her head. While they were there, they called Henry and explained the Probate Court plan. He didn't react right away. He questioned whether there was a disadvantage in letting Pierce file the first pleading relating to the children's trusts since January would have the power and the language of the actual trust documents on his side. "That's very powerful proof. You might want to taint it before the judge reads the document and forms an opinion that might be difficult to alter later on."

Henry arrived and was filled in as to the details of Sinclair's death and the legal analysis among his co-counsel. Henry pointed out that contract law was generally determined by the four corners of the document, and the trusts clearly stated that "in the event of the death of Tyree Sinclair or his inability or refusal to serve, then Daniel January shall serve as substitute trustee." Amy Pierce had the stronger side of the argument for sure. Henry strongly argued that the proposed motion was a big mistake and should not be filed.

CHAPTER FIFTY-FOUR

THE SINCLAIR ACT

Monday September 20, 1999

Davis felt very uncomfortable in the Speaker of the Tennessee House of Representatives' office. He'd never visited the state capitol building before and never intended to be there again. Over the years, he'd left that sort of thing to his law partner. Morty felt right at home; he was a political animal. He'd gotten drunk there many times with members on both sides of the aisle. That was how Tennessee politics had been for more than a hundred and fifty years. Since the days of Andrew Jackson, who'd been a Nashville politician, district attorney, congressman, and senator, there'd been men elected to office and then there'd been the ones behind the scenes pulling the strings. They'd pulled the cork on a jug on many occasions.

Although never elected to office, Morty Steine and his father and grandfather before him had been the man behind the elected Democrats in Nashville and Tennessee for the last seventy-five years. They knew where all the bodies were buried in the state capitol building.

Morty walked in to the Speaker's office like he owned the place. "Bill, thank you for seeing me on such short notice. Calling this special committee meeting to consider sponsoring this proposed bill is an incredible gesture of compassion for Tyree Sinclair. His widow, Rita, greatly appreciates this kindness."

William Montclair had been Speaker of the Tennessee House of Representatives for the last fourteen years. Morty helped put him there, and it was Morty's money and support of fellow Democrats that kept him there. Montclair, born and raised in Chattanooga, had played football for UT in Knoxville twenty-five years earlier and had been a household name in the state and a heartthrob of many young Tennessee girls on campus. He worked his way up in the state legislature to Speaker and now wielded power throughout the state like candy. Morty Steine did not come often, but when he did, his favors were granted.

Montclair remarked, "We've all been following what's happened to Tyree and Rita Sinclair. No one wants to admit that a child could ever marry so badly, but we have no real control over the people selected by our children as mates. As grandparents and future grandparents, we need to guarantee that the courts recognize that those blood relatives have some rights of visitation if they get at odds with one or both of the grandchildren's parents. At the very least a court should have some clear authority to grant access to those loving grandparents. The Sinclair Act will grant that discretion to trial courts. With time we'll let the appellate courts fine-tune the act as circumstances present themselves."

Davis asked, "What's the next step?"

"I'll push the act through committee right to the House floor. There are a lot of grandparents in both the House and the Senate. It should be an easy sell. One thing you can always count on with the Tennessee legislature: if a bill benefits its members, it's pretty sure to pass. I've already started lobbying the older members of the

House. I don't see any problem. Unless we find some special interest group that finds grandparents groups particularly offensive, we should sail right through."

The three men laughed.

Montclair called the members of the subcommittee to meet that afternoon. There wasn't much debate. Four of the members were over sixty, and they understood the dilemma.

"My daughter-in-law hates my second wife. I'd probably file a motion under the act to see my grandchildren more. My son has been willing to defend me. My ex-wife has poisoned the well. I get to see my grandchildren twice a year, and that's it. Maybe with a court order I'd see them once a month or so."

Montclair liked what he heard. The act was relevant. If it was important to legislators, it would be relevant to voters. The act passed nine to zero. Montclair passed it to the Senate and asked that it be docketed in two days, fast tracked.

The act had the same result in the Senate subcommittee. Two senators had special needs related to the act. One of them called Morty with a question. They were old friends and political allies.

"Morty, Tyree Sinclair's daughter has been missing for more than two months and is presumed dead?"

"That's what we believe, Randy. We've got no reason to believe she's alive, or she would have tried to contact her children."

"So where's January?"

"He's got an order granting him sole custody from the court, and according to the existing law, Rita Sinclair has a dead husband and no rights of visitation with her grandchildren. He's got a hearing scheduled for October 20th before Billingsly, but right now he's got custody of the kids."

"What if January and the kids run away to be reunited with the mother?"

Morty paused because the thought had never dawned on him. He'd always thought that January murdered Rachel and kidnapped the children. The question momentarily forced him to open his mind and rethink the entire case. He felt very uncomfortable, but then was able to shake it off. "You're one sick person, Randy. How do you sleep at night? That would truly be bizarre. God, you're a cynical person."

Montclair and several other representatives lobbied hard to get the necessary votes to pass the act. Promises were made and favors exchanged, politics as usual. It was easy to convince older representatives to protect the rights of grandparents. They'd be acting in their own self-interest. Younger ones needed a little more prodding, but most came around.

The next day the Sinclair vote passed thirty-one to two in the senate and eighty-eight to eleven in the house. The bill passed pretty easily. Morty was on the phone to the governor the next day, lobbying for him to sign the bill into law. The governor agreed to sign the Sinclair Act on November 3, 1999, and after he did, at the ceremony, he handed the pen to Rita Sinclair, whose name the act bore.

CHAPTER FIFTY-FIVE

AN IMPORTANT HEARING

Wednesday, September 22, 1999

Davis did beat Amy Pierce to the courthouse by one day and filed a petition relating to Rachel's trust. It was unclear as to whether this petition filed by Rita Sinclair expedited the January probate filings relating to the children's trusts, or if Davis truly won the race. Regardless, all three petitions were set to be heard before the Honorable Robert Rutherford, judge of the Probate Court. Rutherford had been on the bench for more than thirty years, was well respected, and a good friend of Morty Steine. It was agreed that Morty would argue the petition filed by Rita Sinclair.

Rutherford opened court by asking for a moment of silence "for his friend Tyree Sinclair, who was brutally and senselessly murdered."

Pierce made a mental note. It was her first potential error on appeal for bias of the judge, his admission of friendship with the husband of the petitioner. *I can't believe that Rutherford put his friendship with Sinclair right there on the record like that. Talk about bonehead moves. What a gift.*

Rutherford said, "We're going to take these petitions in the order they were filed. That makes logical sense, and it's only fair.

I'll hear the one filed by Rita Sinclair relating to the trust of Rachel January first. Who will be arguing on behalf of the petitioner?"

Morty rose and walked to the podium. "I am, Your Honor."

"Mr. Steine, what say you?"

"Your Honor, my client, the petitioner Rita Sinclair, is the mother of Rachel January, the primary beneficiary of this trust, and the maternal grandmother of Frankie and Gaby January, the secondary beneficiaries of this trust. The primary beneficiary, Rachel January, has been missing since July 4th. Exhibit C establishes that Mrs. Sinclair has spent more than a hundred fourteen thousand dollars of her own money in an effort to locate Rachel January without success. The petitioner moves to freeze the trust for ninety days, as is, earning five percent interest, before naming a new trustee. The funds are currently being managed and invested by a money manager, who has done so since the trust's inception. He has done an excellent job in that capacity as evidenced by Exhibit D." Morty handed up to Judge Rutherford a chart evidencing the growth of the trust over the last six years. "If frozen by the court, there will be no need for any action by the trustee, and therefore no need to appoint a trustee within the ninety-day period. There is no need to expend any funds or to manage any funds. The delay in appointing a trustee will not in any way prejudice the beneficiaries and therefore should be granted."

Morty's presentation was concise. There simply was no reason to name a new trustee at this time. He put the burden on Pierce to explain why there was an immediate need to appoint a trustee.

Pierce worked her way to the podium.

The judge jumped on her immediately, "Do you know where Rachel January is?"

"No, sir."

"Do you know if she's alive or dead?"

"No, sir."

"This trust is for the benefit of Rachel January, right?"

"Yes, sir."

"Your client couldn't possibly provide any benefit to her at this time since he doesn't know where she is or if she's alive or dead, right?"

"He could spend money to look for her."

"The petitioner has already spent one hundred fourteen thousand dollars doing that, right?"

"Yes."

"Sit down. Petition granted. We'll freeze the trusts for ninety days. That seems to be in the best interest of the primary beneficiary, Rachel January."

"You can get back up, Ms. Pierce. The next two petitions are yours, and they are identical. They relate to the January children, Frankie and Gaby, and seem pretty straightforward. Please state your position."

"You're absolutely right, Judge. We rely on the identical language of the trust documents to demand that this court appoint Daniel January, the father of Frankie and Gaby January, as their substitute trustee. The documents are very clear: 'In the event of the death, or if Tyree Sinclair is unable or unwilling to serve as trustee, then Daniel January shall be the substitute trustee.' Unfortunately, Mr. Sinclair died on September 13th. Accordingly this court must name Mr. January as trustee. The word *shall* leaves no wiggle room."

Pierce sat down and smiled at Davis, who walked to the podium.

Before he could begin, Rutherford went for the jugular and asked, "Isn't this basic contract law?"

"No, sir, anything but," Davis said definitely. "Your job is to protect these minors, not just look at a piece of paper written several years ago when Tyree Sinclair thought his daughter was happily married. You need to look at the facts as they exist today, not the fantasy that Tyree thought they were five years ago when he drafted these trust documents. Dan January was an unfaithful husband who, because of that infidelity, has entered into a marital dissolution agreement that is pending in Circuit Court. A hearing is scheduled for October 20th to determine if that order should be finalized. Under its terms, Dan January may receive eight hundred thousand dollars, and Rita Sinclair will receive sole custody of Frankie and Gaby January." Davis made the document an exhibit. "What sense would it make to give custody to Rita Sinclair, yet control of the funds to Dan January? Why give the responsibility of the children to one party, yet the purse strings to another?" Davis paused. He thought he'd made an excellent point.

Rutherford turned to Pierce for her input. What do you say, Ms. Pierce?"

"We accept the fact that Rita Sinclair is a loving grandmother, however, Dan January is in a better position to manage and direct these funds for the benefit of his children than she is. He has a law degree and often performs these same tasks for clients. Tyree Sinclair recognized this when he drafted these trusts. He could have named Rita Sinclair as the substitute trustee, but he didn't. He picked Dan January. It's this court's obligation to honor his wishes."

Davis knew exactly what Tyree Sinclair wanted, and it certainly wasn't that Dan January be appointed trustee for his grandchildren.

Pierce raised her voice and looked the judge straight on as she said, "Finally, I direct the court to the title of both trust documents, 'irrevocable trust.' The definition of the word *irrevocable* is self-explanatory. I submit that the court is judicially estopped to amend these trusts and rename the trustee. No one is in a position to do that. I submit if the trusts could have been amended, Tyree Sinclair would have done so when he was alive, when he learned that his son-in-law was unfaithful to his daughter. He didn't because he knew he couldn't. The removal of Dan January as trustee was only accomplished by a negotiated agreement of all parties as part of the consideration of the marital dissolution agreement. Rachel January disappeared before this document became effective. The petitioner, prior to the death of Mr. Sinclair, filed a motion requesting that the marital dissolution agreement be frozen. They cannot now argue that they should get the benefit of that agreement that they asked to be frozen. You can't have it both ways. The irrevocable trusts should be enforced, and Dan January should be named trustee of both trusts. Thank you."

Pierce sat down, and Davis got up and slowly walked to the podium.

Rutherford put up his hand like a traffic cop and said, "I've heard enough. These are irrevocable trusts. Mr. January was named the substitute trustee. Mr. Sinclair is dead."

Davis interrupted, "He was murdered."

"Don't interrupt my ruling, Mr. Davis. Do you have any admissible evidence that Mr. January had any involvement in the murder of Mr. Sinclair?"

Dead silence.

"I thought not. Unless you have proof otherwise, then Mr. January is hereby named trustee under each of these trusts with the full powers granted under both documents."

Davis retreated to his seat.

"If there is nothing further, I'd ask that Ms. Pierce draw the order as to my ruling on all three petitions. Court is adjourned."

Pierce turned to Davis, "See you at the hearing on the 20th."

Davis walked slowly from the courthouse to the office. He wasn't in any rush to get back to work. He didn't like losing. It left a bitter taste in his mouth. Unfortunately, Bella met him at the door with a handful of messages and questions about the hearing.

"I don't really want to talk about it. Let's just say that Pierce got to draw the order and January's in control of the children's trusts."

Bella knew not to push matters. She'd raised Davis from a twenty-two year-old law student, knew his moods, and figured he'd open up eventually. *Better to let him do so on his own terms.*

"Police chief Neenan called; he emphasized that it was urgent."

Davis shuffled the pile of messages so that the police chief's pink slip was on top. He noticed it was Neenan's cell phone number, not the police administration offices.

"Chief, Ben Davis returning your call, what's up?"

Gerry Neenan spoke for ten minutes, uninterrupted. Davis listened intently and then indicated he understood and would leave the office in the next thirty minutes. When he hung up the phone, he slammed it down. He was profusely sweating, and his blood pressure must have risen a good thirty points. He walked into Sammie's office, came around the desk, and from behind put his arms around her.

"To what do I owe this sudden exhibition of affection?" she said playfully. He tightened his grip,

"There's no good way to tell you this. Chris Addams is dead. He called 911 and then hung himself. He left a note, which Chief Neenan read to me. He assured the police that his death involved no foul play and asked that as his lawyer, I identify the body. I'm off to the morgue now. He mentioned you in the letter. How proud he was of you, and how zealously you represented him. He asked for your forgiveness and asserted his innocence to the charges against him. His last line was 'nobody will remember all the good things I did during my lifetime, just these hideous allegations against me.'"

Sammie, who had not spoken, began to cry. She'd grown close to Chris Addams; he was more than a client, he was a friend. He'd been her first big solo case, and it turned out worse than badly. She was crushed. Davis left her with her head on the desk, crying. On his way out, he filled in Bella , who immediately went to Sammie's aid and comfort.

CHAPTER FIFTY-SIX

IN A FAMILY WAY

Thursday September 23, 1999

Sammie and Victor stared with mixed emotions at the smiling face on the stick. He was happier than she was, but that may have been because she was dazed. Sammie wasn't ready for motherhood or the responsibility of a family. How would she manage work and a child? Her aunt Liza did it. How would a baby affect her practice? How did this happen? Well, she knew how it happened. She took sex education in high school and went to the University of Florida.

Victor tried to calm her down, "Darling, everything's going to be wonderful," she heard. "I'm going to help out. I can reduce the number of my shifts or even quit my job for a while. Remember I'm a nurse. I've got the skill set to take care of a baby. We'll remain on the sixth floor. I'm sure your uncle and Morty will accommodate your work schedule and needs to be a mother."

Victor was making very good points and making it sound easy. *It wouldn't be as easy as he made it out to be, but he was being sweet and that was important.* "You can keep your name. I wouldn't want to make your uncle change the letterhead. But I want my child to have my name. I don't want my child growing up a bastard. Please say you'll marry me." She knew he was joking, or at least half-joking.

Sammie had been listening but heard only every other word. She was still in a fog. She gave him a hug. "Is that the only reason you want to marry me? So your child will have your last name?"

Victor took her hand and said, "I want to marry his or her mother because I love her with all of my heart, and I want to spend the rest of my life with you. Is that reason enough?"

They sealed the deal with a long embrace and a shower together. Sammie dressed while trying to figure out how she was going to tell her uncle and the rest of the office. She figured she'd tell Bella first. Her wise older friend would know how to best proceed.

Davis decided it was a perfect day for the Wilson Vette. He put the top down and drove slowly down West End. *What a glorious day!* He was ready to take on the world. First in the office, he grabbed a cup of Joe prepared by the automatic timer and settled in to look at four days of accumulated mail. He started with a letter from Amy Pierce.

Dear Ben,

I am writing at the request of Dan January concerning the proposed visitation of Rita Sinclair with Frankie and Gaby during the 1999-2000 school year. Frankie and Gaby will attend different schools, and each school has different hours of operation. Frankie's school has bus service; Gaby's does not. Dan believes that Frankie is too young to wait at a bus stop by himself. Therefore, both children will need to be driven to school. As you know, Dan has started his own firm as a solo practitioner, and as you might suspect, he is working long hours.

Please be advised that I have been authorized to offer the following visitation to their grandmother during the 1999-2000 school year: Sunday @ 4:00 p.m. through Friday @

6:00 p.m. three weeks a month, and their grandmother shall keep the children the entire fourth week. January will get the children for five straight days during their Christmas break. The parties will share holidays and will work together for the mutual benefit of the children.

Please advise me if this arrangement is acceptable.

Amy Pierce

When Sammie got in, Davis with pride showed her the letter. "You were right. We gave him a few weeks with the kids, and it proved too much for him. He realized it was easier being a part-time dad than a full-time caregiver. I think you should call Rita Sinclair and give her the good news. It was your strategy that worked. I think you should take the bow. I've got a meeting with George Hopper today at two. Why don't you sit in? Give Rita my best and tell her congratulations from me."

Sammie stopped by Bella's desk and shared her news about Victor and the baby. The older woman got up from behind her desk, and the two women embraced. Bella scolded Sammie about her concerns about disclosing her pregnancy to her uncle.

"Your uncle will be ecstatic over a new baby in the family. Shelly and Larry will be on a plane the minute they hear the news so that they can congratulate you in person. Liza will be planning a wedding with gusto. Just tell them. They'll all be excited."

Sammie walked away from the conversation more comfortable and went to her office. She really was excited about relaying the good news of what happened in the January case to their grandmother. She was equally excited about telling her family about her personal good news.

In her last few conversations with Rita, the woman seemed more and more depressed. With each passing week, it was more apparent that her daughter was dead. The thought of her grandchildren spending the school year with her would certainly brighten up her life.

The Sinclair housekeeper picked up on the first ring. She must have been standing next to the phone. "Sinclair residence."

"Mrs. Sinclair, please, Sammie Davis."

"Sammie," Rita said in a surprisingly cheerier voice. After Sammie described the proposed visitation, Rita began crying uncontrollably. "That's wonderful. They'll be with me the entire week. I wonder why he agreed? It's not like him to think of others before himself."

Sammie decided not to spoil the moment by explaining that January was thinking of himself. He found taking care of her grandchildren too difficult, so he was turning the job over to her. *That is the ugly truth, but why be ugly? The woman is on such a high, why spoil it?* "Rita, it doesn't matter *why* he did it. You'll have your grandchildren during the school year, and that's what counts. These young people need your help to get through these difficult times, and the important thing is that you will be there for them."

"Sammie, thank you for what you and your uncle have done. I'd be lost without you."

They said good-bye and hung up.

The day started off on a high note, but every winning streak eventually comes to an end. At eleven o'clock Davis found himself in front of the Honorable Palmer Stephenson, judge of the Seventh Circuit, arguing a motion to exclude evidence in an upcoming jury trial.

Davis argued, "The purpose of Rule 403 is for the court to weigh the benefit of the evidence against the prejudice of the evidence and to determine in its wisdom whether the benefit outweighs the prejudice. One important factor against introduction of the evidence is whether the same information can be provided to the jury through another source. I submit that the jury need not be shown the photo of Mr. Jones depicting his injuries. Those same injuries are described in detail on the police report and can be described by Mr. Jones and any of the eyewitnesses."

There was a serious question about whether Davis's client Sam Butt started the fight, but there was no question about who finished it. Mr. Jones and three of his friends wound up in the emergency room.

The judge waved the other lawyer off, never a good sign. "Mr. Davis, your client is insisting on going to court, claiming this was self-defense. It was four against one, yet it seems your client gave better than he got. I believe a picture is worth a thousand words. We're going to let a jury decide this one. Motion denied. The picture gets in. Good luck."

The judge left the bench, and Davis left the courtroom in defeat.

When he got back to the office, he found George Hopper telling fight stories to Sammie and Morty in the conference room.

Hopper read from a written report at first: "There have been a number of reported sightings of Rachel January.

1. Gas station—Atlantic City
2. Zoo—St. Louis
3. Macy's—New York City
4. Trader Vic's—New York City
5. Trailer Park—Knoxville
6. Disney World—Orlando
7. Perkins Restaurant—Kansas City
8. Arby's—Davenport, Iowa
9. Bus Stop—Portland, Oregon

"None of these leads were determined viable. We continue to investigate, but I question whether this is a good use of our resources. I believe that Rachel January is dead and that her body is within a two hundred-mile radius of Nashville."

Davis agreed with Hopper's conclusion. He made an executive decision without consulting Rita Sinclair, who was still guided by her heart. "Go ahead and terminate the ten investigating firms. We've spent enough money there. Pay them off and send me a final bill. Let's focus our attention on the local investigation. What have you found out so far?"

Hopper stopped reading, and his report was now verbal, nothing in writing. "Let's start with January's younger brother, Phillip, who twice married older women who died under mysterious circumstances."

That got everybody's attention.

"Both women died of sudden heart attacks. One was fifty-two, and the second wife was only forty-two. The current Mrs. January is younger and is only thirty-two and currently healthy, but you never know."

Sammie broke in, "Do you think the father's involved?"

"I know the dad's got money trouble. He filed bankruptcy four years ago. Your friend Steve Lewis was his lawyer. Based on my research, he's in financial trouble again. So he needs money. Maybe his brother promised his part of the $800,000?"

Davis volunteered, "Under the bankruptcy law, you can only file every seven years. So if he filed four years ago, he was barred from filing again for another three years. That might have been a real problem for the brother. A real motivator to help Dan commit murder."

Davis then asked Hopper, "Has our other source been helpful?"

"He's amazing. I can't yet share the fruits of what he's discovered, but technology beats persistence every time. I can tell you the Kings, the Coopers, and the Gaineses are communicating, and what they are saying will implicate them in a cover-up. We can't yet prove murder, but they are cooperating to protect January. I just need more time. I'm confident they're going to slip up."

Davis responded, "The judge gave us until October 24th. With luck we might be able to get a second extension, but it would be better if we could prove something by then."

The meeting ended, but everyone thought that progress had been made.

After everyone left, niece and uncle were alone. Sammie in a quiet voice started by saying, "I've got big news."

Davis asked, "Good or bad?"

"Great. Vic and I are getting married."

"Congratulations. He's a great guy. I wish you the best of luck. You've got my approval, even though you don't need it." I know your grandparents will be very happy. They've been praying for this to happen."

"There's something else."

"More?"

"I'm pregnant."

"Talk about a short engagement. When did you find this out?"

"Today."

"Let me ask you this: are you getting married because of the pregnancy or because you love him?"

Sammie didn't answer right away. She really thought about the question. "I love him. I'm not sure we'd marry right now if I wasn't pregnant, but I do love him. We might just continue to live together."

Davis considered her answer and then asked, "So why don't you just live together?"

"Because of the baby. He wants the baby to have his name, and so do I. I'm going to keep my name. We agreed we don't want you to have to change the letterhead."

Thinking like a lawyer, Davis asked, "Are you going to have a prenuptial agreement?"

"I haven't thought about it. This all happened this morning."

"Well, you'd better start thinking about it. It's your life and the life of your unborn child. This is serious. I want you to act like an adult and be responsible."

Sammie was less sure of herself than after her conversation with Bella. Her uncle walked out of her office, and Sammie picked up the phone, called her aunt, and shared her news. Liza was very supportive and started crying. When Sammie mentioned her uncle's comment about being responsible and the prenup, Liza flew into a rage.

"That dumb son of a bitch. Where does he come off lecturing you about being responsible? He forgets what he was like in the seventies. He never worried about birth control. If the girls he dated weren't on the pill or some other form of birth control, he'd have fifteen kids by now. Look, honey, forget about him. You're going to be a great mother, and I'm going to help you through this pregnancy. Vic is a wonderful man, and you're going to have a great life together. Let's start planning a wedding. Call Nana Shelly and let's get the ball rolling. Wait till that idiot gets home tonight. I'm going to give him a piece of my mind."

Sammie let her aunt rant a few minutes and then broke in, "Don't be too hard on him. His remarks were out of love. He was just looking out for me."

"He's hypocritical. He's forgotten what it's like to be young and in love, and that pisses me off.

CHAPTER FIFTY-SEVEN

THE GRAND JURY

Tuesday, September 28, 1999

The grand jury process is not judicially fair. It is a rigged system that clearly favors the state. The Rules of Civil Procedure and the Rules of Evidence, not to mention due process, are thrown out the window. No one is present in the room to protect the rights of the accused. It is the closest thing to the Spanish Inquisition that the Constitution allows in this country.

The district attorney, the chief prosecutor for the county, presents evidence to twenty citizens chosen from the voting rolls, who sit for several months hearing as many as a hundred criminal cases from simple assault to first degree murder. The DA in any manner the prosecutor sees fit can summarize these cases. The DA can also present as few cases as he or she wants. The DA controls the flow of information as the absolute ruler of the domain. Sometimes, depending upon the DA's whimsy, he hears witnesses' testimony, without cross-examination. Other times the DA elects to introduce exhibits, and still other times he puts on a full-blown dog and pony show. Other times, maybe because of limited resources, or simply because he is tired or not in the mood, the DA just wings it, reciting those facts he wants the grand jury to hear without any countervailing proof. He calls no witnesses and is not represented by counsel. It is a real one-sided presentation.

This morning DA Johnson Tory was pulling out all the stops and making a full-blown presentation of evidence in an effort to secure indictments of the proposed defendants. He had on his best blue suit with a crisp new white button-down shirt and a power red tie. Johnson Tory, recently reelected to his third four-year term, was forty-six years old, a Democrat, and three times divorced, ready to marry and divorce a fourth time. He was always looking for the next Mrs. Tory. They were usually young, twenty-somethings with large breasts. He loved women, and right now he had his eye on a pretty brunette in his office. Tory knew that would create a new set of problems. He'd avoided co-workers up till now, but he figured he was a big boy, and he could handle it. He was smart except when it came to women. He just couldn't keep his hands to himself. He was a sweet talker both with the ladies and with the juries. He had a way with words.

DA Tory introduced himself, "Ladies and gentlemen, I am District Attorney Johnson Tory. I was elected by the good people of this county to prosecute people who break the law in this county. I don't care if they do that with a gun or if they do it with a pen. In fact most of the time the person who does it with a pen hurts more people than a criminal who uses a gun.

"You are a grand jury. You are not here to determine guilt or innocence. That will be another jury's job. Your job is to determine if there is reasonable suspicion to indict or charge the defendant with a crime. It is a much lower standard than guilt or innocence.

"It is important that you feel like your questions are answered. If after I finish a subject you still have a question, you have a right to either ask me or the witness that question. Now you're not lawyers, but I don't want something important going unanswered.

"Today is the first day of this grand jury, and we are going to start with an interesting case. It is a serious case. It involves the disappearance of someone's mother and daughter. It involves the possible murder of someone's mother and daughter. It doesn't get more serious than that."

The DA paused to let his last remark sink in. "If this was a trial, I would have to prove the charge against the defendant beyond a reasonable doubt. I will admit that is a heavy burden, but this isn't a trial. The police haven't completed their investigation. In fact they've only just started treating this as a crime based on the newly discovered information I will be presenting to you today. You see, the purpose of this proceeding is to ask you to grant an indictment. An indictment is a green light to the police to start an investigation. It tells them you think there's a possibility that a crime has been committed and it's worth spending community resources to determine if these defendants committed those crimes."

He took a drink of water and paused for effect. Johnson Troy was a pretty good actor. It was his job to convince the grand jury to bring back indictments against the defendants. To do so, they needed to understand the much lower burden of proof that he was required to meet at this hearing.

"Here's what we know. On July 4th, 1999, at 7:00 p.m., her parents at Rachel's home saw Rachel January. We also know that when her parents brought her children back at 10:50 p.m., Rachel was gone, never to be seen again. During that four-hour period, Rachel January disappeared."

Tory had abandoned the theory that Rachel had returned to the Sinclair house and left the following morning. It didn't support an argument that January and his co-conspirators were guilty of a crime. A defense lawyer would certainly raise that possibility at a trial. There was no physical evidence that she returned to the Sinclair home, to her childhood room, but it was a good argument to raise reasonable doubt. But that wasn't Tory's concern today, so he plowed ahead.

"The question to which we do not yet know the answer is this: Did she leave her house voluntarily under her own steam, did she leave under violence or force, or was she murdered in her home?"

He let that question linger and then moved on to some of the lesser crimes the grand jury would consider against January and the other defendants who were tangentially related to the disappearance/murder of Rachel January. It was inherently unfair that the same grand jury would hear the evidence concerning the Laura Chapman embezzlement charge by Sinclair & Sims.

The DA spent the next hour presenting evidence. The first charge was against Daniel January for embezzlement from his law firm. The key witness was Benjamin Abraham Davis. Davis was brought into the grand jury room. Tall, dressed in a blue suit with a matching blue vest, he caught the eye of every man and woman on the grand jury. As he was sworn, he made eye contact with each of the twenty grand jury members as if he were about to address his testimony to each of them personally.

After giving his background to DA Tory, Davis described in detail the schedule of sex acts his client had to endure in exchange for legal work. He put into evidence the diary, the time tickets, and the settlement agreement. Davis testified how the time tickets and the diary lined up perfectly.

"It cost January's law firm $260,000 because of his unethical and wrongful conduct. My client Ms. Chapman is very embarrassed by what she's done. Prior to her disappearance, she apologized to Rachel January. If she were here today, she would apologize to you.

I know it seems that she may have acted immorally, but you need to understand that Dan January preyed on Laura Chapman. She was alone and vulnerable, and he took advantage of her. She was going through a messy divorce; she ran out of money. Dan January was her trusted advisor and her attorney. He was her fiduciary. That is the highest and most trusted relationship with another human being. It was January who suggested that they trade sex for legal fees. She did things with him she'd never done with any other man, not even her husband. When she became disgusted with herself and refused to continue, he threatened her with exposure to her husband's attorney, and he threatened to cause her to lose custody of her children. What kind of trusted friend turns on you like that? Only a real slime! He then had the nerve to sue her for unpaid legal fees of $14,000. What a worm! That's when Ms. Chapman contacted my partner and niece Sammie Davis. I was elected to meet with Tyree Sinclair, Rachel Sinclair's father, senior partner of Sinclair & Sims, Mr. January's employer, who'd sued Laura Chapman. Of course, he knew nothing about the sex for legal fees. He was horrified and realized I had him over a barrel and had an excellent countersuit. He settled for $260,000 and returned Ms. Chapman's $5,000 retainer. I agreed to testify as part of the settlement and tell the truth. "

Davis had never been before a grand jury. He was amazed at what he was allowed to testify to. Most of his testimony was hearsay. It wasn't like being in a courtroom. There was no judge, there were no Rules of Civil Procedure, and there were no Rules of Evidence. He could say whatever he wanted to say, The DA had absolute control of the process. He just let Davis run wild.

After Davis's testimony, the grand jury indicted January for embezzlement. That indictment was presented first just to taint the jury. It was placed under seal.

The DA next read the statement of Dan January, which established his alibi for July 4th. He allegedly was having sex with Robin Gaines at the Gaines home between the hours of 6:15 and 10:45 and returned home just after 11:00 after the Sinclairs arrived at his home with his children. This was a sworn statement under oath, subject to the laws of perjury. The DA then read the statement of Robin Gaines, also under oath, which corroborated January's alibi. Her statement established that she was with Dan January on July 4th.

The DA then submitted the affidavit of George Hopper that established the sting on the *Good Ship Lollipop* and the whispered conversation between Robert Gaines and Albert King that contradicted Robin Gaines's affidavit.

The DA introduced the affidavit of Richard Sasser Jr. The grand jury was very interested in the young man from Yale. They asked questions about him and whether his actions were legal. The DA admitted that the e-mails were obtained without a warrant and probably wouldn't be admitted into evidence in the criminal case, but divorce counsel obtained them and a different set of rules applied in a divorce case then a criminal trial. They very well might get into evidence in the civil matter.

The next witness was George Hopper. Hopper's testimony introduced the e-mails he received when Richard Sasser hacked the Gaineses', Kings', and Coopers' computers proving that January paid them $50,000, $25,000, and $25,000 respectively. He then played excerpts from audiotapes and videotapes from the *Good Ship Lollipop.* Finally, Johnson Tory introduced the bank records of Phillip January, Dan's brother, proving a withdrawal of $200,000 on July 5th from Franklin January's trust account that evidenced a wire transfer to Phillip's account. Tory then introduced Phillip's purchase of money orders that he sent to several locations, which his brother used to fund his escape from law. The DA pointed out that the tapes and the bank records were obtained with a properly issued search warrant. What he didn't remind the jury was that if they didn't know about the e-mails obtained by Dickie Sasser, his office wouldn't have gotten the warrant issued. A good defense attorney would later argue at trial that because the search warrant was obtained through unauthorized means that the bank records, the fruits of the search, might be held inadmissible. That certainly would be the argument of Phillip January's counsel, if he'd been criminally tried.

The grand jury brought back an indictment against Robert Gaines and Robin Gaines for accessory before and after the fact to obstruct justice, giving false statements, and criminal conspiracy. The Kings, the Coopers, and Phillip January were indicted on all the same charges except they were not indicted as accessories before the fact because their e-mails were dated after July 4th at 7:00 p.m., so they were only after the fact. These indictments were not sealed and would be served immediately.

In addition to the embezzlement indictment, Dan January was indicted for obstructing justice, giving a false statement, and criminal conspiracy. These charges would remain sealed.

Tory told the grand jury about the brutal murder of Tyree Sinclair and that he had no proof, at this time, as to who may have killed this fine father, grandfather, lawyer, and friend, but that he was going to ask the police to continue to collect evidence. There was no reason for Tory to mention the death of Sinclair to the grand jury other than to taint the well. January was Rachel's ex-husband and the dead man's son-in-law and successor trustee. The announcement of Tyree's death certainly made January sound awfully guilty in the minds of those twenty laypersons.

"Ladies and gentlemen, this is the first of many days we will be spending together. We will be revisiting this case later in the term. It is my intent armed with the indictments you have granted me today to confront some of these defendants to find out what they may know about the disappearance and death/possible murder of poor Rachel January. I promise you, as an elected official, that I will get to the bottom of this matter. I owe this to the county. I owe this to this grand jury. I owe this to poor Rachel January and her surviving two children. Let's call it a day."

CHAPTER FIFTY-EIGHT

LEAKS

Wednesday, September 29, 1999

Nashville at the turn of the twenty-first century was a town where secrets could spread faster than a wild fire. Like any southern town, there were still the remains of the old-time political machine. Fading fast, built on nepotism, favors, and racism, it was losing ground to the progressive South. But traditions and secrets died hard.

The existence of the indictments was first disclosed to the Metro police department, which was entrusted with serving them on the defendants. Detective Duncan was told within the hour because it was her case.

Officer David Tanner overheard two other officers having an innocent conversation discussing the defendants in the cafeteria. Tanner, who was represented by January in a nasty divorce, picked up the phone five minutes later because he heard January's brother mentioned with the others, and his ears perked up. Tanner, a loyal client, made a phone call to his lawyer.

"Thanks, David, I can't tell you how much I appreciate the call. I can't imagine what my brother's got himself involved in, but I appreciate the heads-up. I'll get to the bottom of it. You've got to help family, no matter how stupid they may be."

Tanner thought he was just helping his lawyer deal with a family matter. He never heard Dan January's name mentioned in the conversation because January's indictment was still under seal, and no one outside the grand jury knew of the pending indictment against Dan January himself.

Of course January knew what he'd done or hadn't done. *The shit's about to hit the fan. If they're going after Phillip, they're not too far from going after me.*

"Look, keep your ear to the ground and if you hear anything else, let me know what's going on. By the way, you just bought yourself five hours of free legal work. Thanks."

As soon as January hung up, he dialed Frankie's school and spoke to Nancy Flexor, the assistant principal.

"Mrs. Flexor, Dan January, sorry to call so abruptly, but I need to pull Frankie out of class. I got a call there's been a cancelation for an appointment with a child psychiatrist I've been trying to get him in to see. It's for one o'clock. I need to pick him up right away. Could you feed him a quick lunch and have him in front of the school in fifteen minutes please." *I'm brilliant. What can she say but of course?*

"Absolutely sir."

The story worked so well, he didn't change one word when he called Mrs. Porter at Gaby's school. He picked up both kids at their respective schools and started driving. He had a full tank of gas.

Davis got the call from Duncan after lunch. She wanted a meeting and suggested that Jack Henry be there. Henry was in a meeting. When he called back, he had to rearrange his schedule but assured Davis he'd be at his office by four.

Davis called Duncan and asked, "Detective, would four work for you?"

"That's fine."

"Can you tell me what this is about?"

"Don't you like surprises?"

"Not really. Can't we bury the hatchet? I apologize for how I acted during your investigation of the death of Martha Keller. I was wrong."

"Holly shit. Was that an apology?"

"Yes. Be gracious."

"You're right. Apology accepted. You'll like what I have to say at four. See you then."

By four o'clock Dan January, Frankie, and Gaby were across the Tennessee state line in Georgia. January had stopped in Columbia and traded his Mercedes sedan at a used car dealership, Feeder Used Cars. January dealt directly with the owner Ted Feeder, in a quick transaction that lasted all of thirty minutes. January let Frankie pick out the trade. The boy picked a Sebring convertible. The kids had watched *Honey, I Shrunk the Kids* and *The Little Mermaid* on a small battery-operated TV as they traveled south toward Florida. As an incentive, January promised they'd stop at Disney World. The kids were excited and momentarily forgot the death of their grandfather as they thought about seeing Mickey and Minnie.

Rita Sinclair was in a panic. Both schools repeated January's lies when she went to pick up her grandchildren. She didn't have Tyree to turn to. Already in the car, she drove directly over to Steine, Davis, & Davis.

The meeting with Detective Duncan had begun, and she was in the process of sharing who had been indicted and for what. "We've got Dan January's indictment under seal. It's only for embezzlement so far. We're hoping to squeeze the others and get a confession out of one of them and get January on something more serious. If we're lucky, January will be facing a murder charge, and we'll make it stick. If I were to guess, the brother will be the one to crack. He's most likely the one who had direct involvement in the murder. You know his two first two wives died under mysterious circumstances. He furnished the funds. He's made quite the investment in this little enterprise. January called him several times the night of the murder. What they talked about and if they met would break the case."

Henry asked, "When will you start arresting the defendants?"

"We thought dinnertime in front of their families would be a nice touch. We're not going to play nice. We're going for maximum embarrassment."

Henry voiced the consensus of the group, "You should be as brutal as you can, and go as far as you want. Even if these people played no part in Rachel's murder, they still took blood money. They supported Dan's alibi even though they knew it was a lie, so they must have had a pretty good idea that he killed her.

Just as Henry finished his pronouncement, Bella ushered Rita Sinclair into the conference room. She was hysterical. "They're gone. That bastard took them. They're gone."

She fell to the floor, hitting her head hard. Everyone in the room rushed to her side. Sammie brought her a wet towel and placed it on her forehead. Five minutes later, she was conscious, eyes open, and muttering again, "They're gone." Within a few minutes, Rita told the complete story, and two minutes later, Detective Duncan had an APB out for Dan January. When asked by the desk sergeant, "What for?" she couldn't say, "Kidnapping." After all, they were his kids, so she said, "Murder." She figured she'd sort it all out after he was arrested.

Dan January, Frankie, and Gaby were more than four hundred miles away in northern Florida on their way to Kissimmee. They stopped at a Red Roof Inn, and January paid cash. He had plenty of cash in twenties and fifties. Dinner was at a Mexican restaurant, cash again. Frankie wore a sombrero. After the meal, January filled up the car with gas so they could start out early in the morning.

Back at Steine, Davis, & Davis, the group called in George Hopper to get his opinion about where he thought January might flee. They knew he had about a six-hour head start.

Hopper took a map of the United States and drew a 400-mile radius around Nashville. "They could be anywhere within that circle, but my educated guess is the southwest corner, moving toward Texas. I'd hire men to set up key roadblocks on the ways to Mexico and try to block their access once they're out of the country. I'd be prepared to use force to get your grandchildren back after Davis gets an order from the court . . ."

Davis broke in, "I can get an order setting aside the agreement and granting Rita Sinclair temporary custody of Frankie and Gaby. I may need the indictment unsealed, but I think I can prove him unfit."

"What good is custody if the kids are not in the state? You've got to find them."

Hopper looked Rita right in the face and said, "I'm going to find them. You've got my word."

She kissed the former boxer on the cheek, and he blushed. She believed he'd find her grandchildren.

CHAPTER FIFTY-NINE

THE GREAT ESCAPE

Thursday, September 30, 1999

The kids weren't very happy with their dad, especially with Disney World right down the road.

"I want to go to the Magic Kingdom," Gaby complained. "I could hear the fireworks last night. You promised we could go. I want to see Mickey."

"Not today, maybe tomorrow. Daddy needs to make travel plans right now."

January left the hotel room and stood in the parking lot while he talked on a throwaway cell phone. He'd been calling the Cuban embassy in Bermuda all day, trying to talk to the private secretary of Carlos Santos, the private secretary of the ambassador. The ambassador was a good friend, a schoolmate of the defense minister who was the brother of the president of Cuba, Fidel Castro. January had been told by his source that for a small bribe the ambassador could secure January an audience with the defense minister, who might accept a large bribe to let him and his children into Cuba as political dissidents.

"Yes, sir, my name is Dan January, and I've left several messages for the ambassador. I'm a friend of Don Lopez. He suggested that I mention that I own a lemon tree and that I can offer him a glass of delicious lemonade."

What that meant January had no idea, but he was certain it meant he was an American willing to pay the ambassador big dollars for something that Americans weren't supposed to obtain from Cuba. The Cuban embargo had existed almost forty years, and Americans had been circumventing that law the entire time. The ambassador was not the first or the last Cuban ambassador to do so.

January rejoined his children in the room, and having nothing to do but wait, he suggested, "Let's go to Disney World." *What the hell. Hundreds of thousands of people are there. Who is going to recognize us among all those people? Who is going to think I'd have the balls to take the kids to Disney World right there out in the open? It's the perfect place to hide.*

The kids were jumping up and down in their seats.

"Put on your damn seat belts," yelled January, "or I'm not starting the car."

They were there in less than fifteen minutes. January was careful to pay cash for everything. He got the kids mouse hats and tee shirts. It was less crowded than he thought because of school. There were almost no lines, which meant they rode the rides fairly quickly. Gaby's favorite was It's a Small World After All. The three sang along with the music.

At noon January got a call from Santos. He had the ambassador on the line. "Mr. Ambassador, our mutual friend Mr. Lopez said you might be able to introduce me to Defense Minister Castro. My children and I . . ."

"I understand you own a lemon tree . . ."

January didn't have time for games. Frankie and Gaby were sitting on a bench four feet away and were getting antsy.

"How much for the introduction? That's all I need to know. Let's bypass the discussion about lemon trees and lemonade. I'm interested in how much you want."

The diplomat wasn't prepared for such candor. He spoke perfect English, but he hesitated anyway. "Fifteen thousand dollars for me. The general will set his own price, if any. No guarantees. What crime have you committed?"

"Does it make a difference?" January responded. "I married the wrong woman."

"A common mistake," said the ambassador, "always expensive."

The ambassador gave January the telephone number of a Major Pepe and the wiring instructions for his fifteen thousand dollars. January wrote them on a pad he had with him in his back pocket. He was instructed to call Major Pepe at ten the next morning for further instructions. The January family enjoyed the rest of the day at Disney World and stayed through the fireworks that evening.

The next morning January did as he was instructed and called Major Pepe. "Major, Dan January. My family needs asylum . . ."

"The ambassador has filled me in to some extent, but he was unclear as to what crime you have committed."

"My wife has disappeared, and the police think I killed her. She abandoned her family and left me to face the consequences."

"Where are you from, Mr. January?"

"Nashville, Tennessee."

"I will get back in touch with you in three hours."

January gave Pepe the telephone number of a second throwaway cell phone he'd purchased. He'd bought an even dozen. Then, on another one, he called his brother and gave him an update of his efforts to flee the United States to freedom.

"I want you to send a money order of fifty thousand dollars payable to me to the Kissimmee National Bank. I've got to use fifteen of it to begin my bribery out of the country."

"His sibling asked, "Where are you going?"

"You're better off not knowing. The less you know, the better off for you and the better off for me."

Six hundred miles away, Dickie Sasser listened to January's call to his brother Phillip. Sasser called Hopper and informed him, "January's five miles from Disney World. He just called his brother. He'll be at the Kissimmee National Bank in the next hour for certain. I dinged him off a cell tower near the Magic Kingdom. If there are multiple branches, my guess is he'll be at the branch closest to the park I've got his new cell phone number, and if he stays in the area and uses the same tower, I can listen in on his conversations. The balls of this guy. He's taken the kids to Disney World. He's hiding right out in the open. You've got to give him credit."

Hopper mobilized an army, but it may have been too little too late. He hired sixty-five men to comb the area near the cell tower for January and the kids. They went to the three closest branches of the bank and must have just missed January. While they were looking, Hopper made arrangements two hours later for a temp agency to hire another two hundred persons to canvass the area, including the four theme parks.

Dan January stepped back into the parking lot and called Major Pepe.

Pepe answered and put January on speaker, "Mr. January, thank you for calling back. I now know a little more about your situation. My intelligence service has provided me with a pretty good summary of your situation. Who killed Tyree Sinclair?"

"I don't know. It was a carjacking. It wasn't me."

"It wasn't a carjacking. He was murdered. You became trustee as a result of his death and now control more than five million dollars."

January didn't expect the Cubans to know as much about his business as they did. He didn't realize he'd be dealing with a nation state that had unlimited resources with ready access to information.

"What do you want?" he demanded.

"Who do you think you are, Mr. January? I represent the Cuban government. The defense minister is an official of my country, and he must carefully consider your request for political asylum."

"Major, how much? That's all I need to know. How much? I didn't kill anyone, but I need to get myself and my children out of the country to safety and freedom."

There was a long silence and then a new voice came on the line.

"Mr. January, I am Raul Castro, I am the Cuban defense minister. I command the Cuban armed forces, the military arm of the Cuban government. That is a very responsible position, and I take my duties very seriously. I've read your file, and I can't tell if you're innocent or guilty, but I know for certain that your children are innocent. I also know that young children need a parent and that your children's mother is either dead or disappeared. If she's dead, they'll need a parent and you're it. If she reappears, we can address her reappearance at that later date. Like the laws of the United States, I'm going to presume that you are innocent and I'm going to give you the benefit of the doubt. I will grant you asylum for the payment of two hundred thousand dollars."

"That is a lot of money, but I'm in no position to negotiate, so I will accept your generous offer. When can arrangements be made?"

"Major Pepe will supply you with the wiring instructions. I will provide you with a furnished villa, staff, and protection for an additional one hundred thousand dollars a year. Is that agreeable?"

"I accept."

"First year payable in advance upon landing."

With the deal cut, the call ended. January took the children shopping and bought new clothing for all of them. At the mall they went to the food court and had something to eat.

"We're going on a trip tomorrow," he told Frankie and Gaby.

"Where to?" Frankie asked.

"Our new home. You're going to love it," replied January, and he was convinced they would.

Standing outside the Regions Bank, January called his brother, who was also standing outside the bank where the January children's trusts were held.

"Phillip, I need another three hundred thousand immediately. You might not hear from me for a while. When I can, I'll get back in touch, Love you, bro."

Sasser called Hopper back, "He's going to Cuba. Somehow he's made contact with the Cuban defense minister, and he's flying down there under his protection. I've played the tape for Greene. He thinks we should get the State Department involved. I think we should play the tape for Davis and the other lawyers and let them make the call rather than Greene."

Hopper agreed with Sasser. He was a smart kid. They both trusted Steine and Davis. Greene had his own motives, and they weren't sure his number one priority was about the safety of Frankie and Gaby.

Three hours after it originally occurred, Dickie Sasser, by phone from Fort Campbell, a U.S. Army installation, played the tape of the conversation between Dan January and the Cuban defense minister concerning a several hundred thousand dollar bribe. Present in the Steine, Davis, & Davis conference room were Rita Sinclair, Davis, Jack Henry, Morty, Sammie, George Hopper, Detective Duncan, General Little, General Tory, and Warren Fields of the TBI. The group had been pulled together rather quickly, and there was no clear understanding about who was in charge.

Everybody started talking at once. Morty's voice rose above the pack, "This is my office. I own the building, so I'm in charge. We have a man we believe murdered Rachel January about to flee the country to another country, and this country does not have diplomatic relations with the host country. That's a bad thing. More important, he will be taking two young children with him. He must be stopped. Agent Greene has suggested that we rely upon the State Department to solve our problem. I strongly disagree. This is not the time to be diplomatic. Now is the time to be cunning and strategic. We need someone calling the shots with experience in tactics, who has led men and can make quick decisions without hesitation."

Davis smiled and pointed at his old friend. "I recommend we place our trust in Morty Steine to get this job done." Jack Henry seconded the motion, and it was unanimously agreed.

CHAPTER SIXTY

YOU'D BETTER SAY YOU'LL HELP

Friday, October 1, 1999 and Sunday October 3, 1999

The conference room of Steine, Davis, & Davis was filled to capacity with all sorts of interested people. It was standing room only. There were law enforcement types from federal, state, and local jurisdictions, the DA's office, and of course all of the Sinclair lawyers. The recent widow of Tyree Sinclair, the grandmother of Franklin and Gaby January, Rita sat at the head of the table surrounded by several of her lawyers appearing insignificant, but that was about to change. She was watching the crowd and taking in everything that was being said.

A heated debate ensued as to how best to handle the negotiations with the Cuban defense minister. He was a powerful man in charge of armed forces of the Cuban government and the brother of Fidel. The district attorney's office and the law enforcement officials of Davidson County, the locals, whose interest was prosecuting January, argued for a direct approach: a call from government to government. Official channels, so to speak. An FBI agent said that wouldn't be possible. The State Department wouldn't permit it, at least not officially because the United States had no formal relationship with Cuba. Then he cleared his throat and said, "There are always back channels."

The approach of Morty and Davis was far less direct. They insisted that a well-orchestrated private phone call to Raul Castro from Morty would be more effective, keep the United States directly out of the conversation but use the weight of the superpower to influence the politician. Morty and Davis felt that Castro wouldn't want to be reminded of the Bay of Pigs and the trade embargo as he was negotiating for the lives of these children. His motivation had to be cash and the possibility of embarrassment.

The debate ping ponged back and forth for more than an hour. There were a lot of egos in the room. In the end Morty suggested a compromise plan that seemed to satisfy everyone. Because the safety of the January grandchildren was at stake, it was agreed that despite her limited background as a hostage negotiator, the call was up to Rita. They were her grandchildren. She had the most to lose. She shared with the group her reasoning, "Tyree always told me that the Steine family had been an important reason the Sinclair family and Nashville survived the Depression and that I could trust Morty Steine. I know the lives and safety of Frankie and Gaby are at stake. That bastard January, if he succeeds, may keep them as prisoners in Cuba the rest of their lives, certainly the rest of my life. I want to see my grandchildren again. I'm going to trust that Morty knows what the hell he's doing." She gave the green light for Morty to call the shots. It was not so much a plan as it was a threat.

Morty got Dickie Sasser on the phone, "Dickie, I need you to get me Agent Greene. Can you do that, son?"

"I can have one of my agents request that he call you. He's in Washington, but he's always listening. I'm sure he's listening to this conversation. He'll be getting in touch with you without any further effort on my part. Trust me."

Thirty seconds later, the phone in the conference room at Steine, Davis & Davis rang. It was Agent Greene. "Mr. Steine, you require something of me?"

"Well, sir, it's interesting that you should call. I do require your assistance. I need the help of our government. I need the defense minister of the Cuban government to accept my phone call and listen to what I have to say."

"Mr. Steine, as you know since the Eisenhower administration, this country has not had diplomatic relations with the Cuban government, and since the Kennedy administration, there has been a trade embargo. I'm not sure exactly how I could expedite a phone call between a private citizen and a high-level member of that government."

The phone call confirmed the position taken by the FBI and shot to pieces the direct approach of local law enforcement and the DA's office.

"Cut the crap, Greene. Two little kids' lives are on the line. A murderer is on the loose, and I have a plan to bring everybody back here to Nashville. I need your help. Can I count on you or not?"

"You're a lawyer, Steine. January's not a murderer until proven guilty."

"Okay, alleged murderer."

Greene, who had been jousting with Steine, got serious and said in a very businesslike manner, "I suggest you talk to your own partner rather than to me. He's got the answer to your problem. Ask him about his second honeymoon to St. Barts. That's where you'll find your solution. Good luck, and don't be cheap. January's ante, with lodging, is three hundred grand."

Greene knew all of the details of January's plot, as did Steine, Davis, & Davis through the Dickie Sasser intercepted phone calls. Dickie worked for both parties and was forced to share his information with the NSA.

"What are you talking about?"

"Ask him about Roberto Mendez and his law partner Diaz in Miami."

Realizing Greene in his own way had helped him, Morty thanked the NSA agent and ended the conversation, promising to get right back to him and to keep him informed along the way.

"Don't be silly; you won't have to."

He then turned to Davis, "Who the hell are Mendez and Diaz?"

Davis explained about his chance meeting with Roberto Mendez and his wife Mia and reminded Morty of the five boxes of Cubans he brought back into the country. He explained that Mendez made that happen. He also described how Diaz was from the same village as the Castro brothers and watched them play baseball growing up.

Rita approved Davis making first contact with Mendez because of their past association, but she said, "Ben, this is no reflection on you. I think you're an exceptional lawyer. I've even told your father that, but I want Morty to deal with Diaz and Castro. I'm sitting here trying to do what I think Tyree would do, and I believe he'd want all those years of experience controlling the fate of his grandchildren. I'm sure you understand,"

Davis did, but it didn't hurt any less.

"Rita, if my children were in the exact situation, I'd want Morty Steine in charge of securing their safe return. You're placing your trust in the right man."

Then Davis found Mendez's number and got him on the line, "Roberto, Ben Davis from Nashville."

Benjamin, how are you? How's Liza? To what do I owe the pleasure of this call? Do you need more Monte Cristo #4's?"

"Roberto, this is not a pleasure call, although I'm sure my friend Mr. Steine would always appreciate a few boxes of cigars. I have a life and death situation and I'd like to fly down to Miami to meet with you and Mr. Diaz to discuss the matter at your earliest convenience. Tomorrow if possible."

"Tomorrow is Saturday. Mr. Diaz spends his weekend with his great-grandchild, grandchildren, and children at his villa. His weekends are sacred, especially Sunday. His weekdays are devoted to business. He's a busy man. I may be able to fit you in next week for an hour. I could see you on Tuesday. I'm involved in the sale of a business on Monday."

"Roberto, you're not hearing me. This is a life and death situation. It involves two small kids and a murderer fleeing the jurisdiction of the United States." Davis then told Mendez a half-hour version of the January story. It was a one-sided version. After all, Davis was a trial lawyer. Of course, Mendez understood Davis's background and listened, took his words from where they came, with a filter.

"Let me get back to you."

After the phone call ended, Davis instructed Hopper to hire a private jet and have it waiting at John C. Tune Airport, a small private airport just outside Nashville. Davis also instructed Hopper to hire another hundred investigators to blanket the Orlando area in search of January and the children.

"I want you to have them canvass the transportation hubs: airports, bus stations, train stations, etc. He may try to change cars. Cover every rental car agency you can. We've got him narrowed down to a specific ten-mile radius. Let's close in on him."

Davis felt they were close and shouldn't squander the opportunity. "The more eyes and ears we have working the streets, the more likely we are to stumble on January and the kids. January will be moving south for his extraction."

Morty called Howard Longfellow and asked him to pilot the jet. Longfellow, who had narrowly escaped prison and loss of his license because of his right cross, was more than happy to help his lawyer.

The Davis team couldn't know that the January family was already driving south and had reached Palm Beach, headed to the Florida Keys, as far south as they could get to Cuba for a rendezvous with a seaplane.

The tension in the room was unbearable. The law enforcement types began questioning the Diaz connection, arguing as DA Tory Johnson put it, "wasting valuable time and jeopardizing the lives of the January grandchildren."

Morty shot back, "Talk about wasting time, try working through our federal government. You heard Agent Greene. He works for the NSA. It's the federal government, and he recommended we take this route."

Just then the phone rang. Davis picked it up. Mendez was on the line.

"Benjamin, I am shocked to extend an invitation to you and your guest to the home of Mr. Hermando Diaz this Sunday at 1:00 p.m. for lunch to discuss your life and death problem."

Davis made one last telephone call. It was to Karl Moore, the former DEA agent, who now ran a security agency.

"Karl they need to be trustworthy men, who will use force only when necessary. Most important, their motto must be 'no questions asked.' Do you think you can get the men we require?"

"Mr. Davis, they'll be waiting at John C. Tune Airport Sunday at dawn, I promise. I'll determine what gear they require for the operation, and you'll reimburse me at cost. I'm not sure right now what each man will charge for his services. I'll negotiate hard, but not too hard. You want your men motivated. I'm a freebie. You've done a lot for me, and I want to show my gratitude. "

Davis didn't know what to say, so he just nodded his head and smiled.

Sunday morning at dawn, the Gulfstream 5 was sitting on the tarmac waiting for takeoff with Longfellow at the controls and a surprising co-pilot.

"What the hell are you doing sitting up there?" Davis yelled at his law partner.

Longfellow replied, "He's not hurting anything. I'm certified to fly this thing solo. It's good to have company in the cockpit."

Davis shot back, "He's certified on single engines, and I'm not even sure...."

"Buzz off," the old man yelled in response.

Morty had flown Hurricanes in World War II and for the last forty years flew various small single engine planes. He'd never flown a jet.

Longfellow assured Davis, "Once you're up in the air, they're all about the same. It's landing them that can really be a bitch if you don't know what the hell you're doing."

The group on the plane included Davis, Rita, Karl Moore, Carlos Ramos, another former DEA agent, and three ex-navy seals, Lance, Nick, and Tonto.

Only Morty, Davis, and Rita went to the villa. The rest remained at the plane and ate sandwiches. They were greeted at the door by Roberto Mendez, who escorted them to the backyard where there were three long tables. The entire Diaz family was eating lunch poolside. There must have been twenty-five great-grandchildren ranging from two to ten and grandchildren from ten to twenty-five. He'd had four children. It was quite a crowd. Mendez took them to a sixty-inch round table in the corner that was ornately set with cheeses, meats, and breads, white and red wines.

A small dark man stood and said, "I am Hermando Diaz. It is a pleasure to make your acquaintance, Mrs. Sinclair. My condolences on the death of your husband. From what I have read and heard from Roberto, he was a man to be respected and admired."

Rita smiled and said, "Thank you for those kind words. We had many wonderful years together. He was a great husband, father, grandfather, and lawyer. I am here to get his grandchildren back."

Diaz turned to Morty and Davis. "I've also done my research on you gentlemen. You are men to be respected and not to be taken lightly. Roberto has explained your problem, and I must tell you it is a big one. Mr. January has chosen to run, rather than face justice; that does not mean he's guilty, but it does mean he doesn't trust justice. "

It had been agreed that Morty would take the lead. Diaz would expect to deal with the senior partner and elder.

Morty began, "We also have done our research and understand your relationship with the Castro brothers. We'd hoped that you might make an introduction and I might convince Raul that protecting Dan January was a serious mistake morally, financially, and politically. We have both monetary and political weight behind us."

There was an odd silence during which everyone sipped wine. Diaz took a piece of bread and cheese and popped it in his mouth. He was thinking, or at least he was pretending to do so. The others followed suit and ate some food.

Another sip of wine, and then, "Money alone will not solve your problem. Raul has given his word to Mr. January. You must convince him that he's a murderer and that justice requires his return to the United States. He will argue that his word is his bond. I've heard him use that expression at least two dozen times. His word is useless, but it sounds good. Also, the fact that the children will be returned to this lovely woman will help, and of course, you'll have to match January's money offer."

Morty took in the information. Diaz knew his man.

The meal continued, and second and third glasses were poured.

After an hour and a half, Diaz stood and extended his hand. "It will be my honor to do what I can to secure the return of this lady's grandchildren to her."

With that he kissed Rita's hand and handed Davis and Morty a box of Monte Cristo #4's. They followed Mendez as he walked from his home.

CHAPTER SIXTY-ONE

TWO TOUGH OLD BIRDS

Monday, October 4, 1999

It was a long night spent at the Diplomat Hotel. Rita took a hot shower, had dinner in her room, and went to bed. The men cracked open a couple of bottles of Jack and a case of beer and played poker. Davis ordered room service, and they waited to hear from Diaz or Mendez.

Diaz contacted Morty at nine on Monday and gave him the defense minister's direct office number.

"He's expecting your call. I can't make any promises. He reminded me that 'his word was his bond.'"

Twenty-three minutes later, Morty dialed the number given. He pushed the speaker button.

"Mr. Defense Minister, I am Morty Steine. I have you on speakerphone. I am an attorney from Nashville, Tennessee. I represent Rita Sinclair, the maternal grandmother of Franklin and Gabriela January, ages eight and six, who have been abducted by their father, Daniel January, and are trying to illegally enter your country . . ."

The voice on the other side of the line was firm and angry. "Let me stop you right there, Mr. Steine. I decide who enters legally or illegally into my country."

Morty had intended to identify who was present in the conference room, especially his client, Rita, but the defense minister didn't seem interested in introductions.

"Maybe so. I stand corrected. Then Mr. January is trying to illegally exit the United States and is currently a fugitive of American justice."

"As an American, you can understand that I've made a deal with Mr. January. We entered into a contract. A deal is a deal. You don't know me, sir. My word is my bond."

Morty laughed to himself. Diaz's prediction was true to form. The line came out of the corrupt dictator's mouth too easily.

In the same businesslike tone, the defense minister stated, "My country has little concern for American justice. You see, Mr. Steine, our countries do not maintain diplomatic relations, and for the last forty years your country has tried unsuccessfully with great malice to try to strangle the life out of mine. Why should I care about American justice? What about justice for my people?"

Morty had to change his strategy on a dime. Reason wasn't going to work. Compassion for Rita, the grieving grandmother, was a waste of time and effort. The only thing that was going to have any effect was strength.

"You surprise me, Minister."

"How's that?"

Morty paused for effect. "I thought I would be dealing with a soldier, but you're more a politician than a soldier. I almost believed your little speech about social justice for your people, but then I remembered that you accepted a two hundred thousand dollar bribe to let a murderer into your country, and you knew he abducted his children to boot. You're motived only by greed, not the social justice of your people or the guilt or innocence of Mr. January."

Now defiant and even angrier, the minister said, "How do you know so much about my business? Has Mr. January shared with you our banking arrangements? If so, then there will be no need for American justice. I will have him killed myself, and his children will also pay for his sins."

Bingo, the man just showed his true colors, and that statement will hang him. You can always count on an asshole to come through. All you have to do is give him enough rope, and he hangs himself.

"I've got friends in high places. I've seen the wire transfers. I've heard and taped your conversations with January, so I've documented the fact that you've received two hundred thousand dollars of his children's trust fund money to enter and live safely under your protection in your country. You've also rented him a villa for another hundred thousand dollars. You've already pocketed that blood money. You're protecting a murderer and a kidnapper. That's quite a story, don't you think?"

"Mr. Steine, I don't know who you think you are, but I control the Cuban army, navy, and air force. I could destroy you in a millisecond. Where do you come off making these wild accusations? You're not with the tabloids, are you?"

"I don't have to contact the *National Enquirer*, or one of those less than reputable publications, but then again, why do so when I have listening to this conversation Raymond Burke of the *New York Times*, who is prepared to write an article in next Sunday's paper of how you assisted in the recovery of this fugitive and these abducted children, or how you were a co-conspirator."

There was dead silence from the Cuban end of the line for almost two minutes. Two minutes of silence is deafening Finally, the minister asked, "Mr. Burke, are you really there?"

"At the invitation of Steine, Davis, & Davis, I'm very interested in how this story turns out and will write about it," replied Burke, who had been invited to play poker the night before. The team had been instructed to let him win so he'd be in a good mood this morning.

More silence, and then in defeat, he asked, "Mr. Steine, what do you want from me?"

It was like music to Morty's ears. The entire room began making silent high fives, which the Cuban could not see on the other end of the line. Morty began in an even stronger and demanding voice, "Our goal is to capture Mr. January and have the safe return of the children. Our priority is securing the children. We need you to set up a remote rendezvous with January so we can close in for the capture. He must not suspect anything. He must believe that you are proceeding with your end of the bargain. He must believe that your word is your bond."

Castro was digesting his betrayal and asked, "What do I get for my cooperation?"

Morty appeared to be winging it at this point. The casual observer would conclude that he'd have had no prior discussion with either Davis or the client as to how much of the three hundred thousand dollars Castro should keep in return for his cooperation in the delivery of January. He seemed to stutter on his feet.

"I can promise you a terrific human interest story written by Mr. Burke about how the Cuban government denied amnesty to an American fugitive fleeing American justice with his two young children, returning them to their loving grandmother. The article will feature you as that decision maker."

Morty was just fucking with Castro. He knew he'd have to sweeten the deal.

"You're kidding. Such an article would only get me hated by more than half the world. How much?"

Morty knew they were down to business. "Fifty thousand U.S.

dollars. You must return the other two hundred-fifty thousand dollars immediately. You get to keep the fifty thousand only if we capture January and the children are safe. If the mission fails, you get nothing. I want you to have some skin in the game. Remember, sir, that money belongs to the children, not the father."

Seeing blood, Castro responded, "That is a ridiculous offer. I admit I'd like a positive article by Mr. Burke. Everybody likes good press. But cash is king, and fifty thousand falls way short. I want to keep the two hundred thousand dollars. Mr. January isn't going to be my guest and will not be using my villa so I am willing to return the hundred thousand rental fee."

On cue Rita broke in, "Sir, enough of these games. Two beautiful children's lives are at stake. Put money aside, put your ego aside, and let's get them home to safety. You will keep a hundred thousand dollars and return two hundred thousand dollars, or Mr. Burke will write an article that will expose you as the corrupt man you are."

Rita paused and in a voice that was as hard as steel said, "My word is my bond."

The deal was cut. Castro agreed to schedule through his aide a pre-arranged rendezvous between the Cuban navy and January somewhere within the hundred or so miles between Key West and Cuba. Davis and Rita waited on shore. Davis had never been a big fan of small boats. Morty insisted on being in on the capture.

The team didn't know whether January was armed. He was, but no shots were fired. The ex-seals boarded January's craft, disarmed him, and subdued him. January was taken in international waters twenty-four miles from Cuba. January screamed that he was a lawyer and that his constitutional rights were being violated the entire time of his capture. Ramos eventually placed tape over his mouth to silence his protests. The children, recognizing Morty, ran into his arms. He took them below deck away from their father, who remained topside handcuffed and gagged. There was a very happy reunion when they reached the beach and reunited with their grandmother.

CHAPTER SIXTY-TWO

THE HEARINGS FROM HELL

Friday, October 29, 1999

Dan January sat outside the Sixth Circuit Court with his captors, Longfellow and Hopper, waiting to appear before the Honorable Paul Billingsly. He felt like a slave about to enter the Roman Colosseum. He'd been dragged against his will, handcuffed and gagged, and been forcibly brought back to the United States from international waters. *I'm a lawyer. I know my due process rights have been violated. Forget that I may have violated a few laws along the way. That doesn't abrogate my rights to due process.*

Hopper and Longfellow looked up to see Pierce approaching.

She stopped in front of the trio on the wooden bench and demanded, "What the hell's going on here?"

Hopper responded, "What do you mean?"

"Why is my client handcuffed to the bench?"

"Citizen's arrest. There was an all points bulletin out on him, and Mr. Longfellow and I as concerned citizens have brought him in and have returned the minor children to their grandmother. No reward is necessary. Just the thought that we've reunited the children with their Nana is reward enough for us and that we brought your client in for justice."

"Shut the hell up, Hopper. I know who and what you are, you punch-drunk loser. Get those cuffs off my client this minute."

"I can't do that. I gave the key to Mr. Davis. He wanted to make sure your client kept his appearance before the judge. Mr. Davis asked me to secure him to the bench. He's in the john if you want to talk to him."

Pierce stomped off to the men's room. Davis was standing by the middle urinal, just finishing up.

"Amy, I'm not surprised to see you in here. I've often thought you had big balls. Now I realize you've got a dick as well. Pull alongside. I'm almost finished, but no comparing. I could never live with the fact if yours were bigger than mine."

Pierce ignored his comments and changed the subject. "Okay, you got January here, violating his due process rights. What's your plan?"

"I don't have to share that information with you. Besides, isn't that going to be up to the judge? January failed to appear at the October 20th hearing. He fled the country and took his children. He needs to explain that to the court, and the court will take whatever action it deems appropriate."

Pierce usually had a snappy comeback but was at a loss for words. She knew her client was in trouble.

Winnie Bray, Judge Billingsly's court officer, came into the hallway and announced, "The judge is ready for you now."

Davis handed Hopper the key, and he unlocked the handcuffs. Everyone filed into the courtroom. January kept rubbing his wrists because the handcuffs had been a little tight and left marks.

Ms. Bray called the January case and called court into session.

The judge began, "Well, hello, Mr. January. I understand you've done some international traveling."

Pierce stood and stated, "Good morning, Your Honor. . ."

"You think so, Ms. Pierce."

"I must advise my client to assert his Fifth Amendment rights."

"Ms. Pierce, this is a civil court, and this case is a civil matter. It is a divorce action relating to whether I should continue to freeze a marital dissolution and property settlement agreement. What does that have to do with self-incrimination?"

"The removal of his children from the United States may raise criminal charges, sir."

"Let's put that matter aside for a moment. Why was he not in my court as ordered to do so on October 20th? He's in contempt of my court, and I'm entitled to an answer. I have a right to throw him in the Davidson County jail until he answers that question to my satisfaction, and if he chooses not to answer, he could stay there a very long time."

"Judge, you need to know that Mr. January was brought back to this country in violation of his constitutional rights and due process . . ."

"Stop right there, Ms. Pierce. I don't care how he got here. Whether by plane, train, or mule, he's here, and I want to know why he violated my order. If he doesn't answer my question, I'm going to hold him in civil contempt and order that he be held in the county jail until he does. Why don't you take five minutes and consult with your client? Five-minute recess."

When the court returned, Pierce's position hadn't changed. It couldn't because her client's criminal problems would have grown exponentially.

"Deputy Wilson, please take Mr. January to the county jail until he's prepared to answer my questions. I'll prepare an order of contempt."

Jack Henry spoke up, "Your Honor, may I approach the bench?"

Henry handed the court and Pierce a petition.

"This petition has been filed in the Probate Court to remove Dan January as trustee of Franklin's and Gabriela's trusts and to substitute their maternal grandmother, Rita Sinclair. We ask before Mr. January is taken to jail that he be transferred to Probate Court to answer this petition."

Pierce objected that she was not provided sufficient notice or time to respond to the petition.

"You can take that up with the probate judge, Ms. Pierce. Motion granted. Now, Mr. Henry, what do you want to do with the pending matter in this court, the frozen marital dissolution agreement?"

Henry and his team had discussed their preferred result and figured the judge would agree with their suggestion. "Since Mr. January is in jail and certainly can't access the assets anyway, we propose that the agreement remain frozen while Rachel January's life or death remains uncertain."

Billingsly sat there in silence for a few minutes contemplating the proposed action. With January in jail it made sense. "It is so ordered," and he left the bench.

In the hall Henry congratulated the rest of the team. The hearing went as planned. Davis suggested that they all needed to hurry to Probate Court on the fourth floor because he anticipated that testimony would be required at that hearing to replace the trustee.

Amy Pierce was already inside. She was very unhappy and getting unhappier every moment. Judge Robert Rutherford took the bench, and at the same time a Davidson County sheriff brought in Dan January. No longer was he dressed in street clothing. He now wore the familiar orange jumpsuit of the criminal element.

How appropriate. That quick change was for the better, thought Davis.

Davis could see the outrage on Pierce's face. *It is a beautiful sight to see.*

"Mr. January, I have a petition to remove you from the trusts of both of your children. It alleges under oath that you've spent three hundred thousand dollars as a bribe to a foreign government official."

"Your Honor, my client respectfully must take the Fifth."

"Is Mr. Christopher Addams in the courtroom?"

Davis stood and answered Judge Rutherford, "Mr. Addams is deceased, Your Honor, but for the purposes of this hearing his affidavit should be sufficient. It attaches and authenticates all of the relevant documents to his and authenticates to his affidavit proving Mr. January's withdrawals from the children's trust accounts."

The judge read Addams's affidavit out loud, which established that $250,000 left Gaby January's account in one payment for an account in the Cayman Islands. Sammie cried during the entire rendition. Davis next called Dickie Sasser, who established that the payee on that account was the defense minister of Cuba. Pierce had no questions for the witness. What could she ask? She didn't know what he would say and this wasn't the time or the place.

"Before I rule, Ms. Pierce is there anything you'd like to say in your client's defense?"

Amy Pierce was not one to go down without a fight. She knew that she'd lost this hearing, but the fight didn't end here. It never ended at the trial level. There was always an appeal.

"I stand before you knowing the court is going to grant the petition. I had no choice. My client had to take the Fifth. Taking the Fifth is not an admission of guilt. It's a legal protection under the Constitution. No one should be penalized for exercising it. The real crime was that my client was in court today at all. He was in international waters, and the petitioner used thugs to hit him over the head and drag him back to U.S. jurisdiction in violation of his due process rights. He's in county jail right now, but the judge doesn't want to hear about that. He'll stay there indefinitely under a civil contempt order because the petitioner is wired into our judicial system."

Davis stated, "Objection."

"You can object all you want, but we all know the truth. What the hell. I've said what needs to be said. Remove my guy, and let's be done with this charade. The Court of Appeals will either see what's going on and care, or it won't."

Judge Rutherford cleared his throat. "In light of the testimony and the wrongful conduct of Mr. January, I am confident that the Court of Appeals will have no problem with my decision to remove Mr. January as the trustee of the two January children's trusts. I appoint their maternal grandmother trustee and Benjamin Davis as substitute trustee. What about the disposition of the Rachel January Trust?"

"We ask Rita Sinclair be named trustee for the benefit of her grandchildren and that I be named substitute trustee."

"It is so ordered."

January was ushered out of the courtroom. No one shed a tear because of his removal. Pierce also left quickly.

Rita Sinclair thanked Sasser for his skills, time and testimony. Henry and the rest of the team realized that the prosecution of Dan January and the rest of his co-conspirators was in the hands of the district attorney's office and that they were relegated to being mere witnesses, spectators. That would be very frustrating, especially for Benjamin Abraham Davis, who always liked to be in the thick of things.

CHAPTER SIXTY-THREE

LET'S MAKE A DEAL

Monday, November 15, 1999

When Davis, Sammie, and Morty entered the room, they found seated at the table District Attorney General Johnson Tory and his young Assistant General Belinda Little.

Morty asked the first question, "Who represents the brother?"

"I think you know her. She's a good friend of yours, Amy Pierce." Tory was being sarcastic. He knew damn well that Steine, Davis, & Davis knew and hated Pierce, and the feeling was mutual. Pierce was representing both brothers. A clear conflict of interest. Johnson answered the next question before it was asked. "Yes, she has a signed waiver from Phillip January, acknowledging her prior representation of his brother, Dan."

Morty responded, "The bitch knows how to cover her bases, but she's not as smart as she thinks. She'll paint herself into a corner."

Davis posed the next question, "What were her exact words when she called you to set up this meeting?"

Johnson did not hide that he was annoyed, "I'm not a stenographer. I don't remember exactly what she said."

Little spoke up, "I heard her. We were on speaker. It was something like, 'you'll need Phillip to prove the money. Without him, you don't have a case.' What did she mean by that?"

"She knows about Dickie Sasser's eavesdropping between the January brothers."

Morty would admit that obtaining the information from the conversations was quasi-legal, Davis would vigorously argue that it was highly probable that the evidence was inadmissible, and based upon her extensive research, Sammie insisted that Sasser's actions were illegal. Davis pointed out that they'd secured the evidence under the protection of the NSA and that she could worry but not bother him with such details. She could simply worry for the both of them.

Sammie spoke up. "You might not be worried about the fruits from the poisonous tree, but I am. We learned quite a bit from Sasser's wiretap: location, escape plan, and rendezvous. What if it's all excluded? What if the court holds that the citizen's arrest was an abduction from international waters?"

Morty, who was now turning red in the face, blurted out, "Whose side are you on anyway?"

Pierce arrived, dressed to kill, in a dark blue Armani suit and high heels she used to crush her opponents. "I'm here to make a deal for the brother. I elected not to question your boy Sasser at the probate hearing, but wait until his deposition. He'll never testify at trial. Your use of the NSA to obtain all of that information may have been clever, but it was illegal, and it will be inadmissible. That's a lot of tainted evidence. Dan's taking the Fifth, so you're getting nothing from him on the death claims. His alibis will hold up, so all you have is the charge of embezzlement of the trust funds."

Davis smiled, but Johnson answered, "And the embezzlement from the law firm, plus sex for fees. I think a jury will love that one.

I'm going to let General Little try that case under tutelage of Mr. Davis as an outside consultant because he knows the case. I think a woman's touch is just what that case needs."

"You forget, General, I'm a woman."

"Ms. Pierce, I don't think of you so much as a woman. I think of you more as a man with breasts, missing a penis, but with balls."

Davis began to laugh openly. So did Morty and all of the others. Even Pierce cracked a smile, but was able to hold back her laughter.

Pierce began, "Funny man, let's get down to business. You've lost your key witness who was going to prove the financial crime. Chris Addams is dead."

Little spoke up, "We have his two affidavits. They're a great road map..."

Pierce cut her off, "Those are useless. Not only is he dead, but he's a charged child molester. I promise you I'll get that damaging fact into evidence somehow...."

Davis interrupted, "Alleged fact."

"Where's there's smoke there's fire. When the jury hears about his alleged conduct and how he took his own life, how credible do you think those affidavits will be? Those affidavits will be as valuable as toilet paper. Your entire case will be sidetracked. No, to prove the financial crime against my client and his brother, you're back at square one. Look, I'll be the first to admit that they took the kids' money, but be prepared for a long drawn-out fight and a messy trial. I may even put the kids on the stand. Ask their grandmother how she feels about her grandchildren hitting the witness stand. My client's testimony proves his own guilt and his brother's guilt. It's in the state's best interest that we make a deal. It's in the January children's best interest that we make a deal, and in Rita Sinclair's best interest. So what do you say?"

Davis answered, even though it wasn't his place, "You're one evil bitch. How do you live with yourself?"

"I drink twenty-year-old scotch, and I count my money toward an early retirement."

A candid conversation ensued. Pierce made a proffer of proof: what Phillip January would testify to. Johnson conferred with the others and offered two years with opportunity for parole after eighteen months. Pierce's response was the lightest possible sentence for a felony: one year and one day to turn on his brother. No question she was a tough negotiator, but the death of Addams and suspicion over Sasser's actions made the deal attractive. Neither Davis nor Morty wanted the January children to be called in the Phillip January trial. Franklin's and Gaby's lives were going to be complicated enough when their father was tried for his crimes including the murder of their mother. They saw no point in further complicating their lives.

Three weeks later Phillip January reported to begin serving his one-year term. Due to prison overpopulation, he was assigned a cellmate. As the cell door closed behind him, introductions were made.

"I'm Phillip January."

"Hi, I'm Oscar Brand, nice to meet you."

CHAPTER SIXTY-FOUR

PLEA BARGAIN AND PRELIMINARY MOTIONS

Wednesday, December 8, 1999,
and Monday, January 17, 2000

General Tory and General Little met Henry, Davis, Sammie, and Morty at the front door of the DA office. They looked a little ridiculous: four lawyers pursuing the same case, like a parade. But this case had gotten real personal, more so than the others. First, there were kids involved. Second, everybody admired Rita Sinclair. She was so strong, and you felt a pain in your heart because she loved and lost Ty. Third, you never found Rachel's body or Rachel, so there was the unanswered question of whether she was dead. Last, you had to hate January. He was a real son of a bitch, and he hired Pierce, an even bigger son of a bitch. That's why they were all showing up for this meeting. They wanted to look January and Pierce right in the eyes. It would be hard not to spit.

Johnson Tory greeted them, "Gentlemen and Lady, they're waiting in the conference room. Don't expect to be welcomed with open arms. Pierce has filed charges against us before the disciplinary board. She's filed a civil complaint against George Hopper, Karl

Moore, Rita Sinclair, the four of you, and several John Does, and she's sworn out criminal warrants as well against all of you."

Davis wasn't fazed. "He's still an embezzler and a murderer. The rest is just hot air."

Johnson Tory, more a politician than a lawyer, started in, "I don't know. On appeal, she might be able to get some of our evidence thrown out."

Little argued to her boss, "We'll look at the source of each piece of evidence. If it's questionable, we'll decide how important it is. We'll do a risk/reward analysis before we introduce anything. Davis, Morty, and Henry will help. I'll have more than a hundred and twenty years of experience behind me."

They moved to the conference room where January and Pierce were waiting. Pierce immediately got confrontational, not just for the benefit of her client. She truly hated them.

"What the hell are they doing here? Are you trying to provoke me? Well, you've succeeded. Would the two of you like to be added to the list of defendants in the pleading I just filed, Generals? That could easily be arranged."

Johnson in an angry tone responded, "Don't threaten either me or this office, Ms. Pierce. That will only get years added to your client's sentence. This is my meeting, and I invited these interested lawyers to it. They represent Rita Sinclair, who has a vested interest in the outcome of what happens to your client, who is the father of her grandchildren and who is accused of killing her daughter."

Pierce whispered something to January. He'd been in jail, held under Judge Paul Billingsly's contempt order since October 29th. His bail on the murder charge had been set at $2 million. He couldn't make bail because he could neither provide sufficient property nor pay the requisite ten percent to a bondsman. But that really didn't matter because even if he could make bail, no amount of money would release him from Billingsly's contempt finding. He was stuck in the county jail.

"Let's get the embezzlement out of the way," said Little. "It's a maximum of five. We'll let you off with four."

Pierce replied, "Drop the murder charges, and you've got a deal."

"You're kidding, right?"

"Dead serious. You've got so many problems with your murder charge, I don't know where to begin. No body, no weapon, no motive."

"No motive. What are you talking about? He got access to all that money."

"No, Tyree Sinclair on July 4th was alive and well, and he became the trustee, not my client. My client got nothing. In fact economically my client lost what he thought was a fair and reasonable settlement of his divorce, which he negotiated directly with Mr. Davis. The death or disappearance of Rachel January has caused only trouble for Dan January. He wishes nothing more than that she would turn up alive. One thing he does know is that he didn't kill her, and he's not pleading guilty to that charge. He had sex with Laura Chapman for legal fees. It was unethical and will sit badly with a jury, but he didn't kill anyone. He didn't kill Tyree Sinclair or his daughter, Rachel Sinclair, and the state will have to prove beyond a reasonable doubt that he did commit those murders."

She's a bitch, but she's one convincing bitch, thought Davis.

"And just so there's no misunderstanding, I intend to let the jury know all about your tainted evidence. I don't think the jury is going to appreciate how you acquired your information without warrants and how you invaded my client's due process rights. I know about the NSA and Dickie Sasser and how Steine intimidated the defense minister. We'll be in the appellate court for years. This case will definitely make it to the Tennessee Supreme Court, but I can also see a federal track all the way to the U.S. Supreme Court. Don't worry, Tory, you'll be famous. I can see it now. It will be a reported case with your name as the lead defendant."

Pierce was just trying to scare the politician, and it was working. Little forced her boss to have a backbone, and the murder prosecution proceeded. In the end January pled guilty to the embezzlement charge and received a three-year sentence, eligible for parole after thirty months in consideration from release of the contempt finding. January still had to face the murder charges, which had to be proven beyond a reasonable doubt.

Pierce filed dozens of motions in limine (preliminary motions). The case was randomly assigned to Judge Katherine Russo. It was a cold January morning when the motions were heard. Everyone was in the gallery. Sammie sat next to Rita Sinclair and held her hand tightly.

Judge Russo opened court, "Good morning, ladies and gentlemen. We're here today to hear a number of motions in the matter of the State of Tennessee vs. Daniel January, Docket # 99-23423. General Little, are you ready for the state? Ms. Pierce for the defense?"

Everybody acknowledged being ready.

"Let me emphasize that I've read every word related to this matter, including the cases cited. These are serious constitutional issues, and I've treated them as such."

Davis didn't like the sound of that. Pierce was ecstatic.

Pierce told the entire story. She explained how Steine, Davis, & Davis represented Richard Sasser Sr., then the son, Dickie Sasser. She knew about the NSA employment contract and how Sasser and Hopper worked together to gather the evidence that led to the discovery of January and the children in Florida. She'd learned all this through extensive discovery depositions. She spoke in great detail of January's deal with the defense minister and then Steine's conversation with him.

Pierce took a drink of water. She was sweating through her black Armani suit. "Steine, Davis, & Davis employed mercenaries and with the help of the NSA, our own government, invaded international waters. Mr. Steine and Mr. Davis broke the law, not Mr. January."

Davis was furious, and even Morty, who usually kept a good poker face, was pretty upset.

Little came out of her chair and said, "Objection, Steine, Davis, & Davis aren't defendants in this matter."

Pierce yelled back, "They should be."

"Stop right there, Ms. Pierce. Mr. Steine has been a respected member of this Bar for more than fifty years. I'd watch what I said even though there is limited protection from slander in pleadings. I'll make sure you regret it even though it does not extend to allegations of criminal conduct. The claims against Mr. Davis and Mr. Steine are criminal in nature, and I would be happy to be the one to push you over the edge."

"Sorry, Your Honor, my apologies to Mr. Davis and Mr. Steine."

"Wow, Judge Russo can take control, thought Davis.

"Let me point out that your client fled the jurisdiction of the courts that control his divorce action, the trusts, and the custody of his children. He illegally left this country and bribed a foreign official to remain outside the jurisdiction of our courts and in contempt of Judge Billingsly. I recognize that Steine and Davis violated his due process and his constitutional rights, but if they hadn't, he never would have been brought back to face the embezzlement charge, to which he pled guilty, or this murder charge."

It was the judge's turn to take a drink of water. "Here's what I'm going to do. I'm going to let it all in. The jury's going to hear everything the lawyers try to submit. They'll hear the objections as well and why I'm going to make the lawyers decide what they want to try to get in. This case is definitely going to the Court of Appeals. There's no stopping it. For the record I think Mr. Steine and Mr. Davis did the right thing to get the children back to their grandmother. They are better off living with her than with their father in Cuba. The proof will determine whether Daniel January killed Rachel January, but we do know that he's an admitted embezzler, and not what one would consider a common embezzler. We're going to move these cases along. They're not going to sit and clog up my docket. Two of them should be pled out."

Even though Billingsly was setting all three cases for trial, there was a distinct possibility that some other judge would try one of the lesser cases. More likely they'd settle.

"We can set a trial on the law firm embezzlement case for February 3rd, for the embezzlement of the trust for February 23rd, and the murder trial for March 8th all for 9:00 a.m. Court is adjourned."

A few days later judge Billingsly's predictions came true.

CHAPTER SIXTY-FIVE

JURY SELECTION, INSTRUCTIONS, AND OPENINGS

Tuesday, March 14, 2000

The trial didn't begin on the 8th as scheduled. It got pushed back till the 14th. That was the simple part of how our judicial system works. Billingsly actually did lose the trial, even though he wanted to keep it. As usual, Bella was tied to the office and wouldn't get to see any of it. Sammie as low man on the totem pole wouldn't get to see much of the trial as she'd like, but at least she wasn't going to testify. Davis and Morty were going to attend as much as the law permitted. As witnesses, they were under the exclusion rule. They could not hear the testimony of other witnesses before they testified. They could hear the opening arguments because they did not constitute proof, but after those statements, they couldn't be in the courtroom and hear the testimony of others. So depending on when they testified in the case, they could miss most of the trial.

The delay of the trial also permitted Caroline and Jake to attend during their spring break. Liza sat between her children. She rarely came to court, but she felt compelled to attend this trial. Sammie, who wasn't on the witness list, sat next to her. As it turned out, Russo didn't even want anyone on the witness list to hear the openings. Davis, Morty, Rita Sinclair, George Hopper, and the other witnesses weren't allowed to attend court until after they testified. The judge knew this case was going up on appeal so she was minimizing the issues from the start.

Judge Katherine Russo took the bench, and court was called to order. "Good morning, ladies and gentlemen." She was addressing the one hundred and forty-seven prospective jurors sitting in the back of the courtroom awaiting the possibility of serving on her jury. "I have reviewed and the lawyers have reviewed your questionnaires"

One month earlier each prospective juror had completed a five-page questionnaire with basic questions and then others specific to the January case to ascertain bias that might disqualify them.

"Jurors 3, 5, 8, 34, 36, 45, 56, 59, 67, 78, 89, 91, 102, 105, 109, 115, 123, 145, and 147 are dismissed for cause."

Nineteen jurors based on their answers were gone without any discussion on Judge Russo's call. There was a flaw in the questionnaire that no one picked up on. Question 15 asked, "Do you know any of the witnesses?" Then all twenty-five potential witnesses were listed, including George Hopper and Morty Steine. The prospective jurors took that question literally as had you met those witnesses? They had not. But many of the men had heard of and several of them had bet on or against George Hopper. Pierce should have known that, but she was too busy preparing a murder trial. As for Morty Steine, several prospective jurors had enjoyed his music as a member of Third Coast, a local blues band. Pierce had heard him play and was familiar with his music, but she had other things on her mind.

Judge Russo gave each side six preemptory challenges, where no particular reason for the challenge had to be given. After four hours, a jury of twelve with four alternates was selected. The jury was comprised of five women and seven men. All of the women were over thirty-five, and three were in their late fifties. This was a definite win for January. From Pierce's standpoint, the older, the better because they'd be less likely to sympathize with Rachel's lifestyle and adoption of the Ten Commandments. The men were also on the older side. There were four men over fifty-five, two in their forties, and one twenty-five year-old. Everybody on the jury had been married except the twenty-five-year-old; three were currently divorced. The jury came from varied backgrounds: two housewives, a bookkeeper, a hairdresser, three salespersons, an accountant, a house painter, a waiter, a computer programmer, and an unemployed health care executive drawing unemployment benefits.

Judge Russo informed the jurors that they needed to select a foreman. She sent them to the jury room to carry out that duty. When they returned, she asked the newly elected foreman to stand and introduce himself or herself. Judy Monroe, a thirty-six year-old mother of three stood and identified herself. Pierce didn't like that selection, *not a good premonition of things to come.*

The judge swore in the jury and the four alternates and gave the preliminary instructions. They were the same instructions given in every criminal case warning the jurors not to discuss the evidence until time to deliberate. "It's important that you hear all the evidence before you share your opinions with each other."

Judge Russo went into a long discussion about the witnesses and that most witnesses are biased in some way or another. "Only you are the judge of the facts. I'll tell you what the law is, but collectively you determine what the facts are. And remember, what the lawyers say is not evidence. Evidence is what is testified to and the documents that come into evidence."

Russo smiled. This was her jury. They'd get to the bottom of this case. "Ladies and gentlemen, this is serious business. The rest of a man's life is at stake. If he's convicted, he's going to jail for a long time, possibly the rest of his life. I want to listen to and weigh the evidence very carefully. Always remember there's a very heavy burden on the state to prove its case beyond a reasonable doubt. That means there's no other reasonable cause for the death of Rachel January other than that Daniel January killed her. You've got to hear the proof and decide. Good luck."

Belinda Little got up and smiled at the jury. "My name is General Belinda Little. No, I'm not in the army. I'm an assistant DA, and I work for you. I'm here today because the state has charged Daniel January with the murder of his wife, Rachel January. No, we don't have a body. No, we don't have a murder weapon. We don't have a confession. Those are what we call in the law direct evidence. We don't have any direct evidence that Daniel January killed his wife, Rachel. What we have is Daniel January's conduct after the murder occurred. He acted as if he committed the murder. He abducted his children, he fled the jurisdiction of the Tennessee courts, he illegally left the country, and he bribed a foreign government official to spend the rest of his life outside the United States to avoid criminal prosecution. Mr. January's evasive and suspicious conduct, commonly referred to as circumstantial evidence, proves Mr. January's guilt. An innocent man doesn't act that way. He was nabbed in international waters on his way to Cuba. He would have gotten away if he had not been intercepted and brought back to justice in Nashville by some unorthodox methods. He wouldn't be standing trial nor would his children, the grandchildren of Rita Sinclair, be safe. We will prove through circumstantial evidence that this man murdered Rachel January. Thank you."

Short and sweet, thought Little. *Maybe too short and sweet.*

Pierce rose and looked at the jury. She had the presumption of innocence on her side, and the state had everything to prove.

"Ladies and gentlemen, you've just heard the weakest opening statement ever given in a murder trial in the history of jurisprudence. My client acted guilty, so he is guilty. Let me make one thing clear. The state has to prove its case beyond a reasonable doubt, and if it intends to argue that it satisfies that burden based upon the fact that Dan January looks guilty, we may as well go home right now. When Dan January left the state of Tennessee, he had every legal right to do so, and he had full custody of his children. He didn't abduct anyone. He took his children to Disney World, and the proof will show they had a great time. The proof will show that the person who was unlawfully abducted was Dan January and that his constitutional rights were violated in the process. The state gets to go first. They will present the majority of the witnesses and the proof. That again is because the state has the burden. I will ask some questions, but I will do far less because the defendant doesn't have to prove anything. You must wait until all the proof is presented before making your decision. That is the fair thing to do. That is what is required of you. That is what you've sworn to do. That is what Mr. January and I know you will do. Thank you."

Pierce sat down. Although her opening was short, she appeared to be satisfied. A murder trial was an emotional case, although not for Pierce because she had no emotions. She'd have a couple of drinks and be ready in the morning. January, as tough as he was, wouldn't sleep. There was a lot at stake for him. Pierce was used to fighting about money. This time she was fighting to keep her client out of jail for the rest of his life. Her heart was black and cold. It was just another case.

CHAPTER SIXTY-SIX

THE COP AND THE LAWYER

Wednesday, March15, 2000

The judge welcomed everyone with a big smile. "General, call your first witness."

"The state calls Detective Sharon Duncan."

The Amazon Duncan made her way to the stand and was sworn. Little established her background, a veteran of thirteen years on the force. "I was not called into the case until July 5th. I met with Mr. January about noon that day at the request of Chief Neenan."

"What was Mr. January's attitude?"

"Unconcerned."

"Did he indicate why?"

"He thought she'd left the house on her own, and to use his own words 'she may have hooked up with some guy.'"

"Did he give you a written statement?"

"Yes."

General Little moved the statement into evidence. This might be the only opportunity for the jury to hear from January. With the court's permission, a copy was given to each juror.

Little had Duncan read the statement out loud.

"His statement doesn't mention seeing Rachel that night, does it?"

"No."

"His statement doesn't mention Rachel running into Robin Gaines that night, does it?"

"No."

"His statement doesn't mention that Mr. January and Rachel got into a screaming match?"

"No."

"Have other witnesses come forward, and has their testimony materially disputed Mr. January's statement?"

"Very much so, several witnesses. Robin Gaines places Rachel in the January house when she arrived sometime between 7:20 and 7:30."

"We'll let Ms. Gaines testify for herself, but would it be fair to say that her testimony dramatically contradicts the statement of Mr. January?"

Pierce objected on the grounds that the question called for a conclusion, and Russo sustained the objection.

"After your interview, what happened next?"

"Officially nothing. Rachel January hadn't been gone twenty-four hours, so technically she wasn't a missing person. The interview of Mr. January was a personal favor by Chief Neenan for Mr. Sinclair, a respected member of the Bar."

Did anything happen unofficially?"

"I'd say. It was the most amazing thing I'd ever seen. About a thousand volunteers began canvassing the Forest Hills and Green Hills areas. They began with Radnor Lake and then fanned out. For three solid days they looked, but found nothing. I thought they'd find her body, but they didn't."

"When did the police open its file?"

"On the 6th. We started looking for ways she might have left the house after the Sinclairs and kids dropped her off. We were still proceeding under the lie Mr. January told that she wasn't there when he and Ms. Gaines arrived at the house. We later learned from Ms. Gaines that she was sleeping and couldn't have left the house until at least 8:30, if she ever did."

Little showed Duncan the note.

"Was this note found at the Sinclair house?"

"Yes."

The note was moved into evidence, and a copy was given to each juror. Little had Duncan read the note out loud.

"Did you ever figure out when this note was left at the Sinclair house?

"No, General."

"Do we have any knowledge of Rachel January ever leaving the January house that night?"

"Evidence that she arrived; no evidence that she left."

"Was there any record of a taxi or other public form of transportation picking Rachel up?"

"None."

"Mr. Albert King was paid twenty-five thousand dollars by Mr. January and has pled guilty to obstruction of justice and received a sentence of one year and one day. Isn't that true?"

"Mr. King was a co-conspirator, and he was paid to cover up Mr. January's crime so he could flee the jurisdiction and arrest."

"How does Mr. King's testimony contradict Mr. January's sworn statement?

"Mr. King contradicts Mr. January's alibi as to where he was at certain times on July 4th. Mr. January was not as he claims having sex and alone with Robin Gaines all night on July 4th. The two of them arrived at Albert King's home at 9:15.

"Did anyone else plead guilty to a crime in connection to Mr. January's escape?"

"Robert and Robin Gaines admitted accepting fifty thousand dollars, and each received one year one day. The court let them serve their time consecutively so that one of them would be out of jail to care for their children."

"How did their testimony contradict Mr. January's statement?"

"Like King, they destroyed the timeline of his alibi. January definitely had the opportunity to kill his wife, and he lied about his whereabouts."

Duncan then told the story of how January fled with his kids. How he lied to the schools. How he traded cars in Columbia and drove to Orlando. How he contacted the Cuban defense minister, and how Steine and Davis brought him back.

"Did either Rachel January or Dan January have a gun registered in his or her name?"

"Rachel January had a .32 caliber pistol registered in her name."

"That's the same caliber weapon that killed Tyree Sinclair?"

"Yes."

"Was that weapon ever found?"

"No."

"What was Mr. January's explanation for the missing weapon?"

"Either Rachel took it with her, or it was stolen."

Little sat down and offered the witness to Pierce, who rose with her knife sharpened.

"Your interview of Mr. January was a favor to Chief Neenan, right?"

"Correct."

"But that was Morty Steine's favor, wasn't it, not Tyree Sinclair's?"

"Mr. Steine's on behalf of Mr. Sinclair. It was his daughter."

"During that search on the 5th through the 7th, Mr. January was looking with everyone else?"

"Yes. But he did lie about her being at the house when he and Ms. Gaines arrived."

Pierce asked the judge to have the last portion of the answer struck as no response. The judge did and directed the jury to ignore that portion of the answer.

Pierce hammered Duncan for another fifteen minutes and then sat down. Little felt that Duncan was more of a positive than a negative witness.

Next up was Benjamin Abraham Davis. Little figured she'd establish he was a biased witness right out of the box.

"You represent Rachel January?"

"I did when she was alive and when she was missing."

"Isn't she still missing?"

"She's dead."

"How do you know that?"

"I've spent hundreds of thousands of dollars looking for her, and I know this woman. She's the mother of two children. If she were alive and able to contact her children, she would. She must be dead."

It was critical that Davis convince the jury on this point because if they concluded that Rachel was alive and well, then no one was liable for her murder, not January or anyone else.

"You've also represented Rita Sinclair and her deceased husband, Tyree Sinclair?"

"Yes, I have."

"You're biased against Dan January?"

"I despise Dan January. I'm convinced he killed his wife, Rachel January, and I know he abducted his children and tried to prevent their grandmother from ever seeing them again by taking them to

Cuba. He's a horrible human being. I'm here to convince this jury of that fact. I guess that makes me biased."

The jury actually started laughing. Davis was so brutally honest, it was refreshing. Even Judge Russo joined in.

Davis was asked about how he first met Dan January, and he told the Chapman story. The women on the jury were noticeably shocked when Davis described the sex for legal services arrangements in detail. He apologized for Mr. January's graphic efforts to take advantage of a scared, broke mother of two. "His actions were not only unethical, for which he had to surrender his law license. They were also illegal and resulted in his pleading to embezzlement, for which he received a sentence of thirty months. Furthermore, his actions severely damaged his employer, who had to pay a settlement to my client, Ms. Chapman, of two hundred and sixty thousand dollars."

Russo called for a fifteen-minute comfort break. When they returned, Davis was back on the stand.

Little asked, "Could you explain to the jury the property settlement of the Januarys' divorce?"

"Before Rachel disappeared, Mr. January, who was a lawyer specializing in divorce law, and I worked out a settlement to his divorce. Ms. Pierce wasn't hired yet. It was fair and reasonable. He got the house, his pension, most of the marital property, except for some specific art that Rachel created, and eight hundred thousand dollars, which was being paid by the Sinclairs. In return he gave up custody of the children, resigned as substitute trustee on three trusts totaling ten million dollars, and got visitation every other weekend and a month in the summer."

"Why did the Sinclairs pay the eight hundred thousand dollars?"

"So January would resign as trustee. The trusts were irrevocable. Tyree Sinclair couldn't change them even though he desperately wanted to. His son-in-law didn't turn out to be whom he thought he was. The payment was to get rid of Dan January. The trusts contained ten million dollars. Tyree Sinclair didn't want Dan January to get his hands on that money."

"Did he?"

"Ultimately he did, and he stole about almost four hundred thousand dollars of his children's money after he fled the jurisdiction of the Sixth Circuit Court."

"What happened to the deal you made?"

"It disappeared when Rachel disappeared. Under Tennessee law, the agreement wasn't final until ninety days after it was signed, and Rachel disappeared before that time period elapsed."

"Didn't that hurt Mr. January?"

"You would think so, but soon after that, Tyree Sinclair was brutally murdered, and that elevated Mr. January from substitute trustee to trustee. He was now in control of ten million dollars."

Davis described the death of Tyree Sinclair.

"And there's an actual video of this murder?"

"Objection. It was a carjacking, Your Honor."

Judge Russo stated, "We're not showing the video. We'll simply refer to it as the death of Mr. Sinclair. Move on, General."

"Mr. Davis, describe for the jury how you located Mr. January and how he was returned to the United States."

Davis described how January's cell phone was tracked and how his conversations were eavesdropped. He described January's conversations with the ambassador, Major Pepe, and the defense minister.

Pierce objected throughout the testimony.

Davis then testified about Morty's conversation with the defense minister. Again, Pierce objected, citing a violation of January's constitutional rights.

Russo instructed the jury that the Court of Appeals would determine that issue. She allowed the lawyers to decide how much or how little to let them hear about how the defendant was brought back to this country. Despite that instruction, General Little elected not to play the tapes for the jury. Davis and Morty thought that was a big mistake. Sammie thought they should have avoided the entire subject matter.

Russo looked at her jury. They looked hungry, a little confused by the whole Court of Appeals discussion, and needing a break. She decided to take lunch.

Davis was glad to get off the stand and go to lunch. He left not only the courthouse but downtown with his family, who had been watching his performance. He drowned himself in a big meal: a double cheeseburger, fries, and chocolate malt at the Elliston Soda Shop, Morty's treat. The kids had the same as their dad. Sammie, who was ready to deliver, had a malt and nothing else. Liza, ever the nurse, remained with Rita Sinclair at the courthouse. Rita was a nervous wreck.

Sammie started in, "I know we're not supposed to discuss your testimony, but I think you're making a big mistake going into his capture and return to Nashville. I think the Court of Appeals is going to reverse on that issue."

Davis snapped back, "You're right, I'm not supposed to discuss my testimony. Drink your malt."

At two fifteen Davis was back on the stand. He answered a few more cleanup questions and then was turned over to Pierce.

"Afternoon, Mr. Davis."

Davis grunted an acknowledgment. He really disliked Pierce, and it was hard not to show it. His body language, with his arms crossed, was a clear giveaway. He knew better than that, but he just couldn't help himself.

"You want this jury to find my client guilty?"

"Yes."

"You'll consider it a personal defeat if he's found innocent?"

"I think justice will not have been served."

"How many times have you met Rachel January?"

"Three times."

"For a total of how long?"

"About three hours."

"During those three hours, did she always tell you the truth?"

"Not everything she said was accurate."

"She lied to you?"

"Not accurate."

"You have no medical training?"

"No."

"She was seeing Dr. Virginia Ames five days a week?"

"At one point, five, then later, three."

"Dr. Ames was her treating doctor and is in a much better position than you to form an opinion as to Rachel January's mental health?"

"Yes."

"You don't know if Rachel January is alive?"

"I think she's dead."

"You think. You don't know?"

"Based upon the evidence, she's dead."

"You've not seen a body or a weapon?"

"No, I haven't."

"When Mr. January took his children out of school, he had custody of them by order of the court?"

"Yes."

"The order did not prevent him from taking his children to Disney World?"

"No, it did not."

Pierce peppered Davis for another two hours and made several good points. She was a tough examiner, but he was a good witness. He stayed calm, looking at the jury, not Pierce. Davis knew that it was important to make eye contact with as many of the jurors as possible. He was particularly effective with the ladies.

Pierce turned to the judge and suggested that they stop for the day. She wanted to carry Davis over to the next morning.

That made sense. Russo looked at the clock. It was five fifteen. She called it quits and adjourned court. Davis felt pretty beat up as he descended from the stand. As he reached Liza, she gave him a deserved hug. He gave each of his children a kiss and along with Rita Sinclair and the rest of his team, he walked out of the courtroom.

CHAPTER SIXTY-SEVEN

MORE OF THE STATE'S PROOF

Thursday, March 16, 2000

Davis arrived at court early because he wanted to talk to General Little before he climbed on the stand. Liza and the kids didn't come. They'd had enough. It was hard to watch their loved one cross examined by Pierce. He found the prosecutor sitting alone in the courtroom.

"I think she's made some serious points with the jury. That's why she carried me over till today. What do you think she intends to do next?"

"I suspect she's going to get into Dickie Sasser and your relationship with him." We certainly opened the door."

Davis winced.

"We opened it all the way. Sammie argued we should have kept it closed. Oh well, too late now. After Pierce is done with me, what do you have for me on redirect?"

"So far I've got nothing. I agree her cross has been pretty effective to this point, and I don't think I can clean up any of it. Let's see what she does today, and then we'll powwow..."

"I don't think there will be time."

Before Davis could make his point, Russo came in and called court to order. Davis took the stand.

"Mr. Davis, you used a gentleman named Richard Sasser Jr. to hack e-mails of Mr. January, Robin Gaines, and Albert King?"

"I didn't. My investigator, Mr. Hopper, did, and he turned them over to me."

"That was without a warrant?"

"I'm not the government. I don't need a warrant."

"Didn't Mr. Sasser invade Mr. January's privacy?"

"I suppose so."

"Didn't he steal his e-mails?"

"His e-mails are right where they started, so technically he didn't steal anything. He invaded his privacy. It's more of a trespass."

"Would that be a tort, subject to civil suit?"

"Possibly."

"So Mr. January could sue you and Mr. Sasser for hacking into his e-mails?"

"Mr. Hopper employed Mr. Sasser, but you'd also have to prove damages."

"Don't you think being charged with murder is being damaged?"

"Mr. January is being charged with murder not because Mr. Sasser obtained some e-mails. He lied to the police concerning his whereabouts the night of July 4th. He lied about seeing Rachel."

Pierce reacted quickly, "Objection. Proof not in evidence. I move to strike Mr. Davis's last statement."

Russo ruled, "Sustained. Please ignore Mr. Davis's last statement."

Davis threw off Pierce's momentum. She had to regroup. She called a sidebar with the judge. Little, Pierce, and the court reporter huddled around the judge. Because he was on the stand, Davis could also hear the conversation. The proof would eventually come in through Robin Gaines but wasn't yet in.

Pierce began, "Judge, the General has opened the door by Mr. Davis's testimony and how the defendant was brought back to this country. I intend to play all the tapes. I want to make it clear that the playing of these tapes does not waive my original argument that this trial is in violation of my client's constitutional rights."

"So noted, Ms. Pierce. That position is consistent with my ruling. However, how the Court of Appeals views your playing of these tapes will be up to it. I warn you that you proceed at your own risk."

Everybody returned to his or her respective positions. Pierce resumed her questioning of Davis. "You recorded Mr. January's conversations with the ambassador of Cuba?"

"Richard Sasser Jr. did."

Pierce played the tape and moved it into evidence. Davis could tell the jury paid close attention to what was being said. The evidence was presented in a form different from any other so far in the trial.

"You recorded two conversations with Major Pepe?"

"No, Richard Sasser Jr. did."

"But that was on your behalf?"

"George Hopper, my investigator, asked him to."

"Same thing, right?"

"I turned it over to the DA."

"Sasser works for the NSA? You negotiated his contract with the NSA?"

"That's confidential."

Pierce turned to the judge. "I'm not asking what's in the contract, just if he negotiated the contract."

Russo directed Davis to answer the question.

"Yes, I did. "

Pierce played the first tape and moved it into evidence; and then played the second and moved it in. Davis watched the jurors' faces as they heard the audiotape. They were hard to read. Davis usually prided himself, because of his training from the master, to interpret a jury's reaction to evidence. Not this time, and the master didn't see their faces because he didn't testify yet. Sammie, who wasn't on the witness list did, and she observed them as they took in the proof. She definitely formed her opinion as to its impact on the jury.

"You recorded a conversation between Mr. January and the defense minister?"

"Yes."

She played the tape and moved it into evidence.

"In that conversation, he denied that he killed his wife?"

He'd say any lie to get out of the United States. He used three hundred thousand dollars of his children's money to do so."

Davis didn't like the way the morning was going. Pierce next played Morty's conversation with the defense minister. Morty sounded very cool and collected, but threatening.

"Mr. Davis, Mr. Steine extorted Mr. Castro to set Mr. January up, didn't he?"

"What do you mean?"

Little screamed, "Objection!" She didn't state a reason, which was required by the Rules of Civil Procedure.

Russo waited before asking, "What's your basis?"

Little said, "Mr. Steine didn't threaten criminal prosecution. He referred to simple worldwide embarrassment. Those are two very different things. The U.S. government could not have prosecuted the defense minister for bribery. He had immunity."

Brilliant answer, thought Davis.

Russo paused a moment pondering the general's argument. "Public humiliation and ridicule are effective motivators, sometimes more effective than criminal charges. Mr. Steine's actions, although very threatening, were not criminal and not extortion."

Sammie watched the jurors' faces during the exchange between Davis, Pierce, Little, and the judge, but she never took her eyes off the jurors collectively.

Pierce questioned Davis another fifteen minutes, but she never recovered from the finding that Morty's conduct was not criminal. That ruling stuck with the jury. When Pierce concluded her cross, the judge broke for lunch.

Davis suggested that he not go back on the stand. The jury had enough of him, a day and a half. He suggested that Little get the extraction behind them and put Hopper on the stand and then suffer through his cross. He figured the trip home to the United States had turned out to be the big weakness in the state's case, so get it out of the way. He argued that she should save Morty till the end as one of the last witnesses.

General Little agreed with that strategy except for putting Morty on the stand. She was reserving judgment on that point. Morty, who was furious, kept arguing that he was a critical witness to the case and that his charisma would win the jury over. Little insisted that Morty's testimony was a rehash of Davis's and another opportunity for Pierce to beat them over the head about the recapture of January, the weakest part of their case. The fight continued every time Little walked into the hallway during a break. The next witness after Davis was George Hopper.

Hopper did a great job on direct. He talked about Dickie Sasser and what a bright kid he was and how he could use a computer to extract information. He testified about the hunt for Rachel, and that if she was alive, he'd have found her. He talked about putting his team together to rescue the January children and the capture of their father, and the faces of Franklin and Gaby when they first saw their grandmother on shore. He was confident he'd done the right thing bringing those kids back. Little ended on that note.

Pierce began, "Do you know you can be sued by Dan January for trespassing?"

"So what? I got those kids home. No one was hurt, and they are now with their grandmother."

"What about my client? He's hurt. He's on trial for murder."

"Your client's in jail for embezzlement, a crime he pled guilty to, and he is standing trial for murder. This jury will determine if he's guilty. That's simply justice. Not him sipping rum in Cuba under the protection of some crooked politician." Hopper still had it. That was his knockout punch.

Pierce sparred with him another twenty minutes, but that answer was what the jury remembered.

The two principals got on the stand and testified about the day January picked up the kids. Nancy Flexor angrily said, "He lied right to my face. He said Frankie had a doctor's appointment. There was a cancelation, and he got fit in."

A lawyer generally asks no questions when he or she wants the jury to think that the witnesses' testimony hurt the client. For both, "No questions."

Richard Feeder, the used car salesman/car lot owner from Columbia, Tennessee, who was on the other side of Davis in the Brandon Tell swimming pool case, testified that he traded January's autos in record time. "It was the fastest transaction I ever had. Less than five minutes. The son picked out the car in less than two minutes. Neither son nor father asked me any questions about the car they were purchasing, and the transfer took about five minutes of paperwork. He was definitely in a rush."

Another witness where there was no advantage to prolonging the agony of having him on the stand. Pierce again asked no questions, hoping to send the message to the jury that this testimony was not important. Pierce asked for and the judge granted another fifteen-minute break.

Little made the mistake of leaving the courtroom and was accosted by her old friend Morty Steine.

"I want in. You need me. I'm the one who can win this case. The judges on the Court of Appeals know me and respect me, and I'm the one who can convince them that violating January's due process rights to recover those two small children and bring a murderer to stand trial were the right things to do. I can plead your case. I can see your appellate brief now. It will contain long quotes from my testimony and from Rita Sinclair's testimony. That's what will carry the day, and the conviction will be affirmed."

Little looked at the old man hard. He had many years of experience under his belt. She was new at the game. He gave her a knowing wink and then a broad smile, an irresistible one that he'd used many times successfully. She was a goner.

"Okay, we'll do it your way. You'll be my last or next to last witness. I want to think about whether you or Rita should be cleanup."

"Well, that's at least a start. I'll convince you that I should go last. We'll talk later. You've got a trial to win."

Albert King entered the courtroom in his orange jumpsuit.

Pierce insisted he not be permitted to change into a suit and tie. She wanted him to appear as the rat he was in his prison garb.

After he was sworn, General Little asked, "Is this your sworn statement you gave to the police in connection with the murder investigation of Rachel January?"

"Yes."

"Is it accurate?"

"No."

"How is it inaccurate?"

"I was paid twenty-five thousand dollars by Dan January to say that Robin, January, my wife, and I were together all night on July 4th, but Robin wasn't with us. My statement claims that Dan brought Robin to our house around ten. That's not true. I picked her up at the January house around 8:30, without Dan. She was all shaken up and told me that she'd witnessed a fight between Dan and Rachel. I lied in this statement to support Dan's alibi."

"You've pled guilty to obstruction of justice and providing a false statement and you are serving a year and a day?"

"Yes."

Little had King describe his swinger lifestyle and specifically his relationship with Dan January, Robin Gaines, and Robert Gaines.

"So you were all lovers?"

"Yes."

"Together and separately?"

"Yes."

"Rachel didn't participate?"

"She watched, if you call that participating. I think she enjoyed it."

Little objected as to speculation, and the judge sustained the objection.

Little spent another fifteen minutes and ended her questioning of King.

Pierce asked King only a few questions, "Rachel kept watching all of you have sex again and again, didn't she?

"Yes."

No one held a gun to her head?"

"No."

"She seemed to enjoy watching?"

"Very much so."

"No further questions."

Pierce decided the orange jumpsuit damaged King's credibility enough. She passed on questioning him.

Dr. Phillip January dressed immaculately in a suit and tie was called next by the state, and his rehearsed testimony took less than twenty minutes. It was part of his plea bargain and went as smooth as could be. He proved that he and his brother, Dan, conspired to steal more than three hundred thousand dollars from the children's trust funds to first assist in Dan's escape from Tennessee and then his efforts to gain access to Cuba. Phillip was very matter of fact as he told his story to the jury.

He showed no emotion as he admitted, "I told this truthful testimony in exchange for a sentence of one year and a day. My brother was caught and was guilty of embezzlement, but I don't believe he's guilty of murder."

Little moved to strike the last portion of the answer, but Russo let it stand.

"The jury has a right to hear what his brother thinks as to the man's guilt or innocence. They can weigh his bias against that opinion."

Little and Davis thought it was a weird note to end the testimony, but that's where it ended.

Maria Lopez testified that she worked as the bookkeeper at the OK Corral Gun Range and that in the first six months of calendar 1999, Dan January came to the range six times and purchased ammunition for a .32 caliber pistol five times. Ms. Lopez testified that since January 1999, the only five purchases for .32 caliber ammunition at the range had been by Dan January. Pierce asked Lopez no questions.

Judge Russo looked at the clock. It was after six and time to stop for the day.

"Ladies and gentlemen of the jury, we've had a full day. This case has moved along. So far you have only heard from the state. Hold off making any conclusions. There's more proof to be presented including what the defense has to say. Wait to hear from your fellow jurors. You are a collective body. Have a good night. Court is adjourned."

CHAPTER SIXTY-EIGHT

CLOSE OF THE STATE'S PROOF

Friday, March 17, 2000

Judge Russo stopped by the jury room and looked in on her jury. She asked, "Do you need anything? I think the case is moving along."

Foreman Monroe spoke up, "Do you think we'll be done by tomorrow?"

"The lawyers know better than I do, but after the state finishes, the defendant gets to go. Then we have closing argument, my instructions, and you have to deliberate. I think we'll be here a few more days." The jury seemed disappointed. The jury's impatience bothered the judge. She left for the courtroom.

Russo began the day, "Good morning. I hope everybody had a good night. I'm ready for a productive day. Is the state ready, General?"

General Little stood and nodded.

"Call your next witness.

"Dr. Jackie Samuels."

General Little established her qualifications as an FBI agent handwriting expert. She'd been the head of that department in the Chicago office.

"Did you examine the note that was found at the January residence?"

"Yes."

"Is this the note, which is already in evidence?"

"Yes."

"Was this note written by a man or a woman?"

"I can state with ninety-eight percent certainty a man wrote this note."

"Can you explain why you hold that opinion?"

Samuels described in detail based on how the letters were formed why she held her opinions. How the *s* was shaped or the *y* was formed, and so on.

"Were you provided with printed samples of Rachel January's handwriting?"

"Yes. I was provided with samples from 1975, when she very young, only five years old and then one from 1997. Her mother, Rita, had saved her early samples from childhood. It was interesting to have that childhood sample for comparative purposes, but the adult sample was principally used. Based on those samples, I can state with a reasonable degree of certainty, ninety-eight percent, that Rachel did *not* write the note."

"Did you review any printed samples of Dan January?"

"Yes. I reviewed fifteen samples. Mr. January worked for Sinclair & Sims, so printed samples were readily available. I can state with ninety percent certainty that Dan January wrote this note."

"Can you explain why you hold that opinion?"

Samuels went into detail why she held her opinions and why it was only ninety percent.

Little sat down.

Pierce stood and asked, "Is two percent reasonable doubt?"

"I don't know what that means."

"Is a two percent chance that Rachel January wrote the note reasonable doubt?"

"I don't know."

"What percentage is reasonable doubt?"

"I don't know."

"You can't quantify it?"

"I guess not. That's not for me to say."

"I thought you were an expert?"

"I'm an expert in handwriting analysis, not what constitutes reasonable doubt."

"What about a ten percent chance that Dan January didn't write the note. Is that reasonable doubt?"

"I don't know. That's for the jury to decide, not me."

Good answer, thought Davis.

Pierce ended on that note.

Little asked, "So, if there are a hundred people in this courtroom and half of those are women, it's possible that one of those wrote the note?"

"Yes."

"And of the fifty men, it's possible five, one in ten?"

"Yes?"

"Let me ask you, of those six people in the room how many lied to the police on July 4th?"

"None."

"How many of them got into a screaming match with Rachel January and was the last person to see her alive?"

"None."

"How many of them got to control ten million dollars?"

Pierce objected, "That didn't happen until after the death of Tyree Sinclair."

General Little sat down. As she sat, she said, "I think the jury understood my point."

Pierce had nothing further. Samuels started weak, but ended strong.

Judge Russo announced that she had another matter requiring her immediate attention. "Despite the early hour of ten thirty, we'll break for lunch and be back at 12:30." Everyone cleared the courtroom so her emergency hearing could proceed.

In the hallway Morty and Davis grabbed Little. Morty asked, "Who do you have left?"

"Robin Gaines and Rita in that order. I don't plan on putting you on the stand." Morty was devastated. He thought he'd already won this argument, and now he was back at square one. Davis was ambivalent. Sammie had worked on him so hard he didn't know who was right, but truth be told they'd already committed to the strategy so they might as well roll the dice and put the old man on the stand. So Davis argued, "Robin will be a powerful witness, but I'm not sure about Rita. She's strong and will be good on direct, but Pierce may hurt her on cross. Do you want that to be the last witness the jury hears as the state closes its proof?"

Little had thought about her witness list and whether to put Steine on the stand. "I don't want to get into the entire extraction thing again. I think we come off like mercenaries, and you led the capture. You're the one on tape threatening the defense minister. Pierce will eat you alive on the stand."

"Darling, I can turn all that around and make it right. Please let me."

"It's a judgment call, and it's mine. I'm ending with the grieving mother. I'm leaving the jury thinking about her over the weekend."

Robin Gaines took the stand. Despite the orange jumpsuit, at forty-five, she still looked good, real good. Every man on the jury would want her, despite her checkered past.

There must be a gym at that prison, and she gets plenty of time to work out, thought Davis. *She looks just as good as the day I tried to interview her, and she was outfitted in spandex.*

General Little established the marital and family background of Robin and then her connection to Rachel and Dan January. It was interesting to watch the jurors' faces as she explained the Ten Commandments. They'd heard it before, but hearing them read from a seductive blonde who'd lived them made all the difference in the world. She was hot and all of the men on the jury fantasized about being with Robin Gaines, and so did two female jurors.

"How long did the four of you abide by these Ten Commandments?"

"A little over two years. It worked pretty well. All four of us were happy. On a few occasions we invited another couple into the ménage, but for the most part, it was the four of us, putting the children first. Always putting the children first."

"What changed?"

"Dan and I developed strong feelings for each other, and Rachel got jealous. She demanded that it end. A year later, they were involved in a similar relationship with the Coopers, but that didn't work out either due to Rachel's jealousy."

"Did you continue to see Dan?"

"Yes, with my husband Robert's knowledge. We'd have threesomes or other group involvements."

"Never one on one?"

"Occasionally we'd have a rendezvous, but it wasn't a secret. Robert would know."

"Is this your statement given to the police in the January murder investigation?"

"Yes."

"Is it accurate?"

"No."

"It says you were with Dan January from about 7:15 until 10:00 on July 4th, 1999, having sexual intercourse in his bedroom. Is that an accurate statement?"

"No."

"In your own words, tell the jury what happened that night." General Little had practiced this question and was confident that Robin would give a graphic and detailed answer.

"Dan picked me up around seven at my house. We planned a night alone together. Robert had planned to have a barbeque threesome with the Kings, ribs and sex. I was really looking forward to being alone with Dan. We'd not been one on one in a long time. We arrived at his home about seven fifteen and started undressing as we walked into the house. By the time we got to the bedroom, I was down to my panties only. At that point we saw Rachel sleeping in the bed. It angered Dan. He said, 'What's that bitch doing here? She's supposed to be watching fireworks with the kids at her daddy's office. This is my bed.' I said 'Let's go to one of the other bedrooms.' I just wanted to have sex. That didn't suit Dan. He wanted her out of his bed. It was some sort of territory thing. He threw me on the bed and started screwing me with her next to us. She didn't wake up. We quickened our pace, and she still slept. It was pretty amazing. Finally I held the bedpost, and Dan came from behind. The bed shook so violently that Rachel woke up."

Davis was watching the jury. They were shocked. Even the most promiscuous couldn't believe the testimony.

"That's when the fireworks began. They started screaming at each other. I can't remember the exact words, but they were very heated and threatening. I know Rachel said she would kill Dan. I don't think I heard him say those words to her, but he kept saying 'It is my house now.' She was trespassing and had no right to be there. He could have her arrested. I grabbed my clothes and called Robert, who picked me up and took me to the Kings. I was pretty shaken up."

"What time was that?"

"Before 8:30."

"You're serving one year and one day for obstruction of justice and giving a false statement to the police?"

"Yes."

"No further questions."

Pierce got up and stood there a long time. The jurors began to wonder what she was doing. So did the judge, who prodded her, "Ms. Pierce, do you have any questions?"

"Yes, Your Honor, I do. Ms. Gaines, I was wondering when you have group sex, does one man put his penis in your mouth, another in your vagina, and a third in your anus?"

General Little ran to the podium. Russo didn't even wait for her to say the word *objection.* "Ms. Pierce, what are you doing?"

"I'm conducting cross-examination. The general opened the door when she asked about group sex and the Ten Commandments. I think this jury has a right to understand who and what this woman is. She's a disgusting slut, and that reflects on her credibility as a witness."

Little argued, "Who her partner is and how she has sex should have no bearing on her credibility."

Pierce came right back, "Whether it should or not is not the question. The question is whether it does. To the average Nashvillian, this type of conduct has an impact on credibility. Therefore it is admissible."

Russo paused and then ruled in Pierce's favor.

"So on many occasions, your husband and you had group sex while your children were sleeping upstairs?"

"Yes."

"At one time you were in love with Dan January?"

"Yes."

But you're not in love with him anymore?"

"I still care about him, but, no, I love my husband."

"That is the husband that you cheated on dozens of times, right?"

It's not cheating. He knew and was often there."

And you care so much for my client that you ratted him out?"

"I'm telling the truth."

Little had prepped her for that question.

"You're a cruel person, aren't you?"

"I don't think so."

"You had anal sex next to Rachel while she was sleeping?"

"It wasn't anal."

"Does that make it less cruel?"

"No, it was wrong. It was cruel, you're right."

"So you are a cruel person?"

"That was a cruel action."

"No further questions."

Russo decided to take a lunch break. "Let's take an hour for lunch. General, how many witnesses do you have before you close?"

Little hesitated before saying, "One."

Disappointed by that answer, Davis whispered to Morty, "Big mistake."

After the break, Rita Sinclair hit the stand. General Little spent the first half hour humanizing Rachel and telling the jury about her. She started with her childhood and her education through motherhood. She showed pictures of her with Frankie and Gaby and testified that "she was a good mother."

"Tell the jury about her marriage."

"At first it was good. At least Tyree and I thought it was good. Tyree and I knew nothing about the Ten Commandments or group sex. I'd say Dan and Rachel are equally at fault. Until he stole his children's money and tried to abduct them to Cuba, I thought Dan was a good father. He may have been a bad husband, but I thought he was a good father. I was wrong about a lot of things I guess."

Bad answer, thought Davis. *She didn't even answer the question.*

"Did Rachel have depression?"

"Yes. I think part of that was because of how Dan treated her. How he treated her didn't help."

"Was she taking medication?"

"Yes, and it was helping her."

"Was she in therapy?"

"Yes, and it was helping her."

"Was your daughter capable of committing suicide?"

"Absolutely not."

"You spent over a hundred thousand dollars trying to find Rachel after July 4th, 1999?"

"Yes, I hoped she was alive, but I now realize she's gone. I'm convinced that's she dead." Rita talked about the murder of her husband and how the burden of continuing the fight of finding Rachel fell on her shoulders. She explained that with the help of Steine,

Davis, & Davis and others, she had the strength to fight on and to bring Dan January to justice, but that it wasn't easy.

"I know that we used unconventional methods, but I had to get my grandchildren back. That was my number one priority; I didn't give a damn about Dan's due process rights, and if you were a parent or grandparent, neither would you. You'd want him back here to face justice for the murder of your little girl too; not sipping a drink under the protection of a dictator on some island.

Rita looked at the jury, and a very strong woman started sobbing. This was no act. She just broke down from exhaustion and emotion.

Little looked at the jury and decided to close her proof and turn her vulnerable witness over to the devil.

"No further question. The state closes its proof." It was only two o'clock; Little had miscalculated on the time. There were still three hours before the end of the day and the beginning of the weekend. She was adamant that Morty wasn't hitting the stand. Davis cringed and Morty's hopes were dashed.

Pierce stood and walked to the podium and asked, "Do you need a tissue, Mrs. Sinclair?"

"Please," she said between sobs.

Pierce waited and then began, "The relationship between a mother and a daughter is often a complex relationship?"

"I don't understand."

"A mother and a daughter often fight about everyday things, right?"

"I suppose."

"You and Rachel often disagreed and fought?"

"I suppose, like every other mother and daughter."

"In fact you had a pretty serious fight the morning of July 4th, 1999?"

"Yes."

"She'd stayed out all night?"

"Yes."

"Never called to see how her children were doing?"

"But she knew her children were with Dan and then later with Tyree and me."

"She elected not to go watch the fireworks with her family because she had a headache?"

"Right."

"That could have been an excuse?"

"I don't know. She said she had a headache."

"But she lied to you before, hadn't she?"

"I don't know how to answer that."

She lied about her sex life and the Ten Commandments."

"We didn't know about what they were doing. We were shocked."

"You didn't teach her to act like that, did you?"

"No, we didn't."

"Your daughter surprised you?"

"Yes."

"I guess you didn't know your daughter as well as you thought you did?"

Little jumped up. "Objection, speculation."

"Sustained." Russo took pity on Sinclair.

"You don't know if Rachel committed suicide?"

"Same objection," Little argued.

"No, General, that's a fair question, overruled. Please answer, Mrs. Sinclair."

"Rachel didn't have suicide in her."

"That's your opinion as her loving mother?"

"Yes."

"Who she kept in the dark?"

"Yes."

"No further questions."

General Little looked at Rita Sinclair. She was worn out. You could look into her eyes and see that she was drained and that she had nothing left.

"No redirect."

Russo adjourned court. "We'll start with the defense on Monday. Let's break early today, and everybody enjoy the weekend. I remind you not to discuss the case with anyone, not your families, or each other. You've only heard half the proof. The defense now get its turn. You need to wait and see and hold off drawing any conclusions. Have a great weekend."

CHAPTER SIXTY-NINE

THE DEFENSE AND CLOSING ARGUMENTS

Monday, March 20, 2000

Judge Russo began the morning by stopping by the jury room with breakfast. She said, "Morning. I've got some ham and biscuits, sausage and biscuits, and eggs and biscuits for you all. Remember, breakfast is the most import meal of the day."

The jury thanked her and then dug in. "I hope everybody had a restful weekend. We start the defense today; we're nearing the end of the case and you'll soon have completed your civil duty. As an added bonus..."

She produced two-dozen Dunkin' donuts. She figured not all of them were dieting. The sixteen jurors and alternates ate the donuts within five minutes. Apparently none of them were dieting. By nine fifteen everybody was in the courtroom ready to begin the day's proceedings.

Judge Russo smiled at her jury, and said, "Friday the state closed its proof. Today the defense is afforded an opportunity to put on proof. It's also important that you remember that the defendant does not have to prove anything. Mr. January doesn't have to put on any witnesses. Mr. January doesn't have to take the stand in his defense and testify because he doesn't have to prove anything. With that said, Ms. Pierce, does the defendant have any witnesses?"

"Your Honor, the first thing I need to do is make an announcement."

"Let's have a sidebar."

Little and Pierce moved to the front of the courtroom, and the judge turned off the mic. In whispers with the court reporter continuing to preserve the record the conversation ensued.

"What is it Ms. Pierce?'

"The defense can't find Dickie Sasser. We've looked everywhere. We've tried to serve him with a subpoena, but have been unsuccessful. We've tried using both the sheriff's office and private process servers, but no luck. He's hiding, and I suggest the NSA is helping him hide."

"What do you propose, Ms. Pierce?"

"I would request that the court issue a capias and have it served on the NSA."

"My jurisdiction is exclusive to the state of Tennessee. My judicial powers do not extend to Washington."

"Serve the local office here in Nashville at the federal building downtown."

"Do they even have a local office?"

Pierce handed Russo the address, and it was agreed that the subpoena would be issued. This would become another issue on appeal.

"Call your first witness, Ms. Pierce."

"Yes, Your Honor. The defendant calls Dr. Virginia Ames."

Pierce established Dr. Ames's educational and professional credentials and moved her resumé into evidence.

"You were Rachel January's psychiatrist?"

"Yes."

"At one point, for months, you were seeing her every day, right?"

"Yes."

"It would be fair to say that you knew and understood the mind of Rachel January better than anyone else?"

"I'm professionally trained, yes."

"Better than her parents?"

"She had a difficult relationship with her parents, so yes."

"In your professional opinion in July 1999 was Rachel January suicidal?"

"I last saw Rachel on July 1st, and she was not on that date, so no."

"Well, what about June?"

"In mid-June she was in crisis through June 24th. During that time she was suicidal."

"So the week before, in your professional opinion, she could have killed herself."

"Yes."

"Was Rachel January depressed?"

"Yes."

"She was on Valium, Wellbutrin for depression, and Ambien for sleep?"

"Yes."

"In July she was very unhappy with her life? She wanted out?"

"She wasn't happy, but I can't say she wanted out."

"You can't say with a reasonable degree of professional certainty that she didn't run away, can you?"

I don't know if she ran away or not."

"You don't know if she's alive or dead, do you?"

"I don't know one way or another."

"You don't know if Dan January killed Rachel January?"

"I do not."

"You have reasonable doubt, don't you?"

"I don't know."

"You've got doubt?"

"I guess I do."

"No further questions."

Pierce sat down.

Judge Russo offered Dr. Ames to the state as its witness.

Little got up and asked, "Do innocent persons run away?"

"What do you mean, General?"

"Do people who are accused of a crime flee the jurisdiction where that crime has been committed?"

"As worded, accused persons who are innocent would be better served not running. It makes them look guilty."

"Dan January would know that?"

Pierce objected as to speculative about what January would know. Ames agreed that a reasonable person would recognize that fact. Little sparred with Ames for another twenty minutes, but she couldn't really dent the crux of her testimony, which addressed the mental instability of Rachel January. She finally sat down, frustrated that Dr. Virginia Ames could possibly create doubt in the minds of some jurors. *One damn witness, and all of my hard work could be thrown out the window in vain.*

"I have no further questions, Your Honor."

Russo proclaimed, "Let's take an early lunch before closing arguments."

Davis and Morty consoled Little after court was adjourned. Morty commented, "She was admittedly damaging. She probably swayed a few jurors, but the rest won't forget all the rest of the proof. That just means there will be a fight in the jury room. You expected that, right?"

The three went to lunch together. Davis was pretty nervous. He ate a double cheeseburger with fries and a chocolate milk shake. Little picked at her Cobb salad. Morty picked up the tab.

When they returned from lunch, Russo called court back into

session, and Little walked to the podium. "Dan January is an admitted embezzler. He pled guilty to that crime. He wasn't the traditional thief who put his hand in the cookie jar and got caught. He used his position of trust to take advantage of a young, vulnerable mother of two, who was going through a divorce. She was lonely, broke. His job was to protect her. Instead he screwed her both literally and figuratively. He took advantage of her sexually and then sued her. He cost his firm two hundred and sixty thousand dollars. That's because he lied to Laura Chapman, his wife, Rachel, his partner and his father-in-law, Tyree Sinclair. He lied to the police in his statement. He claimed that he didn't see Rachel at their house. You remember Robin Gaines's testimony. Dan January is a cruel man. He treated Rachel inhumanly. He had sex with Gaines lying next to Rachel. How would you feel if that happened to you?"

Little walked closer to the jury to emphasize her next point. "You heard Robin Gaines state that when she ran out the door, she left Rachel and Dan January screaming at each other. What do you think happened next? It got physical, and he killed her. He was back at the house by 10:45 and then lied to the Sinclairs and the police about the whole story. If Robin Gaines hadn't come forward, we'd never know of his cruelty or the lies."

Robin Gaines was just as cruel.

"Tyree Sinclair was murdered, and we don't know who killed him. As a result of his death, Dan January got to control more than ten million dollars. He lied to Nancy Flexor and kidnapped his children. He stole about a million dollars of his children's trust funds and bribed a foreign official so that he could illegally leave the United States. He ran and tried to remain outside the jurisdiction of the state of Tennessee because he was guilty of the murder of Rachel January. You don't run unless you're guilty."

Little returned the podium. She looked at Rita Sinclair and then back at the jury. "Rachel Sinclair didn't commit suicide. She didn't run away. She was murdered, and I commit to you that Dan January beyond a reasonable doubt committed that murder. We've proven he's cruel enough, had opportunity and motive and that on July 4th he and Rachel fought, and she lost her life at his hands. Thank you."

Judge Russo turned to Amy Pierce, "Your closing, Ms. Pierce."

"Dan January is an embezzler. Dan January was unfaithful to his wife. Dan January was an unethical lawyer. Dan January is and was a liar. Dan January was cruel and inhuman to Rachel January on July 4th. Given all of those facts, you have a right to dislike him, even hate him, but you don't have the right to deny him of his constitutional rights of due process and right to presumed innocence. Just because you don't like him, you can't switch the burden of proof from the state to him or lower the burden of proof to a preponderance of the evidence like in a civil trial. The state must prove its case beyond a reasonable doubt. Dr. Ames knew Rachel January better than anyone else on earth, and she has doubts. Rachel may have committed suicide, or she may have run away. You've never met Rachel. You've just heard about her. You must have some doubts too. If so, you must find Dan January not guilty. It's your only choice. Thank you."

It was three thirty, and Judge Russo elected to adjourn early for the day. All that remained was to give closing instructions and then turn the jury loose to deliberate. Juries were hard to read. The jurors paid close attention during the trial. The state did most of the talking, but it had the burden, so that made sense. The question of Dan January's guilt or innocence would soon be in the hands of twelve of his peers, and the alternates would be set free to go home to their families.

CHAPTER SEVENTY

FINAL INSTRUCTIONS AND THE VERDICT

Tuesday, March 21, 2000

The judge looked at the eager faces of the jurors, and she began, "Today's your big day. You start your deliberation. You've heard all the proof, the lawyers have given their closing arguments, and in a few minutes I'll tell you what the law is and what the law expects of you. I want you to know that you are providing a guaranteed constitutional right to a jury trial. Dan January has a right to be judged by his peers."

Judge Russo described several aspects of the law and how they applied to the January case. She spoke slowly so that the jury would understand how the law applied to the particular facts of the case. She spent a great deal of time on the credibility of the witnesses. "Their demeanor was important as well as their words. You are a collective body. Talk about the evidence. Each one of you may have noticed something different, and you bring your collective knowledge back into your deliberations."

There were many legal terms defined in the instructions but none had more emphasis than the standard of care that was required in order for the juror to find guilt of the defendant. It imposed a finding 'beyond a reasonable doubt', which meant that there was no other logical explanation for the murder other than the defendant's act.

A copy of the jury instructions was given to Ms. Monroe, the accountant, who was the jury foreman. The four alternates were excused. Judge Russo's last words to her jury were, "This is a difficult task. A man's freedom is in your hands, but you are responsible citizens of this county. Do your duty."

The jury began their deliberations at ten thirty. Little met Davis, Morty, and Rita Sinclair in the hallway. The general announced, "Now we wait."

"How long?" Rita asked.

Morty answered, "No one knows the answer to that question. They first will review all the testimony and documents, and then take an initial vote. Depending on the split, they'll negotiate till it's unanimous."

Davis suggested, "Rita, let's wait back at Steine, Davis, & Davis. General Little will call us if there's a verdict."

As usual Morty was right, the jury did just as he predicted. They reviewed a list of all the witnesses and summarized their testimony and looked at the exhibits in the order they came into evidence. That was so predictable. There were several arguments as to what particular witnesses said and what particular documents meant.

At five o'clock they got a call from General Little that the jury told the judge they wanted to go late till seven, and then they intended to start fresh in the morning. The next day everyone reconvened, and the mother of three, foreman Judy Monroe took charge.

"Let's go around and share some of our thoughts about the case. Raise your hand, and I'll acknowledge you."

"I think he killed the father, Sinclair. He owned a .32 caliber...

The foreman stood and said, "Mr. Baker, focus. This is the murder trial related to the daughter, not the father. That proof was a red herring, not relevant to the case."

Roy Baker, a house painter, took the rebuke in stride. Katie Poe, a thirty-three-year-old dental assistant, went next, "Robin Gaines is a real slut. Can you imagine waking up and having two people having sex right next to you?"

Monroe jumped in, "That's the wrong question. The right question is what happened after the screaming match and Robin Gaines left the house and was picked up by Albert King?"

Poe replied, "Rachel was alive when Gaines left the January home. She was the last person who saw Rachel."

The discussion went back and forth for three hours, and then they broke for lunch. When they resumed, the arguments continued.

David Jackson argued, "He'd made it. He was in international waters. It wasn't right that Davis and his thugs brought him back and violated his constitutional rights."

"How can you say that? If he was allowed to carry out his escape, those children would have wound up in Cuba the rest of their lives. They'd never see their grandmother again. She was a loving woman, and that certainly wouldn't have been fair," insisted Tonya Parker, a grandmother of six.

"He had custody of those kids. He had a right to take them to Disney World in Florida when he did. He was trustee of their accounts and had the right to withdraw money. He had the right to take them into international waters, and he could make whatever deal he wanted with Raul Castro he wanted. It's a free country."

Judy Monroe decided she needed to exert control over her jury. She took her job as foreman seriously. "Mr. Jackson, you may have been right until your last statement. Mr. January didn't have a right to seek asylum in Cuba. But this is a murder trial, not about Mr.

January's extradition back here from trial. The question we must answer is do we think that Dan January murdered Rachel January beyond a reasonable doubt?"

At four the judge called the jury and the parties into court and asked for a status report. "Where are we? What's the split?" asked the judge. "Don't tell me which way, just the number each way."

"It's nine to three, and I'm not sure the three are going to budge. We may be a hung jury."

"I want you to keep working. Don't give up yet. Listen to each other's arguments both ways at least for a few more hours."

The jury ended at six and returned the next day. At noon the judge called another status report, and when she was told it was nine to three, she declared a hung jury. As required by law, Russo directed Monroe announce the split in open court. "Ms. Monroe, please tell the state and the defendant how the vote was split between guilty and not guilty."

"It was nine for guilty and three for not guilty."

The judge thanked the jurors for their service and dismissed them.

"General Little, does the state wish to empanel another jury in light of the reported jury split? "Does the state wish to further prosecute Mr. January on the charge of murder of Rachel January?

General Little knew the answer before she turned around and looked at Rita Sinclair. Her boss, Johnson Tory, wouldn't authorize the cost of another trial from either a monetary or a political perspective. "The state will not be prosecuting any further, Your Honor."

Rita Sinclair began to sob. So did Sammie, who was three days short of her due date. Davis and Morty were visibly shaken, and their confidence in the system was shaken.

Dan January and Amy Pierce embraced. January had a weight lifted off his shoulders. He still had to serve the remainder of his thirty months, and he had two years left. By March 2002, he'd be a free man.

"Mr. January, these charges against you are dismissed. Court is adjourned."

Sammie whispered to Rita. "They didn't find him innocent. Nine jurors found him guilty. She just couldn't convince three others that he was guilty beyond a reasonable doubt. It's a tough burden."

That wasn't any solace to Rita Sinclair, who continued to sob. Sammie squeezed her hand tightly just as Sammie felt a strong pain in her side.

The Davis group remained in the courtroom as it cleared out. Rita Sinclair didn't want to face the cameras waiting outside. Under Tennessee law, TV cameras were barred from the courtroom. However, court was now out of session. If she didn't come out, they'd come in.

Pierce was already out there taking a well-deserved victory lap. She told them, "I knew the jury wouldn't allow the Constitution to be trampled on and let justice be abused like that."

Davis couldn't believe that Pierce of all people got to rely on the principle of the Constitution. *It makes me want to throw up.*

"I knew that the jury hated my client. I admitted that and threw that right back in their faces. I made this case not about his right but about every American's rights and the protections the Constitution grants all of us in general. I pointed out if the jury let what happened to him stand, they would have to stand by and let it happen to you or even them. Jefferson made it clear that due process was put in the Constitution to protect the worst of us and to protect the best of us. Today we proved him right. Thank you."

Ms. Amy Pierce strutted toward the elevator. Davis volunteered to go out so his client wouldn't have to. Someone had to face down the cameras.

"Mr. Davis, how does Mrs. Sinclair feel about the verdict?"

"Very disappointed! We thought General Little proved the

state's case, and so did a majority of the jury, but the law requires a unanimous decision, and that wasn't going to happen."

"Do you know why?" a reporter asked.

"I do. With Judge Russo's permission, I was allowed to talk with Ms. Monroe, the foreman, who shared with me briefly a summary of the deliberation of the jury. It seems that the three dissenting jurors never would have changed their vote because of how Mr. January was brought back into this country to stand trial. They were adamant that his due process rights were violated, and it was their opinion even if he was guilty of the murder, they wouldn't convict him. That's why the jury declared a deadlock because of the attitude of those three. No matter how much discussion occurred, the jury was going to be hopelessly deadlocked."

The same reporter asked, "Do you regret how you got January back to stand trial?"

"No, sir. If we hadn't acted when we did, as we did, those children would be stuck in Cuba the rest of their lives. I'm proud of what we did. I have one regret. I would do only one thing differently."

Several reporters shouted out, "What's that?"

"I'd have gone with my partner, Mr. Steine, on the boat ride into international waters to capture January and rescue those children. I would have liked to be able to tell my future grandchildren about seeing his face when he realized he'd been caught and the children's faces when they'd been saved. Instead I was safely on shore."

Everybody laughed, and Davis returned to the courtroom. He wasn't laughing. He was crying on the inside.

Davis and Morty walked over to Sammie, who was consoling Rita. The three stepped away for a private conversation. Morty was elected spokesperson.

"You were right. We should have given General Little different advice, more consistent with your research. Your uncle and I learned from this experience. In retrospect, I'm glad I didn't testify. Based upon what the foreman said, my powers of persuasion wouldn't have succeeded. I would have just embarrassed myself. I'm proud that you stood up to us and strongly voiced your opinion. Keep up the good work. We love and respect you."

Sammie couldn't have been more proud. Morty's words struck a nerve. Just then Sammie's water broke, and Vic took charge. The entire group rushed from the courtroom through a sea of reporters to their cars so they could go to Baptist Hospital. Three hours later, Abby Victoria Browne was born, six pounds three ounces, eighteen inches long. Morty was the proud godfather. In a gesture of goodwill in the moment, Sammie asked Rita Sinclair to be the baby's godmother, having lost her daughter, husband, and the criminal trial against January.

Three months later Davis and Sammie met with Pierce at Steine, Davis, & Davis in an effort to resolve several outstanding issues brought about by the dismissal of January's criminal charges.

Davis opened the conversation, "Your man gets out in twenty months. As a convicted felon, he won't be practicing law."

"He's already surrendered his law license. He'll need to find gainful employment that will be a condition of his six-month probation. Any suggestions? In light of his embezzlement conviction, it will be difficult for him to get a job around money."

"I suppose so. I imagine he owes you quite a bit of money."

"That's confidential."

"You're among friends."

"Right, I forgot," she said sarcastically. "Since my fees are relevant to our negotiations, I'll tell you. He owes me a little over three hundred fifty thousand dollars."

"Is that for everything?"

"Criminal, custody, the trust dispute, divorce, the entire shooting match."

"Boy, that's a lot of money. Maybe you can work out a payment plan. It could take a hundred years. You'd be only a hundred forty-five."

"I'd be a hundred forty-four."

"Sorry, I thought you were a year older than me."

Davis pressed his advantage,

"What about sex for legal fees? Maybe you could use the same fee schedule he used with Laura Chapman? Maybe he'd give you a discount, since it would be him rather than you having to work off the fee?"

"Funny man."

Pierce ignored Davis and got back to business. "Well, since he'll be entitled to the entire divorce estate, and the trustee for all three trusts and have custody of his children when he gets out, he should be able to pay me. I can wait. Under the new statute that your friend Morty rammed through the legislature, Rita Sinclair might get visitation every other weekend and a few weeks in the summer. You know Morty Steine is an amazing man. He should have prosecuted the murder trial. If he had rather than General Little, you might have gotten a conviction. She should have at least put him on the witness stand. What a waste! He was on the list."

Pierce was now trying to get Davis back, and she was hitting a nerve with the unknown. Davis remarked, "I guess we will never know."

Davis hated that Pierce knew that he was debating the truth and was concerned that she was probably right. Davis wanted to end this meeting as soon as possible. Pierce was getting under his skin. Davis proposed, "Here's the deal. January gets a million dollars to start a new life. Sinclair remains trustee on all three trusts. I'm substitute, and Sammie is second substitute, with January declaring he will never have an interest in any of the trusts. January gets every other weekend with the kids and three weeks in the summers."

Pierce came prepared, "January gets two million. Everything else is fine, except he wants a month in the summer. Most important, Sinclair can't poison him with the kids. He was cleared on the murder charges, and she needs to reinforce that fact with the children."

Davis knew all they were arguing about now was money. He knew a deal would be cut, and Rita Sinclair would get sole custody of her grandchildren and control of the trusts. It was just a matter of how much she would have to pay this bastard.

"A million to January, and Rita will pay your fees."

That was music to Pierce's ears. Her fees were going to be paid. No matter what, she got paid in full. Davis knew exactly what he was doing. Her predictable response came quickly, "A million two to January, and my fees get paid."

"Deal."

They shook hands, and paperwork was prepared and signed. Twenty months later, January was a free man. Davis never felt good about the outcome of the January case, but he felt good that the January kids were brought back to the United States. He knew that he had done the right thing in getting them home to a grandmother who loved them. The outcome wasn't perfect, but capturing January in international waters, having him plead guilty to embezzlement, serving thirty months and stand trial for Rachel's murder were the right thing.

EPILOGUE

Friday, March 25, 2005

It was a big day in the Browne/Davis family celebrating the fifth birthday of little Abby Browne. She and her baby brother, Larry, had spent the night with their aunt Liza and uncle Ben so their parents could be free to get ready for her party. As an added bonus, cousins Caroline and Jake were in from college but not specifically to attend the big event. They were on spring break. Caroline, age twenty-one, was a first-year law student at Yale, while Jake, age eighteen, was a sophomore at Princeton. Davis complained about the cost of their tuition, but he could not be more proud of his children.

The firm of Steine, Davis, & Davis was prospering. Morty split his time between his 288-acre farm Squeeze Bottom and his sixth-floor apartment. He occasionally worked a case, but most matters didn't keep his interest for long. He did love Sammie's children and particularly felt honored that she had named her firstborn after his grandfather Abe Steine. He was very much looking forward to her birthday party.

The party started right on time. Nana Shelly, who'd recently moved to Nashville following the death of her husband, Larry, had baked the chocolate birthday cake, and there were six candles. The family sang "Happy Birthday."

Her mother said, "Blow them out, honey. There's one for good luck. Make sure you get them all. Jake will help you."

Davis was using his new video camera he'd gotten as a birthday gift from his children. It was small enough to fit in his jacket pocket. He recorded the teenager holding her up and the two blowing the candles out. Morty sat in a chair talking with Vic. Over the years the two of them had gotten close. They were in a heated political debate when Vic's cell phone rang.

"Yes, he's my wife's uncle. He happens to be here right now. Small world. I'll get him."

Vic walked toward Davis. "It's Saint Thomas Emergency Room. There's a Dr. Nelson looking for you. Someone on staff knew I was married to a Davis who was a lawyer, so he called me looking for you." Vic handed Davis his cell phone.

"Ben Davis, can I help you?"

"Mr. Davis, I'm Dr. Gary Nelson, Saint Thomas Emergency Room. I've got a gunshot victim admission, Tommy Hamilton. He's asking for you"

Nelson paused, waiting for Davis to say something. When he didn't, the doctor continued, "He says you're his lawyer, and he wants to execute a new will. It may be a dying declaration. We have a notary here on staff."

"I'm not his lawyer. I was his deceased mother's lawyer. A guy named Littleton represents him."

"He wants you. It's my medical opinion the man will be dead in three hours. How about you come down here and honor his last wish?"

Davis was shamed into going to the hospital. He jumped in his new Bentley convertible, white with tan interior, and drove with Morty to Saint Thomas. They both hated to leave the party. Morty ate his cake in the car, with Davis yelling not to get any on the seats.

When they got there, they were met by Nelson, who took them to a cubicle where Tommy lay on a gurney. Nelson whispered to Davis, “We’ve done what we can. All we can do is make him comfortable.”

Davis warned, “I’d hold off with the heavy-duty drugs if possible. He’s got to be competent if he is going to execute a will.”

“Understood.”

Despite his condition, Tommy was surprisingly alert, but his speech was a little jerky. “Steine and Davis, I presume. I’m about to make your day.”

Morty bluntly asked, “What happened to you?”

“I owed the wrong people money, and it turns out that their collection methods were a little drastic for my taste. I would have preferred if they charged much higher interest rates.”

Morty scolded him, “You need to stop gambling, Tommy. It’s a pretty dangerous habit.”

It’s a little late now, old man. I think this habit is going to be the death of me.”

Getting to the point, Davis said, “I’m here to redo your will. We can do a handwritten one and have you sign it before the hospital notary. Are you leaving me your share of the Keller fortune? If so, we’ll have to get someone else to prepare the document. It would be a conflict for me to prepare it. Morty can’t prepare it either. That would be a conflict also because he’s my partner. We’d have to get someone else.”

“As much as I know you like money, this is even better. I want to confess committing a crime.” Tommy started coughing and couldn’t stop. The coughing jag lasted three minutes, and he spit out some phlegm. When it resolved, he finally said, “I’d get some credible witnesses to what I’m about to say and quick.”

“Like who?”

“Law enforcement.”

"Davis called Belinda Little and put his cell phone on speaker. He remembered his video camera was in his pocket, and with the notary present, he started filming.

"My name is Tommy Hamilton, and I know I'm dying, so I have no reason to lie. I'm trying to clear my conscience. I met Dan January in the men's room at a Sounds game on July 3rd, 1999. We were sitting next to each other at the game, and I overheard him complain about his wife to some motorcycle types during the game. In the bathroom I approached him with the idea of my disposing of his wife if he disposed of my mother. It was a brief conversation, no more than five minutes, and then we returned to our seats and our respective guests. We met later that day after the game and finalized our plans. I waited outside the January house and murdered Rachel January. Dan January pushed my mother down the stairs at her house. It was an even exchange."

Both Davis and Little had a million questions, but neither wanted to interrupt Tommy's narrative. It was apparent from his voice and his appearance that he was getting weaker by the moment.

"I also killed Tyree Sinclair. That was a freebie on my part. After the 4th, a couple of weeks later, I met January for a congratulatory drink at the Palm bar. We were celebrating getting the deed done, and he was bitching about Sinclair. I was so thankful he got rid of my bitch of a mother, I figured I'd help him out. Why not help the guy? He simplified my life. I thought if I did that, he might later take care of Maureen for me. It was just a thought. We never discussed it. I thought I would bring it up with him later after Sinclair was gone. How could he have said no?"

Little asked, "Did he know you were going to kill Sinclair?"

"He didn't ask, but when I mentioned it in passing, he didn't object either. He just knowingly smiled, and we moved on. That was enough of a green light for me."

Little started asking questions, but Tommy started choking. A minute later his death was recorded on tape. He managed to get out forty minutes of story and lived about two hours from when Davis arrived. He never provided all of the details of the January murder like where he stashed the body. What weapon did he use? Little and Davis had so many unanswered questions.

The medical staff made no effort to revive the patient. He'd flat lined and was not coming back. Out of respect, Dr. Nelson asked them to leave, and they regrouped in the hallway.

Little asked, "What do we do next?"

Morty looked to Davis and then said, "Belinda, I think you should first show this video to your boss, Johnson Tory, and get his feedback. With his permission we should show it to Jack Henry and Rita Sinclair, so they know what happened to their client and loved ones. Finally we should invite Amy Pierce and Dan January to the movies."

Three days later, Amy Pierce and Dan January were sitting in the Steine, Davis, & Davis conference room. Popcorn was on the table.

Pierce looked across the table at Davis, Steine, Sammie, Henry, Hopper, Duncan, and Rita Sinclair. She'd beaten them all, and she felt a sense of pride. She decided to begin with a jab. She said, "Morning, Mrs. Sinclair. The last time we were together was when you paid my bill."

Davis answered for his client, "I'd hold off sending another bill. I figure you won't be sending a bill because you'll be subpoenaed as a witness. Have some popcorn."

Angrily Pierce asked, "What the hell are you talking about?"

Davis started the video. It played for thirty-one minutes. When it ended, Pierce turned to January and said, "Don't say a word. We have nothing to say."

Little stood and said, "Daniel January, you're under arrest for the murder of Martha Keller, as a co-conspirator in the murder of Tyree Sinclair, obstruction of justice in the investigation of Tyree Sinclair, as a co-conspirator in the murder of Rachel January, and for obstruction of justice in the investigation of the murder of Rachel January."

Duncan read January his Miranda rights.

Davis taunted January, "I guess you've been afforded your constitutional rights, this time, Mr. January. Steine, Davis, & Davis always tries to do the right thing.

Fourteen months later, a jury convicted January for the murder of Martha Keller. He received a sentence of life with parole after twenty-five years. Twenty-one months later, January was convicted as a co-conspirator in the death of Tyree Sinclair and received a sentence of twenty-five years. Four years later, January was convicted as a co-conspirator in the death of Rachel January and received a sentence of twenty-five years.

Every appeal was denied unanimously, with the appellate courts writing extremely short opinions. Rita Sinclair raised two wonderful grandchildren, who became productive adults and contributing members of society. The overturned trial conviction of the murder of Rachel January by Dan January in Judge Russo's court and the extraction of January, Frankie, and Gaby were unquestionably the right courses of action. Sometimes the right thing to do isn't the legal thing to do. Steine and Davis were smart enough to know when to exercise good judgment and do the right thing despite the law.

GLOSSARY OF LEGAL TERMS

Affidavit—a sworn statement, under oath, signed before a notary.

Answer—the responsive document filed by a defendant to a complaint.

Bad faith—when an insurance company has an opportunity to settle within its insured's policy limits and fails to do so.

Beneficiaries—the parties who receive money or property under a will.

Beyond a reasonable doubt—the burden of proof in a criminal case. The highest possible burden of proof, no other logical alternative.

Co-trustees—two or more persons who hold joint fiduciary duties to protect the interests of the beneficiaries of the trust.

Complaint—the document that starts a lawsuit and spells out what the defendant did wrong.

Contempt of court—an action in violation of a court order or an instruction of a judge.

Counterclaim—when the defendant turns around and sues the plaintiff who brought the lawsuit.

Cross-examination—when the opposing attorney asks a witness questions.

Defendant—the party who is sued.

Deposition—the opportunity pre-trial for an attorney to ask questions under oath of a party or a witness.

Direct examination—when an attorney puts a witness on the stand and asks questions.

Fifth Amendment—a party's or a witness's constitutional right not to testify, as that testimony would tend to incriminate that witness for the arrest of a crime.

Interrogatories—a set of written questions posed to a party pre-trial, which the other party must answer in writing under oath.

Motion in Limine—preliminary motion filed by a party to resolve evidentiary issues prior to trial.

Overruled—the judge disagrees with the objection made by an attorney.

Plaintiff—the party that brings the lawsuit.

Plea bargain—an agreement reached between either a state or the federal government and a defendant as to their guilt and an agreed upon sentence.

Preponderance of the evidence—the burden of proof in a civil case. The successful party must tip the scales of justice just over 50%.

Probate of estate—the filing of a will so the assets can be distributed to the beneficiaries.

Recross examination—when an opposing counsel gets to question witnesses.

Redirect examination—when an attorney gets a second chance to ask his witness questions.

Reversible error—a ruling by a trial judge that is so significantly wrong that the appellate court either dismisses the case or orders a new trial.

Sidebar—conversation between the court and the attorneys in the courtroom, on the record, but the jury cannot hear it.

Sustained—the judge agrees with the objection raised.

Ten Commandments—A moral code adopted by Rachel and Dan January as to how they would conduct themselves during their marriage.

ABOUT THE AUTHOR

A. Turk was born in 1954 in Brooklyn, New York, and he grew up on Long Island. He earned a BA from George Washington University, and an MBA from the Vanderbilt Owen Graduate School of Business, and a JD from Vanderbilt School of Law. He was licensed to practice in Tennessee in 1980. In 1983 he also was licensed, but never practiced, in New York because of a promise he made to his mother.

A. Turk, for more than thirty years was a prominent Nashville attorney and a veteran of fighting courtroom battles. He garnered national media attention in 1994 when he won a unanimous US Supreme Court decision, which held that 2 Live Crew's parody of Roy Orbison's song "Pretty Woman," did not require a copyright license. With the support of NBC, HBO, Time Warner, *Mad Magazine*, and others, A. Turk won this landmark case preserving the right of commercial parody under the Fair Use Doctrine.

A. Turk in 2010 retired to begin his second career as an author of courtroom dramas based upon his personal experience. *First Do No Harm,* A. Turk debut novel, told the story of a rash of medical malpractice cases that Turk fought to save a rural community from two unethical and incompetent doctors and a corrupt county hospital. His next novel, *Second Degree,* described the downfall of a young surgeon, who was given everything life could possibly offer and threw it away for sex and drugs. The third installment of the Benjamin Davis Series, *Third Coast*, a prequel, provides the reader insight into the life of Davis's mentor Morty Steine, a great man and a mensch. It also affords the reader an opportunity to observe just how a jury operates; how it weighs the evidence admitted at trial, and how it deliberates to reach its verdict.

A. Turk has been married to his wife, Lisa, for thirty-eight years, and they have two adult children, Jessica and Ben, as well as two pugs, Neuman and Cosmo. A. Turk currently splits his time between Nashville, Aspen, and Palm Beach. Mr. Turk has already begun working on the next installment of the Benjamin Davis Series.

ACKNOWLEDGMENTS

I'd first like to thank my family: my wife Lisa, my daughter Jessica, and my son Ben. My family and my faith define me as a person.

I'd like to thank my editor, Dimples Kellogg. She understands my voice and has been instrumental in the development of the Benjamin Davis Series. She is a true partner in my writing effort. There would be no series without her.

I'd like to thank Dan Swanson for his cover honoring the great state of Tennessee, which has been my home for over forty years. I'd like to thank Darlene Swanson for her formatting of the manuscript so it could be read in digital form.

I'd like to thank the members of my focus groups:

Brandon Bubis, Martin Bubis, Robert Denny, Amy Eskind, Anita Dowdle, Douglas Dowdle, Oliva Faziani, Thomas Forsythe, Karen Goldsmith, Steve Goldsmith, Elliot Greenberg, Jay Lefkovitz, Steve Lefkovitz, Laura Little, Paula Milam, Thomas Milam, Scott Newman, Lisa Silver, Miriam Silver, Jania Tiner, and Jessica Turk for their thoughts and constructive criticism.

As an attorney, whose clients did not have the funds to hire fancy jury consultants, I conducted very rudimentary mock jury trials. During these exercises I presented evidence to random citizens and then videotaped those mock jurors' deliberations. Those videos provided me great insight and helped me to prepare for the actual trials. By submitting a draft manuscript to my focus groups, I believe I gained insight into the reader's perspective of my manuscript, and I'm afforded an opportunity to improve the work that is eventually released to the general public. At the very least, I think everyone involved in the process has a good time. We eat, drink, and argue about characters' strengths and weakness and what changes I should make to the book. We engage in lively debate. I used this process for the first four books in the series and plan to employ the same when I write my fifth.

Thanks again, focus group members.

A. Turk